Claire McGowan publ... ...ved
it up with many othe... ...as
in women's fiction – w... ...ree
radio plays broadcast o... ...*You
Did* and *The Other Wi*... ...lle
in the US and UK.

Praise for *This Could Be Us*

'About halfway through this beautiful, expertly-stitched novel,
I thought to myself, "Every woman needs to read this book"; by
the end, I thought, "every human". Moving, thought-provoking
and profound, it's one of my favourite reads of the last few years'
Louise Candlish, author of *Our House*

"Such a complex and original take on the thorniest
sides of families and relationships'
Justin Myers

'This poignant and moving story signals a heartfelt and
thoughtful change of direction from thriller writer McGowan'
The Bookseller, 'One to Watch'

'Captivating … A beautifully structured novel with the
complexities of family at the heart of it, *This Could Be Us* allows
the reader's impressions of each character to shift throughout, as
we are left to wonder what we might do in the same situation.
As heart-warming as it is thought-provoking, the steady pace as
the past slowly catches up to the present ensures you might be
tempted to read just a few pages more, and more'
Irish Independent

'The author's own experience of having a disabled
sibling makes it an emotive read'
Good Housekeeping, Book of the Month

'McGowan, an acclaimed writer of crime fiction, drew
on her own family experience of caring for a disabled sibling
to create a complex and ultimately forgiving story'
Irish Times, The Gloss

Also by Claire McGowan

Are You Awake?

I Know You

The Push

The Other Wife

What You Did

The Lost

The Dead Ground

The Silent Dead

Controlled Explosions

A Savage Hunger

Blood Tide

The Killing House

The Fall

This Could Be Us

CLAIRE McGOWAN

corsair

CORSAIR

First published in the United Kingdom in 2023 by Corsair
This paperback edition published in 2024

1 3 5 7 9 10 8 6 4 2

A CIP catalogue record for this book
is available from the British Library.

ISBN: 978-1-4721-5719-5

Typeset in Garamond by M Rules
Printed and bound in Great Britain by
Clays Ltd, Elcograf S.p.A.

Papers used by Corsair are from well-managed forests
and other responsible sources.

Corsair
An imprint of
Little, Brown Book Group
Carmelite House
50 Victoria Embankment
London EC4Y 0DZ

An Hachette UK Company
www.hachette.co.uk

www.littlebrown.co.uk

Author's Note

I was in my twenties before I realised something my character Kate discovers in the book – that you can't really talk about disability as a standard experience. It's such a broad term, meaning so many things to different people, that it's hard sometimes to find anyone whose viewpoint matches your own. In this book, Kate's daughter Kirsty is born with a genetic condition so rare it doesn't have a name. This was the truth for my family, when my brother was born in the early eighties with a chromosomal disorder that still hasn't been named. We don't even know if anyone else in the world has the same condition, and it makes it that much harder to find a community, or explain to people how profound his disabilities are, how he still needs round-the-clock care at almost forty and that, no, it's nothing like Down syndrome, although that involves a whole extra chromosome and my brother only has a section of one inverted. He will never walk, or talk, or feed himself, and we aren't sure if he knows who we are or not. Guilt, pain, secrecy, loss – all of those I have experienced. It's also true that people within a family can feel very differently about the same experience. And that if you try to articulate a negative emotion about it, especially in the Catholic environment where I grew up, you can encounter judgement, censure, and isolation.

My family's experience has been a harsh one – years of caring for someone with multiple and complex needs, without being sure if they can recognise you and not able to help them when they're suffering pain they can't tell you about. Once I left home in Ireland, I understood that not everyone experiences it this way, and that even people with serious challenges can live full and happy lives and bring great joy to their families. It was a surprise to me, to learn this, and it compounded my own feelings of guilt and injustice, to know that even in this niche world there are layers of difficulty. I've tried to reflect here something of what it's like when joy is in short supply, but also to give a more nuanced and hopeful portrayal than the one I've lived as a sibling. This story is only meant to show one particular situation with disability. It may not match yours. My intention is to shine a light on families like mine, and like the one in the book, who often struggle on for years with so little support, broken by love and by pain. I hope that for some people it may highlight an experience that resonates.

Kate, present day

To begin the story near the end, a woman was driving. Like everyone in this city, she wore jeans, Converse, sunglasses, a black jumper (*sweater*, as she still hadn't learned to call it), although the day was hot. It was always hot there. Her hair was blonde but it used to be something else. She was driving on a Los Angeles freeway, dodging between lanes of traffic as if she hardly saw the other cars, the blare of horns and near-miss of fenders an everyday occurrence. She took an off-ramp, swerving over two lanes to get there, then drove up a twisting road, the city spread out below her in a sizzling haze, although she didn't notice. Here and there, hillsides lay scorched from the previous years of wildfires, and on any other day she couldn't see them without that dip in her stomach, the fear that destruction was almost at your door and still kept coming. The houses on either side of the road were large and architectural, built into the hillside, which was half in shadow, half in knife-edge sunshine. Here and there the kingfisher flash of a swimming pool, but she didn't see this either, she was too angry. Down the winding canyon road she lived on, buzzer at the ready for the gates – no need to get out of the car in this city. They opened with a click and she drove up to a low-slung white house, surrounded by fragrant pink flowers. Home.

Inside, her feet clattered on the cold tiles, a chill wind of air conditioning blowing her expensive hair. 'Conor. *Conor!*'

A man appeared at the top of the stairs, annoyed at the

1

interruption. He was tall and flat-stomached for his age, which like hers was fifty. He had sandy red hair that had faded from a more youthful ginger. 'What are you doing home?'

'I need to talk to you.' She took her phone from her bag, and wished she had something to throw at his feet that was less breakable. Stupid paperless world. 'I saw something. In the daily email, you know, the *Variety* one. You optioned a book? You want to make a film of it?' Even as she said it, she wondered if it was a mistake. Because wouldn't he have told her, if this was really happening? 'Is it – it's not what it sounds like?' She had barely taken it in. 'It's not about – what I think?'

He began to come down, one step at a time, deliberately slow. 'Your daughter.' The word itself was a shock in Conor's mouth – concepts of family, belonging, ownership, none of them seemed to fit with this Teflon man.

'What about her?'

'Did you know your husband wrote a book about her?'

There he went again, with these words, implying relationships between people where they no longer existed. She hadn't seen Andrew in fifteen years; to refer to him like this felt like a slap. '*You're* my husband.'

'You know what I mean, don't be obtuse.' He raised his eyebrows at her, and she recognised the look, the one that meant he was waiting for her to calm down and be rational.

'Of course I didn't know he wrote a book. He was always trying to, but I didn't think he'd ever finish anything.' Even now, having seen it with her own eyes, she didn't really believe it.

'Well, he did. A memoir about her.'

It was like a dream, where people who have no business knowing each other casually walk through the same rooms in your head. 'Why? And you optioned it?'

He shrugged. 'You saw the announcement.'

2

But she still didn't get it – even without the connection to her, so red-raw it was embarrassing, what about this story could possibly be appealing to him? 'Who'd want to see it – a film about *that*?'

'Well, that's just it – you see, she's learned to speak. It's actually a great story.' He was already writing the pitch in his head, she could see – heart-warming drama, hope wrung from despair, overcoming the odds ...

Kate was so angry, hot spurts of it leaping from under the protective crusts she'd applied years back, in order to stay sane and living. The ground was moving under her feet, although not literally, as was often the case in LA. This felt worse. 'She can't speak. You must have the wrong people. For God's sake.'

'Read it yourself if you don't believe me.' Conor's attitude was baffling – he seemed irritated with her, as if he hadn't just done something that disturbed the entire foundation of their lives together.

'You really want to make it,' she said faintly. A film about her. Her family. What she'd done.

Conor made an odd gesture. 'I'm flying to London tomorrow to sign it off.'

Later, Kate lay on her bed, the white duvet (*comforter*) stretched taut and perfect beneath her. The ceiling fan revolved over her head, even though they had air conditioning; it was just a design feature. She tried to process what had just happened, as her therapist in the expensive house in Santa Monica, paid for by the misery of shiny Hollywood people, had taught her. As she lay there in her movie-star room, where Conor did not visit, she felt the tectonic plates in her, grinding and shifting. It had always seemed cruel to her that you couldn't shed your memories in the way you shed skin cells, so the body that lived through things

3

was not the same one you were in now, and yet you were stuck with remembering everything that had happened to you. It was still there inside her – Andrew, Kirsty, the painful soup of emotions those names swirled up. Olivia, Aimee. David. And Adam. He'd be twenty-two now. A man. It was Adam she was most fearful about as she lay in bed, the sunlight fading into an LA night howling like coyotes, shaking with the realisation that time had finally caught up with her.

Kate, 2002

Kate woke early on what would turn out to be the last day. She had set her alarm to make sure she'd have several hours on her own to get the house perfect. Andrew was sleeping in the middle of the bed, his mouth slightly open, his breath wheezy from hay fever. She wouldn't be annoyed with him today, she had decided, and to confirm that promise to herself, she dropped a kiss onto his clammy brow, reflecting that it was sometimes easier to love people when they were asleep, vulnerable and still. He didn't stir. She wrapped her silk dressing gown around the bulk of her stomach, feeling it settle in cool folds about her. It was going to be a lovely day, the sun already straining gold through the curtains. May in England was untrustworthy, but it was always nice for Kate's birthday, and this was her thirtieth. She'd made it to the finish line of her uncertain twenties; she had everything she'd wanted. Andrew, who was at least a kind man, a loving man, with a good job. A tasteful, welcoming house, ready to be showcased today, her two-year-old and the second baby due in a month.

At work, she had broken into being on screen, just about,

4

covering a few local news items while Chiara, the main reporter, was on maternity leave (how ironic that a woman being forced aside by pregnancy so often allowed another in, and now it was her turn to reluctantly cede her place and go). But she'd be back in six months to pick it up again, until she took over as studio anchor in another year or so, when Mary-Ann finally retired. What else was there? Maybe she'd get really into hobbies, make her own candles, learn sugarcraft, arrange flowers. Tidy the garden. She'd have time for that now the main things were sorted. To develop the edges of herself, fill in the details. Standing in her quiet bedroom, looking at her outline in the mirrored wardrobe doors, Kate allowed herself a surge of joy under her ribs, where the baby lay, and was answered by a small kick that made her gasp. It was a miracle, it really was, even with heartburn and swollen ankles and back pain. She forced herself to appreciate it all.

She decided to shower later, so she'd be as fresh as possible for her guests, so she went noiselessly onto the landing and pushed open the door to Adam's room, hoping he'd still be asleep like his father. He was standing up, totally silent, clutching the bars of the cot. 'Hello,' said Kate, taken aback. 'Are you waking up by yourself now?' He was such a good-looking child, with his bright blue eyes and shiny black hair, the bloom on his cheeks that she loved to stroke. She was proud of him, of course she was. She just hoped he'd behave himself today and not throw one of the tantrums that so embarrassed her.

Adam didn't say anything. He didn't talk much yet, something Kate resolutely declared did not worry her, though it did. There was no nappy smell, and he wasn't crying – would it be wrong to leave him there for a little while, just to enjoy the silence, the clean house? 'Mummy will be back,' she said, slipping out again. Adam didn't make a sound. Perhaps he was finally becoming less clingy.

5

In the kitchen, she stooped to pick up a few stray toys, tutting as she spied the dirty mug and plate Andrew had left on the coffee table overnight. Would it kill him to take them to the sink, seeing as he actually passed through the kitchen to get to bed? But no, she wouldn't have words with him. Not today. He'd been working so hard, commuting up to London every day on those crammed trains, never getting a seat. She wouldn't shout at him about a cup left out; she would be Nice Kate, Loving Wife, Kind Mummy. A pleasing sense of her own nobility buoyed her to her tasks.

The house was clean with bleach and polish – she'd corralled Adam into his cot and set about scrubbing furiously at 7pm the night before, Andrew urging her to sit down and 'take it easy'. Only one of them could afford to take it easy, she had wanted to say, and clearly it was going to be him. But now it was worth it, to rise and see the place shining, a smell of beeswax and the lilies just unfurling in the fat glass vase, which Andrew would say set off his allergies. She opened the fridge, looking at the cling-film-wrapped bowls and plates of food she'd prepared yesterday. No breakfast, she decided – she couldn't bear to dirty up the kitchen in its sterile perfection. Her mind was playing out uplifting scenarios of how people would arrive, and they would say *oh Kate the place looks great, oh Kate you're blooming. The food's delicious. What a great party.* She looked around her home, the clean hardwood floors, the shampooed carpets and sofa, the dust-free furniture, the pictures she'd hung herself when she got tired of waiting for Andrew to pick up a hammer, and she thought: I've done it. This is it. I won.

Andrew woke up, groaning, at nine thirty. 'I think I've got a cold coming. I don't feel so good.' Andrew and his colds. An Ebola patient could not suffer more. But his job was taking a lot

6

out of him, she had to be understanding. Or so she told herself several times a day.

Kate was standing at the sink washing the dishes from the cream she'd just whipped. Jellies were setting, salads chilling. She wanted everything to look perfect when people were ushered in the door, but here he was rummaging in drawers, fiddling with Lemsip and spilling the sweet gritty powder on the worktops.

'Could you put the packet back, do you think?' She wiped up the powder and wrung her cloth out clean. Andrew leaned against the counter to take his medicine, grimacing. 'Did you get the trampoline down from the attic yet?' She knew he hadn't.

'Oh. I will.' He was back at his Blackberry, a sort of fancy pager, and the most infernal device ever invented. When it was in his hand, she and the child and the house might as well not exist. Sometimes she thought she'd invent a function that could flash her words up on the screen. *Put fucking trampoline up, thx bye.*

She forced a smile. 'Thanks. Just ... before the party starts would be great.' She was Good Kate, a supportive wife, a loving mother, a successful reporter. She had it all. No need to get annoyed by trivialities.

From the next room there was the sound of something ripping, and an ominous silence from Adam, who she'd left in front of the TV. Again, she waited, eight months pregnant, to see if her husband would notice. No.

'Could you get him, please? Sweetheart?' Andrew dragged his gaze vaguely from the screen, but it was caught again just as fast, like a fish on a hook. His work was so busy, she could almost see the tightness settle in his chest as he scrolled through the messages they'd expect him to answer even on a Saturday. Kate wasn't going to fight today. It was her birthday. She was as far as she could get in pregnancy before she'd be incapacitated, and if he wouldn't help her, she would put together a party for thirty adults and children all by herself. She *could* do it, of course. It was just that she didn't see why she *should*.

Olivia was the first to arrive. She'd offered to come early and 'lend a hand', but Kate suspected her co-worker was in fact often lonely. She knew Olivia had moved to Bishopsdean from London when she took up her researcher post at *Look South*, and it wasn't the best place for a young single woman, the nappy belt, with the double-sided buggy jams in the aisles of the town's shops.

She opened the door and leaned over her bump to kiss the air near Olivia's cheek. 'Lovely to see you!' It was already setting in, the paradoxical feeling she got whenever she'd spent hours arranging a party. She'd stand, looking round at the row of wine bottles, the food arranged on pretty plates, the balloons and flowers, and she'd think – why are they coming? Why do I have to entertain these people? It was all she could do not to retreat upstairs with a whole trifle under her arm. But Olivia was here and so the party smile had to go on.

'Gosh, the place looks wonderful. I don't know how you do it.' Olivia unrolled a long cardigan from her thin white shoulders. She was so tiny and Kate so huge. But it was alright. Once the baby came, she'd go to the gym, bounce back, as they said in the magazines.

'No trouble,' Kate lied. 'Oh, you shouldn't have.'

Olivia was unloading gifts from her raffia shopping bag – a pink orchid, a cold-beaded bottle of Prosecco, and white roses wrapped in purple paper. Too much. Annoying. 'This is for you' – the flowers – 'and a little something for Adam in case he feels left out, with the baby and all.' That was a small tissue-wrapped parcel.

'So kind of you.' Was that a dig, that Kate should have bought something herself for her first-born? She hated the idea she was doing it wrong, failing in any way. She felt the same unsettling under her feet that she always did with Olivia. The woman had no child living with her, but all the same she was a mother. Kate wondered sometimes if that was why, despite her cakes and hand-made cards, Olivia was not well-liked at the TV studio. No one knew quite where to place her. Then, of course, there were the rumours, about why the little girl – well, she was just a baby – didn't live with Olivia. But Kate had to be nice. It couldn't be easy, not having your child around, even if Kate did sometimes fantasise about booking herself on a long spa break, all by herself. 'Maybe you'd like to give it to Ad? He's in his cot still and I can't really lift him.'

'Of course.' Attentive as always, Olivia flew to the task and, alone again for a brief moment, Kate passed a hand over the lilies, the wrapped platter of charcuterie. Her party anxiety was in full force now – what if no one else came, what if they did come and didn't get along, what if people had a horrible time and blamed her?

The doorbell rang and her heart surged.

'Liv? Could you grab that?' No answer, silence from upstairs. Irked, Kate dragged herself the ten steps to the front door. The bell rang again, she stretched out her smile. Outside were Chris and Kelly, whose two-year-old Jordan went to nursery with Adam. 'Hiya!' Kelly looked anxious in a too-small maxi-dress that revealed the tattoo on her shoulder. 'We brought, eh – Chris?'

'Oh!' Chris, in a Burton polo shirt and cropped khakis, fumbled over a bottle of supermarket white.

'How lovely! Hello Jordan!' She thought about kissing the little boy, but he had a scaly rash on his pinched face. The parents had seen fit to pierce his ear and dress him in a mini England football kit – the bloody World Cup, and polyester on such a hot day. 'In you come then.' She'd been worried about inviting nursery people – what had started as a lovely community plan seemed, as she lay awake at night, a folly of social mixing. For a moment she hovered with Chris and Kelly (*why are you here?*), cursing Olivia and Andrew for not being around to help. Then the bell rang again and it was Zoe from work, then the older couple from next door, and the party had taken hold and sustained itself and it was all going to be OK.

'Alright for Pimm's? Food?' Kate floated between groups, balloon-like. One of the neighbours had taken over from Andrew's attempts at barbecuing and was serving up a stream of charred burgers and sausages. As it was Kate's barbecue, there were also vegetable skewers, prawns, bowls of couscous. Not like her parents' idea of one – a bottle of Heinz and a ripped-open pack of sub rolls on a folding table. Adam had thrown a small tantrum because he didn't want his salad, so she'd shut him in the living room for a time-out. His wan face looked out at her through the glass, but she was determined to leave him there for five minutes, as the parenting books advised.

In years to come, when she recognised this party as the last day of her old life, Kate would play a game with herself, trying to count the people who'd been there. She always did this anyway, and if it passed a certain number she could relax, saying later, *there were about thirty people, that was a good turnout, wasn't it?*

But the truth was she could never remember exactly who had come. She spoke no more than a sentence to each person, a stately procession all in herself, ensuring drinks, chat, food for all. There'd been a few shaky moments – when the chunky eight-year-old of a nursery family slapped the young son of

10

one of her colleagues, and when she heard someone ask Olivia, who'd spent hours crawling in and out of the Wendy house, which child was hers.

But Olivia just said, 'Oh, none of these, actually.' She didn't give the response everyone at the TV station had already heard, neatly packaged – *I have a daughter, but she lives with my parents.* Despite probing, no one at the station knew why. When Kate started at *Look South* a year ago, Olivia had already been on maternity leave, then simply returned with no word of where the child was. People speculated about it, in the kitchen and at work drinks, but Kate was no nearer to knowing.

Otherwise, people were mingling, smiling, laughing. The party was a success, and Kate was relaxed, and even took a few sips of Prosecco, telling herself it couldn't hurt this late on. She was a good hostess! People liked her. She even leaned into Andrew's arms, letting him hold her up. A few feet away, Adam was playing with Jordan, kicking a little ball around. See, he was happy, he was fine. Everything was fine. 'It's a good party, isn't it?' she asked Andrew, who by now knew the correct responses.

'Of course. You've done an amazing job.'

So the party meandered on, candles lit inside stylish hurricane lamps, the garden lights she'd nagged Andrew into hanging glowing beautifully, jugs of Pimm's collecting sodden fruit in the bottom. It was all going fine until Kate took a step, and fell down.

'Oh!' Suddenly she was looking up at the garden from where she sat heavily on the patio. She could feel its cold stone through her dress, and a babble of voices and heads surrounded her. 'Andrew?' Where was the man? She didn't even realise it hurt for a moment. It was more like trying to keep your footing as an immense swell picked you up and carried you. Then pain smacked her like a wall. An awful noise was coming from deep

11

in the layers of her own body, and, as if from miles off, she heard Adam crying. Someone should take him away, he shouldn't see her like this. She tried to speak. 'Araga. A-grew.'

In the blur of noise and pain, something cut through – Olivia's hand in hers, cold as icy water. Olivia's voice, high and clear. 'Kate, I think the baby's coming.'

That was impossible, it wasn't due for over a month. She clung to her friend's hand, trying to say with the press of her fingers what her tongue could not frame. 'Ar – agrew?' Why didn't he come to help her, when she needed him most?

'It's OK.' Olivia's face a pale oval. 'It's all going to be fine. I promise.'

Afterwards, Kate would wonder if what happened could somehow have been Olivia's fault. As if her promise, so entirely misguided, there and then took on the poisonous cruelty of a curse.

After, it was just fragments. The pain was too much to keep it all in.

There was the grain of the car seats, a check of grey and blue. There was one of Adam's toys under the seat in front, shiny red plastic, yellow wheels. She could see it because she was sprawling over. She was vomiting into her hands, ropy and slimy. Andrew was in the front trying to drive. 'Oh God. Oh God, I don't know what to do. Hang on, please, we're almost there!' She was thinking *Adam*. Where was Adam? Who had him? Olivia surely – she would take care of him. It wasn't like this when he came, the gentle onset of labour allowing plenty of time to get to hospital and settle in with a book, wait grumpily for the ordeal ahead. What was happening now? Why did it hurt so much?

*

12

Later.

Gentle hands were touching her. It made her want to cry. An anaesthetist in green scrubs, kind eyes. When she winced as he pierced her hand he said, 'I'm sorry to cause you pain, Kate.'

Kate, Kate. They were all saying her name, but she couldn't answer. The voices at her head. *Breech. VP. Brain cert.* Incomprehensible. They moved her body like meat. There were bells going off. She sank back, important, carried like a priestess to the grave.

Later still.

There was Andrew sobbing outside the door, and she was afraid for him, for her, for both of them, under all the pain and screaming. She was also irritated, around the edges. What did he have to cry about? Then she lost all feeling below the waist. Gone. Then it was night somehow, and she was alone, the harsh lights burning like spent candles. No one was coming. She clenched her fists. Below the waist was a river of red pain. Her nose itched and she focused on that because it meant she was alive. No one was coming. She had no strength to shout, so she was dying. She wished she could pray. But for what? Adam, Andrew – she couldn't grasp onto their faces. Her home. Her furniture, the lamps casting pools of light. It wasn't fair she would never see it again. Then more voices over her, lights dripping and dimming, the killing relief of being wheeled along. The waffle blanket made her think of her own baby crib, or was it her sister's, Elizabeth's? Someone else was in charge now, and she could surrender her body. *I give up*, she tried to say. Andrew was somewhere behind, flapping anxiously, half into a blue gown. She felt some terrible fear, as she had in the car – he could not protect her. Some part of her that had trusted him, been soft towards him, hardened and calcified. She knew now she could not rely on him, not really.

A face swam into view below four lights, blurring dark in the middle like the sun. 'Hello, Kate.' A surgeon. God-like. 'The baby's in a bit of distress, so we're going to do an emergency Caesarean. When you wake up it will all be over.'

Over. She held onto the word like a raft. She didn't care how. As long as this could be over.

So much later, or earlier, she had no idea.

Andrew was sitting in the chair by her bed. His head was bent over his steepled hands. He wasn't asleep. She was floating. Her body had gone and she was very happy about that. Her hand throbbed, and looking down, she saw a tube had been put in the vein. A tug on her arm suggested a drip too. So this was how Gulliver felt, tied down.

Her throat cracked and she looked at the jug of hospital water with longing, until the clacks of her gummy mouth made Andrew start. 'You're awake?' He tried to follow her eyes. 'I'm not sure you're allowed ... Well ...'

He looked about for a glass, then finding one, held it for her, spilling water on the bedclothes. He had to hold her chin because she couldn't lift her body at all. The water choked her, she gulped it so fast. Andrew dabbed her face.

Dimly, she remembered. The baby. There should have been a baby. Andrew pushed back his hair so she could see how his hairline had receded in the years since she'd known him, and the smears on his glasses, his tired eyes. 'They're coming to talk to us. They wouldn't tell me anything.'

'Where—'

'I didn't see. They sent me out.' He looked at the floor. 'Kate – I don't know if ...'

The door swung open with a rubbery belch and in came a stocky white-coated man. Salty hair, rings on fingers.

14

'Mr and Mrs Waters,' he said, flipping the chart. It was still strange to Kate to be called this – she used her own name for work, and on most of her documents. Behind him hovered two younger doctors, a girl with a chapped nose and red ponytail, the boy gulping a large Adam's apple. She wondered how her Adam was. Who had him. Olivia, she remembered. Olivia would not leave him, and this gave her the same overwhelming relief she'd felt being wheeled into surgery. Someone else was in charge, could be relied on. The doctor – Dr Cameron Fraser, his badge declared – gave a small sigh. He rested his burly hands on the edge of the bed. 'I'm sorry to tell you I have some bad news.'

'No, no, no,' Kate was saying, though she couldn't speak. *Don't tell me, don't make it real.*

'You may notice I have some students with me today. I can ask them to leave if you wish, though it's important to their learning experience.'

Andrew was looking unsure. 'I suppose if . . .'

'NO.' Kate found her voice, lodged somewhere in her chest. For God's sake. Couldn't he see this was not a moment they'd want an audience for?

Dr Cameron Fraser sighed and dismissed his minions with a rattle of his Rolex. 'Mr and Mrs Waters. Can you tell me, is there any family history of genetic disease, disability, that kind of thing?'

Andrew looked blank. 'I don't think . . .'

'A history of stillbirth, or infant death?' They were both staring at him. He coughed. 'Well, no matter. We'll aim to get to the bottom of this, though we can't always, in these cases.'

What cases? *Say something!* Out of the corner of her eye, she could see Andrew's pale clammy face. *Say something!* 'But, ah, Doctor . . .' She could see he didn't want to speak the words, make them true. 'The baby – she's alright?' She. It was a girl, then. They'd said they didn't want to know, although Kate secretly had,

15

so she could plan, paint the nursery, imagine the rest of her life. Why would you not want to know exactly what was coming? She had hoped for a girl. One of each, her family complete, everything done and ticked off. So why did she feel such terrible growing dread, hijacking her mind and shutting off all rational thought?

Dr Fraser snapped the chart shut. 'It depends on your definition. She's breathing fine, and healthy enough in her way – but. Well. I'm afraid you need to prepare yourselves for the fact your daughter isn't quite what you will have expected.'

Adam, present day

Long ago, when he first left home and began to endure weekly phone calls with his father, Adam had started counting the pauses in the conversation. This one was going on a long time. Four seconds, five. Six. 'So what?' he said finally, snapping. 'What's the big deal?' So his mother had got in touch. She wasn't dead, it made sense she'd come back sometime.

'So what—? It's her, Ads. After all these years. She sent me an *email*. It was there when I woke up. She's in America.'

Adam shrugged, which his father wouldn't be able to see down the phone. Downstairs in the kitchen of the house share, he could hear Barry arguing with Ilona over the butter. *It wasn't me left those crumbs, you must have used it, even if you say you're vegan.* Tedious. 'I knew she was in America.'

'How?'

'There's this thing called the internet, Dad. You never looked her up, in all this time?'

'Well – no.' He didn't want to know, that meant. Easier to pretend Adam never had a mother, or that she'd walked out the

16

door when he was seven then vaporised. 'You haven't . . . talked to her?' said his father, with great trepidation.

Jesus Christ. 'Of course not. So why's she messaging now?'

'It's the book. She says we need to talk.'

Adam gritted his teeth. It was a source of some annoyance that his father, as effective as a chocolate condom, had not only finally written a book but got it published, for a lot of money, a bidding war even. Meanwhile Adam couldn't get his band signed. 'What about the book?'

'There's a film producer who wants to make it – in Los Angeles. Of course, most of these things don't go anywhere, but all the same, it's nice . . . '

He cut in. 'What's it to do with her, Dad?'

'Well that's just it. It seems she's married to this producer. Your mother. She's his wife.'

'What? You didn't know before you signed the contract?'

'Well, no. I looked him up online of course. But it didn't . . . well, I didn't know.'

A few seconds of pause from Adam now, his world shifting, all the anger threatening to break through, just a tinge of it enough to scorch his insides. 'I still don't see the problem.'

'We might have to see her, Adam. He's coming over to meet me – I assume she'll come with him. She wants to *talk* about it.'

Adam hung up. Just ended the call, no goodbye, no explanation, and it gave him some satisfaction to think about his father staring at the phone, wondering if it had cut out. Then the familiar wave of guilt – why did he take things out on the parent who'd actually stayed? Adam lay back on his unmade bed and thought about what his mother would see, coming into his life after fifteen years. A son of twenty-two, living in a house share with three other people, two of them members of his barely-breaking-even band. The shower sprouting new species of mould,

17

not enough towels to go around, an endless parade of girls tip-toeing down the dirty hallway and out into the dawn. Living off his dad, who he couldn't stand but also loved in a sad way.

He didn't like to sit with such thoughts, so he got up, flipping himself restlessly off the bed. He'd go out. Not hang about in the kitchen buttering toast with Barry and listening to his hilarious bantz about the difference between competing brands of non-dairy spread. Outside the sky was a pale white, dreary and featureless, litter blown into their neglected front garden. Nothing like LA, where his mother had been all these years (and who pronounced the whole name of the city like his father just had, *Los Angeles?*). Married to a film producer. She must be rich. Glamorous. Adam bashed his head just once against the condensation-thick glass of his window, the slight pain distracting him from thoughts of her – the day she left, everything that happened after – and went downstairs, throwing his phone into the pocket of his hoody, slipping in his wallet. His hand hovered over the sprawl of masks on the hall table, but no one was bothering now, not really. Not even him, despite what he'd lost from it, despite what he knew. He thundered past the kitchen before Barry could say a word, his mouth formed in an 'o' around his toast. Out into the day which wasn't cold or warm. As he pounded along the dirty pavement, all he was thinking about was Delia. How she would react. What this would mean for her. For them.

Kate, 2003

Kate felt almost drunk on the joy of being out alone. How she'd taken this for granted, once. Just to be a woman in a café, on her own. Again it started, the film always running in her head these

18

days, as if she were watching herself on a screen. *The woman has put on two stone. She has only been able to zip up her knee boots halfway. Her hair is going dark at the roots, and new lines of pain have been sculpted into her face.*

But at least she was out, and it was quiet, thank God, there was no one to wipe or nurse or soothe, just for an hour, and it was good, in that moment, to be able to lift her coffee and taste the foam, without Adam whining and pulling on her arm, or having one and a half ears cocked for Kirsty's choking cry. It was hard to get much done when your child might be dying at any given moment, and the sheer effort of keeping her alive was wearing Kate down like an old watch. She thought she'd done OK with Adam – he had tantrums, yes, and hadn't learned to speak that early, but her figure had bounced back, as if human flesh was a squash ball, and she'd ignored his crying like you were supposed to until he eventually stopped. But this time. This time had broken her.

She half-closed her eyes and let the café wash over her, the clatter of cups and hiss of steam. The place was full of young people, lounging low in their chairs with little white head-phones in their ears. Didn't she used to be young too? She was only thirty-one. She adjusted her leggings and sweatshirt. A Bishopsdean mum, that's what she looked like. One step away from a Range Rover.

Life felt hard at the moment. Andrew came in every night from the train, flopping on the sofa, expecting dinner and sympathy, all because he got to leave the stink of crap each day and go to a place where people didn't bite you and if they wanted something wouldn't just lie on the floor and shriek, or deposit pale yellow poo on the sleeve of your cardigan. *Be nice, Kate.* It was harder and harder to summon up Good Kate these days. Yes, it was bad for him, commuting and working long hours for a horrible boss and rushing home to help with baths and bed, but surely it was worse for her, stuck at home all day. Andrew's way of handling their new life was to carry on as normal. In those terrible days after the birth, he'd kept things going. Washed her hair for her when she couldn't move. Pulled together terrible meals, too salty or burned. Invited round friends and family, when Kate didn't want to see anyone, didn't want anyone to see them. Andrew had refused to break. They had a baby, didn't they? They had to feed her and clothe her and love her all the same, he had to go on earning, Adam had to be kept alive too. She didn't understand that way of thinking – an outrage had happened to them, and there must be something they could do to protest it, surely? But there wasn't.

Kate swallowed the sweet coffee, more foam than anything else. There had been so many options on the menu. What was a latte – wasn't that just Italian for milk? She was ashamed not to know. A girl had approached the till. She wore her jeans low, almost like seventies flares, and as she leaned over the counter to pay Kate could see her pants ride up above them. The entire gusset was visible. Kate thought of her own underwear, high and stretchy, running from her mid-thighs to her still-misshapen navel. She hadn't looked at herself naked for over a year, and when she had a shower, she rubbed soap over deep red ridges in her flesh. It was a whole new world of underwear. Before – even after Adam – there'd been lace, satin, balcony, French. Words like that. Now it was beige and elastic and nursing and cup shields. She seemed to be wearing someone else's body as a suit. Even her hair had changed, gone wispy and thin. There was no money or time now for hairdressers, since she'd not been able to go back to work. She had to walk past her old salon on the high street with her head down, wheeling the buggy as fast as she could, Adam clinging onto the back.

The girl at the counter turned, as if feeling Kate's eyes on her. Her hair fell in blonde waves, the way Kate's had once done, and the shiny mock-football top she wore was strained tight over full breasts. Kate flinched her eyes away. She decided she'd had enough time out of the house. As much as she sometimes felt the walls were closing in on her, it was even harder to be out there among people, in her new suit-body, scrapes of dried vomit on her jumper.

A light rain had started as she left the café, fumbling her money and the small talk of the waitress clearing the table. She'd forgotten how to speak adult. She pulled up the collar of her old rain jacket as she walked home. Without realising it her pace had slowed to a crawl. She had to get back. Andrew had been alone with them long enough, and there was no one else to ask. They'd already been through all the registered child-minders in Bishopsdean, and not a few of the unregistered. There was a social worker assigned to their case, a nervy woman called Amaryllis with a permanent cold, but so far her main contribution had been to explain they could apply for free nappies.

The door to the house was the same as when they'd bought it – smart royal-blue paint, the number 24 securely screwed in. It was just everything behind the door that had changed. Kate stood on her doorstep, hands in the pockets of the old coat, shivering in the unseasonable drizzle. She had to will herself to put her key in, and at once it hit her – the wailing in such harmony that for a moment it was almost beautiful. Her hand convulsed on the doorknob, but she made herself shut the door behind her and walk into the living room.

The middle-pitched wailing was coming from Adam, of course. A fractious baby, he had become a hostile, angry three-year-old, always howling over banged knees or lost toys. Jealous if they picked up Kirsty, who was often choking or being rushed to hospital, Kate disappearing with her for days on end. She understood why he was this way, but it didn't make it any easier.

The highest-pitched crying came from Kirsty, her one-year-old daughter. It was a sound Kate had become almost inured to, as if she'd gone deaf on that frequency. Kirsty still didn't look that different from other children when wrapped in blankets and knitted hats, but if you peered closely you would see it in her face. Kate noticed it all the time when people leant over, hoping to admire a sweet baby in her pram, then the slight frown, the look up to Kate and the fake smile – *oh, isn't she lovely?* She could hear them falter over the pronoun.

The bass note of the wailing symphony was coming from Andrew. Sitting in the middle of the floor, the baby cradled to his chest, Adam clawing at his back, Andrew had clearly come to the end of his tether. As Kate stood there, trying to parse the scene for what had gone wrong, she saw that Kirsty's face was blue, and then the wailing abruptly stopped, her little body convulsing as if it would break in two. Kate was across the floor before she even knew it. 'Put her on her front. Her front, Andrew!' There wasn't time to think. She pushed her fingers into the child's mouth to stop her swallowing her tongue, laid her over her arm in an approximation of the recovery position, and counted the seconds. A baby could do without air for one, two, three seconds. *Oh God, come on, breathe, breathe.* The absolute terror of a life in your hands.

Then, a gulping sound. A thin mewling cry from Kirsty's mouth. The seizure was over, for now. She hadn't died. They'd have to up her epilepsy medicine again, though it gave her terrible side-effects, including constipation that meant they were always having to shove her full of suppositories. Andrew was crying, his head in his hands. Too late, she realised that Adam had seen it all. His sister almost dying yet again, his parents breaking down, his father weeping and mother shouting. And he was standing frozen, three years old, a very adult look of shock on his pale little face.

After Kirsty's arrival, the first month had been about keeping her small red body alive, swallowing what gulps of milk they could get into her with tubes and pipettes. Kate could almost never put her down, afraid she would simply stop breathing and die. It was as if a part of her own body, a fragile beating organ, had somehow ended up on the outside. There hadn't been much time to wonder why their child was this way.

After that day at the hospital, when the doctor explained there were some 'abnormalities' with the baby, once Kate recovered they'd been sent home to figure it out for themselves. No name for the condition, if that's even what it was, no map to follow. If Kate let herself think at all, marinating as she was in desperate shock, all she could feel was a sense of outrageous unfairness. *Why? Why me?* But unknown people in their labs were at work, testing vials of blood and peering into microscopes, and soon she and Andrew found themselves back in the geneticist's office, warm and subdued. Kate had wondered if it was soundproofed, to shut out the storms of desperate weeping that must take place inside those walls. She noticed tissues on the doctor's desk as she gently said lots of numbers and long words, something about inversions and duplications and mutations. That word had snagged Kate's attention away from the poster she was studying, ghostly pairs of chromosomes like wriggling worms. 'Mutant?'

The doctor gave a kind but impatient smile. 'It just means a change in the DNA. A lot of mutation is beneficial – it's how we get diversity on earth.'

'Yes, I know that. I did go to university.'

Beside her, she heard Andrew breathe in but he wouldn't challenge her rudeness, not in front of the doctor. The geneticist was conciliatory. 'Of course. Well, then you'll know that sometimes these changes are not for the better – it's like the copying goes wrong somehow. As if the DNA is a malfunctioning photocopier.'

Kate blinked. Was she really going to use an office metaphor?

'What does it mean, doctor?' Andrew had the right tone – deferential, a little scared. Kate just felt furious, at the woman's sibilant tone, at the drug-company Post-its on her desk, at having to be there at all.

'It means Kirsty is going to be disabled, you know that. What we can't say now is how severely. These chromosomal disorders are often unique – there could be no one else in the world with that condition.'

'It doesn't have a name?' said Andrew.

'No, it's too rare for that, I'm afraid.'

'Did it happen in her?' Kate's voice was angry, used-up. 'This *mutation*?' The ugliest of words, like a rip in the world.

'That's what we need to discuss today.' Hesitation. A click of the drug-company pen. 'We've tested your blood, and I'm afraid, Mrs Waters, the gene is present in you. It's likely come from your side of the family.'

'That's ridiculous. There's no one disabled in my family.'

The doctor clicked her pen again. 'In the past, these things often went unnoticed, because the children would not survive. There may have been stillbirths ...'

Suddenly Kate was picturing herself and Elizabeth, sitting in a hospital corridor in scratchy frocks, kicking at each other's legs. Their father in with their mother, who was mysteriously ill and crying, and didn't come home for what seemed like months. The bad time.

24

'... Or your mother may have had miscarriages. There's often a pattern, when you know what to look for.'

Kate would have liked to bring her fist down hard on her desk, or scream. She had not cried since the birth, and wouldn't for another two years. Instead she bent back one of the longer nails on her left hand, until it snapped and she gasped in pain. Then it was Andrew asking a string of brittle questions – *I see, doctor, and what does this – what's the name of it? There isn't one, I see. And do we know what might have caused it? I see. I see. And will she ever – do we know what she'll be able to* ... on and on, while Kate sat there, parts of her tearing open, and all she could think was how she'd like to slap the doctor in her stupid face.

'What about our son?' Andrew was asking when she tuned back in. He was just centimetres away, but she hadn't the slightest idea what he might be thinking or feeling.

'The law changed a few years back, meaning Adam can't be tested until he's older and can give consent. There's a 50 per cent chance he will carry the gene. I can refer you to a counsellor and they'll help you draw up a family tree.' The doctor said this almost jauntily, as it if might be a fun ancestry project for them to try. Then they were getting up and Andrew was thanking the woman, thanking her for delivering the worst news she'd ever received, and they were leaving, even though she wanted to scream that no, it wasn't fair, it wasn't true, and demand a recount on those blood tests. And that had been it. Every day they waited to see if Kirsty would learn to sit up, or laugh, or talk, or remain as she was, floppy and mewling, wracked with terrifying seizures that stopped the air in her lungs.

There'd been other terrible moments. Lunch with friends who had a baby born two days after Kirsty, healthy and bright-eyed. The questions from everyone, even friends who should have known better, often so rude they took Kate's breath away. How, why, whose fault. What would she be able to do. What was her life expectancy. Did Adam have it too. She even saw them shepherd their own children away, as if it might be catching, and every moment tore her heart with pain and rage. Even worse, the ones who said, *but she's beautiful*, as if judging Kate for not being grateful. *She's still your little girl*, Andrew's mother had said, and Kate had walked out of the room to stop from screaming.

Telling her own parents, bewildered and hostile. Too exhausted and heartsore to bring up her mother's long hospital stays, the crying behind closed doors. Telling Andrew's family, who at least had a better understanding of the science, scanning their faces for judgement, knowing it came from her, this thing. When it came to telling Elizabeth, Kate tried to marshal the same soothing clinical tone as the doctor, but it didn't last. Her sister – not a genius but no dope either – seemed to wilfully misunderstand the biology, even when Kate drew lines on Adam's colouring book in fat red crayon. 'But how could I have what Kirsty has? I'm fine!'

'You can carry the gene, or you can actually have the condition – it depends if you have the good copy of the gene to protect you.'

Elizabeth's blue eyes, milder than Kate's, had gone wide and filmy. 'Oh Kate! This is awful!'

'For fuck's sake, it's me who's dealing with this, not you. Chances are it'll just be one of us who carries it.' And of course Elizabeth's test had come back negative, and she'd phoned up crying with relief.

'I was just so scared. I'm not like you, I could never cope.'

That was the trouble with having a reputation for capability. It was very difficult to take it back when you realised you couldn't in fact cope at all.

*

26

Now, Kate looked at the scene before her, the broken husband, crying children, and knew she needed help. Andrew was on his third written warning from work about lateness, and early leaving, and vomit on his shirt, and they couldn't afford a nanny on one salary.

She took out her Nokia phone, recently acquired, and dialled a number. The old polite Kate would never have followed up on offers of help, assuming they were not actually meant. But the voice of New Kate spoke through her mouth, like a tunnel through a rock. There was only one person who had reacted as she'd wanted to Kirsty's condition, offering practical help, babysitting, unobtrusive favours. Who had never said anything insensitive or cruel. Who might be able to rescue them now.

'Hi, Olivia.' She pushed the pleasantries through her granite face. 'You said to let you know if there was anything you could do to help. Well, actually there is. Are you still on the late shift at work?'

Andrew, present day

Olivia was staring at him over the kitchen island. The furrow between her brows had grown deeper over the years, and sometimes he itched to lean across and smooth it out with his thumb. If touch between them were not so fraught, so loaded with meaning, like a language neither spoke with fluency. 'So, what will you say?'

'I don't know!' His heart was still pounding with the shock of it, Kate's name appearing in his inbox after fifteen years, like someone dead coming back to life. Was that too long to have the same email address – should he have changed it, updated himself – would she judge him?

'Andrew.'

'Sorry. What did you say?'

'We have to think what this means for the children.'

'Well, I have, obviously. I called Adam already.' And his son had hung up on him. Andrew didn't really blame him. Adam had not asked for any of this, to be abandoned by his mother. How was he supposed to react when she suddenly reappeared?

'What timing, too. Today of all days.'

'I know.' When he'd seen the name in his inbox, jolting him back to the past, his first thought had been that Kate somehow knew tonight was his book launch. The day he'd waited for all his life, and of course Kate had to surface and ruin it. *We need to talk*, she'd said. *About your book*. He felt a fear approaching from far away, its shadow already falling over him. 'I think – Liv, I think she's annoyed about the book.' Kate had used the phrase *life rights*. He didn't know what that was. He had deliberately not included her in the story, simply saying she'd left when the children were young. She wasn't even named. And why hadn't the producer told him he was married to Kate, before optioning Andrew's book? Would he have said no if he'd known? It was a lot of money. He could pay it back, maybe, but the idea of causing such a fuss made him cringe.

Olivia's brow creased further. She seemed to be holding herself together by sheer force of will. 'Isn't that for the producer to sort out? Or your agent?'

He still loved that phrase, *your agent*, even in the middle of all this. 'I've no idea. Kate just says we need to talk.'

'Does she mean in person – will she come back *here*?' Olivia was looking round at the house. Swiftly, he catalogued all the things that were the same. The walls the same colour, due a repaint for years. The kitchen island Kate had been so proud of, chipped around the edges from Adam's tantrums and Kirsty's flailing legs. Had they bought so much as a chair since she'd left?

'I don't know.'

28

'I take it she doesn't know about – Kirsty.' She said the name as if it was a wrench, which he knew it was.

He winced. 'She didn't exactly leave a number to keep her updated.' Even the divorce had been conducted without speaking, at a distance through lawyers. Doing whatever it took to shut his eyes to the situation, all these years. 'I ... I'm sorry, I can't do this now, I have to ... prep my speech.' He was so relieved he'd thought of a good excuse to leave the room, he almost gasped. When he went upstairs, though, he didn't go into his office, but instead turned left and pushed open the door to Kirsty's room. His head was reeling. Kate! After all this time!

He still wasn't used to seeing the room empty, the mattress bare, without Kirsty's little face behind the bars of her bed, sometimes staring miserably out, soaked in tears and snot. Or beaming at him, pleased to see him for no obvious reason, when there was nothing he could offer to make her life better. The tug of love at his heart, instinctive, a cord between them bound so tight her pain could always tear him. And she had such a lot of pain, Kirsty, for such a small person. The dank smell of the room had never lifted, and her chair stood at an awkward angle, a cumbersome thing with multiple Velcro tabs to keep her upright, heavy as a dining table. Pushing it straight, he felt a twinge in his back from years of lifting her, and then he realised he was crying, a quick yelp of tears caught in his throat. Oh God. It was too much. He was too old for this. For all of it.

Kate, 2004

After the incident, Olivia began coming at eight each morning, in the noise-whited hour after Andrew left for the train. Trailing scarves and hand-sewn bags, her arrival was like balm on the chapped day. She knew the only hold that would lower the decibels of Kirsty's demented howl, how to make Adam cease his angry rolling of toy cars along Kate's arm, tearing flesh. She would stay to the afternoon, then slip on her cardigan and leave to work the late shift at the station. On the nights she didn't work – she was part-time, and Kate sensed she didn't work for the money – when Andrew came home at 9pm, Olivia was the one with the patience to serve him a meal and ask about the ongoing feud with Phil in Accounts over what constituted an allowable lunch expense.

Most of all, she was a pair of arms into which Kate could pass things, children and dishes and laundry, before ducking with tearful gratitude into the next room and closing the door. The sound of wailing would dip like a siren going by, the smell of nappies and fish fingers fade, and Kate could unclench the permanent crick in her back and breathe again. It crossed her mind that Olivia was doing too much for them, of course it did. She could hardly have any time for herself, always at work or at Kate's house or asleep. But then, she reasoned, Olivia didn't have much of a life. The knitting and card-making could only go so far. Perhaps she was glad of the company. Anyway, when your own need was so palpable and shrieking, it became hard to worry about anyone else. If Olivia was willing to come, Kate would not question it.

It was strange, how completely she fitted into their lives. Before the party when it all changed, Kate would have called Olivia at most a work friend. They had lunch sometimes, rolled their eyes at each other in meetings when male producers said clumsily sexist things. But they weren't close. Somehow, Olivia being there that day of the party, the first one to reach Kate when she fell, it had roped them together.

Two years had gone by since Kirsty's birth, and the country was at war, though Kate, once so ambitious to be a reporter, drinking in every news development, had failed to grasp the thread of it, the protests and coffins arriving with flags draped on top. She had never gone back to work, since no one could be found to look after Kirsty, and even when she ventured out, Adam knocking over displays in shops and having tantrums when she wouldn't buy him a Pokémon, Kirsty attracting pitying glances when people peered in her buggy, the world felt sealed off from her. These moments were the hardest, seeing other people frown at her child. A terrible defensiveness, a shame, a rage at the unfairness of it all, so intense it made her gasp. It wasn't Kirsty's fault, was it?

Kate and Andrew were downstairs, him slumped mindlessly in front of *Newsnight*, her in the kitchen stirring the stew Olivia had made. It was one of Olivia's nights off from the station, so she'd stayed late. Kate couldn't even remember if they'd discussed it. It just seemed normal that she did this. Olivia crept downstairs from settling Adam in bed, and Kate heard the meek clearing of her throat and felt a surge of irritation – *speak up, woman*. But that wasn't fair, Olivia was so good to them. She had to find Nice Kate in there somewhere, Grateful Kate.

'I'm sorry,' said Olivia. 'I can't come next week.'

It didn't go in at first. Then it did, and Kate splashed hot stew up her arm. 'Shit! What did you say?'

'Next week – you see, I have it booked off, from a long time ago.'

For a moment Kate was enraged, as if Olivia were a nanny they paid. 'But what will we do?'

Olivia looked miserable. 'I'm sorry – it's just, my daughter's coming.'

*

31

Kate could hear him. The bathroom routine of lengthy piss-ing, the hocking of mouthwash, the deep honking nose-blows. Andrew always felt the need to evacuate all his cavities before bed. She waited as he checked on the children, standing in their doorways for longer than seemed necessary, gazing at their sleep-ing heads. It irritated her, his sentiment for them, and then she hated herself and became even more irritated. What was wrong with her? Her husband knew how to love the children, even when they were impossible, and she didn't have the knack. She worked so hard at it, dropping kisses on their sweaty heads, holding them close when their bodies were rigid with rage, but it still didn't come, like breasts that would not express milk. She still counted the minutes till she could go into another room and shut the door.

Finally done with his gazing, Andrew padded in, leaving the door carefully ajar, as if they wouldn't hear Kirsty wailing through a concrete bunker. She put her book down. Her hands were slick with cream. 'What will we do?' she said.

He knew what she meant. It was all either of them could think about. 'I'd forgotten she even had a daughter. I suppose she's just been there. She's a rock really, isn't she.'

'Mmm.' Why did Kate feel so angry? Olivia was certainly not obliged to help them – she had already done far too much, more than either set of grandparents. Kate's own parents were too nervous of Kirsty's seizures to offer any care, and Andrew's simply pretended nothing was wrong, buying clothes and toys that might suit an average two-year-old but were all wrong for the one who actually existed.

He sat down heavily on the bed. 'I can't take any more days off. I can feel it when he looks at me. I'm on thin ice as it is.' 'He' was Martin, a man Kate had never met, but who dictated more of her life than seemed possible.

Kate contemplated the wasteland of a week alone. Seven in

the morning to nine in the evening. The children and her and no one else. 'Maybe Olivia can bring her round.'

'The kid? What's her name?'

'She calls her Delia. I think it's short for Cordelia. I'll never understand why people name their children after fictional characters who've died horribly.' Where had that remark come from? Old Kate, Nice Kate, would never have said things like that, or at least not out loud.

'Delia. That's nice.' She could almost see the thought forming in his head – *if we have another ... when we have another ...* Kate panicked. Anything to stop him speaking the words.

'I'll ask them over.'

'And she never said why the kid's not living with her?' Andrew got into bed and reached for his own book. She was reading, or pretending to read, *The Curious Incident Of The Dog In the Night-Time* (a child like that, perhaps she could have managed, and the flood of guilt and jealousy this thought caused made her catch her breath), and he had the same copy of *Shantaram* he'd been struggling through for over a year.

'I didn't like to pry.' And actually, she'd never cared much before, if she was totally honest, too taken up with her own misery. That was what happened when you let someone in. They made you care about their lives, they took up your interest.

Andrew was blowing his nose again. 'It seems strange – a mother leaving her child.'

'Don't leave that tissue there.'

'Sorry.' He balled it up. 'I mean, it's not easy – we know that better than most, but doesn't she miss her? I'd feel like I'd lost a limb without our two.'

Her arm lay under her, dead and numb, like something you could easily walk away from. Kate turned a page with her other-person's hand. 'I don't know if I'd say that.'

33

Andrew looked surprised. 'Oh. Well I know that you – that it's hard.'

It hung between them, leaden, the weight of unsaid words. Could she try to explain how much she was struggling to love her children? She'd been able to hide it with Adam, because he was a difficult baby and she was just adjusting to motherhood, but this was twice now. Two children, two chances to feel that flood of love. 'It's more than hard, it's . . . ' The words were in her mouth, but she swallowed them down. He wouldn't under-stand. He loved the kids, even on the hardest days. 'She's in so much pain, and it hurts me, the way people look at her. The things they say.'

'I know.' He rested a hand on her bare thigh. He was attrac-tive still, hadn't lost his hair or spread round the middle like so many men his age. She could lean into him, breathe in his skin. Ask him to help her, explain the worst and darkest thoughts of her mind. Be a different person.

But no. She couldn't. 'Don't read too long,' she said, and turned over to sleep.

Olivia, with her hippy hair and watery smiles, her echinacea pill-popping, was not firm. She gave way to Kate on every issue – politics, what to feed the children for dinner, what hairstyle would suit her best. So it came as a shock when she very politely but equally resolutely batted away Kate's attempts to meet Delia. They had plans already. Delia was shy with new people. Another time, perhaps. It was like pressing into a soft toy to find the unexpected hardness of the voice box.

When she did it, Kate wondered how long she'd been plan-ning it without realising. When she woke up that morning to the dual wails of her children, the smoke alarm sounding from Andrew's burnt toast, was it then the plan had formed? Or was it when Olivia said she couldn't see Delia? Was she already stamping her feet then, stubborn as a child? The morning, the five hours of it alone, felt entirely intolerable. By twelve she had dressed both children for the outdoors, pulling a hat far down over Kirsty's face. People didn't always notice anything was wrong when she was bundled up like that. She could be just any toddler, not one with . . . a condition that didn't even have a name. People always asked what it was, and Kate had nothing to tell them, and often they would look at her as if she was a bad mother, to not know the name of what afflicted her own child. If you name a thing you can understand it. You can find people in the same boat. You can fight it, and yet they didn't even have that. It felt so unfair Kate sometimes balled her fists and screamed into them.

'We're going to see Livvie,' she told Kirsty. Now and again, shamed into it by Andrew's efforts, Kate talked to her. Sometimes there was a flicker, a sense of anxiety or sadness or even joy, the occasional fit of giggles at nothing, that made Kate think her daughter was in there. But was it just projecting? No way to know. 'She doesn't want Mummy to meet her little girl. And why's that? We'd like to know, wouldn't we?' Kirsty's gaze, blue like Kate's own, drifted off into the distance. Of course she couldn't understand. A terrible tenderness washed over Kate and brought tears to her eyes. It wasn't fair, any of this. And every day she woke up and it never got better.

Adam was in the living room, playing with fierce concentration with some Duplo. Kate always praised what he built – *that's so good, darling* – but privately she worried. Should he be so solitary, so silent? He could talk well enough, but rarely said much. Perhaps he was simply drowned out by the noise and needs of his sister, so often on the brink of death. When he went to school in a few months, that might help. 'Come on, we're going.'

'Don't wanna.'

'Well, tough. Put your shoes on.'

With Kirsty squirming in the buggy, and Adam dragging mutinously behind on his wrist-strap, Kate marched them through town to the flats where she knew Olivia lived. She'd never been invited in. A burst of righteous anger spurred her on to press the doorbell. Inside she could see clean carpet and a pot plant in the hallway. Of course, Olivia's father would have set her up somewhere decent. He was something big in the government, Kate knew, one of those faceless men who sit on boards and quietly determine the lives of millions.

Kirsty began to wail, that broken-glass shriek Kate just couldn't bear, and Adam started to whine. 'I don't wanna go here, Mummy. Don't *wanna*.' His favourite phrase. He was set in his ways, uncomfortable with new places or people. Afraid almost, though Kate couldn't think why. She switched off from the noise of her children, as she had learned to do. Nothing to do with her, an irritant like a road drill or a car backfire. Olivia's figure, seen through the frosted glass, was nebulous. As the door opened, Kate realised Olivia was wearing jeans, something she'd never seen her in before. With her hair tied back and a grubby T-shirt on – was that *yoghurt* on it? – she looked different. Like a mum.

Too late, Kate realised she hadn't even prepared an excuse for dropping by. She just looked at her friend, as Kirsty's howls reached a snot-plugged crescendo and Adam also began to shout, 'Livvie, Livvie, I hate Mummy.' It was the sound of Kate's captivity. She had wanted it, hadn't she? Being a mother was always in her plan, two kids by thirty, bang on time. But did anyone ever picture this? This feeling that you could never again, ever, not even for a second, think only of yourself?

'Bring them in.' Olivia held the door open, and Kate felt most decidedly the shift in power. Usually it was her welcoming the other woman into her space.

'Do you want me to ...?' She worried suddenly about shoes. The door of Olivia's flat had opened onto an oasis of cream carpet.

'If you wouldn't mind.'

She struggled out of her trainers and coaxed Adam from his over a din of complaints. Olivia was saying something about drinks.

'Maybe a juice or something, for Adam.' Her eyes darted hungrily, as her ears were occupied by the noise of both children. Olivia's flat was tranquil and lovely – pictures, books, incense burners, all in harmony. And at the table, paused over the slices of cucumber she was eating with tiny hands, was an angel.

Later, Kate realised she'd vaguely thought there might be something wrong with Delia, a reason she couldn't be around people. When she saw the child, it hit her like a slap. It was the opposite. Olivia had hidden her child from Kate because she was perfect. Beautiful. A helmet of golden hair, a confused smile, little denim dungarees with a duck on the front. She'd laid her food out on her plate like a lady hosting tea, and the mere act of picking it up – healthy food! – spoke reams about her cleverness, her sweetness.

'You didn't tell me.' It was out before she meant it. *You didn't tell me your child was beautiful.*

Olivia moved over to her daughter, standing behind the chair the girl knelt on. Her feet, in their striped socks! Her pink ears! Olivia spoke to the child, not Kate. 'Darling, this is Mummy's friend. And there's the little girl, and a boy to play with. Say hello.'

'Hello,' said Delia obediently. 'Would you like to play with me?' She spoke like a child two years older, and as if to highlight the disparity, Kate felt Adam – four to Delia's three – pull on her arm. His nose was also thick with two slugs of snot.

'I don't wa-nna.'

'You don't want to what?'

'Muh-mee, I don't wah-na play here! I want to go home!' Why was he like this? Couldn't he be a nice child, a normal child?

'I don't care what you want, Adam.' Disengaging, she bent down to undo Kirsty, who was about to strangle herself on the buggy straps. As her back was turned, she sensed Adam lurch across the room.

Weakly, Olivia said, 'Now Ads, remember what we learned about sharing?'

The cake. He'd gone for the cake by Delia's plate, her after-lunch treat that she was waiting for, like a good girl. Something surged in Kate. Why did it have to be her who had this life? With Kirsty on her hip, floppy and distressed, she went for Adam and seized his arm before he touched the pink cupcake. 'No. No, Adam!'

Adam convulsed. 'Let me go, Mummy! It hurts. It hurts!'

Then it was already too late. Adam's free hand was flailing as Olivia tried to move the cake away, blindly lashing to get free – Delia was too close and she cried out in fear. This changed a second later to a howl of pain, as Adam's fingernails, unclipped by his lazy mother, gouged a chunk out of Delia's perfect soft cheek.

Adam wounding Delia – disfiguring her lovely face, so that she'd always carry a scar – wasn't even the worst thing about that day. The worst was what happened to Olivia. Neither adult moved for a second, as Delia held a hand to her face and blood ran over her small fingers, and Adam scuttled behind the armchair. Yes, scuttled was the word for it, like an animal.

Kate started to speak but her voice was flattened in her throat. 'I – Uh ...'

As she watched, a small drop of blood splashed onto Delia's plate, right in the middle of Thomas the Tank Engine's face. Olivia let out a noise like a balloon going down.

'Christ Olivia, I'm so, so sorry. He's not normally – he's never ...' Except Olivia would know that wasn't true, wouldn't she?

Delia herself had stopped screaming after the first howl and was crying quietly. 'Ow,' she said. 'Ow, ow.' She was holding her ear, as if she didn't know where the hurt was.

Olivia was rocking against the wall, down on her hunkers. 'It's my fault, it's my fault. My baby, my poor sweetheart, my baby.'

Kate snapped into action. She had anti-bacterial wipes in her bag, as always. She strapped Kirsty into her buggy, then whipped them out and approached Delia. 'Let me see that, love. You're a brave girl, aren't you? Yes, you're a brave, brave girl.'

'Ow,' said Delia again. Clear tears welled in her blue eyes. 'He hurted me.'

'Yes, he's a bad boy, but it will be better soon. Let's just clean you off.' She cupped the child's soft face. It must have stung but she bore it quietly. Kate realised she had plasters in her bag too – an indication of what her life had become – so she offered them brightly. 'Look, Delia – Thomas plasters! Let's put one on you, good girl.' The cheerful train marred Delia's cheek like a slash in a painting, both adorable and awful. The gouge had been deep, still oozing, and Kate was sure it would scar. Thinking of that made her pop with rage, so when she smoothed the plaster on, resisting the urge to kiss the child's warm head, she seized Adam by his arm and dragged him away. He was still crying. 'I didn't mean to, Mummy! Ow, Mummy!'

'You've been a very bad boy! We're going right home. You

hurt the nice little girl, look at her!' Tightening her grasp, she forced him back into his wrist-strap, the one that was supposed to stop him running away, and took the brake off the buggy. Kirsty had gone limp from exhaustion, drooping like over-cooked pasta. Kate turned to apologise once again, but what could she say? Olivia was still at the wall, heaving slightly.

Delia, with her ruined face, got down from the chair and toddled over. 'Don't cry, Mummy.' She put her chubby arms around Olivia. Kate dragged her own children out and shut the door. She bent down to Adam.

'We don't hurt people like that. We don't do that. Do you hear me?'

He started to cry. He was sorry, she could see, and probably it had been an accident, but he didn't know how to say that, or stop himself lashing out in anger. And wasn't that like her too? She could see the hurt she did to those around her – Olivia, Andrew, Adam himself – and yet she could not stop herself.

When Andrew came home at 8.47pm she was waiting for him at the kitchen island. She hadn't been able to sit down, and was holding her own elbows as if for support. Andrew was as usual train-stale, breath sour, exhausted. He dumped his MP3 player on the table, earphones trailing, as she asked him every night not to. 'Hi,' he said shortly. 'Christ, what a day. He's such a tyrant, I swear.' He stopped. 'What's wrong? Are the kids . . . ?'

She shook her head. Not the kids. Or not in the way he meant. She opened her mouth but found she couldn't explain what had upset her so about the day.

'Christ, are you alright?'

Kate realised to her horror that finally, two years too late, she was crying.

*

40

Four days passed. Kate struggled through them, each one a conveyor belt of nappies and screaming. On Saturday Andrew was at home – she'd never experienced such joy at him walking in the door on Friday night – and she cajoled him into taking both children out. Actually, she cried until he did it. Since her weeping that day after Olivia's, Kate had discovered tears, and was using the full spectrum. Angry, do-not-fuck-with-me tears. Self-pitying, alone-in-the-toilet tears. Silent, shaking, rocking-back-and-forward tears.

'It's cold out – I'm not sure we should.' Andrew looked reluctant, standing in the doorway with Kirsty in her buggy and Adam perched on the step of it, already emitting a high-pitched noise of complaint.

'I don't care. Just get them—' She welled up. 'Just get them away, OK?'

'OK. God!' They went, and blissful silence rained down. Kate drank it in like the finest wine. She would wander the rooms, strewn as they were with toys and dirty clothes – alone time was too precious to waste on tidying – and savour it. She was beginning to think about making coffee, when the doorbell went. Not Andrew, no – he'd had the keys in his hand, and surely even he couldn't have lost them already. She opened it. On the doorstep, dressed in baggy linen trousers and a shapeless jumper, was Olivia.

For a moment, Kate almost didn't let her in. It was as if all the rules of their friendship had been suspended.

'Is Delia OK?' she said stiffly, as she backed away, allowing – but not asking – Olivia in.

'She's gone back to her grandparents.' Olivia had her hands in front of her, twisting them.

'Oh. And?'

'Her face is alright. I'm afraid it might scar. But it wasn't Adam's fault.'

Kate switched on the kettle. 'Well, it was his fault, he scratched her.' Worse than scratched. He had totally lost control, his body bucking, desperate to be away from her grip.

'He didn't mean to, it was an accident.' Olivia hovered by the kitchen stool. 'Kate – I'm so sorry for how I was. I need to tell you why I reacted like that.' Kate waited. Olivia sighed. 'It's rather hard to explain.'

Kate didn't help her. The kettle clicked off but she didn't move.

'Delia's father – he didn't want to be involved with us. He's married, he has a family. We had an affair.'

'I see.'

'When I found out she was coming, well, I was a little … unwell.'

Kate squinted at her. 'Unwell?'

'I thought he would come back to me, you see, when she was born. Then when he didn't and I was alone in my little flat – and, well, I did it.'

'Did what?' Kate eyed the kettle. She wished she had something, a prop to fiddle with.

'I left her on his doorstep. It was March. Did you know babies can survive being really quite cold?'

'No-oo, I didn't.'

'Well, she was alright. He – her father – they weren't even home, but someone saw her and called the police. They kept her in hospital overnight and then my parents took her.'

'And you?'

'Oh, I have this thing – bipolar, they call it.' Olivia laid her hands on the table. 'I'm not mad, Kate. I would never hurt your children. I have medicine, of course. Mostly I'm just down – depressed, at times. Very, very occasionally I'm manic. I don't know what's real and what isn't. It hasn't happened since then, but she will never live with me, not

42

permanently. I can't risk it, her getting hurt. It's the worst thing I can imagine.'

'But—' Kate didn't understand. 'You've been here, with mine, all this time?'

'It's different. With Delia it's more just – the terrible fear. Of what I did to her. And you're always here, and it's as if – I know I can help. I hope so, anyway?'

'Of course.' She was already dreading it, a terrible fear blooming, that she would have to lose Olivia's help.

'Even with Delia, I know it's mostly in my head. We're fine just the two of us, for short times, but I need to control it very carefully. It's how I get by.'

'Oh.' Kate thought for a while. 'I thought it was Kirsty. I thought you were afraid she'd scare Delia.'

Olivia laughed in a way Kate didn't understand. 'Oh Kate. Kirsty will never hurt anyone. That's something you must know.'

She nodded, not getting it. 'Thank you for telling me this.'

At the door Olivia turned. 'I'll come back next week as usual? If you're sure that you're alright with – everything.'

'Well, OK. If you want to.' Kate accepted it as if it was somehow her due. 'I'm glad I saw Delia, you know. She's an angel.'

Olivia winced. 'Yes. She is.'

Kate would not see Delia again for another eighteen years.

Kate, present day

It was early, the clean washed-out part of the day she had always liked. When she first came here, she used to wake up before the sun rose, in a hazy dawn, and she'd never lost the habit. She'd been up most of the night texting friends: Suzi, the women from

43

her activist group, her circle of TV people, all of whom had been on her side. How dare he. *He* being both Andrew and Conor in this situation. How dare they do this to her, these men. The support of the women bolstered her – she would stop this film from happening, somehow. Now Kate was driving along the Pacific Coast Highway, or the PCH as they called it locally. Such a romantic name, with its connotations of the wind in your hair, a convertible and all the time in the world. Instead, Angelenos spent most of their time complaining about the traffic on it. She passed the Getty villa, a new temple to the old, and headed towards Malibu, where the hills that surrounded the city hid shadowed valleys. LA didn't sprawl like London, out into the home counties. You could be suddenly alone here, all too easily.

She'd made this journey many times, but today her mind was on other things. The sudden shock of the past, back in her life. Her husband was going to London to meet her ex-husband and, if the film was green-lit, they might be working together for years. Conor had wanted the story and despite the fact it was Kate's life, *her* story, he'd gone ahead with the option anyway. What did that mean? Was their marriage over, finally? You can push someone very far, but there is always a tipping point. It wasn't as if she hadn't thought of it before. The practicalities of leaving him. Finding a house. Filing papers, her own residency at risk. Trixie. Where did that leave her, the two of them? Would they just be nothing to each other? She couldn't quite believe she had emailed Andrew, in the dark squirming hours of the night – it felt too easy, too dangerous, reaching back into the past through the screen of her laptop and pulling him out. A terrible fear in her chest now, what he might say, the anger she'd avoided for fifteen years. *We need to talk* she'd said. Hoping what? That she could persuade him out of this film? He had not replied overnight, and she was glad of that.

Kate pulled off the highway into a forested estate, green from sprinkling, trees growing up the side of the mountain, a pleasant chalet-style building ahead. She showed her ID to the guard on the gate, and only the small sign – Mountainview Treatment Clinic – revealed this place for what it was. She parked in the same spot she had the week before, reflecting on what creatures of habit people were. It took a lot to change your life. She had done it once, become a different person. Could she again?

Inside was like a country hotel. She went through the ritual of temperature check, hands rinsed in sanitiser, QR check-in code scanned. They were so afraid of being sued here that they carried on, when everywhere else had abandoned the theatre of safety. The staff, who wore green tunics, spoke in restful tones, and there was a bowl of apples on the counter, sunlit from the picture windows. They even remembered who you were. 'Mrs Ryan?'

So many times in her life people had called her by the name of one man or another. 'Well, no – it's McKenna. Just Kate is fine.'

'You're here to see Beatrice? Wonderful. She's in the day room.' Kate was led along a hushed carpeted corridor, following the distant sounds of flute music. Conor must be paying through the nose for this place. He'd always been happy to paper over feelings with money.

Trixie was in an armchair by the window, covered in blankets and wearing a beanie despite the heat. Her pinched white face moved at the sight of Kate. The nurse – because that's what she was, not a spa employee – left them. The room was beautiful. There was a top-range coffee machine on a wooden table, magazines, organic snacks. All the same, this was not a place anyone came to voluntarily.

Kate sat down. 'How are you?'

Trixie shrugged, a small gesture with her fingers. 'Alive.'

'I'm glad to hear it. Did you eat anything today?' The question you weren't supposed to ask, but there came a point when you had to because you couldn't think about anything else.

'They make me. And no, I didn't do drugs, because I can't get them.' Kate met her eyes, the glint in the green of them. Somehow, this weak, ailing girl was one of the few people she could really be honest with, and how strange that was. 'He's not coming?' said Trixie, her voice hoarse. Stomach pumps, and vomiting.

'I'm sorry. He's not.' Best to be honest. She laid a hand on Trixie's cold white one. No response. Kate knew better than to try and excuse her husband.

Trixie looked her over. 'Something's happened? You look like a crazy person.'

'Thanks. Yes, it has. Your father . . . ' Trixie made a small movement. 'Conor,' Kate corrected herself. 'He's optioned a book.'

'He does that.'

'Yes. But this one – it's different. I'm *in* this book.' Or perhaps she wasn't. She wasn't sure which would be worse.

'Oh?' That had caught Trixie's attention, which was rare.

'My ex wrote it. About – about our daughter.' She could hardly say the word. It felt like a lie, especially to Trixie. Kate had never discussed it with her, but the girl must know what she'd done to her own children, must feel on some level that Kate could not be entirely trusted. 'You know she's – how she is. Well, she learned to communicate, apparently, with sign language. I didn't think that was possible. He wrote a memoir about it.' She was still trying to process this information. Kirsty had learned to speak? How?

More importantly, what would she *say*?

'And Conor wants to make a heart-warming movie out of it? He knows it's about your family?'

'Oh yes. That won't stop him.'

Trixie pulled herself up in the chair, with difficulty. She looked like a cancer patient, yet all her suffering was self-made. 'Another classic Conor moment. You should totally leave him.'

Kate sighed. 'I don't know what to do. If I should go and see them in England, or try to sue or something – or even if I should . . .'

'Run again.'

'Well. Yes.' That was her main impulse. And yet she was here, though she didn't have to be. That had to count for something.

'You think they'd want to see you?' Kate thought about it, the family she'd fled from fifteen years before. Andrew, her husband. Adam, her angry son. And Kirsty, and here was where her thoughts always failed her, a river of rushing pain under a sheer coat of ice.

She sighed. 'Honestly? I have no idea.'

Kate, 2005

'Why are we doing this again?'

Andrew used his 'Kate' voice to answer, as he always did these days. It sounded like someone straining reasonableness out through a sieve. 'They say it's good.'

'Oh, it'll make Kirsty better, will it?'

'I just think it might help. With . . . everything.'

Andrew turned the car round a corner, gentle, safe. She knew he was right. Yes, they had to do something, they could not go on as they were, slowly drowning in misery. He had suggested various things over the years – couples counselling, a privately paid support worker, selling the house and moving somewhere cheaper. None of them viable or anything she could face, and so she had agreed to this instead.

Kate turned to look at her daughter, whose half-closed eyes were fixed on her own fingers, apparently the most fascinating thing in the world. They said it was because of the patterns it made on her starved retinas. It was obvious now that she wasn't like other children. That she would never talk. That she hadn't the muscle tone to walk. When they took her out, the stares came quicker now. No matter how much Kate brushed her fine blonde hair, dressed her in little dungarees or cute pinafores, there was clearly something wrong. The way she held her body, floppy and boneless. The shape of her face, her unfocused eyes. The noise she could make, ear-shattering for someone so tiny, when in distress, and not able to tell them what was wrong. Kate had almost given up trying to speak to Kirsty, feeling stupid when the child's eyes drifted away, looking at nothing. She had almost accepted her daughter would never do most things. But that didn't mean she wasn't furious about it, the unfairness, the raw hand her child, and she, had been dealt. *She didn't ask to be born*, was something Andrew had started saying a lot, but that was meaningless. No one ever asked to be born. He still spoke to Kirsty. He still kissed her on the forehead, and picked her up for hugs, and bought her toys and books. Books! It made Kate want to cry, the bright pictures and cosy stories of a world where nothing bad could happen.

Her eyes flicked to her son, who sat in his car seat bundled up in his coat. Adam was clutching his Action Man and scowling deeply – he still spooked at new places, new people, new sensations. Sometimes Kate couldn't bear to look at him, so clearly did she see her own thoughts reflected in his identical blue eyes. *This is so stupid.* He was five now. Kirsty was three and still alive, somehow. Kate was thirty-three – her birthday forever the same day as her daughter's, always mired in the memories of that day.

She wasn't sure she would ever celebrate it again. Thirty-three and her life felt over. She hadn't gone back to work, likely never would. Where once she'd looked over her shoulder, a little smug, as if winning a race at school, strides ahead of her competitors, she had now been left behind. The anchor job at *Look South* had gone to a twenty-six-year-old with shiny highlighted hair, while Kate's world was the house and the park and the gates of Adam's school. Kirsty might get some day care when she turned five, though it wasn't clear how many days a week it would be. But it wasn't her fault. Kate reached back, pushed aside Kirsty's damp hair. She'd put her in denim overalls, a bee embroidered on the front, a sweet outfit made for a child two years younger, she was so small still. Kate clung to her anger, because tenderness was harder. Anger kept her going, spurred on like an automaton. If she allowed herself to soften, imagine how it felt to be her daughter, she might break down entirely.

'Here we are,' said Andrew cheerfully, pulling into the church hall car park. He always drove so anxiously, as if apologising to the other cars. Kate sat for a moment and so did he, as if neither of them could face taking off their seatbelts and going in. The church hall was a low grey building, pebble-dashed, an orange light burning in one barred window. 'Come on, everyone.' Andrew undid his belt resolutely.

It was possible to ignore it sometimes, if they were speaking of the children or watching something interesting on TV, or making the effort on a family day out. But in the shower, in the middle of the night, waking to the ridge of Andrew's tired back, the truth of it clutched at her. *I don't love him.* She didn't love her husband, after six years of marriage. She knew him too well, perhaps. There was nothing else to find out, no new pages to turn in the book of them. They had become people who cared for children together, that was all, and there were the next fifty years stretching ahead. There'd been a day, a few months back, when the Tube had exploded, and she hadn't even thought to worry about Andrew being on it until he'd called, emotional and panicked from the office. What did that mean, that she heard about a terrorist attack in a city where her husband worked, and didn't even think of him?

Andrew never said anything about the yawning gap between them, beyond the suggestions of therapy, holidays, workshops, groups. He went to work, then came home and got down in his suit to tidy up the flour, or toys, or shredded newspaper from the floor, or on one bad day, actual shit. On weekends he took the kids to the park, or soft play, or trailing round improving National Trust properties. He was good. He worked hard, it wasn't his fault he had to stay in the office so late or that the train, with its electrified third rail, was so often delayed by ice or wind or heat. Nor was it his fault she was so angry all the time, directing her rage at him since she couldn't take it out on her children. But all the same, Kate wondered how far she could let things slide before he would speak. They hadn't even touched in a year, beyond hands brushing to pass over money, or plates, or children. It was a lurch like missing a step on the stairs, to reach for that love and find it gone. As if she'd found herself unable to breathe, or some other simple human act everyone took for granted.

Her life, once so carefully curated, had become something she didn't want people to see. So she had agreed to come here. To find those who might possibly understand.

The church hall smelled of lino and soiled nappies, which was to be expected when you invited parents to 'bring the kids – siblings and all disabilities welcome!' In a group like this, 'kids' encompassed a pretty, scowling teenage girl, slumped against the wall by the tea urn, all the way to a boy of indeterminate age who was strapped into a complicated upright wheelchair. He wore a helmet buckled under his chin, and was giving out a sort of low, loud moan. Kate had never seen someone this disabled before – well you didn't, did you? When was that ever on TV? – and felt a pulse of distress, immediately berating herself. It wasn't his fault, poor boy, and for all they knew their future looked the same. Kirsty was in her arms, warm and strangely light, clutching her hands in Kate's pea coat like a little monkey. Would she, could she, feel some sort of kinship here – were these her people?

A woman was coming towards them, lumbering on orthopaedic sandals. She was swathed in floral prints as if she'd become entangled and had to climb her way out of Laura Ashley. A line of fuzz darkened her upper lip. 'Welcome!' This, Kate inferred, must be Margaret, who ran the group. She had formed her own opinion of Margaret from the latter's emails, misspelled in blinking Comic Sans, on a variety of novelty backgrounds. Kate felt a gust of cold air as Andrew shut the door behind them, holding Adam by his hood as the boy prepared to bolt. They were in. Her fate was sealed.

Margaret introduced Kate to the 'gang', as she insisted on calling them. She had a strong Birmingham accent that reminded Kate shudderingly of her childhood. Margaret's disabled child – adult, really – had died a few years ago, a boy called Billy. Billy's dad had 'done a runner' after the child was born, and it seemed the gap in Margaret's life could now only be filled with people who knew what she'd been through. Kate nodded through this sad spiel, which was delivered near the 'refreshment station', though she didn't see how Margaret's experience could be the same as, say, that of the family with the engaging little boy with Down syndrome, who was pealing with laughter at a jack-in-the-box he'd found. But that was the

51

thing about disability, it was different for everyone. You couldn't assume anyone understood. This boy could expect to live a full life, have hobbies, have friends, perhaps even live away from his family one day. It wasn't the same.

The 'refreshments' on offer were coffee granules and value tea bags, plus a variety of cheap baked goods set on coloured party plates. This jaunty touch hit Kate somewhere very raw and painful. She looked at Andrew, who fumbled in the pockets of his coat for coins to pay the subs Margaret insisted on – 'I like to keep everything straight'. She knew he hated things like this, walking into a room where he didn't know anyone, but he was trying.

Kate tried to keep track of everyone, while maintaining two lists in her heads – whose child had what condition, and which of the women had the nicest clothes. Part of her must have hoped after all that she'd make a friend, someone she could invite round for coffee without having to excuse Kirsty's howls or seizures. But she could never be friends with anyone who wore a North Face coat because of a light amount of drizzle. She'd given up hope of finding anyone – a similar feeling to her twenties, when she would scan a bar for eligible men and see none – when the door opened with a muffled curse and a woman fell in, smoothing rain from her hair, which was short and spiky. She was dressed in clothes Kate would never wear – a silver Puffa jacket, and underneath a crop top and Adidas tracksuit bottoms, as if she'd come from the gym – but she had an air of style, of refusing to be downtrodden, that Kate could relate to.

'Aimee,' sighed Margaret. 'You're late again.'

She couldn't have said how, but Kate and Aimee became friends right away, that very night. Aimee gave you little choice, really. She would just start talking at you, spilling it all out like she was upending her handbag in search of her keys. Her bouts of clinical depression, the affluent Essex childhood with a pony and Range Rover, all that disrupted by drugs, kicked out by her family, her twenties as an acid-house casualty, finding herself pregnant by Keith, who owned a chain of gyms and had installed her as an aerobics instructor. Aimee understood the narrative of her own life. She'd learned how to structure a hard-luck tale from watching Jeremy Kyle. Even the birth of her son with severe disabilities hadn't daunted her for long. 'I still loved him, know what I mean Kate? He's still my boy. But Keith, he couldn't see that, he just wanted some little tyke he could sit on his shoulders at the football.' So Keith had left, or rather insisted Aimee and Dylan leave, and now they languished in a flat in the cheap end of Bishopsdean, and Keith had moved one of his Pilates teachers – 'Vikki, bony bitch'– into the five-bed mansion that had once been Aimee's. None of this had broken Aimee. You could see it in her, stamping her feet in over-sized trainers against the cold outside the church hall, but as Dylan got older and more challenging, it seemed to Kate that cracks were starting to show. She didn't even bring him to the meetings now, in case he hurt the younger kids.

'Couldn't face this group shit when he was younger,' said Aimee, eyeing the dank concrete walls of the hall. 'But I don't know what to do with him now. He could punch my lights out if he wanted to. He wets himself, he gets these bad dreams, and you hear him blubbing and screaming all night long. It chills you, Kate.' She was one of those people who put their hand on your arm and say your name, as if assuring you of their attention, and Kate was surprised to find she liked it. She realised that all her old friends – the ones who'd melted away after Kirsty – were middle-class, polite, used to veiling their feelings behind shiny hair and tight smiles. Here was Aimee, nervy and unstable, exposing her still-honed navel on this winter night, but she was the first person in years who actually seemed to understand.

A light showed in the door – Margaret, in her floral frock. 'Who's out there? I'm afraid we don't allow smoking.'

'We're *outside*,' said Aimee, eyeballing her like the unruly girls in upper sixth who Kate had always wanted to be friends with.

'Well. It's time for Circle Talk now.'

'Come on, then, Kate,' said Aimee, grasping her new friend's arm, stubbing out her cigarette on the wall with her other hand, and Kate felt an old long-forgotten sensation. In this ill-matched and motley group, she was actually cool.

'Now he's eighteen I have to fight for everything,' said Aimee. 'The nappies, girls, they'll bankrupt me. His buggy, his grab rails, his carers – I never know what they're going to cut next. It's scary.' They had met for coffee in town, along with another mum from the group – Kate had been slightly miffed on learning she was not the only one invited into Aimee's confidence. Sarah was pretty and artless and not even thirty yet. Her voice was accented from St Lucia, still unusual in the white-washed town Kate had somehow found herself living in. Her son Alexis, aged six, had Duchenne's, was already in a wheelchair, and would likely die by his twentieth birthday. He sat nearby, eyes darting around with a quick intelligence, though he was already struggling to speak. Kirsty was in her buggy and Dylan, Aimee's son, at a nearby table in the helmet he had to wear to stop him bashing his head. Kate could see how people shot him glances, and felt a familiar protective rage, along with a terror of what lay ahead for Kirsty.

Heart racing with what she was about to admit, Kate now said, 'Do you ever think, you know – why me? It's so unfair. Everyone else just has these kids who are fine, they're going to

54

grow up and live their lives and we've got . . . well. I just, I can't, I don't – feel the same. All these happy mums. I just can't feel it.'

She'd caught it. A brief look from Sarah to Aimee. So even between them, some things could not be said. Sarah hesitated. 'I always feel he was sent to me for a reason.' Too late, Kate spotted the crucifix resting on her smooth chest. Of course. That would make a difference. 'God knew I could cope, and so I do. And he's so special! He's so full of love, and joy, he really is.' She meant it too. Her eyes softened into a smile, looking at her boy, perhaps thinking how hard she had to love him in the little time she would get.

Aimee said, 'I know it's tough, Kate. But they're still ours, aren't they? It still works the same, if you see what I'm saying? The love.'

Kate was nodding vigorously. 'Oh of course, I didn't mean otherwise! God, of course not.' But it didn't work the same. Not for Kate. And it wasn't because of Kirsty, was it? Because she hadn't felt it with Adam either, this love they were talking about. She tucked the thought away in the dark place, pretended they had misunderstood her, and not long after Sarah said she had to take her boy home, and Aimee got up too, beginning the long process of getting Dylan ready to move. She pressed a rough kiss onto Kate's forehead, but Kate knew she had been judged. Even among people worse off than her, she was not good enough. She sat, knowing she should take Kirsty home, as her daughter began to cry, building up to her full-blown shrieks. She had failed. This was something she simply could not do. Being a mother, a wife. Loving.

'Kate? Is that you?'

It took her a moment to come out of her fugue, rocking the buggy up and down. When she looked up to see who was there, she was acutely aware of her lank hair and baggy jeans. 'Oh!

Hello.' David McGregor. Her old boss at *Look South*, the one who'd hired her in the first place. He was wearing a suit, trim and handsome although he was, what, ten years older than her? She hadn't seen him since her birthday barbecue, three years before. She remembered being pleased he had come to see her house, how well she'd managed everything at the party.

He was trying not to wince at Kirsty's off-key crying. 'You've your hands full, I see.' She saw him look in the buggy in that way people did when they knew, not sure what to say. It made her want to hide the child under her jumper, out of shame, protectiveness. *It's not her fault! Don't look at her like that!* 'We were very sorry you didn't come back to work, Kate. A big loss.'

'I meant to but – I can't.' She gestured towards the buggy.

'You were so good. Especially when we got you on screen those few times – perfect.'

Kate was horrified to realise she was going to cry. She swallowed the tears down with her last cold dregs of coffee. 'I loved it. It was just so – it was what I'd always wanted. But they'd hardly take me back now, I'm in such a state.'

'You're still beautiful,' he said, and he flashed her a sudden look, one she had not seen from a man in a long time. Desire, but tinged now with sadness, with loss, and her body began to react, shocking her with a knowledge it seemed she'd always had. He was standing so close she could almost breathe in the smell of his skin. His pale wrist under his watch. The silver threaded through the hair above his ear. *David.* Of course. Why hadn't she realised?

It seemed to shock him too, because he fumbled out the next words. 'Er, anyway, it was nice to . . .'

Kirsty's wails kicked up a notch; she was hungry. There was never anything she could eat in cafés or restaurants – Kate was used to asking for soup and maybe a potato to mush up in it, if they had any. To strange looks, always. To being different. 'I'm sorry, I better . . . '

'Yes, yes, of course. I'm just getting mine to take away.' He paused. One of those moments your life can go one way or the other. 'Maybe a catch-up sometime though?'

Kate sucked in air, suddenly breathless. It was a small thing to ask. Just coffee. A chat. But there was a dangerous charm in life-altering acts. If she said yes to this apparently innocuous request, she knew somehow her marriage, her life would be forever changed.

Lightly, she said, 'Maybe sometime. Email me?' Andrew was less likely to see an email. As Kate walked home, a new snap in her step, she told herself it was nothing. A work catch-up, maybe a job in it. Sensible, really, to meet him. Nothing she should feel guilty about at all.

Adam, present day

The latest iteration of the band – Pete having gone solo after a row about the takings from a gig at Lancaster University – met three times a week to practise in a room behind a pub on Shoreditch High Street. They tried hard, but they'd lost almost two years of gigs and practice, and Adam could already see how it would go. Tom was starting to talk about getting a proper job, not just shifts in the Costa at Liverpool Street. Matt was good, and girls liked him, so Adam worried he'd leave too. Barry would never leave the band, but was at best a glorified roadie. Maybe Adam should go solo too, get out before he was left behind. That would be the worst. But he wasn't much of a guitarist, if he was honest. It was so hard. He just wanted to have made it already, not constantly scrape to climb an unassailable mountain of unpaid, poorly attended gigs, gormless venue owners, reviews in free papers, pennies for Spotify plays.

'You OK, mate?' said Barry. Adam had played the wrong note three times.

'Yeah. Head's not with it today.' Adam hated admitting this, or any sign of weakness. 'Bender last night, you know.' That was a lie; he rarely got drunk, not liking to lose control.

Matt nodded shrewdly. He was a quiet guy, his talent speaking for itself. Kept Adam on his toes. 'We can break for five, if you want.'

'Thanks.' Putting down his guitar, sweaty under the strap, Adam picked up his phone, which was sitting on a bar table, ringed with the ghosts of old drinks. A flurry of messages from this girl or that, texts and WhatsApps and emails and Tinder matches, but he hadn't the energy to flirt right now, so he flicked them to dismiss. Then her name. *Delia*. His heart began to pound, flooded with dopamine and adrenaline and something else. Fear. Why was she getting in touch, when they'd agreed several months ago (thirteen weeks and four days, not that he was counting) that it was a bad idea? Whatever was going on between their parents, and after what the family had been through the past year, they were a little too close, so they had to walk away. But here was her name and his heart was banging right out of his chest.

Can we talk? Three words guaranteed to strike fear into a man. It meant a hard discussion of some kind. It meant drama. *I wish you would . . . why can't you . . . can you just . . .* But Delia wasn't like that, was she? When she'd said, in that terrible time, *let's not be in touch, it's too painful, it'll hurt them too much*, she had stuck to it, leaving Adam gazing for hours at their message stream from before, pathetically saved to read over and over. Maybe she knew about his mother, coming back from the

58

virtual dead. He signalled to the boys he was going out, and then, on the draughty high street, over the blare of traffic, he pressed Delia's name to call her. Phoning, like it was 1997, as if he'd ever answered a call from a girl in his life. As he waited, he recognised and almost welcomed the doubt. He really had no idea if she'd pick up. And that was unusual, for him. It energised him, the not-knowing. 'Hello?' That clear posh voice of hers, from the expensive schools her grandparents had sent her to while her own mother was busy raising Adam.

'It's me. Adam.' Didn't she know that, had she deleted his number or something? No, she'd just texted him. 'What's up?'

'I meant more we should talk in person.' He couldn't read her tone.

'Sounded urgent. Is it about Kate?'

'Kate?'

'My – my mother.' The word cramped in his mouth. 'You haven't heard?'

'Heard what?'

'Oh, it's a long story, but basically – she's been in touch. After all this time.'

'OK.' He listened to her down the line, the soft release of her breath, and wondered where she was now, in her bedroom in the shared house in Hackney maybe, silk scarves and vintage teacups scattered artfully about. Lying on her small bed where he'd been so happy for a while. 'No, I didn't know. I should call Mum. She'll be a wreck.'

'You didn't want to talk to me about that?'

'No.'

'What, then?' Adam hated suspense. Hated waiting, hated uncertainty.

'I can't tell you over the phone.'

'*Delia.*' It felt good to say her name, even in this situation.

'I'm sorry, it wouldn't be right. Can we meet? Where are you?'

'Shoreditch. Band practice.'

'Oh! I should leave you to that then.' She had the greatest respect for his creative time, as she called it. So much that it made him ashamed, because he hadn't yet lived up to what she believed he could. Maybe he never would.

'No, it's – we're about done here. I can come to you.' A lie.

'Not now. An hour or so.' Stupid. He'd lose all respect for a girl who dropped her life and ran to him, and here he was doing the same. With someone else, he might try to claw back control, either not turn up or cancel two minutes before, when she would already be there ordering a coffee. But he couldn't do that to Delia. This was part of the problem.

'OK.' Adam hung up and went inside for his hoody. Despite his worry about what she was going to say – chlamydia? – and the looming asteroid of his mother coming back, his heart felt light. He was going to see her again.

Kate, 2006

Kate checked and rechecked the map she'd drawn for herself on a piece of Adam's sketching paper. Even then she was so nervous she took a wrong turn, going round and round the industrial estate, which seemed to be full of car showrooms. Her hands felt slippery on the wheel, and when she finally saw the Travel Express sign and pulled into the car park, she had to sit for ten minutes breathing. Her stomach was roaring like the back of a bin lorry – was she really going to do this? For a moment she thought about driving away, going back to the house and fitting both children onto her knee for a hug, chatting to Olivia who now looked after them sometimes by herself, to allow Kate time, time to do the terrible thing she was about to do. And then when Andrew came home going up to him, smiling, kissing him full on the mouth, starting again. Being a different person.

It was the impossibility of doing this that sent her scrabbling from the car and into the shabby lobby of the hotel. *If you can't go back, you must go forwards.* This was the mantra crocheted onto the cushion her sister had sent her for her birthday. Kate had hidden it in the spare room, unsure if it was pointed, or just another thoughtless gift from a sister she knew less and less as time went on. Elizabeth rarely came to visit, or help with the kids, didn't understand, and Kate couldn't even blame her for that because she barely understood herself. The hotel smelled of stale coffee and floor cleaner. Eyes cast down, Kate said someone else's name to the woman behind the desk, who had a frizzy perm and greasy skin, pores huge. She was given a key on a chipped wooden holder, and asked about newspapers or wakeup calls. Blushing, she murmured no. They wouldn't be here more than three hours. The thought made her obscurely sad as she went to the smeary lift, very aware of her lack of luggage. Room 425. She walked along the corridor, which smelled of ash. There it was. She couldn't go in. Trembling, she fumbled the key in the lock. A cool quiet descended on her, the hotel room fresh and unused if run-down. She put her bag down on the bed. She thought about making a cup of tea, but there was a clattering at the door. She froze, then moved very slowly across the frayed carpet. It might not be him. Of course it was him.

David was slightly hunched in the hallway, as if the place was too small for his size. He was dressed strangely – tracksuit bottoms and a white polo shirt. She had only ever seen him in a suit or smart jumper, sometimes with the arms rolled up to show his tanned forearms, the strong wrist encircled with an expensive watch. 'I'm meant to be running,' he said, seeing her look, and then he leaned in to kiss her, not on the cheek as she'd expected, but full on the mouth. She was taken aback and didn't respond; the door wasn't fully shut. She flipped the 'do not disturb' sign onto the handle and firmly turned the lock.

'Um. You want tea or something? Coffee?' Maybe he could figure out how to work the machine.

He was pushing back his hair, already sweaty as if his run had been real. 'What? No, I'm fine.'

She didn't know where to place her body in the room. Nervously, she lifted the tiny stupid kettle and couldn't think how to perform the next step. There was no socket anywhere it could stretch to. 'I was thinking I might have some, but I don't know, and there's only one packet of biscuits—'

'Kate.' He was beside her and his hands were on her waist. 'What's wrong?'

She bit her lip. 'I'm really nervous. Sorry.'

'I'm nervous too. I felt like crap leaving today.'

'Me too. It's awful.' Were they going to compete over their guilt? Glumly, she moved to sit on the bed.

He sat in the desk chair – the kind you might get at a conference, with wooden arms – and moved it so it was facing her, and he took her hand. His was warm, slightly clammy. 'Let's have some contact, at least.'

'OK.' She entwined her fingers with his, still not able to look at him. 'I never knew this place was here.'

'No. Funny how you can miss bits of your own town. You find it OK?'

'I got lost. I was so nervous.'

'I had to go back for my keys three times.'

They chatted until she was finally able to look him in the eyes, cool and green and kind. 'It's so good to see you.'

His mouth curved. 'You too. Christ, I missed you.'

'I missed you.' She reached out and he kissed her, hesitantly, cupping her face. It was the slowness that got to her, the holding back. She found herself clawing at him, his hair and back and T-shirt. It smelled damp, as if it hadn't been laundered properly, and she had a flash of his home life, his wife and children and washing machine. She'd met the wife a few times in the past, an angular, bony woman who worked part-time as a teaching assistant, and had felt pleasantly superior. But this wasn't about the outside world, it was about blank spaces, a room for rent.

They walked, glued at the mouth, to the sagging bed. He stopped to take things from his pockets – keys, wallet. Was this really going to happen? She was going to be unfaithful? Hadn't she been set on this path since they met in the coffee shop last year? Her mind couldn't take it in, but it seemed her body could, because her legs were opening and wrapping round him, and her mouth was on his neck. 'I want you,' she heard herself say. 'I want you so much.'

'You drive me crazy, Kate.'

'Say it again!'

'Kate.' He kissed her, 'Kate Kate Kate.' She loved her name in his mouth. Then they were at the farthest point they'd been, and then further. He unbuttoned her top with shaking hands, laying her open, and she tried to say something to announce her body, apologise for it, not let him unwrap her like a gift with no message. 'I'm not – I mean, since the kids—'

'You're beautiful.' His accent thickening, pure Glasgow. 'Look at you. Perfect.' He ran hands over her stretched stomach and up. His mouth travelled down her neck and chest, and with one finger he scooped her nipple into his mouth.

'Jesus!' Kate, who'd been imagining this for months, arched her back. 'Oh God, oh God.'

With rapt concentration, David was removing her shirt and bra and she was half-naked. 'Slow down, slow.'

But her jeans were off – lifted clear, ungainly peeling – and she was in her pants, and he was fumbling off the awful tracksuit bottoms and the white sports socks, bobbly on the bottom, moving faster and faster. To be wanted so obviously was like a drug. Was that really all it took? Different hands, a different mouth?

David took off his askew glasses, looking blank and dazed. 'Should I get the, eh—'

She didn't understand, then she did. 'Yeah. I suppose.'

He got up and fumbled in his tracksuit and then he was shrugging off his underwear, rising up, and stripping open the foil packet, breathing hard. And then, all of sudden, she had crossed some kind of line and it was happening. She was unfaithful.

She hadn't expected to have an affair, of course – does anyone? Yes, she hadn't slept with Andrew since she was four months pregnant with Kirsty, but that wasn't the reason. It's never the reason, not really.

The reason, when she looked back on it after – at her leisure, when all she had left to her was time – was that she'd become invisible. The second birth had left her ripped in places she hadn't even known existed. For years after she was still finding angles it hurt to bend into, or bizarre twinges when she peed. And that was just her body. She was also still piecing together the fragments of memory from that day – her own blood blooming poppy-red on the hospital sheet, the baby's fast-emerging head, monstrous from the wound opened up in her stomach. All the same, she tried, made approaches to Andrew even though her body felt like someone else's, a site of trauma. *I'm tired*, he would mumble. *It's the commute. It's the stress. I have a cold.* She considered toys, outfits, light bondage, weekends away – the defeat-admitting rota of 'spicing it up'. But she didn't want that. She wanted just the magnetic force of true, early attraction. And that was why seeing David that day in the café was so very dangerous. When she looked back at the start of it – which she would do often, not to deny herself this essential pleasure of lovers – there'd been a spark between them from the moment she walked into the *Look South* newsroom, all heels and smiles and eager to please, doing her best to hide the fact she had a young baby at home. He'd been flirtatious in a safe, avuncular way she had enjoyed. But she had never expected this.

After that first email, after the coffee shop, they'd started meeting, in moments thrilling with terror. Kate suddenly had to see Aimee a lot more, meaning she barely saw her at all. David had an elderly red setter that was dragged for lengthy walks, and made to sit in the back of the car while David and Kate held hands under the table in the Wig and Pen, a rundown pub on the edge of town. And then, after, he would be pressing her into the cold car, his tongue in her mouth in a way she hadn't been kissed in years, and whispering in her ear how much he wanted to be in her, and on her, and over. Sex was all prepositions, it seemed to Kate. The frustration was what made it all so enjoyable, like a lavishly wrapped present under the Christmas tree. But in all this wanting, there came a time when they actually had to do what they'd longed for so vociferously.

And now here she was. What she'd dreamed of for months. Silently, fitting together. Gasps from them both. 'Oh Kate. I've been waiting for this.'

For a few moments, it was the most right she'd ever felt. He was panting into her neck, struggling with the rhythm. When she opened her eyes the ceiling above them was stained and cracked. His face was very close, dripping with sweat – drops of it were falling on her chest and mouth. 'David,' she said. She wanted him to say her name back to her.

'Oh. Oh.' He seemed to have retreated into himself, eyes glazed, and Kate suddenly arrived at the point where she realised it wasn't going to work for her. She tried to quell her disappointment. Now she just wanted it over, the wet slap between them, the torn-silk rasp of his breath. Then they passed another point and she realised it wasn't going to work for him either.

'What's wrong?'

'I'm sorry. I don't know.'

Things deflated between them and she felt him slip out. 'I'm sorry.'

He was still panting. He pushed back damp hair. 'It's not you.'

Vulnerable, Kate sat up and pulled her knees to her chest. Between her thighs was wet and chafed. She wondered if she'd have cystitis in the morning.

'Hey, don't look so sad.' David was trying to kiss her, clumsily, the condom still hanging from him. His mouth was salty with sweat. 'You're so beautiful. It's not you. Please don't think it's you. I'm just – the guilt you know. And I'm not used to these.'

Of course, because he could make love to his wife with no fear of babies or infection. Because that's what marriage was. Sex without fear. She hugged her legs.

Kate had imagined showering together, but the bath was chipped and the shower curtain mildewed. It clung to her as she stood under spitting water, bringing back unpleasant memories of recently encountered limp rubber. The shower was not erotic but purposeful, scouring away traces of him, his mouth and hands. She used the tiny bottle of gel and found it left her body with slick, nasty patches. The mirror was rust-stained and in it her face looked thin and exhausted. The face of an adulteress.

66

When she came out, clutching a threadbare towel round her, David was replacing the phone on its cradle, a just-been-caught look on his face.

'Shower's free.' She pretended not to know he'd been talking to his wife, with whom no doubt he never failed to finish. Three children were proof of that.

'I have to go,' he said.

'But don't you need to . . .'

'Oh, I'm meant to be sweaty, if I'm running. I'll shower before I . . . well.'

He was really going to leave? She stood there in her towel. There was something peculiarly sad about putting the same clothes on again, in daylight. Her mouth felt tacky and she wished she'd thought to bring a toothbrush. But how to explain that to Olivia, who had waved her off, supposedly to a doctor's appointment? The thought of her faithful friend at home, taking care of children not even her own, made Kate gasp as the wave of shame hit.

He stood jangling keys, not touching her. Time was short now. In thirty seconds, he'd walk out and this moment, this one chance, would be over and shattered.

'I'm sorry,' he mumbled, looking away. 'I fucked up.'

'It's OK.' The disappointment crushed her chest.

But they both knew it wasn't.

She waited in the rumpled, used room counting to two hundred, and then she went out and shut the door. In the lobby she learned that David had not pre-paid for the room, as she'd supposed, and had to scrabble in her bag for £30 in cash. The realisation that he could have left her having to use her debit card, traceable, began a slow burn of resentment that hurt more than the ache between her legs.

*

When she woke up the next day, for once she didn't see his name in her inbox – he tended to email late at night, when his wife was in bed. It didn't mean anything, she told herself. Throughout the day she checked the computer every hour, forcing herself to ration it. Nothing, nothing. And the next day, and the next. She went through them like a deep-sea diver, slow and clunky, fear blooming in her stomach. Giving vague answers to Olivia and Andrew when they asked her things about the kids, dinner, the house. It was over. She'd failed him and he was gone. So what would she do now? What did she live for? When the phone rang at midday on the fourth day, she jumped and ran – he did call sometimes, when Andrew was out during the day. But it was Aimee, wanting to meet. Alright, said Kate, restless. If she went into town, she could walk past the *Look South* offices. Maybe she'd bump into him. She put the phone down angry that he'd driven her to such desperations.

Aimee was late. No big surprise. It was often hard to park in town. Kate used the time to think obsessively about David. What if he never called again? Was it really over? It couldn't be. She needed it not to be. When her friend arrived, Kate could see at once something was wrong. Aimee was ashen, her hands shaking, eyes glassy and distracted. She'd lost weight in the while since Kate had seen her, her face becoming carved and bird-like.

'Aimee?'

'Sorry.' She hovered. Aimee was not a hoverer. She was decisive, even when her choices were bad.

'Come here, sit down. What is it?' Terrible thoughts were going through her mind. Dylan was sick maybe, or Aimee herself.

'It's the day care.' Aimee cleared her throat, thick. 'When he turns nineteen it's going. That's what the social bitch said.'

'What? They have to find you something!' Kate had started to think about special schools for Kirsty, the kind that collected the kids in a minibus with a ramp on the back. Once she was school-age, they'd been told they would have day care, the occasional respite holiday. The idea of losing that, the hope of some future support that had got her through the past four years ... well, it was unthinkable.

'Not if there's no places.'

'So what ...'

'Carers. Maybe one day a week.' She laughed, a bitter and dry sound Kate had never heard from her before. Aimee had a generous laugh, encompassing all the ridiculousness of her situation. 'Kate, I can't cope.'

'Oh love. They'll find you something, I know they will. Or his dad can pay ...'

'I already asked. There's no money. Gyms are going bust – he reckons there's some downturn coming. Him and little miss perky-tits are relocating to Spain.' Aimee put her head in her hands. 'It's never going to get any better, is it? It's like this, forever.'

Kate opened her mouth to contradict this, but it was true. Unless Dylan died, it would aways be like this, and no one was coming to help. 'We'll write letters. There must be a charity or something.'

Aimee nodded dully while Kate made suggestions. 'Yeah. I dunno.' She raised her head. 'You ever think it's just too much? Like ... too cruel for them, for you. Like you just want to take them in your arms and go to sleep? Dyl – he's in so much pain every day, you know? He hits me sometimes, when I can't make it stop. It's getting worse and worse all the time. And now it'll just be me and him in that flat and ... sometimes I want it all to be over.'

'Like Sylvia Plath,' said Kate, absently. Later she would wonder why on earth she'd said this. Maybe she didn't realise exactly what they were talking about, or how far from hypothetical it was. She was too distracted, trying hard not to face the fact David was gone from her.

'Who?' said Aimee. For a second Kate had the thought – *Olivia would know.*

'This poet. Her husband left her, she was depressed, so she wrote this poem where she thought about taking her kids with her.'

'And did she?'

'No. She put her head in the oven, but she stopped up the kids' doors, so they were OK.'

'And her?'

'Oh, well, she died.'

'Oh.' Aimee raked two hands over her face, stretching the skin. 'Jesus Christ, Kate. You've got all this ahead of you, eh?'

Kate reached out and squeezed her hand. 'There must be something we can do. I still have some press contacts, even.' She thought of David, pushed the thought away. 'There's always hope.'

'I don't know.' They ordered tea. Aimee didn't drink hers and Kate left feeling concerned but sure that she had helped, somehow, made her friend see things in a different light. Perhaps she had even felt good about herself, realising she'd neglected Aimee the last while.

She walked the long way home around the outskirts of town, almost twice the distance. A light rain was falling and Bishopsdean looked grey and provincial. The *Look South* offices were near the courthouse, and Kate slowed down as much as she could bear to, hovered outside. Loitered. Then she saw Bob the camera guy come out for a smoke break and realised she was pathetic, so she made herself go home. But she couldn't resist a final backwards glance at the building which had contained her job, and now her love. Both gone from her.

The next day she was up and on the treadmill of life. Olivia didn't come every day now – she was at the station more, and there had been a tacit understanding she was doing too much, perhaps, after Delia's visit. Kate took Adam to school, wrangled Kirsty, cleaned and tidied, changed nappies, picked him up from school again, trailed them both round the supermarket and to the park. When she came in the door, she knew something was wrong because Andrew was there, along with Olivia. It was far too early for him to be home, and a knife of fear cut her stomach. Did he know? She was already composing her lies as she took off her coat at the door. It was strange too that Andrew came right up to her; usually they maintained a strict exclusion zone of at least a foot. She was annoyed, then afraid. 'What?'

'Sweetheart. You should – I'm sorry, this will be hard.' He never called her that any more.

'I don't – what is it?' And she knew. There must be some part of a human heart that can sense it's about to break, some nub of bone or strand of nerve deep down in the base of the spine.

'They found them earlier,' Andrew was saying. 'They called me at work, you weren't home, your mobile's off . . .' She had left it behind, from some stupid superstition that if she didn't check it constantly, David might get in touch.

She couldn't forgive Andrew for this, the length of time it took him to say the words that would correspond to the dread she was fumbling about in. Olivia was hovering in the background.

'Aimee,' he said at last, 'it's Aimee.'

71

'No,' Kate was saying, as if she could argue him out of it.

'I'm sorry. She gave him all his medicine, then she took the rest. They were on the sofa.' She had done a Sylvia Plath, Kate thought, fists balled as he tried to grasp her elbows, tow her grief into his harbour. *Like I told her. She did what I told her.*

'Both of them.'

'Yes. I'm sorry.'

It's never going to get any better, is it. Aimee's last message to her, that she'd failed to hear. She had suggested instead a solution, a terrible one. But she hadn't meant to. She hadn't meant to! The guilt was almost frightening, and she pushed it as far away as she could.

Kate was able to channel her grief after the first sucker punch that made her slowly sink to the floor. She took comfort in it, the wailing, the hard tiled floor she laid her head on. That was how you were supposed to grieve. Then the English in her kicked in and she was contacting Dylan's father and funeral homes and Margaret, who said, 'Oh dear. Such a shame she felt the need to do that. What an example for the younger parents.' Then she burst into tears, and Kate found herself weeping with the other woman, mourning with her. The sheer bloody unfairness of it all.

She even spoke to the news – they'd got wind that she was Kate McKenna, former reporter, and she stood on the doorstep and delivered a eulogy to her friend, a searing indictment of the public services which had so let Aimee down. She understood now why some people thrived in a crisis. When the worst had already happened, it gave you permission to break. Shattering on the floor of rock bottom, that was so much easier than holding yourself together for years, an inch above it.

Andrew remained in the background, putting the children to bed and cleaning their teeth, trying to explain to Adam what

72

was going on, while she paced the living room as calls came in. At one point the landline went as she talked on her mobile, and Andrew held it to her ear and a voice said *Hello,* and she realised with detachment that it was him, it was David.

'I hope it was OK to call.' Already it was a shock to hear his voice, as if it had been over for months.

'I'm a bit busy.'

'I wanted to say I was sorry about your friend. She sounds – she sounded a wonderful person.'

No, thought Kate, you'd have hated her, with her non-stop over-sharing and lack of culture and her garish clothes, but she had more courage in her little finger than you will ever have in all your life.

'Also – you were wonderful on TV. You always were. You know, if you decide you might like something permanent – we'd love you back on screen.'

Kate looked up. Andrew was pretending to tidy the kitchen. Did he know? Right now, she didn't care.

'I can't, I'm afraid,' she said, her voice cold and distant. 'You see, *my* disabled child is still alive. So I have to take care of her.'

David said nothing. Perhaps she could have forgiven him for going quiet these past few days, perhaps it was just a temporary guilt and nerves and he did really want her. But she wasn't going to hang about to see, open and raw.

'Thanks for calling.'

She hung up. Andrew looked up as if he might say something, finally. The phone rang again. She picked it up. She'd made her choice. She'd made her choice.

In bed that night, she watched herself on TV, standing in front of her house in jeans and gilet, her hair loose. She looked angry, and quite beautiful.

'Aimee loved Dylan,' she said, on TV. 'There will be some

73

who ask how a mother could do that to their child. Well, you have to understand what it is to have a child you love, who lives in constant pain and confusion, who is taunted and stared at every day of their life. Who will never tell you they love you or call you Mummy or be able to go to the toilet alone. Dylan was almost nineteen but still wore nappies. He was strong enough to knock Aimee down, but he couldn't speak or feed himself. His body went through puberty, but his mind stayed like a baby's. Ask yourself, before you judge, if you could live with that.'

She paused, hair flying in the breeze. She said: 'I didn't know Aimee that long, but we understood each other. I have a daughter who is four and will never grow up. Camus once wrote that humans can get used to anything. Well, I believe what we cannot bear is to know nothing will ever change. That we'll be like this, forever. So I ask you to understand that, and think how you can support us, the parents like Aimee.' She stopped. On the screen her name, as in olden days – *Kate McKenna. Journalist and mother*. As if her old self had somehow returned, a different person.

'Are you OK?' Andrew was coming in to bed, tired and rumpled.

Kate pressed pause on the remote. 'I'm fine. I'm not the one who's dead.'

'It's just … even before this, you've seemed unhappy.' He was trying. She knew what it cost him to bring it up, the most conflict-averse man in the world. He was giving her the chance to confess her affair, maybe, the horror of Aimee and Dylan allowing her some leeway, an amnesty. 'I'm worried that you – you aren't coping. I want to help, if I can. I know it's hard, being here all day with her. But we're *married*, Kate. We have to pull together somehow. I sometimes think you don't know what being married means.'

74

Kate turned away so he wouldn't see the tears filling her eyes. For Aimee, yes, but also for David, for the loss of possibility. How selfish she was. Her friend had asked for help, and Kate had failed to give it, failed to see what she needed. If only she could go back a few hours, say something different. Go home with Aimee and make sure she was alright. Give her some hope to cling to. One more second, she knew, and Andrew would hold her. It would be a fresh start. But she couldn't. So she snapped, 'I'd be happier if you'd taken the bins out like I asked you to.'

And she ached even more at his slow blink and retreat, but there was no choice. She'd done many bad things, terrible things that would haunt her for years, but she wasn't going to cry for her lover in the arms of her husband. Whatever else, she wasn't going to be the woman who'd do that.

As the days went by and she appeared on radio and TV and wrote articles for the *Guardian*, she would remind herself of one fact and draw comfort from its extremity. She wasn't dead. And if you couldn't go back, you could only go forwards, as the stupid cushion said.

Andrew, present day

Andrew had come to think that the best and worst thing about being human was the ability to get used to things. Take his years of working in London, commuting to his law firm every day – he had accustomed himself to waking at six, heading out in the cold biting air, cramming onto a train where he often didn't get a seat, standing up for an hour trying to read his *Times Literary Supplement*. Then ten hours in the office, staring at a dusty computer, eating sandwiches made soggy with low-fat mayonnaise, sometimes looking out the window and realising the world was still there. Home to Kate's boiling-over rage, and the smell of nappies and howls of children. Clinging to scraps of comfort in his life, like the sneaked brownie on the way home, the snatch of music through his headphones as he walked to the station, the book he might read standing up on the train and dream of his own name on a cover like that.

And now it had happened, although not quite in the way he'd imagined. There was a page on Amazon with his name, his photo, his book cover. He was scheduled to do events, bookshop talks, even a festival or two. Tonight was his book launch, the long dreamed-of moment of triumph. And today, at 8am West Coast time, a producer was calling him about making a film of his book. He tried to imagine it and failed, an actor playing him, up on billboards, on cinema screens. Who would they get – John Cusack, maybe? Perhaps they'd have to hang out so he could learn Andrew's mannerisms. Here his mind would usually fail him, because surely a person's life could not change that much. But it already had. He had everything he'd wanted for years. An agent, a publishing deal that was written up in the *Bookseller* magazine. He was no longer caring every day for a severely disabled child, something he'd thought would be his life forever, although even thinking that caused a spike of guilt like heartburn in his chest. Adam ... well, Adam was always a worry, but at least he didn't live at home still, like so many young people, and he had his band to keep him busy. There was Olivia, and yes, their situation was strange to say the least, but she was a partner for him in many ways, a mother to his children. He'd been able to quit his legal job, hated for years, with the money from the book advance, and that moment of giving notice was one of the best of his life. So Andrew should have been happy.

You could get used even to miracles, he realised. For years, before at least, he had taken it for granted that Kirsty could signal what she wanted to eat, or say goodbye or I love you, though this had once seemed impossible. Already he complained about his agent not answering emails the same day, or a low-balling from a foreign publisher, or the dappiness of his publicist, a girl of twenty-four called Felicia. Already he worried about the enormous tax bill that was the result of an enormous advance. Perhaps people never changed. If they weren't happy, if they were always vaguely worried, maybe they would be forever. Perhaps Kate hadn't changed either. Maybe, for all her mansion in Hollywood (he imagined) and her job on American TV and her film-producer husband (how strange to think of her with a husband, when surely that was him), Kate was as she'd been before she left. A cyclone of anger and disappointment, nothing ever quite enough. Once, he'd thought it was Kirsty's birth that had broken her, but that wasn't true, was it? Even in the happy years, she had only functioned when she was running fast to stay ahead, buying a house, getting married, having kids, getting to the top at work. She had loved him – if she ever had – only when he was running beside her, a training contract, a good job, a five-year plan.

He settled himself in his study far ahead of time for the call. Olivia, ever considerate, had gone out for a mint tea and brisk walk around the park. Her selflessness made him itchy at times. It was more comfortable to compare himself to Kate, who had gone, leaving him the eternal high ground. He keyed up the video call link. Amazing to think he'd never even done a video call before 2020, and now they were the norm. He looked at himself in the screen, a middle-aged man with receding hair and uncool glasses, wearing a shirt and tie. That was stupid, he now saw. Hollywood people didn't wear ties. Quickly, he started to take it off, but got stuck and almost throttled himself, and so when the screen contracted and began to ring, he was red-faced, slightly out of breath.

A man in the reflected square of his computer, pale and red-haired but handsome, in an open-necked blue shirt. No tan, despite living in LA. He was in a light airy room with dark wooden floors, shelves behind him full of books and DVDs and awards (Andrew squinted to see if the Oscar was there). 'Hello, Andrew?' He had a sort of mid-Atlantic accent. The name *Conor Ryan* in the corner of the screen.

'Yes, yes, hello, that's me! Can you hear me?'

A slight delay on the line that made him nervous. 'I can hear you.'

'Well, hi! Great to meet you at last. Virtually.'

They both did a small fake laugh. 'Ha ha.'

'Ha.'

'We loved your book. Just loved it. So pleased you chose us for the adaptation.'

'Oh, well, no, that's – I felt you'd do a good job with it, like you understood it.' He hadn't known of course just how well Conor Ryan did understand the story – or whatever version of it Kate had told. Conor was leaving later today (for him) to meet Andrew in London tomorrow (for Andrew). He had always struggled with time differences and part of him could not believe the voodoo of it, that air travel could whisk someone so easily across the world, that he would be in the same room as this man tomorrow. His ex-wife's husband.

'Excellent. Excellent. We're very excited about this project. I've already pitched it to a few studios. But before we go further, Andrew, there's something we should get out of the way. An elephant in the room, if you will.'

'Oh?' He knew what was coming. For a moment, he felt a

spurt of anger. The man should have told him sooner. It seemed dishonest somehow.

'Yes. Here she is, the elephant, not really, ha ha.' Conor spun his laptop, and Andrew was looking into the face of his wife, not seen for fifteen years.

Kate, 2007

'Your dad was wondering about lunch, love.' Kate paused in washing up the dishes from the breakfast she had cooked what felt like only minutes ago. Her mother was standing by the kitchen island, glasses on a jewelled string, dog-eared Christmas *Radio Times* in hand.

'Oh, was he?'

'We like to eat early, you know – he can't manage it later, like you, so continental.'

Responses streaked across Kate's mind like comets. *Make it your bloody self then. Eat some of the approximately ten thousand foodstuffs currently crowding my fridge and cupboards. Or better yet, go home. Or don't come in the first place!* But really, this was entirely her own fault.

The situation had unfurled with the implacability of a Greek tragedy. Her parents, John and Ann McKenna, stolid with the breath of the Midlands. Irish stock cooked down into sturdy Birmingham accents. Matching North Face anoraks, the AA road atlas, Terry Wogan on Radio 2. Kate had been trying to escape them since her teens, when she'd left for university and Elizabeth had climbed into her suitcase, complaining she was being abandoned in deadening suburbia. So what had possessed her to invite them for Christmas? An offhand offer, desperate to avoid another year of snow and motorways and trying to soothe howling children in frigid early-morning kitchens where she couldn't find the mugs. But dear God, she hadn't meant it! And they weren't supposed to accept, those home-loving Midlanders whose idea of a good holiday was somewhere you could take your caravan. And Elizabeth, of course, had to come too, since she'd broken up with her dull boyfriend, Patrick, the month before. But there wasn't space so she'd have to sleep on the sofa, and her new-found 'clean eating' meant she'd be insufferable about booze and cheese and the smoke Andrew's father would blow from his pipe.

Ah yes. Andrew's father. And mother. And brother! Because it wasn't enough to have the McKennas. The Waters had to come too. They usually went to stay with Laurence, Andrew's brother, or Ingrid was working at the dog shelter, or Michael, an academic specialising in a really boring area of finance, was on a lecture tour of the US. But this year there was no charity, no lectures, and Laurence's perfect marriage had imploded when he was caught sexting one of his students. Kate wasn't sure if she blamed him – feeling the silent kinship of adulterers beneath the skin – but a student, come on. The girl was barely nineteen and he was likely to lose his job too.

So Kate, exhausted and heartsick after a year where she'd had an affair and lost a friend, had to entertain and cater for eight adults, two children, and Ingrid's border terrier Max. The resentment was like carrying round a five-ton weight, as she made lists of food and bedding and presents. Her parents would eat only the driest of white turkey meat, and insisted on having Christmas dinner at twelve thirty, sprouts and carrots arranged in colour-coded pyramids, crackers pulled and party hats donned in silent concentration. They asked for cash limits on presents and stuck to them rigidly – *I'd have got the nicer one, but we did say thirty pounds*. The children had to be quiet while they watched the Queen's speech and drank a small glass of sherry. Whereas the Waters would either do no presents because they were sending all their money to Ingrid's donkey sanctuary, or exchange weighty tomes on Stalin which they would then argue about long into the night. They ate venison, or goose, considering turkey vulgar, and they wouldn't dine until late, which would then dissolve into the kind of port- and pudding-soaked night that had the McKennas reaching for the Gaviscon. The idea of uniting the families made Kate clutch her head in confusion, like trying to see both halves of a Magic Eye puzzle at once.

After the affair, after Aimee's death, everything was frighteningly monochrome. Her mind cycled over and over that last day, still believing there was some way to take it back, to return and save her friend. Say, *I'll help you. Don't give up. Things can always change.* Even if she didn't believe it. It seemed too cruel that it would forever be too late now, that just one moment of selfish distraction meant she would blame herself always. Time stretched, pegged out only by tired pleasures – Christmas, Sunday lunch with friends, a rare trip to the cinema. She pushed the buggy and lugged shopping with the weight of pent-up tears in her limbs. She knew conventional wisdom would say have it out with Andrew – own up, cry, come clean – in the confidential tones of the problem page. But that was also cheating, taking comfort in a pretended honesty.

He had tried – he'd suggested counselling again, in a heavy tentative voice. He booked a night in a spa hotel, got Elizabeth to mind the kids, although she plagued them the whole time with calls about every little thing, and Kate slept from 9pm right through to check-out. He was there and trying and she could have responded. She missed David too, a dull and boring ache. In the modern world, people could have anything anytime. Affairs were the only real chance to feel truly denied. The intimacy that had thrilled her with its absence – no idea of his middle name, or what his feet looked like – began to haunt her. She was sad for the things they'd never do, like a trip to the cinema or waiting in a doctor's surgery for bad news, or even growing tired of each other. Intimacy, it got you that way, both coming and going.

So all through that autumn of crisp days and soggy leaves, a cold leaching winter and a joyless Christmas, she was too dispirited to do anything but survive. There were times she thought maybe not even that. She thought over and over how it had been for Aimee, gulping in breaths, waiting for the last moment when she still knew what was happening, when she could have stopped it. Her mind was plagued with methods. Pills maybe – the Bishopsdean doctors were more than happy to dole out handfuls of Valium. Nothing painful, she was a coward about that. She couldn't cut into her skin or put her head in a noose. But pills – if she could just go to sleep and this would no longer be her life? Maybe. She stopped taking her sleeping meds, let them sit in the bottle. A small and ugly secret, a dark thrill only she knew about. Would she? Not really. She didn't have it in her, channelling despair into rage instead. But the pills were there all the same.

The Christmas of that year was the hardest Kate had ever known. It was then, amid the silver wrapping paper and turkey leftovers and beeping toys, all hope seemingly drained from the world, that she understood the bottom of her heart was cold. That she had to do something, or she was going to die. That she would likely start another affair out of sheer calculation, survival instinct. *Yes*, she thought, most nights, lying in bed beside a man a million miles away. *This is the worst possible way to live your life.*

*

It was hard to say what drove her over the edge in the end. The image she had was those coin-slot machines in arcades, glimpsed as a child before her mother had pulled her away from the shiny lights and music. Push, push, push, until finally you fell over. It was December 27th, 2006, and after four days of a joint family visit, Kate was right at the edge. With supreme effort, she was able to fob off her mother's request for lunch with a promise to 'sort it soon.' Her sister then came in, setting down the plate she'd just eaten breakfast off, all of them on a varying meal cycle which Kate somehow had to accommodate. The plate held toast crusts and bacon rind – after Elizabeth's insistence on a vegetarian menu for every other meal.

'Can you put it in the dishwasher?'

Her sister raised her eyebrows. 'Alright, no need to snap.'

Kate bit her lip so hard it hurt. 'Dad wants lunch already, apparently.'

'Oh, I won't want lunch for hours yet.' Her sister liked to make such announcements, proud of her own ability to stop her body's hunger. Kate had done the same once – they'd learned it from their mother, who liked everyone else to eat but didn't do it much herself.

'Any chance you could finish these dishes? If I don't get Kirsty down to sleep, her schedule'll be off all day.'

'It's Christmas, Kate! Let her enjoy it!'

'What do you think she's enjoying, exactly? Deep in the themes of *Doctor Zhivago*, is she?' She could hear the strains of the very, very long film from next door, where Laurence and Michael were insisting on watching it, though Ingrid kept talking over it and Kate's own father couldn't follow it and was rustling his newspaper loudly and saying something about mixed nuts. Andrew was playing with Adam, a maddening game Laurence had brought, which emitted loud gun-like noises that sent shudders of anxiety down Kate's spine. Kirsty was in the cloth-sided cot they placed her in during the day, where she would sit slumped looking at her hands. She had been bought toys for Christmas, as always, but it wasn't clear if she understood how to play with them. The sight of them, bright plastic and soft plush, make Kate want to cry.

Elizabeth sighed. 'I know it's hard, Katie . . .' No one called her that now.

'It's more than hard.'

'The thing is, you're not the only person with problems. At least you have two children. There's plenty of people can't even have that.'

Kate opened her mouth to discharge some of the lava in her veins, but stopped. Thinking of the sudden breakdown of Elizabeth and Patrick, not long after her sister's thirtieth birthday, the baffling speed of it. The way Elizabeth sometimes looked at Adam, a hunger or anger or something in her eyes. 'I – yes, I know.' She could have asked for more details, and maybe then they could have talked like they used to, like sisters. But she had no pity to spare for anyone else, was the truth.

She peeled off her rubber gloves, making a decision that was better than setting her entire family on fire. 'I'm going out.'

'What? Where?'

'To the shops. We need a few things.'

'What about the kids?'

'Andrew's here.' Plus their aunt and uncle and both sets of grandparents.

'Yes, but . . .'

Kate stared her sister down, daring her to say something about Andrew needing a break from work, or how good he was to take care of them. Something tore in her. 'It's just so hard. Do you understand how hard it is? It's not just having two kids, it's

84

a child you can't look away from even for a minute, and she'll always be like this, always. She'll never grow up and live her life. Do you get that?'

Elizabeth sighed, and Kate even detected a small eye-roll, and that was it, she was done. She picked up the car keys and went, without even brushing her hair. And found herself, somehow, driving round the quiet M25, following signs for Heathrow. She didn't know why. Maybe because, if she couldn't get on a flight and leave, she could at least come close.

Kate liked to think of herself this way. The kind of woman who'd sit at the bar on a stool, so you could admire the slenderness of her legs. Who'd sip champagne in the middle of the day as if on the way to somewhere mysterious and important. Perhaps that was who she could have been, if she'd kept working – a top reporter, the kind you saw profiled in the Sundays. National TV maybe. It wasn't so impossible. They'd all said how good she was on screen, a natural, smart but approachable. If, if. *If I hadn't had children. If I hadn't got married.* If she hadn't discovered mothering was the one thing she was incapable of. That love was beyond her, for her husband and even for her children. She let herself think that was it, the single fork in her life where it all went wrong. That choice to marry and start a family. Which hadn't even felt like a choice. It was just something you did, like buying a house or getting a job. A train you were on and suddenly you couldn't get off.

She hadn't even realised why she was doing all this until she met him.

This was the script, as he would write it.

A WOMAN sits alone at a bar. Thirty-something, fairly attractive blonde. Air of sadness.

Actually, it was the first thing he said to her.

85

She looked up. '*Fairly* attractive?'

'It's how we say it. Means not some Hollywood stunner, a real woman.'

'Oh.' She had no idea if this was a compliment or not, and that in itself was a thrill. The man who'd come up behind her at the bar was tall, in a white open shirt and grey jacket. He had red hair, dark like the coat of her childhood dog, the imaginatively named Rusty.

'I work in film,' he offered. 'It's a habit. You sort of narrate your own life into a screenplay.'

'You write?' She turned away from him, so he appeared only in the corner of her eye, like a gift saved in a cupboard until Christmas. Andrew had always wanted to write. It seemed to her that wanting to write, yet not actually putting pen to paper, was an activity that could take up decades of your life.

'Used to. No money in it. Now I produce.'

Kate knew Andrew would term this selling out. Andrew, who'd not so much as picked up a pen in five years. She sipped her drink, tapping a nail on the glass. 'How interesting.' That coruscating sarcasm which Old Kate had always found entranced men like him.

He laughed. 'You're right. But it paid for a mansion in Hollywood.'

'Hmm.' She tried not to show she was impressed, but also jealous.

'And what is it you do yourself?' He was Irish, she realised from the construction, but probably many years gone from the country.

'I do what I like,' she said, mysteriously. A lie in every way.

'On your way somewhere nice?'

'Maybe.' She would have to go home soon, lay out yet another meal, put the washing on, referee the choice of evening viewing.

He tapped his credit card on the bar. Gold. She couldn't read the name. 'Can I shout you another? I like a woman who drinks champagne at lunchtime.'

She picked her glass up. 'I'm fine, thank you. I like to be sober on flights.'

'I like to be rat-arsed,' he said, and smiled like a wolf, and despite herself she turned to look him full in the face and it was like a slap, his grey eyes and the waft of cologne from his neck. Something rare, she could tell, expensive.

His whiskey came with a silver tray for tips. He laid down a tenner like it was nothing and drained the glass in one gulp. 'Well, it was nice not meeting you.' And he was gone. Kate turned, suddenly terrified – she'd fucked it up – and then he was there again, leaning confidentially on the edge of her stool. 'I'm back in eight days. The LA flight. In case you're around and you'd like to *actually* meet.' And he went, his hand leaving a cooling indent on her seat, right near her thigh.

Kate lay in bed that night, thinking idly of the man in the airport. Of course she wasn't going to meet him again – ridiculous – but just to be seen like that, to be noticed, had filled her blood with a golden-pink mist, her heart light and fluttering for the first time since David. With the Waters in the spare room and the McKennas in Kirsty's, the child was on her front in her parents' bed, each wheeze of her breath squeezed into a scream. A hard night in a series of hard days, trouble with her lungs meaning one of them had to be awake with her always. Her small body juddered with the effort of staying alive. She would be five soon, she would start special school next year, and Kate would get her days back, maybe. Who would she be then? Her old self felt too far gone. She moved her hand mechanically from patting her child to turning the pages of the book she wasn't reading. Beside her, Andrew slept, his hands curled in on themselves. Small rustling snores lifted the bedclothes from time to time, as he breathed deep and easy in his sleep. How trustingly he leant on her, on their marriage. As if it would always be there, immutable, like the ground he stood on. Her eyes moved over the fabric of the curtains, lit softly by the lamp. They'd chosen them in John Lewis, Andrew earnestly checking out the length of guarantee and blackout depth. It was the same with every item in the house, every inch of skin on her body. To rest her gaze on it was to conjure up a life with Andrew in miniature, how and why it came to be in the house, the discussions before, the online links emailed to each other and her anger when he bought the wrong thing anyway. The marks their children had left on her body, seen and unseen. The story of them. The trouble was they had so many things. They were the kind of people who owned three different types of balsamic vinegar. Of course they were, she'd made sure of it. How could she leave all that?

Sometimes she couldn't contain her anger at Andrew for not seeing. Or did he see and not know how to stop it? Almost more though, she hated herself for who she'd become. Angry at him for everything, from forgetting the milk to how he loaded a cup into the dishwater. There had once been a thing called leeway. When they were in love, it had stretched wide as a continent. As the love dried up so had the leeway, eroded by the desert of their resentments, growing day by day until she felt she was choking. She thought a lot about her life before, and what might lie ahead, if she lifted her foot and stepped over the divide. It was dramatic to think of it like that, but what you did with your life *was* dramatic. Stay or go. Have a child or don't have a child. Small choices, but enough to set you on a different track altogether. She was so tired of the indecision, that was it. Marriage or divorce. Leave the children, take the children. Go back to the moment she'd thought

88

about getting pregnant with Adam, and not do it. That, of course, was impossible. But she returned to it often, lying awake at night listening to Kirsty's thick cry – that fork in the road of her life, the other side shining and unused, just waiting for her to cross back to it. Aimee's death had offered a cast iron argument-winner: you're not dead, but you might be if you don't change things. All the same she remained stuck, imagining what people would say about her. *She left her kids.* There was no coming back from that.

Now, as Kate lay there turning it over in her head, Kirsty jerked beside her. It was a sound, a gulp and gasp, that Kate knew so well that her body was reacting before she even had the thought. Kirsty wasn't breathing – another of her seizures, supposedly now controlled by medication that left her consti-pated and fractious. Her lips were already blue, her body floppy. Not now. Not now! 'Andrew,' she hissed, trying not to wake the sleeping guests. He didn't stir. She turned Kirsty on her stomach, stood over her, loosened her pyjamas, which were for a child three years younger. She pressed her mouth to her daughter's blue one, blew air into her lungs. 'Come on, Kirsty. Come on!' So many times this had happened, and each time she'd come back, but the seconds seemed to last forever, not breathing. Not breathing. Not breathing. 'ANDREW!' She hardly had air to scream between breaths. Breathing for two. That's what motherhood was and she had no air left. He started awake. 'Call an ambulance!'

He was awake, fumbling on his glasses. 'They take too long. I'll drive.' They rushed her to the hospital like that, Andrew at the wheel, Kate kneeling on the back seat forcing air into her daughter's slack body, all of them in night-clothes, firing off messages to her mother and sister in between, telling them what had happened and to check on Adam. The familiar swerve up to A&E, into the blaze of lights, shouting garbled words about what had happened. In a few minutes Kirsty had a tube in her throat and was saved, not dying today, yet again, the world back on its rails and an alternate life, briefly glimpsed, now averted. She thought sometimes of Dylan, in these moments, Aimee's son. His mother had ended his life and her own because she couldn't bear the burden of his life. Kirsty was young, and small still, light enough to lift and carry, but her needs would only grow. It was what Kate feared most, getting to that point herself. Unable to bear it any more, breaking under the strain. She sagged into a plastic chair, restarting her mind and her normal everyday worries, her marriage, her affair, the man at the airport, her misery. One thought surfaced, clear as a bell. She could not do this again. She could not. There was a freedom in realising you'd simply come to your limit, and no more.

January had started, the dreary ramp-up to the year, slushy and frugal. The families all gone home, thank God, only for her to find she missed the company, because now it was just her and Andrew and the kids and nothing to look forward to. Maybe that's why she did it. The flight from LA, the man had said. God almighty, which did he mean? Which airline? What time? Kate spent a lot of time making surreptitious calls to airlines, who all seemed baffled.

'I'm sorry, ma'am, did you want to *fly* to LA?'

'No, I want to know if you have one landing tomorrow.' She could hardly tell the truth – she'd met a man in a bar and had no idea of his name or anything about him, except that she'd felt something remarkable when he looked at her– *oh yes, there you are.*

Eventually she had it narrowed down to three flights. One at 5am – well, that was impossible, she could never make it, though for a mad moment she thought about faking a break-down in the middle of the night. The others were at 2pm and five. She could manage those if she left immediately after the one at five.

Thursday came. Absurdly elated, she tried on six different outfits, a pile of discarded skirts and tops building up on the floor like choices of self. *Who do you want to be, Kate?* Olivia arrived to babysit, supposedly while Kate went to a job interview. Olivia was alarmingly supportive about this. 'How wonderful. You were so good, I'm sure you can break back in.' Kate was so keyed-up she missed the turn off the M25, circling the airport past warehouses and hangars. She did not drink her champagne once she'd found the bar. She had to make it last over three hours, potentially. She also had to pay cash, as she and Andrew had a joint bank account and she couldn't explain why she'd been at a bar at Heathrow in the middle of the day.

Two pm came and went. Her eyes flicked to and from the screen announcing flight arrivals. How long could it possibly take to collect bags? He'd be in first class, he was that sort of man. She allowed herself to drift off into a fantasy where they were together and always went first class, and when they passed through airports he'd turn to her, laughing at the memory of their meeting – *champagne, darling?* Then she realised it was 2.30pm and he wasn't here and she'd have to wait for three more hours, but couldn't leave the bar just in case he did come and she missed him. She took out her book – *Anna Karenina* – and only belatedly realised the subject matter. So many great works were about adultery, when you thought about it, when you too had that stain and pick it up on others like a scent.

Her nerves were frayed, head whipping up at every garbled announcement. She was in the right bar, wasn't she? Had she got the time right, the day? What was she *doing*? Once again waiting for a man who wasn't her husband. This time a total stranger, whose name she didn't even know. Waiting for him to

91

give her something, take her somewhere, just in some way that she couldn't articulate save her from her life.

The girl at the bar had pointedly wiped around Kate six times, leaving a slick of disinfectant, and she was no more than ten pages into *Anna*, when the 5pm flight landed. At 5.10pm she threw back the drink in one desperate swallow. What an idiot she was. A whole day wasted, more lies to Olivia, who took them generously, like inappropriate gifts. She set down the glass and was picking up her bag when he suddenly was there. Tired, his linen jacket crumpled. 'You're here.'

'I have to go now.' She was appalled to find tears thickening in her throat. 'I have to go. I shouldn't have – I'm sorry.'

'Hey, it's OK. I never thought you'd be here anyway.'

'I was. But it's too late now.'

She was fumbling for her jacket, eyes filming, when he stopped her by catching her arm. Into one palm he pressed a business card. 'It's only too late when you're dead,' he said, mock-serious. 'I'm here, you're here. There's always next time.'

She glanced at it quickly, her mouth forming the shape of his name. *Conor Ryan*. Him. Kate drove home, the card burning a hole through from the compartment of her bag she'd zipped it into. It's only too late when you're dead, he had said, and the idea made her gasp for breath. Freedom, dangerous freedom, was filling up her nose and mouth, as if she were drowning and never coming up for air.

Kate, present day

Kate drove back down the Pacific Coast Highway, hands gripped on the wheel in rage, the snarl of traffic raising her anger

92

even more. Conor hadn't gone to see Trixie, after she'd begged and begged. Was this it, her line, her limit? She'd often thought, over the years, that she was at it, but she always crossed over, let him get away with it, or just in time he'd do something nice, pay something into the account of their marriage, depleted by every fight and thoughtlessness and wound. But this wasn't her, this was his daughter. A vulnerable young woman, little more than a child. She'd tried to call his mobile, but he never answered when it was her. Investors, directors, stars, they could always reach him, even at Kate's work functions, in the middle of her speech to the association of women journalists, mid-flight, on holiday, not that they'd taken a holiday – *vacation* –in four years.

Funny how terrified she'd been to drive here when she first arrived, chanting over and over, *turn on the right, turn on the right*, ignorant of what the road signs meant. Now she did it on auto-pilot, blaring on her horn when SUVs swerved too close, part of the constant anger of this city. She let herself into the house, the icy blasts of the air conditioning raising goosebumps on her arms. 'Conor?' Any number of other people might be in the house, writers he was working with, twentysomething men who'd stare at her legs; producers, cleaners, cooks, gardeners. She was used to seeing strangers here. A buffer between them.

A door opened upstairs. 'Can you come up?' His voice muffled.

She wasn't going on his summons. She looked through her post – *mail,* he would correct her – nothing of interest; she had no one who would write to her these days, having left her entire life behind. She slipped off her sweaty sandals, washed her feet in the small bathroom. Conor hated her doing that, but she didn't care. Leave the dust trails in the sink. Let him get annoyed. Only then did she walk upstairs, small damp outlines of her feet evaporating behind her on the dark wood. She could hear the low rumble of his voice – was he on a call?

Did he expect her to wait until he finished? Well, screw him. She pushed on the door to his office. Conor was behind his huge wooden desk, his laptop angled towards him, on a video call. 'Hang on,' he said to whoever was on the screen. He beckoned her over. She shook her head – she was too angry to go and smile at whoever it was, prop up Conor's image as a happy family man, which he liked to wheel her out for sometimes. Not when his daughter was in a rehab clinic and he hadn't even been to see her. He beckoned again, and, irritated, she stepped forward.

It was surreal for a moment. She was looking at a room she recognised – she had chosen that wallpaper, that chest of drawers. And then she realised: the balding man with the glasses on screen, that man was her ex-husband. Andrew.

Kate fled. She'd seen the look cross Andrew's face at the sight of her, his mouth open to say something, and she couldn't bear to hear what it was, so she ran. Across the hall, stumbling over the little up-and-down stairs, into her own room. They had separate rooms, she and Conor. He slept badly, was the excuse they used. Didn't want to disturb her. She sat down on the neatly made bed, shaking all over. Stared at herself in the mirrored wardrobe doors – she looked good, didn't she? If someone hadn't seen her in fifteen years? Of course her skin had been aged by the California sun, but she was thin, her clothes were well-chosen, her hair expensive. Would he have seen her and felt a pang, that he'd lost her? Or did he hate her for running, dashing to save her own life, with no thought for those left on that sinking ship? He must hate her and Kate wasn't sure she could bear it, felt it skitter up and down her arms like insects.

Conor appeared in the doorway. 'There was no need to run. I thought we could just deal with any problems here and now.'

She was shaking. 'I can't believe you'd do this to me. Actually, I can. You still haven't visited Trixie, after all.'

His back stiffened as he rubbed at a smudge on the mirror. 'You should stop going out there. It won't do any good. She's past our help.'

'For God's sake – she's your daughter!'

'Is she?' So icy-polite, and it scared her, how he could turn his love on and off. No one should be that much in control of themselves. 'And, as I seem to remember, you walked out on *your* daughter, a helpless child. Trixie is an adult who's had every privilege and chooses to stick it up her nose. So.' He moved back, neatly sliding the door into place. 'I was going to order lunch. Let me know if you'd like anything.' And that was it. He wouldn't engage with her, wouldn't fight, wouldn't shout, wouldn't be cruel. Wouldn't be anything. And that was why she always lost every round with him. It hadn't been like that with Andrew – she could run rings around him and had. And yet she had panicked at the briefest sight of him. Poor Andrew. How old he looked. Such a shock to see his face like that, in live time, across the ocean and the decades.

Kate was still shaking. Andrew was out there. That meant the rest of them were, too. Olivia. Her sister, her parents. Her children.

Andrew, 2008

Andrew closed his eyes. At that moment, 11am on a Saturday, he could hear:

In the kitchen, the cleaner's vacuum, howling over the blare of Kiss FM.

In Adam's room, the kicks and beeps of the violent computer game he'd tried, and failed, to stop his son from having.

In Kirsty's room, the stuttering wails that precipitated a full-on crying session.

And from the garden, the roar of the chainsaw from the men he'd hired to chop down the ash tree which was now rotten through, leaning at a dangerous angle, and which he really ought to have cut down himself. He could feel their mocking deference, thinking just that.

And, from inside his chest, his own heart pounding with the stress of it all.

If he asked, Olivia would make all this stop, but she was out, buying the expensive bread and cheeses she liked from the farmers' market. He tried holding one side of his nose to breathe, yoga-style, as she had taught him, but it only triggered an asthmatic wheezing in his lungs. In front of him, the computer screen, the cursor winking slowly like a one-eyed Joker. In the past hour he'd written one word: *the*. The the the. What came next? What noun, definite or abstract? What gerund? What adjective, even? He sighed and switched it off, saving that one word, 'the', in the grandly titled file NOVEL. Started, 1994. Finished – never, probably. Perhaps, he thought, getting up, the title of the document was the problem. Perhaps if he called it 'stuff' or 'total rubbish' it would give him the freedom to actually write something. The word *novel* was so overwhelming, so many different sentences required, and all in the right order.

As he opened the door of his office, the noise level suddenly and magically dropped like a calm wave moving through the house. The radio had gone off, the hoover stilled. Adam's computer noise abated, with a small amount of complaining, and then Kirsty's crying stopped dead. Olivia was home. Andrew shut his eyes again and gave thanks, in the fumbling way of someone brought up without religion, simple gratitude for the fact of her presence.

In Kirsty's room, Olivia was stooping down to the child, who was lolling on a sensory mat, grasping a doll to her chest. Now six, the differences between Kirsty and other children were increasing every day, a cruel ongoing wounding. She had never learned to speak, or walk, and there was no hope of toilet training, though she could certainly wriggle and grab and pull things onto the floor – Adam had been trained from a young age to watch her around cups of tea, bowls of porridge, heavy lamps. Her health problems too had worsened, and she'd already had four operations to break and reset various parts of her body. She had trouble holding herself up, and always seemed slack and melting. Poor kid. His love for her hurt a place deep in Andrew's heart, that he would never have admitted to. He hunkered down to stroke her soft fair hair, and she held the doll as if offering it to him. She did understand enough to do that, didn't she? She recognised him and knew he was there? It wasn't always clear. Sometimes she smiled at a cartoon on TV, or laughed when Andrew came into a room, or waved her hands towards Adam, and he'd think, maybe. There was just no way to be sure.

'Problems?'

Olivia turned and smiled up at him. She always smiled when she saw him, no matter what terrible trauma was in progress. 'Nothing serious. We couldn't find Sophie, but she was under the bed.'

They had named the doll Sophie for her. Kirsty of course could not name anything, even herself. Olivia cleaned the child's face of snot and tears with one of the wipes they kept in every room. Fresh. Sanitising. 'Get much done?'

'A bit,' he lied. 'It's been noisy with Mary here.'

97

'She does love her pop music. I could ask her to come Fridays instead? It's just her other clients wanted her to do then.'

Typical Olivia. It would never occur to her to do something to suit herself. She stood up, her pale hair falling down her back. 'Why don't you write some more? I can handle things here.'

'Oh, it's alright. There's so much to do.'

'All done. Shopping, supper, nappy change – I have it under control.' She gave him her bright smile, the one that hurt his heart, because she offered her labour like a gift. Please like me, please need me. And he did need her, that much was clear.

Cursing her helpfulness, he returned to the study, the scene of his private hell. Back at his computer, Andrew watched the blinking cursor. If you did this enough, you started to see it as a heartbeat, ticking your life away. He was thirty-six now and still no book. Also, no wife any more. So he was actually back-sliding. He'd given up his City law job, at Olivia's gentle urging, and she'd somehow found him another one with a local solicitor who knew her father. Dull as hell. What he needed. It was so good not to be getting up at six for the packed freezing train that a strange sense of material wellbeing filled his body each morning, which was bewildering when coupled with the pain he felt at the ongoing fact of Kate's absence. Should have felt. Did feel. Yes.

In fact he felt rich, these days. Rich in time – extra hours at home, Olivia spiriting the children away for long periods; rich in people to take care of Kirsty and the house and iron his shirts. Olivia, raised by paid strangers, believed in outsourcing work, and knowing Andrew's squeamishness at having people in the house, for the most part arranged it unobtrusively while he was at work. For someone so diffident when it came to herself, she had fought for extra care and support from the council, and Kirsty now went to her special school five days a week and even had the offer of respite holidays. She'd found after-school clubs for Adam, and was looking for a child psychologist who could help him 'process' his mother's departure. Even the friends who'd drifted away on Kirsty's birth had come back after Kate left. Mostly the women sending messages. *Andrew I can't believe what she did. She really just left? And her friend is staying to help you?* Perhaps they wanted gossip, but it was useful to have lifts and after-school care for Adam, even if Adam himself would loudly complain that little Hugo or Jacob were boring and dumb and he hated it.

And yet Andrew found himself, a year after Kate had left, still looking at the blinking cursor. Some weekends he'd do nothing on the book at all, telling himself he was busy with the children or mowing the lawn, taking the bottles to the bottle bank or sorting bank statements. Other times he would run out of dis-placement activities – the whole world of not-writing – and be forced to sit at the computer he'd bought for this very purpose, sifting through what he had like overcooked pasta. The story had remained the same since he was twenty-two – three boys, post-university, in a variety of dead-end jobs, falling in love and watching ironic films all the time. This had been him, at law school, living in Clapham, trying and failing to ask girls out – he'd been born too soon, really. Internet dating, the safe anonymity of it, was made for someone like Andrew.

Then he'd met Kate, in a bar after work, the way people used to. Poised and ambitious and knowing exactly what she wanted, Kate had sucked him up a slipstream of better jobs and property ladders, then a move to the country and a baby and second baby and – that was it. Their determined swarm up the monkey bars of life had been halted, and now Kate was gone, and Andrew was back to who he was meant to be – a small-town lawyer sitting in front of the computer, failing to write. If you ignored the two children and the woman who was not his wife but who unaccountably lived there, dishing out yoghurt in the kitchen, he was still that clueless twentysomething who'd dreamed of nothing more than cracking the spine of his own book, his name on the front, maybe in a trendy sans serif font, doing self-conscious writing in ink on paper at a large desk in front of an open fire, and a wife baking scones and herding kids away with loving buttery hands. The woman in these daydreams was not Kate – he didn't know who she was. Kate would complain that the ink left marks on his shirt cuffs, and she had only baked when trying to impress people. Strangely, he rarely thought of her at all; in fact, had never tried to find her, or make contact with her, or divorce her. It was easier to simply turn his back on the whole mess, the fact she had left him and their children and was clearly not coming back. Close his eyes, keep going, try not to think about what it said, that he was a man whose wife could stand him so little she had just walked out one day, without even taking her children or her winter coat.

The woman in the dreams was not Olivia either. He didn't like to think about Olivia too much either, for all he saw her every day.

He stared at the cursor.

The first line had been reworked so often it had the texture of drying cement. *Dominic moved aside the arm of the naked sleeping girl, and took a swig from last night's champagne.*

Oh God! It was awful! He'd tried to capture the zeitgeist and it turned out that was shallow and derivative, full of brand names instead of humour, and thinking it was transgressive to receive a blow job in a night club. Andrew hadn't had any type of sex in years, after so long of trying and failing to get through to Kate. She would initiate matters, sometimes, with the grim determination of someone cleaning out the gutters, and he

100

found he couldn't go along with it. His penis had crawled back inside him like a traumatised mole. He set his fingers on the keys, tapping them slightly with a sound like falling rain. He'd always associated this with happiness, the glowing screen, the heater at his feet, the mug of tea, the rain outside, but somehow having actual time to do it made it terrifying. Finally, he had the bucket to draw up that untapped water inside him, and there was nothing there.

Olivia was just so damn supportive. She subscribed to writing magazines for him, she offered to edit his work, she read books about unlocking the artist within and left them lying around. He wasn't locked. There was nothing there to unlock. After a while, he realised it was Kate's voice telling him this – you're useless, you can't write, you'd have done it by now if you could, you never finish anything, I told you not to waste your time. It was her face he could see in the doorway, her hair loose and shampooed, her face cross and beautiful, in her old red dressing gown with hand cream crusted around the sleeves, telling him to take the bins out, and all he wanted to do was follow her gratefully out the door. She had absolved him from trying. But Olivia, she just kept on believing in him, and sometimes he thought that was the hardest thing of all.

Andrew and Olivia had never discussed her moving in after Kate left. They never discussed anything, Andrew being conflict-averse and she taking it to a whole other level. She just glided in and glided out, leaving things quieter, clearer, tidier. It was Olivia who'd broken the news about Kate's escape, when she'd phoned him at work that day a year ago.

'Andrew?' He'd never spoken to her on the phone before, so it took a moment to recognise her voice. 'I've just come back to the house and well – Kate's not here.'

'Where is she? Did she take the kids out?' Already he could see his boss watching, glancing at the clock, displeased.

'No, the children are with me.' Olivia always said *children*, not *kids*. He knew no one else who spoke like she did. 'I—' Olivia's voice hitched. 'I think you should come home.'

He felt that panic, the tightness in his chest. 'I can't! I'm already on borrowed time as it is. My boss—'

She cut across him, her voice as pale and flat as she was. 'I'm sorry. But you really do need to come.'

It took a long time that night to process it all – ring the police, who read the note Kate had left and exchanged a wordless glance before handing back the piece of Adam's drawing paper. 'Sir, I'm not clear what you want us to do.'

'Something might have happened to her!' The note, addressed to him and Olivia jointly, had explained simply that Kate was going and would not be back. She just couldn't do it any more. She did not say she was sorry – maybe there were things so enormous sorry could never cover them. She was going, and could Olivia please make sure they were alright.

'It says very clearly she's gone, sir. Do you know if she was seeing someone else?'

'Of course not!' Andrew felt the ground being stripped away, falling piece by piece beneath him. All this time, he'd known how shaky it was, how unhappy his wife was. Then there'd been that year where she was always out, returning flushed and hectic, but he hadn't wanted to think about what that meant. He'd chosen to march on, as if looking down meant he would stumble and die. There was his job, which sucked up so much of him, and the kids, the endless worry for both of them, and the bills, and Kate's unhappiness had been bottom of this list and now it was too late. 'She – maybe she wants me to go after her. I—'

Olivia took the note from him and held his hand. He realised no one had done this for years. Certainly not Kate. Her fingers were cold. 'I'm afraid she's gone. I think there was someone else, yes.'

'You knew?' He wasn't stupid, he'd realised she was unhappy, of course, they were all unhappy, life a daily struggle, but this? To walk out and leave them with only a note? He couldn't take it in.

'I – no.' Olivia dropped her head. 'I knew nothing for sure. So please don't ask me. She's my friend. It wouldn't be right.' And she had never said a single word against Kate, only that she 'must have been terribly unhappy'.

Andrew sat staring at the note, while she discreetly saw the police out, and put the children to bed – Adam knew something was wrong, of course.

'Did Mummy go out today?' Andrew asked, when the boy was in bed, pyjamas on and teeth brushed.

Adam just watched him, almost scornful. 'We were at the park with Livvie.' She had waved them off, according to Olivia, giving no sign of what she planned. When they came back, soggy from the rain and cold, there was a clean house and note and no mother.

'Did Mummy say anything? Before you went?'

The boy just shrugged. He was such a good-looking kid, all hard edges and cold blue eyes and glints of rage. Kate's son. Andrew hugged him, awkwardly, breathing in his son's smell of toothpaste, the peanut butter from his bedtime snack.

'I'm sorry, mate. It's going to be OK.'

'I'm tired. Can you turn the light off?'

'Alright.' Sighing, Andrew switched it off, and in the dark heard the child say, 'Mummy's gone, Dad.' As if he had already accepted it.

Then Olivia had seen Andrew himself into bed and tiptoed out. 'I'll be here,' she said. He'd never thought to ask what she meant. She'd found tenants for her flat, moved a few small things into the spare room, and inhabited all the corners of his life he hadn't known were empty. That was a year ago, and she had never moved back out. In all that time, no one had heard from Kate, and Andrew had no idea where to even start looking for her. It was as if she'd died.

A blast of noise from downstairs, Adam protesting at what he'd been given for lunch, the whirr of the expensive coffee machine Olivia had brought with her. Really, he couldn't work in this din. With something close to relief, Andrew closed down the document, his day's work still consisting of just that one word. *The*.

Adam, present day

He didn't much like going to Delia's place, which was dirty and chaotic from her array of housemates, but he went all the same when invited, because she was there. Adam, who was legendary for sending Ubers to pick up girls and bring them to his place in the middle of the night, so he never had to shuffle around an unfamiliar bathroom looking for a toothbrush. Ah well. Even the mighty fall. It was a large house with a number of bedrooms in it, he'd never been sure if it was five or six. Lots of up and down in-between floors and steps everywhere to trip over if you had big feet, as he did. Always strangers in the kitchen strumming Radiohead B-sides on knackered guitars or skinning up in the garden. The living room no longer existed, having been turned into another bedroom, and there was no table in the kitchen, so when they ate it was balanced off their knees in Delia's room. Adam also didn't like having sex with the smell of vegan spaghetti all around him (of course she was a vegan). But he did it. Because of her.

Every time he arrived, she was doing something beautiful and interesting. He'd thought at first she was setting herself up, acting a role, but it happened even when she didn't expect him, so he'd had to conclude she really was just beautiful and interesting. He'd almost have preferred it if she was like him, an emotional grifter, a fraud. But she wasn't. This time he was let in by a guy with a scratchy beard and one of those patterned tunics hippies wore at festivals. When the band had played festivals, for one glorious summer pre-lockdown, Adam stayed in a BnB nearby. No way was he queueing for a shower among people's manky foot water. Adam nodded to the guy, who had the glazed eyes of the professional stoner. No idea who he was.

Delia was in the garden, among the uncut grass on her yoga mat – a hundred quid, made from recycled bottles – in a lotus position, her fingers and thumbs in circles. 'Hey.' Her eyelids shifted at his voice, but she didn't open them. Making him wait. That was fine; he knew it was the secret of his enduring interest in this girl, the way she always seemed to be looking past him at something not quite in reach. That, and the fact she was almost, but crucially not, his stepsister. The only person who could understand the mess of growing up in that family. After a few moments, she opened her eyes, the startling grey of them, and a serene smile spread over her face. 'Hi.'

'Finished?'

'Just a sec. Will you?' She held out her iPhone to him and he snapped a picture of her with her eyes shut, apparently unaware of the camera. She would upload it to her Instagram with some kind of inspirational quote. He'd thought it was dumb at first, basic, but she had a hundred thousand followers and every week got offers to showcase products, candles, protein bars, athleisurewear. He handed back the phone, and at last he had her attention.

'Did you speak to them?' he said, as she stretched out her shoulders prettily.

'Yeah. Olivia wouldn't say much but I think she's spinning out.' Delia called her mother Olivia sometimes. Not all the time. He didn't understand the logic, but that was yet another thing he liked about her.

'I still don't get why she'd be upset. It's not like they're together.' He clung to this, for reasons of his own. Olivia and his father were not a couple, so there was nothing to keep him and Delia apart, was there?

'Because, silly.' Delia turned her wise eyes on him. 'What's her role been, all these years? Unpaid nanny?'

'She chose it,' muttered Adam, not exactly sure who he was defending. He didn't care what people said about his father.

'But she loves him. You can see that, can't you?'

'Um, not really.' His father with his constant nose-blowing and anxious kindness: could anyone really love him? Presumably his mother had at one point, or thought she had. He was decent enough. Never a dick, never cruel the way Adam knew he sometimes was to girls, but he couldn't stop himself. Maybe for some women that was all it took.

'She does. And if your mum comes back, where does that leave her? High and dry?'

'Look, she buggered off, she can't just waltz back in. She didn't want to be our mother, or his wife. So why now? She has this high-powered life in LA, her own slot on a TV show for God's sake! And he's her husband, you know, this producer? She's married to this guy who wants to make the film. So. There's nothing for her here.' Another wise glance, and he knew she knew he'd googled Kate, that this wasn't the first he was hearing of his mother's new life. Annoying, to be so seen.

'And the book launch?' Oh God, that was tonight. He'd been

ignoring it. That was all they needed, his father and Olivia and him and Delia and however many other people, all cooped up in a bookshop, trying to deal with the fact his mother had resurfaced. Delia turned stern. 'Adam, you have to come. You just have to.'

He sighed. He'd never said he wouldn't. 'Fine, I'll go. Would that make you happy?'

'Thank you.'

'You can fit it in, can you, with all your *training*?' She just raised her eyebrows at this snipe. On top of her degree in Fine Art, which she was finishing at a distance, Delia was training to be a life coach and yoga teacher and dietitian and various other made-up things. She didn't need to work, of course, her granddad was completely loaded. Not that Adam could support himself with the guitar lessons he gave. But he refused to work in a dead-end job with a twenty-five-year-old manager who read Alan Sugar's autobiography at night before wanking himself to sleep. He was an *artist*.

'Will you see her?' said Delia.

'Hm?' He'd drifted off into fantasy, living the LA canyon life, girls in floaty dresses around swimming pools the colour of cheap turquoise jewellery.

'Your mother. Will you see her when she comes?'

'She's not coming. Where did you get that from?'

Delia opened her eyes wide, her sign for when he was talking rubbish but she was too polite to say. She put out a hand and he helped her up from the mat, unable to stop himself admiring the line of her thighs in Lycra. 'I thought the producer was coming over to meet your dad.'

'He's coming here anyway, I think. Not just for Dad.' Why did he feel the need to point this out? Because he couldn't accept that his embarrassing dad had actually sold a book, become

107

someone people wanted to meet? He was jealous, that was it, of someone who had actually done what they set out to.

'Whatever. Won't she come with him? If she's his wife? I mean, won't it be a bit weird otherwise?'

Adam had not thought about this. Would he have to see his mother, after all this time? Would she cry? Or worse, what if she didn't want to see him at all – she hadn't for the past fifteen years, had she? 'I've no idea. She left us – she hasn't a leg to stand on, has she?'

Delia shrugged her long hair over her shoulder. 'Olivia left me too.'

'That's different.' This was a common, contentious subject between them. 'You still saw her.'

'Not very often.'

And Adam knew he was at least partly to blame for that, something he didn't want to dwell on either. 'Anyway, never mind that coachload of escaped lunatics. What did you want to tell me earlier?'

Delia hesitated and he saw something cross her face. Was that fear? Nothing scared her normally. If she met a violent mugger, she'd probably namaste them into submission. 'Let's get a coffee first, OK? It's no big deal, I just . . . have something to tell you.'

If it was really no big deal, he reflected, as she rolled up her expensive mat, she would have told him right away. Something was wrong.

Andrew, 2009

'What do you think?' Olivia asked. They had taken to eating what she called 'supper' in the evenings. Something light with eggs or fish, served at the kitchen island Kate had longed for so much when they bought this house. As if islands, either kitchen or tropical or no man being one, could really make you happy. After this 'supper', they would move into the lounge, reading or talking by the fire until it was time for bed. It was Olivia who'd started lighting it, buying wood and firelighters and sweeping it clear in the mornings. In her quiet way, she had repeatedly told him she disliked TV, until he woke up one day and thought it was his own idea. Often Andrew crept off to bed early and watched things on his laptop, *Top Gear* and *Late Review*, and sometimes, furtively, porn, with the sound muted and one sweaty hand on the device, leaving what looked to him like incriminating fingerprints. His shame was great, but it had been years without touching a woman. He wondered sometimes if he ever would again.

'I don't know,' he said, forking at the scrambled eggs, thinking it was strange to have them for a meal other than breakfast. 'I'm not sure I want someone else in the house.' It was hard enough to work under Mary's reign of noisy terror.

'I think it would really help.' She poured him out a beer, leaving half of it in the bottle like a waitress, and he had a flash of wondering why – why did she wait on him hand and foot? He'd never asked her to. He'd never asked for any of this, but still she gave and gave and he didn't know how to tell her to stop. He had tried a few times to bring it up – *you know, you don't need to stay, Olivia, you must have lots of things you'd rather do* – but she simply refused to hear him, and so she was still there, in the spare room, possibly forever.

'But – Kirsty can't speak. They told us she never would, I mean.' So what good would a speech therapist do?

'I know,' said Olivia patiently. 'But I was thinking of Dylan. Aimee's boy. There were signs he used – he didn't speak but he

109

could ask for things. A drink, the lavatory. I looked it up. It's not standard sign language. It's called Makaton, for disabled people.' She had this idea, she'd said, of asking the council to provide a therapist for Kirsty. She was good at asking for things, as long as they weren't for herself.

'I don't know.' Part of him was annoyed. Kirsty was his child, his sole responsibility since Kate had fled, and it wasn't Olivia's place to suggest that she could learn to communicate. Surely she couldn't – they'd been told enough times it wasn't possible, to give up all thought of hope.

'Do you know some children don't speak because they physically can't form the words? The speech centre, you know in the brain. Anyway, they do sometimes understand the concepts. But this sign language – it's not like for deaf people, it's simpler – they can sign words like 'bed' and 'milk' and so on – even your name.'

To Andrew, who had privately wept a few times over the fact his daughter would never say 'daddy', this felt very painful. He grunted. It was suddenly overwhelming, all these boulders he was trying to shove uphill. His novel, which seemed to shrink rather than grow, tangled in on itself. All he'd done that month was write and delete an excruciating scene where one of the boys got drunk then threw up in a job interview. Adam, whose behaviour was always a worry, when barely a month would go by that they weren't called into his school because of him fighting, or insulting the teachers, or refusing to do his homework. Was it Andrew's fault – should he have taken the boy to a therapist when his mother left? Did that kind of thing scar you for life? And now this – the idea of Kirsty somehow learning to talk. Was it even possible, when she couldn't use a toilet or feed herself?

'I'll think about it.'

'Alright.'

He hoped that was the end of it, but:

'It's 2009,' said Olivia, after a few quiet moments pushing about her egg.

Andrew wondered if he'd drifted off and missed the whole start to this conversation. 'Yes.'

'March.'

'Mm-huh.'

'I was thinking.'

He put down his fork. When she began sentences in this way, it was inevitably the first pebble in what would become an avalanche of small comments on the same topic, until he gave in.

'Next month it will be two years.'

Andrew honestly didn't know what she meant at first. He began running 2007 through his mind. Then he remembered, and his stomach flipped into his mouth. April. The rainy day, the note. Kate gone. 'Of course. I didn't realise.'

'It's a long time.'

'Time races by, doesn't it? Adam's nine now. I can't believe it.'

She wouldn't budge from the topic. 'Legally, you don't need any grounds after two years. If you've lived apart all that time.'

'Oh?' He could almost understand what she meant but shied from it.

'So, it would make it a lot easier. The divorce.'

Andrew stared past her at the fire, its crackle and dance. It was almost hypnotic, and you could imagine early humans doing exactly this, the fire at night, man and woman. Except this was the wrong woman. This was not his wife, not anything. They had never touched, even. 'I didn't realise that.'

In fact, he hadn't looked into divorce at all. It was two years since Kate had left. Andrew wasn't sure what he'd expected at first – an immediate return, a phone call at least, perhaps a snarling split where they had the kids alternate weekends – but she had vanished so thoroughly, he sometimes had dreams that she was dead and no one had told him. He could even see himself at her funeral, holding the children's hands, Adam in a cut-down suit behaving well for once, Kirsty in a little dress, maybe grey since she was young for black. In his dreams, he often spoke to Kirsty and she spoke back. He never heard her voice though. The words just seemed to drop into his head.

Olivia straightened her cutlery on her plate. Rarely did she approach anything so forcefully, and he was scared. 'I just feel you should sort it out. It's like a ... vein between you. Still pumping. Do you think she'll come back and be with you again, is that it?'

'God!' He almost recoiled. 'No, I never think that.' Kate was like a mythological person now. He imagined her in a variety of exotic scenarios, but never back here in the kitchen. This home had clearly been intolerable to her, she would never come back.

'Then why?'

'It's so expensive – things are tight just now.' That wasn't the reason and they both knew it.

'It needn't be expensive. The court fees are only a few hundred pounds.'

'I suppose.' What was the reason? Perhaps just the fear of being in touch with her, of having to face the reasons she'd left. Why living with him had been so terrible that she'd run and never looked back, not even at her own children. He would do it one day, yes, surely – but for now it just felt like signing over the deeds to a house that had burned down. Pointless, even a little offensive.

'So why not? Don't you want to be free of it, and able to move on, perhaps even marry again?' She halted, as if the conversational train had thundered through the station she wanted and out the other side.

Andrew held his breath. She was looking down – he realised this was one of those moments where the veil they drew over their life together had almost lifted, you could see feelings press through it ... faces, edges ... Was that what she wanted, to marry him? To be with him?

He looked at her, the fine bones of her face, her thin gentle hands that worked so hard to arrange his life, the waves of her hair colourless in the firelight. He could reach over now and push aside that lock of it. Change their entire lives. But there was Adam upstairs, crying himself to sleep most nights and kicking dents in the wall, and there was Kirsty, so helpless, and somewhere there was another child he hadn't even met, Olivia's daughter. All of these children depending on them, like a lifeboat on pitching seas and he was only just keeping it bailed out. Any change in their circumstance might overturn them, and he knew from Kate Olivia wasn't always stable, that she didn't have Delia living with her because of some breakdown after the child's birth. Did he have even feelings for her? She was attractive, yes, soft and gentle and desperate to make him happy in a way Kate had never been. Certainly his brother and even his mother had hinted strongly they thought Olivia was his girlfriend, inviting her on family visits and holidays, though she always politely declined. No one would blame him, since Kate had taken all the blame with her. But there was just too much weighing on it. She was his wife's friend, who had moved in to help him and never moved out. He couldn't be the man who'd pounce on her, take advantage of her kindness.

He waited, saw her eyes close slightly, sensing the veil fall back into place. 'I'll think about it,' he said again, noting his faltering tone, hating himself for his cowardice. 'It's a lot to take in.'

'She isn't coming back,' said Olivia, but the moment was

over, and she stood up to gather his plate. Andrew looked at his watch. Soon he could escape upstairs, and forget this conversation, and he'd not have to get divorce forms or face the idea of Kate. He was beginning to think he'd won, when Olivia made one last sortie. 'I do think you should look into the sign language. Don't you want to try everything?'

Andrew drank his beer and, as if drawn on strings, she reached forward to pour more for him. 'You really think Kirsty could learn it, this thing?'

'Why not?'

'Well, she's – I'm not sure her brain works like that.' He always felt guilty having to say what Kirsty could not do. But the facts were inescapable. They'd been told she didn't understand speech, most likely could barely recognise her parents. The smallest aspects of being human, even those were not allowed to her.

Olivia shook her head. 'She knows things. I'm sure of it. She turns her head when you speak. She can't form words with her mouth, but maybe she can think them, sign them. Being her – I imagine it's like being locked up in a big canvas bag, and not able to properly see, or hear, or talk to any of us.'

Andrew put down his glass, a little sick. It was too easy to think of Kirsty as being almost like a pet – you could babble to her, and cuddle her, and even love her, but she couldn't understand or answer you. Imagining an alternative gave him an ache in the pit of his stomach. 'If you think it will help,' he said. He didn't. But he could hardly say there was no point in trying. And just like that, Andrew had lost in a different way.

'I'll phone them tomorrow.' Olivia poured out the last of his beer. He drank it.

Giving up all hope was not a natural human state. When Kirsty was born, Kate had begun the process of stripping out what

114

they had left. She sank to a base level of assuming their child would never do anything – laugh, or talk, or walk, or be toilet trained. It was a colossal betrayal the world had perpetuated on her, and she was determined never to trust anyone or anything again. Andrew had found himself in the strange situation of having to play the optimist. After all, they still had to keep the child alive, feed her and change her and love her. If one person has claimed all of the negative ground for themselves, you have little choice but to take the other side.

Over the years it became easier to manage people's expectations of Kirsty. When they cooed into the pram, trying to be generous, talking to her, you heard yourself say, 'It's OK, she can't understand.' And sometimes people would look at you as if you were cruel, to say such things about your own daughter. It was one thing he understood about Kate – when you were the parent, you had to push through the cloak of soothing lies to find the truth. Otherwise the disappointment would kill you. If Kirsty was not in pain, and as happy as she could be, that would be enough for him. He'd decided it early on, to have no expectations beyond that.

And then, of course, Olivia. Her quiet, firm, intensive ways. He wondered sometimes if it was easier to be upbeat for a child who was not yours, so you couldn't be as terrified of all hope being utterly snuffed out, a sensation so painful few people could carry on rekindling it.

So that explained Sandra the sign-language teacher. She appeared in the house several weeks after that 'suppertime' conversation, and he heard her voice all the way upstairs. A local accent which got on his nerves in any case, shredded and roughened as if gone over with a cheese grater.

He heard Sandra before he saw her and then, coming cautiously downstairs, felt assaulted by the very look of her. The dyed, frizzy red hair, the reek of cigarettes and hairspray – how was it that she didn't go up in flames? The tight leggings and the wobbly spindle-heeled shoes she staggered about in. Sandra was fifty if she was a day, but dressed like a teenager who'd run through Topshop on a coke binge. Kate would have been absolutely horrified – or at least Old Kate, the one he'd known before she struck up the friendship with poor Aimee, and hadn't that surprised him, his class-conscious wife who'd tried so hard to upgrade her own accent and style, caring so much for a woman who talked incessantly about horoscopes and dance music? Perhaps he had never known Kate at all. Poor Aimee. He didn't like to think about that, so he moved forward, not for the first time feeling like a stranger in his own home, awkwardly uninvited to the party which had shown up in his kitchen.

Kirsty was wearing dungarees and a pink T-shirt, pretty clothes for a much younger child, smeared in banana and dribble. She was in her walker, one for toddlers, except she was by then seven years old. She seemed to like it in there, in as much as she could be assumed to like anything. Sometimes she would move around the tiled floor, her clenched feet pedalling like someone treading water in an invisible sea. Music was playing from a portable speaker on the kitchen island. Something full of bass and pop and women screeching about stopping right there. The woman with dyed hair was holding his daughter's hands and dancing them like a puppet master.

Olivia stood by, not exactly clapping her hands, but clasping and unclasping them to the tune. 'That's it!' the woman was shouting. 'Good girl, Kirsty. You have a little dance there.'

Andrew wished to do something to announce his presence, but there were no doors nearby to slam. He settled instead for raking his hands over his face. Fucking hell. Couldn't they just

116

accept Kirsty as she was? She would be frightened by this surely, the noise and shouting and strange woman.

A prickling in his neck alerted him to the fact his son stood behind him on the stairs, holding a toy that had once been a rabbit – Kirsty's. Not that they were sure she even recognised it. It now lacked eyes and ears, subject to a kind of cuddly toy myxomatosis.

'Hey mate,' he said, from habit, though Adam rarely spoke back to him.

The child stared. At nine he was growing tall, his face hardening into the same lines as Kate's. He would be handsome, grown-up soon. 'What're they doing?'

'They're making your sister dance.'

'She can't dance.'

'I know.'

'She can't feel music. Mum said. S'stupid. She won't like it.'

Andrew blinked. It was both the longest statement he'd made since Kate went, and the first time he'd mentioned her. 'Hmm. Do you want to go down?' He held out his hand, very hesitant, as if to a wild deer, though Adam at nine would hardly hold it, in fact he would not have done so even when younger. The boy ignored it, then turned to go back upstairs.

Andrew descended. The woman did not stop the dancing for a full minute after he appeared.

'Hello,' said Oliva nervously. 'Er, this is Kirsty's new therapist.'

'Sandra,' she supplied. 'So what's the situation here?' Sandra stared him right in the eyes and he began to sweat. 'No sense beating about the bush. Liv, you ain't Kirsty's mum?'

Ain't. She couldn't even speak English, and he was supposed to trust his child to her? 'Her mother isn't around,' said Andrew, stiffly.

'Stepmum then?'

He could see Olivia's eyes glaze with awkwardness, and deflected like mad. 'Olivia is our very good friend. What were you doing there? She doesn't really respond to music, we don't think.'

Sandra patted Kirsty's forehead in a way that seemed annoyingly proprietorial. 'Oh, it's been shown they can feel stimulated by it, like in their brain, and it helps with communication. I have a doctorate.' She hitched up her leggings. 'Oof, these are right up my crack.'

That was her all over. She was loud and she was coarse, and she had absolutely no fear of anyone or anything. She called him 'my love'. She had tattoos up each arm, smoke lines around her mouth, leopard-print leggings, three teenage boys with different dads – but she was also smart and tough. She'd been a social worker before training as a therapist. Olivia, he suspected, was a little afraid of her. Andrew sometimes worried that they were so different, her mere presence in the world might somehow obliterate him entirely. But all the same, he paused that night on his before-bed rounds to look in at the kids. Adam was already asleep, curled into a tight ball. Andrew would smooth his covers and sometimes his hair, though Adam often jerked away in his sleep, muttering. As every night, he pushed on the open door to Kirsty's room, finding her awake. She was on so many medications to make her sleep and wake and control her seizures and bowels and blood flow. Olivia had rigged her up a mobile, a drift of coloured sea creatures over the wall, a soft nursery tune. Her eyes did not seem to follow it, just stared at nothing. The patterns of light and shade on her retinas. They weren't sure how much she could see, even after operations on her eyes as well as ears and hips and heart. So much effort into keeping her small body alive.

'Kirsty,' he said, keeping his voice low. She didn't look round. She didn't know her name. Did she? 'It's me. Dad. Daddy.' His voice choked up on the word, and suddenly he was enraged with Olivia. He had long given up on these most simple things – that his daughter would know him, would look at him, call him Daddy. How dare she give him more of it, that oh-so-dangerous hope.

Andrew, present day

'Ready?'

'Almost. Just looking for my cufflinks.'

'In the little box in the nightstand.' Olivia stepped into his room, because it was still just his room – she'd never spent a night there – and slid open the drawer in question. Her movements were graceful, considered, and she had found the very thing he wanted in a second. It was annoying, how dependent he was on her. She came around to fasten them for him without being asked, smiling up at him. 'You'll be great, you know. Don't worry.'

'I'm not worried.' He was, though.

'It's so exciting. But you know, big parties . . . '

They always made him anxious, and indeed he was very nervous, thinking what if no one came, or what if too many people came and the venue was stuffed, the wine ran out. He'd asked for RSVPs but nobody under forty seemed to understand those any more. His stomach lurched, a ball of fire in his chest. Olivia had thought of that too. 'There's Rennies in my bag, in case you need them. Train's in fifteen minutes.'

'I know. Look, I'll be down in a minute.'

'Alright.' She turned, and he realised too late he should have complimented her dress, a flowery one, and the way she'd done her makeup and hair, extra shiny somehow.

'You look very nice, by the way.'

'You too.' She paused, put a hand on the knot of his tie. He held his breath. They had so rarely touched, in the fifteen years they'd lived together. 'I'm very proud of you, you know.' And she went out, leaving a trail of perfume, faint as a dream. Andrew looked at himself in the mirror, balder and more lined than he had imagined himself at his first book launch, in a suit and tie. Too formal? God, he didn't know. The kids from his writing class always wore ripped jeans and fraying jumpers and beanies over unwashed hair. They'd probably laugh at him.

Olivia reappeared with her coat on and held out his. 'Come on, superstar author.' The phrase made him squirm. Her naked praise and support, it still felt so strange. Kate's exacting coldness had been more comfortable for him somehow. An expectation of failure that meant he didn't have to try. Outside, a light rain was falling and Olivia put her umbrella up, taking his arm as they walked to the station. He wasn't used to going out at night, up to London, and it was odd to pass the commuters coming the other way, weary-eyed and stale, like he'd been for so many years until she saved him. They went in and bought tickets from the machine, in companionable rhythm, stood on the platform waiting. He wished he'd brought a drink to calm his nerves, gin in a tin perhaps, but Olivia was funny about drinking, funny about so many things. They sat opposite each other on the quiet train, strewn with abandoned *Evening Standard*s. He was going to his book launch. The day he'd dreamed of so many times, imagining the speech, the enemies from his past he'd invite to watch his triumph, it was now. It was today. Remember this, he told himself. Soon time would spool away and it would also be a memory, like everything.

Olivia kept asking if various people would be there. 'Anyone from work?'

'Um – I invited them, but not sure.' He'd had a desultory response from his old City law firm, as if they didn't really believe he'd done it, or were faintly astonished someone would prefer writing to the pleasures of contract law. It would be nice to see his evil former boss Martin, force him to watch as Andrew was feted. 'The writing class, of course.'

'Oh yes. Letitia?'

'Yes.' Why did it irritate him, that she remembered the name of his teacher from ten years ago? That was what a partner did, except she wasn't his partner. And that was a point in itself. How would he introduce her to everyone, his editor April, all of twenty-six, the publicist who was even younger, his agent Simeon, a red-trousered type with a home in France? Who would he say she was? Since they never went anywhere, the question had only arisen on the odd awkward occasion when they had someone round to do work at the house. And Sandra, of course, who'd gone straight for the jugular and never stopped.

'Is Adam coming?'

'Oh, who knows. He knows it's happening.' Adam could just as easily come and be charming, come and cause a scene, or not turn up and never mention it again. Was it humiliating, to have no family there? Or was Olivia family now? 'What about Delia?' he asked, hopefully. Delia would be perfect at a book launch, clever and lovely, proud of him.

'She said she'd try.' Olivia's face took on a familiar vagueness as she spoke about her daughter. She didn't like to talk about her own child, did she? Only his. 'And everyone from the publisher's coming, April and Felicia and Jon?'

'Who's Jon?'

'The cover designer.'

'Oh yes.' Why did she know this and he didn't? Her anxiety was feeding his and vice-versa. As they lapsed into silence, the fields of Surrey speeding past, Andrew felt like he was going to his execution. What had made him think he wanted a night devoted to himself? He wasn't worthy of it, would only stutter and look stupid. And he realised, as he picked up a free paper and pretended to read it to avoid talking any more to Olivia, that when he'd pictured his book launch – even after she'd walked out, even when fifteen years had gone by since he'd seen her – he had always imagined Kate there, across the room, applauding coolly. Nodding to him as if to say, yes. You did it at last.

Andrew, 2010

'So we're all set? Do I need to have a talk with Adam, about how to behave?' Andrew was on edge. Delia had never been to stay with them before – Olivia went to see her from time to time, but that was that – and she was coming this weekend. The years of taking care of Andrew's children without mishap seemed to have healed something in Olivia, so she could now actually contemplate having her daughter around her.

'They'll be fine.'

'Didn't he injure her last time they met?'

'Well, yes, but he was only little then. He didn't mean it, it was just an accident.'

There were a lot of accidents around Adam, lashing out in his temper tantrums. Broken dishes, enraged parents of other children who'd been hit or kicked, supposedly accidentally. 'I'll talk to him.' They both also knew Adam didn't listen to a word his father said. But these were the lies they passed between them, like currency. 'You're sure she's OK in your room with you?'

Olivia turned her face. 'Of course. I'm on my own in there, after all.'

This conversation had many hidden depths. It felt like walking with leg weights. 'Alright. It will be nice to finally meet her.' He had suggested it many times, that Olivia should see her daughter, should visit her more, but Olivia always resisted it politely. Things were fine. Delia had a routine, it would upset her to break it. Andrew needed her. And then, a few months ago, Olivia had finally agreed to it. He didn't know why he was so uneasy. Of course Olivia should invite her daughter here, to the house where she lived. But it made things concrete somehow. It made them a *family*. It stirred up topics that had settled down again after the discussion of him divorcing Kate, which he had still not made any move to do, still could not face. After all, you didn't divorce a dead person.

Delia's visit was set for a weekend in April. Andrew couldn't believe he was actually going to meet the little girl – right until the moment the car pulled up in the street. Delia always took town cars, Olivia had explained. Her mother didn't drive and her father had been told not to while on medication, so the child was ferried everywhere by liveried drivers. Andrew hadn't wanted to delve too much into Olivia's finances, despite the fact they'd been essentially living together for three years now. She insisted on paying half the bills and mortgage, but beyond that they had never talked about her wealth, or why her daughter didn't live with her. They had never talked about so many things.

Now, Andrew moved to open the door and realised Olivia

was frozen stiff in the kitchen. 'She's here,' he said. Sounds outside, an engine idling, a door slammed.

Olivia wrung her hands, trembling slightly. Andrew sighed – so this would be up to him, now she'd shut down at the crucial moment. On his doorstep was a pale child in full denim, jeans and a jacket pinned over with metal badges, and a denim baseball cap set on her head, out of which came a long fair ponytail. She was standing with a large black hold-all.

Andrew looked at the driver, executing a three-point turn. 'Do I need—'

'Oh no. Granddaddy pays it all on account.' The tones crystal clear, even though the child was slight and shivering in the breeze.

'Come in, Delia. Do come in. Er – I'm Andrew, of course.' He tried to think what his relationship to this girl could be, and his mind blanked and reset itself. 'Your mum's in the kitchen.' He was amazed by how grown-up Delia seemed. There was already an adult sway in her walk, totally unconscious, a way of holding herself. Adam was ten but he was a boy, and Andrew couldn't believe all ten-year-olds were as wild and angry as him, with such an adult understanding of the complexities of things.

'Olivia, here's Delia!' God, he hated the heartiness of his voice. Not for the first time, Andrew had the dizzying sensation that he'd stepped into the wrong life. This woman, this child, even his own children – where had they come from? Wasn't he still twenty-five, living in flat shares like the boys in his long-gestated novel?

Olivia blinked several times, as if resetting herself. 'Darling! You're here.' She cupped the child's face with her hands.

'May I leave my jacket, please?' Delia was so polite.

Andrew took it. 'Of course. And would you like juice or something – Coke?'

'I normally have tea around this time.' Delia consulted the plastic watch around her wrist.

'Um – of course.' At what age did they start drinking tea? Adam would only drink pop from the supermarket, the cheap, additive-filled kind. Adam. God. Where was he? Andrew's muscles weakened with fear. 'I'll make tea then.'

'Thank you,' said Delia formally. 'Are there other children? I know about the little girl. Don't worry. I'll be understanding.'

'And there's Adam. He's about your age, a bit older.'

Delia touched her cheek, where there was a very thin white scar. 'I remember. He hurt me one time.'

Olivia said, 'He was very little, darling. He didn't mean it.'

Delia looked at Andrew, as if for confirmation of this, and he couldn't give it. 'We'll go to the cinema tomorrow,' he said. 'Harry Potter. That'll be nice, and we can go for walks in the forest – sometimes there are deer.'

'Granddaddy owns some deer,' said Delia vaguely. Her eyes wandered to a packet of Hobnobs on the kitchen island.

'Let's make tea,' said Andrew, even more heartily. 'Nice cup of tea!' Soon he would be actually rubbing his hands together.

'You use teabags.' Delia looked startled as he took the packet down from the cupboard. 'Um ... could I please just have water?'

'Of course, but don't you want—'

'No thank you.' She almost shuddered. 'Will I see Adam sometime?'

'I can see you now,' came a spectral voice, from under the dining table, and a loud hollow laughing. The adults jumped, but Delia just looked politely interested. Intrigued, even.

Looking back, it was only a matter of time before Adam hurt Delia again. She had a curiosity about him. Of course she did, she was nine and he was ten, a boy. His feet already smelled and he had hair coming under his arms. She asked lots of questions about him. Did he go to school? Did he have friends? Did he play football? On a trip to a castle they were having a picnic, sandwiches in Tupperware, crisps, a thermos of coffee for the grown-ups, juice boxes. The five of them out in the sunshine, and there were daffodils, a fresh spring smell in his lungs. Andrew felt hopeful, almost. Something to do with the niceness of National Trust gift shops, all that jam and soap in the shape of flowers, made him feel maybe life wasn't totally awful. A blow had been absorbed. Kate was gone, but life went on, and maybe this lovely child would be partly his too.

She'd asked questions all day. What's that, Andrew? Did Anne Boleyn really live here? When did her head get chopped off? Do you think it hurt? He told her about the Tower of London and her eyes went wide. 'Can we go there, please?'

We. He imagined a future in that one word, where she'd live with them – and why not? Olivia was her mother after all – and Adam would calm down with Delia about, surely, and they'd be what he'd barely dared say for years – a family. They were having lunch, Olivia feeding Kirsty, who had mashed potato smeared over her face. It was always hard to find anything in cafés she could eat, so they had a lot of picnics. Andrew was answering Delia's chattered questions. Adam was roaming the picnic area, over by the bins where wasps swarmed. Delia looked at them nervously. 'What if they bite me?'

'They hardly ever do, and even if they do, it's just a little sting.'

'A girl in my school, if a wasp or like a bee stings her, she'll die.'

Adam perked up at the mention of death. 'Why will she die?'

'I don't know.' Delia started, shocked to be addressed directly by The Boy.

126

Andrew explained what anaphylaxis was, glowing with pride as both children listened intently. It was highly likely this would never happen again. Then his son was up again, restless, shoving pickled onion crisps in his face.

'Does he like juice?' whispered Delia.

'Why don't you ask him? He's just there.'

She giggled slightly. 'Andrew, will you and Mummy get married?'

He froze. Adam had heard too, though he carried on roaming, doing something secretive over at the bin. 'Mind the wasps,' Andrew said reflexively. 'Erm – what makes you say that, Delia?' Olivia had gone into a kind of trance, pretending not to hear.

'Grandma said I wasn't to ask, but I thought that's why she lived here.' Of course, everyone must think that he and Olivia were a couple. And what were they? There wasn't a word for it.

'Er, well, I . . . '

'Do you love her?'

'Erm – your mother has been my best friend these past years. Of course I – care about her.' Olivia bent over Kirsty, wiping her face, as she had done every day for years now. Too much, far too much, and yet every time he'd given her a chance to go, she stayed.

'Caring's not the same as loving.' Delia frowned. 'It's what people say when they don't really love you, but they think they should.' How could she know this, at nine?

For once in his life, he was actually pleased to see Adam approach with his crisps held out, which he thrust at Delia. 'Want one?'

Adam sharing? The girl looked at him mistrustingly, then put out her small hand, glitter polish chipped off around the cuticles. Adam had his fist clenched round the bag. Just then Andrew realised the bag was buzzing. Delia screamed. A wasp emerged from the bag, angry as all hell, and on her finger a swelling red lump. 'Oh!' she screamed. 'It was in there, I felt it, I felt its *wings*!'

Adam cackled. 'Just a little sting, Dad says.'

Andrew realised later he'd been almost grateful for what happened, so pleased was he to not have to finish that conversation.

Andrew knocked gently on the door of Olivia's room, which had once been the guest room. It hadn't changed much since then, the same anonymous cream bedspread and curtains, bowl of pot pourri on the dresser. Delia was propped up in the camp bed, a bandage round her finger. Her face was swollen and she kept sniffing as her eyes let out a slow leak of tears. 'I brought you some hot chocolate,' he said. Olivia was in the garden, having some kind of private meltdown, and he dreaded the discussion ahead.

'I've cleaned my teeth already,' sniffed Delia.

'It's OK. Special treat.'

She sat up and took the cup, blowing on it, brown foam round the edges. 'Thank you.'

He sat awkwardly on Olivia's bed. As always, it was made up as neatly as a hotel, and there was no sign of her corporeality, no rumpled duvet or impression on the pillow. 'I'm sorry for what Adam did. It was mean.'

She quivered. 'I *hate* wasps. Its wings. I felt them on me.' She made a fluttering motion with her fingers. 'Is he not a nice boy?'

'Um ... he's angry, a lot of the time.'

'Because his mum went away?'

God. The child's acuity was like an arrow in the throat. 'Maybe. I'm sorry about your finger.'

'It will be better. At least I don't have the thing you told us about, the ana thing.'

Anaphylaxis. She'd remembered. 'That's true. So really, you don't need to be scared of wasps.'

Another tear juddered and fell out into the cup. 'Is Mummy alright, Andrew?'

'I think so. Why?'

'She doesn't like it when I get hurt. She cries and says it's her fault.'

'But it was Adam's fault.'

Delia shook her head. 'She thinks it's hers. Will you tell her it isn't? Otherwise she might not let me come again.' A tear trembled on her lashes. 'And I want to come. It's so much fun here.'

Oh God. Oh God oh God. Fun, this house? The poor kid. For the first time it truly hit Andrew, that Delia's mother had left her too, just as much as Kate had. To raise his children. And why? He'd never asked her to. Why couldn't she live with her own child – what was this terrible fear that her presence would injure Delia, when she was fine taking care of Adam and Kirsty? He didn't understand. 'Of course I'll tell her. Try to get some sleep.' He wanted to call her some pet name, sweetheart maybe, the kind of words he used to Kirsty but mostly in his head. It didn't seem right.

Outside, Adam was sitting cross-legged on the floor, scowling at nothing. 'Well?' said Andrew, wearily.

Adam didn't bother saying he hadn't meant it. Obviously he had. Instead he said, in a low flat voice, 'You like her better than me.'

'What?'

'Her. Kirsty too. Everyone likes everyone better than me.' Andrew was so very tired.

'Mate, of course that's not true. I love you very much, and Olivia does too.'

'*She* didn't,' he said, barely audible, and Andrew knew which

129

she he meant. Not Olivia or Delia, or even Kirsty. His mother, so rarely mentioned. He hesitated.

'Is that something you want to talk ...'

Adam leapt up, ran to his own room, slammed the door. Andrew sighed. As he turned away, he saw something had been left on the floor, half pushed under Delia's door. A scrap of paper, which held a huge comical drawing of a wasp with fangs, and in capital letters the word SORRY. He left it where it was.

Andrew went back downstairs, feeling trapped in something, the need to give a thing he did not have. Olivia was in the living room with the TV on, which he knew to be a bad sign. Her eyes were glazed. He said, 'I'm sorry. Adam, he – we need to get him some help, maybe. I'll look for another therapist.' Adam had refused to tolerate any that the council offered. 'Delia's fine though.'

Olivia said, 'She won't come here again.'

'Oh, but she must – I've loved having her.' A happy child, a loving child. 'Olivia – look, she wants to be with you. There's no reason she can't visit more, or even ...' He ran out of steam suddenly. If he suggested Delia live with them permanently, it would be to bring up all the other unsaid things. Like just what they were to each other, this woman who lived in his house. A storm of justifications rose in him – he'd never asked her to move in, she was Kate's best friend so of course he wasn't going to jump on her right away, she'd never actually *said* if she felt more for him than just a friend – but all were quickly suffocated under a tidal wave of guilt. The fact was, Olivia had given up everything for him, even her own child, and still, from some fault in his nature, some diffidence or fear or guilt, he couldn't give her this so tiny thing in return. 'You should see her more,' he said, lamely. 'I know it isn't my business, but it's what she needs. She's your daughter, you can't just abandon her.' For a lurching moment, it was as if he'd said it to Kate.

'She'll get hurt.' Olivia's voice was so low he could hardly hear it. 'She's better off without me.'

'She won't, she loves . . . ' Olivia had fallen forward, her head and chest flopping onto her lap, a high-pitched keening coming from her mouth. 'Olivia? I'm sorry, I didn't . . . I shouldn't . . . ' But the noise carried on, and Andrew realised, panic filling his nose like water, that he was now the only functioning adult in the house, all these children depending on him.

In the end he rang her parents, and they came in a large Bentley, defying the no-driving rule. Her father was a silver-haired posh-voiced seventy-year-old clearly used to getting his own way. As his wife, also silver-haired and spare as a rail, twittered upstairs packing Delia's things, the father – Ronald – stood in the kitchen with Andrew.

'She's ill, you know.'

'I know.'

'It can be controlled. Years since she had an attack. But she won't live with us. Too afraid she'll do something to the girl.'

'Yes.' Useless to say that was an unfounded fear. 'Should I – her work will need to be told?' Did they know she was ill already? Kate had known, but only because Olivia told her, the last time Adam hurt Delia.

'The boss chappy knows. How she is.'

Adam tried to remember the man's name. Oh yes – Kate's old boss too, who he'd never liked, a bluff over-confident man who'd test you on the finer points of obscure whiskey. 'David?'

'That's the one. McGregor.' Ronald's mouth tightened. 'Appreciate it if you could tell him. It might be a while.'

131

Delia was being hustled downstairs by her grandmother, crying quietly. Olivia was already in the car, and he hadn't even said goodbye. 'Delia could have stayed,' said Andrew wretchedly, wishing he could make his apologies to the child, though he didn't know what for. Olivia's father fixed him with a steely bloodshot eye, and Andrew wanted to defend himself, say he'd never touched Olivia, never asked her to be here, never asked for any of it. But all the same it was his fault and he knew it.

The next morning, Andrew, having been up all night with a screaming Kirsty, was trying to give her a bath, water all over the floor and on his jeans as she splashed and squealed, Adam throwing a tantrum in the corridor about who would take him to football now Olivia was gone, when the doorbell rang. He went down cursing, sopping wet, Kirsty squirming in his arms in a towel.

'Oh dear,' said Sandra, taking him in, her jaws working with chewing gum. 'Big night, Andy? On the sauce?' She held out her arms for Kirsty. 'Give her here.'

He hated it when she called him Andy. 'Does she have a session today?' Olivia kept track of all that. 'I'm afraid Olivia – she's gone away.' He'd no idea for how long, or how he would cope without her. 'So I don't think we can – today's not good I'm afraid.' Not that the therapy seemed to be doing any good, since Kirsty still showed no signs of making any communication.

Sandra cocked her head at the noise of Adam, wincing as Kirsty squealed in her arms, and peered past him at the mess from last night's dinner and this morning's breakfast, the porridge on Andrew's jumper and holes in his socks. 'Never mind a session, Andy, looks like things have gone to shit around here. Why don't I come in and make you some tea, eh?'

Kate, present day

The parking space she drew into said *Ms Kate McKenna* on a little white sign. How proud she'd been on the first day, to have her own space, her name. A name she had given up for a time, allowing herself to be called *Mrs Waters*, or *Adam and Kirsty's mummy*, then reclaimed. She pulled her car into the space and opened the door on a crushing ceiling of heat. In the few steps to the door of the studio, she was already dazed by it, sweating into her linen dress. Then the sliding doors enveloped her in a whoosh of cold air. The receptionist, some new young girl with pink hair, greeted her by name and reminded her, in a strong upward inflection, of the need to report any covid symptoms. The temperature check machine they'd bought at great expense sat already abandoned to the side, bottles of hand sanitiser hardly used. How soon things became normal. Kate took the lift – *elevator* – to her floor, where again she was greeted, this time by runners, producers, camera people. Her main producer, Tristan, a slight young man from Brooklyn, waved her over. 'I wasn't sure you'd show.' She had run out in a state the day before, after reading the news about Conor's book acquisition. She was hardly fit to be here today either, but her career was really all she had left and she couldn't afford to miss a show.

'I'm sorry. Something came up – family emergency.'

He knew all about Trixie and her issues, not that American workplaces were particularly sympathetic about health or family, or anything that showed you weren't a robot. 'No worries.'

'What's on today?'

'Some prairie housewife who wrote a book about surrendering ... the trend for keeping bees ... a chef showing how to cook with foraged foods ... ' The usual then. She could handle this, she told herself. It was her daily bread (and that bread would be homemade and sourdough). Just because Andrew was back in her life, and she'd seen his face briefly on a computer screen, that didn't mean anything had changed. She was still successful, with her own segment of a nationally screened chat show. She had her own makeup artist. She had *made it,* incontrovertibly. No one could take that away from her.

'Great. I'll go get my face on, then.'

'Maybe a little more blush today,' he said diplomatically. Kate flushed with shame. She looked terrible, clearly, past the age where shock left no marks on her. Luckily the studio had some of the finest makeup artists in Hollywood.

An hour later she sat under the lights of her set. Kate was one of three anchors on the afternoon show, a sort of rotating interviewer. She was never quite sure how they assigned segments but suspected it was in the hope of a bust-up that would go viral. She was to talk to the housewife, which she imagined was deliberate. She was often given the more controversial stories, women's rights and healthcare and gender roles, anything where her liberal spin might make for fireworks. She liked it – it reminded her of that brief period after Aimee's death, when she'd felt she might be able to make a difference, be a serious journalist raising serious issues. And Tristan knew she had been married in the past, and rejected a traditional marriage with Conor, made sure to earn her own money, keep her independence. She'd never go back to the early days of squatting in his house, helpless and dependent, and they'd always been free to live their own lives. Even if in practice that meant him making a film about her family without even asking her.

When the housewife was led out, dazzled by the lights and sense of frantic activity in the shadows, Kate pasted on a smile.

They'd once told her she made good TV because she had no poker face, and there were memes all over the internet about her Resting Bitch Face. She didn't mind. She'd rather be a successful bitch than a kind loser. The wife was about thirty, wearing an oversized floral dress that fell to mid-calf, and her hair was braided around her head. She looked unsure, gaze darting about, almost stumbling as she stepped onto the raised platform with the chairs facing each other. On the table, a vase of flowers, water carafe, cup of tea in a saucer for Kate – part of her British image, though really she drank coffee and the stronger the better. American tea wasn't worth the hot water.

'Hi! Lucy, is it?'

'Yes. It's so crazy to meet you – I'm such a fan!'

'Thank you.' It had ceased to mean anything, people saying that, which was sad. 'So I'm just going to ask you a few questions about your book and your lifestyle, and I hope you won't mind if I play devil's advocate a little? Just to keep it interesting.'

'Of course!' She blinked hard. 'Golly, it's warm in here.' Kate had never before met anyone who said the word golly non-ironically. The book was on the table between them, the title *Submit and Be Happy*, with a photo of a woman smiling up at her big strong husband. Irritating. But all the same Kate didn't mean what happened next. She'd swear that afterwards. Tristan was in front of her then, and the makeup artist whisking some last powder over her nose, and then the camera was on and so was her smile.

'I'm here today with Lucy Waterhouse, aka the Submissive Wife, who's written a book about finding happiness by becoming a traditional wife to her husband. Lucy, what does that mean?'

'Um ... it means I gave up paid work. I take care to make a beautiful welcoming home for my husband Keith, I always have his dinner ready and prep his lunch for him in the morning. I get up to cook him breakfast before he goes out to work, and I defer to him on all big decisions, like where we live, what we spend money on, and when we'll have children.' She beamed. For a moment Kate let herself imagine it, getting up to make breakfast for Conor, even though he only drank protein shakes and coffee in the morning. Smiling and waving him off to his office. What a joke. On any given morning they were just as likely not to be speaking to each other.

'So – you have no income of your own?'

Lucy smiled widely. 'Our income is joint, of course. We're married! I think sometimes, as a society, we've forgotten that's what marriage means.' Hadn't Andrew said something very similar to Kate once, in the distant past?

'But tell me, Lucy, don't you ever have disagreements? I mean you're only human, you can't want the same as your husband all the time.'

'Well, we have conversations. I tell him my wishes, but ultimately I trust him to decide for us. And honestly, Kate' – she leaned forward earnestly – 'it doesn't work when both people in a marriage try to make choices. You just end up pulling in different directions, like mules. This way we're one, the way God intended it.' She'd wondered how long it would be before God showed up.

'But not everyone believes in God, of course.' Kate caught a flash of Tristan's face, drawing a hand over his throat. Mentions of atheism were to be avoided at all costs. 'If I can just go back to what you said about your husband choosing when you have children – what do you mean by that?'

Slight blush. 'He's in charge of the birth control decisions.' Not very religious, then, but Kate wouldn't go there again.

'That sounds a bit dystopian to me, Lucy. He literally gets your contraceptive pills for you?'

Furious blush. 'Well, yes. It's his right.'

'To decide what you put into your body and when? And what about feminism? You don't agree?'

'I honestly believe feminism has brought women nothing but sadness. Look at my mother – maybe yours too, Kate – they didn't expect to have jobs, they had enough to do raising the kids and keeping the house. And now we're expected to fly high at work, look after our kids ourselves, and also have Instagram-worthy homes. I mean it's not possible, is it? And the men don't help – just look at the stats for the division of labour in the home, it hasn't improved in decades.' Kate frowned. This wasn't right – the nervous young woman actually had a point, and the figures to back it up.

'There's always paid help, of course . . .'

'That's just outsourcing your labour to poorer women. I don't call that feminism.' She set her jaw firmly, and Kate suddenly saw why the book had sold a million copies. This Lucy had dared to say what most did not – the new way of living for women, having everything but needing to be perfect all the time, didn't work either.

'Alright, but isn't it possible to have an equal partnership, where you both earn and both do housework and childcare?'

'In a dream world,' Lucy said, earning a laugh from the audience that Kate really had not expected. They were on her side, this homespun young woman. 'Does *your* husband tidy up, Kate?'

They had daily cleaners for that. Kate blinked; she had never really grown used to thinking of Conor as her husband. 'Well, he's very busy . . .'

'And childcare – I've never known a man do the bulk of it. They just don't remember things like school forms, and new shoes, and all the thousand little details a mom has in her head. Do you have children?'

She'd asked Kate a personal question. They never did that, only wanting to talk about themselves. Kate froze. She had never talked about her family on air. Did she have children – yes, of course she did, but she had left them with their father, who presumably had been obliged to do all of the childcare, since she'd given him little choice. And it was true, wasn't it, that her marriage to Conor was far from perfect. She might like to tell herself he didn't make all the decisions, but he did, didn't he? By dint of caring less than her. By always being ready to walk away, which was something she'd never been able to countenance.

'Well . . . ' The silence hung there. Dead air, a cardinal sin. Tristan waving like a drowning swimmer. 'I . . . to be honest, Lucy, I don't think that's any of your business, and nor is it your business what other people do with their lives. You should be ashamed, pushing the women's movement back to the fifties like this. You have no idea of the damage you'll do.'

The monitor showed Kate they had cut to an urgent commercial break. The studio was in silence, stunned at what she'd said. And the woman opposite already had a filmy sheen of tears in her earnest eyes.

Andrew, 2011

Olivia was saying, 'I'll need to order the turkey soon – or goose, if you prefer. But the deadline for the butcher is Friday.'

It was Christmas again. To Andrew it seemed an unwanted intrusion, a guest who wouldn't leave even when the hosts were weeping in the bedrooms. He tried again, 'Are you sure you want to be here? Don't you want to go to your parents – spend it with Delia?'

If Olivia wasn't here, he could ignore the holiday, shut himself up with the kids and watch cartoons. Kirsty wouldn't know the difference and Adam, unlike every other child in the world, seemed to have something of an aversion to Christmas. Andrew and Kate had taken him to Santa in the local shopping centre the year he was two and, rather than sit on the man's lap, Adam had bitten his finger, causing the failed actor in the fake beard to drop his *ho, ho, ho,* voice and scream out some very child-unfriendly words.

Olivia's jaw had set in a way he'd come to recognise meant she wouldn't budge. 'I'll visit Christmas Eve, that's our main celebration anyway. And you'll need me here on the day.' There had been no more talk of Delia staying over since the incident. Olivia had returned after a month at her parents', moving back into the spare room and taking up the reins of his life. Andrew had tried to talk to her about it, break this hoop they were lashed onto, but she wouldn't. And he did need the help – that month on his own, working full-time while caring for two kids, one disabled, had been intolerable. Strangely, it was Sandra who'd saved him. A godsend, Olivia had always called her. A thorn in his side, Andrew had privately thought, filling the house with noise and clamour, her teenage sons ringing the bell for her asking where their jeans were, her monosyllabic husband dropping her off in a car with a rattling engine, even her loud yappy dog on occasions. The anti-muse. But she had corralled her son's girlfriend into looking after Kirsty while Andrew was at work, collecting her off her school bus; she'd found a therapist Adam seemed to tolerate, even though he insisted it was stupid and wouldn't discuss a word of the £70 sessions with Andrew. She'd sent the silent husband round to cut the overgrowing grass, even.

'Honestly, we'd be fine.' There was something about the

idea of Olivia being there, her blinking determination to make things nice, that was unbearable. The gap between the lovely family Christmas everyone held in their heads and the loneliness of the reality, the rubbed-off shine.

Both sets of parents, the McKennas and the Waters, had invited them, along with his brother Laurence who had now set up a second home with his former student, all of twenty-three and pregnant with his child. Neither family, for all they exclaimed how much they wanted to see their granddaughter, had any idea of her needs or interest in adapting their homes or routines to her. He compromised on a one-night visit to his parents in York just before Christmas, stopping off with the McKennas on the way back, which coincided with one of the worst snowfalls in a decade. Olivia would not come, of course – she always extricated herself from any family occasions, though they were all convinced she and Andrew were a couple – so Andrew found himself, exhausted after being up all night with Kirsty, staring out the window of the McKennas' terraced house in dismay at the flakes coming down. Adam, who'd slept in the living room at his grandparents' and openly watched unsuitable TV all night long, came to stand beside him. 'Snow.'

'Yes. I hope we can get home OK.' Adam was now eleven – perhaps he'd be excited about a blizzard and Andrew's adult concerns would ruin it for him.

But the boy just said, 'Me too. I hate it here.' Andrew looked at him, surprised to find himself and his son in accord. He was right – it was horribly awkward, having lunch with Kate's parents and sister without mentioning her. Elizabeth was married now, to a man called Paul who did something in IT, and pregnant at last. Kate wouldn't even know.

After it happened, he'd had to phone her parents to tell them, and once he'd talked through their refusal to believe it, Ann had said, 'Oh Andrew. We can only say sorry.' He realised they meant sorry for bringing Kate into the world, sorry that they had a daughter who would do such things. She might as well be dead, at least then they could have talked of her fondly. 'I miss Livvie,' said Adam, unexpectedly. Andrew sighed. He did too, he had to admit. She made everything so much easier.

They did make it home, and on the day it was all fir branches up the stairs, candles burning and carols on the stereo, silver wrapping paper with bows and tags, the kind Kate had some-times bought and then forgotten about. They only tear it up, she said. It was nice. It would have been nice, at least, if they were a normal family, if his novel wasn't still unfinished, if the woman passing out the gifts was not his missing wife's work colleague – a woman who would rather act as a sort of unpaid companion than see her own child at Christmas.

For Kirsty, the gifts Olivia had bought were plastic, brightly coloured, so that she might at least be able to see them, or practical, like a holly-red sweatshirt that would wash well. For Adam, the best. A guitar, a real one, sized-down. When the boy opened it, Andrew felt an odd pang shoot through him, pain, envy, and guilt that he had been exactly like his own parents and not able to realise what would have been the best gift of all for his son. All through dinner his blue eyes slid to the box and Andrew spent the evening tuning it up, not that he even knew how. Adam even played a few bars with him, and it was one of the nicest times he remembered having with his son. And all because of her, now washing up so unobtrusively in the kitchen.

'Thank you,' he said later, when children slept and they drank an adult gin in front of the fire, Olivia permitting herself a very weak one for Christmas. She seemed to fear that any stimulant – excitement, alcohol, upset, even sugar – might set off another episode. 'This was – it was perfect.' He didn't mean that. It could never be perfect. 'It was a wonderful gift. The guitar. It must have been very expensive? I should pay you back.'

Olivia blushed and set down her glass. 'Oh no. There is a little something, I – well.' And she was taking a silver envelope from the mantelpiece and he realised, *oh no, she's got me a present too.*

He unfolded it. A piece of paper. He read it. 'A writing class.'

She was scarlet. 'It starts in January. I thought it might – you know, sometimes a kick-start ...'

He had paused slightly too long and her face was falling in. 'Olivia. How do you do all this? So thoughtful. And I didn't – Kate and I never ...' They had given up on gifts once Kirsty was born. The last present he'd bought Kate would have been for her thirtieth birthday, a necklace he had never seen her wear and which she'd left behind when she went.

Olivia was flustered. 'Oh no, no, how could you, you have so much on and you ...'

'I'm sorry.'

'I don't mind.'

He balled his fists. He would have liked to kick something, stride about the room. 'You should mind. You get so little – you do so much – and ...' Andrew realised he was crying, his breath laboured and angry. And Olivia was holding him in her sparrow arms, murmuring that it was OK, it was alright of him to be such a selfish, thoughtless git. And Ghost Kate looked over his shoulder – *I always said you were useless.*

He became suddenly aware of how close they were, he and Olivia. The intimacy of a fireside at Christmas, children asleep upstairs. She drew back, eyes darting nervously to his face. Really looking at him for once. Her face thin and pale, cheeks flushed from the heat. Soft hair falling in waves. Her hempy, hippy clothes. Her kindness, hovering around him like a cloud of butterflies. Sometimes too much.

142

'Olivia – Livvie – I ...' He'd never called her that before, a pet name that Adam sometimes used. 'What ...' His mouth froze up and he couldn't say any more. This was it, the moment he'd thought about so much over the past four years. To talk to her, finally. To each understand what the other felt. If she lived in his house because of him, or just because Kate's note had asked her to take care of the children. He was sure Kate had only meant for the day, yet Olivia had stayed ever since. Finally, he managed to say, 'Is this what you want, being here with us all the time? I mean, you're young.' She was only thirty-three now, and he suddenly wondered if her birthday had been and gone, because he couldn't recall when it was. Oh God. 'Don't you want to ... live your life?'

She stiffened. 'I thought ... you needed me.'

'I did! Christ, I'd have gone under without you. But it's been years, and you do everything for us. You don't owe us anything.'

She pressed her lips together. 'I feel if I can help you, well, it might make up for it a little. What I did to Delia. That I can't take care of her. And maybe, if I'm alright with them, I can trust myself with her, one day.'

'But Olivia, there's more to life than being needed.' Was that it – she felt she only had value if she could be of service? Her whole life an atonement for letting her own child down? 'And Delia – well, I can't cope with it, knowing you're here and not with her. It's not right.'

Her voice was very small. 'I want to be here with you.'

What did that mean? Did she want him to take her thin red hand and lead her up the stairs to his bed, on the other side of the wall from hers? What if he did and he'd got it wrong, and she ran screaming and never came back? It would break Adam, to lose her too. And did he want that even, could he face being in another relationship, amid the ruins of Kate's leaving? Did he

143

love this woman beside him, her life so threaded through his? God, he didn't know. 'But – why?'

She balled her hands in her lap. 'You're so good. So kind, and you *see* me, you need me, and the children, I can love them, I can actually help them, I can have a *family*. You're my family.'

Seconds ticked on. Neither made a move. They held their breath. The moment stretched and buckled. And Andrew, in his usual way, backed down. 'You're so very good to us. Thank you for this class too – what an amazing present.'

Her face softened. 'I'm glad. You'll be wonderful, you know.'

The sense of some crisis averted, heart hammering. Then he realised he would have to go to the class now, and let people see his writing. Oh bugger.

Andrew found he was dreading the first writing class more than anything. He walked as slowly as he could to the room, down the draughty second floor of an adult education college, on a street in central London. It was January and the whole concrete building seemed to rock with coughs and splutters. The students jittery post-work, sour-breathed, the teachers pushing glasses up weary, running noses. It seemed unlikely that any great art would ever come from this room, next door to Yoga 101, where the linoed floor echoed with the slaps and footfalls of Downward-Facing Dogs.

He opened the door, apologetic and late, the train up to London as always delayed. He scurried into the only free seat, beside a bald man who reluctantly moved his rucksack. 'Now,' said the teacher, in a cough-strained voice. 'I believe that's everyone. I am Leticia Crowley. Miss.' She watched as if expecting them to write this down. A few did so, anxiously, while others rebelliously refused to uncap their pens. 'Welcome to Introduction to Writing. I myself have been writing for over

144

fifty years.' Immediately the mind worked it out – that meant she was how old? She could have been any age from forty to eighty. She wore a high-necked blouse with a green tweed skirt and odd, fey high heels in turquoise blue, her hair in a large blonde-tinted bun. 'Together we will workshop your poetry, prose, and memoir, and turn you into stronger and more successful artists.' The bald man next to Andrew was nodding knowledgably, as if he'd helped shape the curriculum.

Across the room a young woman spoke up, in an American accent. She was plump with smooth, well-fed skin and an abundance of auburn hair. 'Will we be required to write in every genre?'

At this technical word, several people looked frightened. Letitia Crowley looked annoyed. 'There is no genre in this class, dear. You write what moves you. From the heart. Then we pass judgement.'

'But isn't—'

'Please, no questions yet. Let us say who we are.' Letitia deliberately started on the other side of the room from the intense American girl. The class was as follows: Pam, a fiftyish housewife working on a chick-lit novel. Derek, City trader in pinstripes, impatient with metaphor and poetry, working on a thriller about a City trader. Tam, the bald neighbour, who was Scottish and wrote poetry about otters, that actually turned out to be about his penis. Rupa, a beautiful girl with a nose stud and flared jeans, who had a memoir of her family's travails under Partition. Everyone flashed their eyes nervously at her, she was the one to beat. Marjorie, an intense loud woman with a thatch of red hair, who was writing erotica under the pseudonym Veronkya Lace. Pete, a smiley twentysomething in hip glasses, who could have stepped from the pages of the novel Andrew had been incubating since he was that age. There was Candace, late thirties, smart with very long nails, who was worried she might not make it to many classes. She was writing a business book. There was Sammi, a dreadlocked performance poet who Andrew suspected was a lesbian. And there was Madison, the confident American girl, a veteran of what she called MFLA courses, writing an intense campus novel. Then, there was Andrew himself, lost, his pen already busted and leaking all over his untouched notepad. 'Very good,' said Letitia Crowley. 'Let's begin.'

Adam, present day

Delia was beside him on the bus. It was a very normal bus – in fact worse than normal, as some guy was playing his mobile at top volume, shitty R and B, in the back seat, and there was a layer of litter collecting about his ankles as they swayed around corners. But it was the best bus he'd ever been on all the same, because she was sitting beside him, in a green print dress and (vegan) leather jacket, her hair in an artful top knot. Did it just fall like that, or did she work at it? He wanted to know, but also didn't. 'It's on Marylebone High Street?' she said.

'Yeah.' Adam felt vaguely annoyed he'd had to travel here, to this nice part of London, the bakeries and baby shops. It wasn't part of his edgy image.

'He'll be pleased you came.'

'Mm.' Also annoying. Adam wasn't in the business of pleasing his father, he didn't want to create expectations. 'So you're not gonna tell me the thing yet?' Despite his trip to her house, pathetically running to her summons, she was still insisting he had to wait. He was starting to think the whole thing was a ruse to get him to the party, and hated that she had so easily played him. He was annoyed at the hope which had started to grow inside him, that maybe she'd changed her mind about their agreement. He'd pretended to think the same, of course he had, but these last few months without her had been really shit, and that was just the truth. He might even be prepared to tell her as much. If she would make the first move.

She gave him a long cool glance. 'It's not the time.'

'For fuck's sake, Dee, why the mystery? What are you, the last series of *Lost*?'

'Great retro reference.' She didn't care if he got frustrated, she just withdrew into herself until he was forced to say sorry to get her back out. Exactly like Olivia. 'I will tell you, I promise. After the party. Tonight's about your dad.'

Adam let out a groan. 'It's gonna be so lame. I might die.'

'There'll be drinks at least. Come on, this is it.' She dinged the bell and stood up, weaving gracefully down the stairs of the still-moving bus.

The window of the bookshop was full of Andrew's book. *Your Hand in Mine*. Stupid title. The picture on the front, a child's hand in an adult one, was so dumb. Kirsty would never have held out her hand like that and if she did, it would have been smeared in snot or banana. The shop looked full, to his surprise, with the tinkle of laughter and rumble of conversation. Adam suddenly didn't want to go in, baulking at the door.

'What's wrong?'

What if people looked at him, *oh yes, that's the son*; what if there were bits about him in the book? The way he'd been in his teens, a total nightmare? He'd been given a copy of the book, his dad proudly beaming and calling it an *ARC*, but he hadn't been able to read it yet. 'It'll be lame. I won't know anyone.'

'You know me.' She took his hand, and he couldn't help but

147

follow her, into the warm interior, the lights inviting, the bright colours of book jackets and calming smell of paper everywhere. Delia, conscientious, doused her delicate hands in sanitiser and Adam grudgingly did the same. The shop extended deep into the back, and there were a surprising number of people. Not just awful ones from Bishopsdean either. There was Sandra, in her leopard-print leggings, her voice cutting through like a buzz-saw. She'd already done a few interviews about the book, since she featured quite heavily in it, the miracle worker who'd taught Kirsty to speak. He'd have liked to talk to her actually – he'd always enjoyed the way she riled his father – but couldn't face it just now. She had a way of seeing everything you were trying to hide. He quickly spotted a group of young creative types, a girl with an undercut and a nose ring, another one in a patterned jumpsuit. If not for Delia, he might have been over there already trying to chat them up. But there was Delia. He saw her smile at him, as if knowing what he was thinking. She made her way to the drinks table and asked for a sparkling wine, confident, in her element. Her grandparents were rich, she was always going to parties. 'I don't want this,' he complained, when she handed it to him. 'Are there no spirits?'

'The sparkling is always the best,' she said. 'They really skimp on the rest, believe me.'

'Oh, believe you, with all your knowledge of book launches?'

Delia just laughed, as she always did when he was grouchy. 'There's Mum.' She crossed the room, dodging party-goers – how did his father know so many people? – to Olivia, who was clutching an undrunk glass of the same wine and looking miserable.

'Oh darling, you came. Hello, Adam sweetheart.' She didn't kiss him, which he'd trained her out of over the years. He took a swallow, felt the fizz slide uneasily to his stomach.

'Where's Andrew?' Delia was looking around, even waving to one or two people. How could she know people even here?

'Getting ready for his speech. Terribly exciting.' Olivia's misery seemed to deepen. She hated parties, hated any kind of limelight, and Adam knew she probably felt she didn't belong here, like he did. Who was she, after all? Not his father's wife, not his partner even. His friend? No different to Martin over there, his dad's old boss with the shocking breath. Once, loitering bored about his father's office, Adam had put a packet of mints on Martin's desk with a Post-it saying YOU NEED THIS. Clearly it had done no good.

Olivia's expression became even more sorrowful and, noticing a slight tremor in her hands, Adam couldn't stand it – her worry, her pain – and turned away to look at travel books. Blue, so many shades. Beaches. Places he should be having fun right now. A squeal of feedback interrupted him. Andrew was up on the balcony with some young woman in a print dress with a posh, high-pitched voice.

'Darling, you don't have a drink,' Olivia whispered to Delia and Adam realised that yes, it was weird she'd got one for him and not herself. But then he forgot about it, because his father was being introduced.

The woman in the print dress, not much older than Adam surely, said she was his father's editor, but he didn't catch her name over the hubbub that took a few moments to quieten down. Martin's boom could still be heard a second after silence had fallen. 'I'm so pleased to welcome you here to celebrate the most wonderful book, one which will break your heart and build it up again ... ' Adam tuned out as she praised Andrew, standing awkward and sweating beside her in a shirt and tie, the only person here dressed like that. He looked at Delia, an arm's length away. She was pale. Was she alright? His mind played a few notes of fear – she was sick, she'd fallen for someone, maybe that hippy from earlier, and she'd tell him after this stupid party – and he gulped down the already-warm drink. It was fine. They'd made the choice together to end it, and anyway people didn't leave him, he left them. Except his mother, of course. He was well aware of the psychology.

Andrew was now awkwardly taking the mic. 'Er hello, can you hear me?' God. Lay people using mics was always a shitshow. They should have got Adam to sort the PA. He supposed he could have offered, made the effort, as Delia would say. It really was something, having a book published. He'd tell the old man that later. Delia would like it, be proud of him and give him that special little look, the tilt of her chin when he'd done something good. 'It's so overwhelming to be here and see you all. My book is published! Wow! So many people I need to thank. My writing group, and Letitia, my teacher, who set me on the right path.' The cool group raised some applause and whoops. So they were the writers. His dad actually had some non-embarrassing friends. How irritating. 'My editor, April, my agent Simeon, who took a chance on me . . . ' Some more names. Adam stopped listening. He was sick of standing here now, squashed uncomfortably by the bookcase, Martin's halitosis filling the air. ' . . . I must thank Kirsty, of course, my beautiful daughter, who sadly isn't with us tonight.' His voice broke a little. A low murmur of sympathy, applause. Adam gave an audible *huh*, and Delia flashed him a look. 'My wonderful son, Adam.' Oh God. Why was he being thanked? He'd done nothing. 'Delia, I see you there too, thank you for coming. And really just everyone. Um . . . I think that's it, I can't . . . '

Wait. He hadn't thanked Olivia. Oh God. Was he really not going to thank Olivia? The person who'd sent him on the bloody writing class in the first place, bent over backwards to

150

give him time and space and quiet? Normally Adam enjoyed a good social faux pas, but Olivia deserved better. A whirlpool of tension was spreading out from her, engulfing him and Delia. He tried to catch his dad's eyes, signal. *Thank her. For fuck's sake thank her.* His father looked past him, flustered. 'Um, um, I'm sure there's some other people, but I left my notes in the taxi, ha ha! Thanks everyone! Have fun!'

The hubbub of chat resumed. Oh God. He had forgotten to thank Olivia.

Andrew, 2012

Andrew closed his eyes. 'You want what?'

'I want them chopped off. Chucked away. I'm never gonna use them.'

Andrew took off his glasses and stared across the dinner table at his son. Tall, handsome, piercing blue eyes that were pure Kate, black hair falling over his forehead with a crow's wing gloss. Adam was twelve now and Andrew didn't know, he really didn't, how they were going to get through the next six years with him. 'That's not how it works. You don't chop – well, they sort of snip the tubes. You know with the—'

'Whatever,' said Adam, with withering scorn. 'I'm never having kids, so I want that vasect-what's-it, so I don't have to use condoms. They're shit.'

He'd given up trying to stop his son swearing. 'No one will give a vasectomy to a twelve-year-old.'

'But I don't want kids!'

'You might change your mind, you see. A lot of people when they're your age, feel they don't . . .'

151

Adam was making the noise he sometimes emitted, almost an animal-like growl in the back of his throat. Anger, frustration. 'Do most people have that shit in their sperm?' He jerked his head at the third occupant of the table. Kirsty was in her special high-chair, looking at her fingers, moving them in gentle patterns like a dancer. These days, Andrew found himself watching and watching for anything that could be interpreted as language, a gesture attached to a meaning. But after several years of Sandra filling the house with her smell of hairspray and fags, Kirsty still showed no signs of understanding. She was bigger now, but still the size of a five-year-old. Still not walking, still not feeding herself, though she could sometimes grab for a banana or biscuit and mash it near her mouth. She could smile and laugh and look up when you came into a room. That was something, wasn't it? There were people who had it worse.

'Kirsty isn't shit,' said Andrew, feeling his voice falter as it always did when he tried to be positive.

'Jesus!' Adam pounded the table, making the spoons jump. 'I never said she was. It's not her fault, is it. The gene shit, I mean. I'm gonna have it too.'

'We don't know that.' It was true – Adam could not be tested until he was eighteen, and able to give informed consent. 'In a few years, we'll help you through it, you'll be fine—'

'You and Dap-brain? Sure. I'd really rely on you to help me make this oh-so-important decision.'

'Please don't talk about Olivia that way. She does a lot for you and it would hurt her feelings if she heard.' Andrew lowered his voice, hoping she couldn't hear over the sounds of cooking in the kitchen. It was horribly early for 'supper' in Olivia's book, but she had nobly brought dinner forward so Andrew could eat before his writing class. She was so silent he suspected she did often overhear the brutal things Adam said. But she never commented. She'd never brought up the divorce again either, or her relationship to Andrew, or Delia living with them. There'd been no further breakdowns, and she did now see Delia more regularly, but otherwise everything remained the same. Stuck, unchanging.

'I'm sorry, OK?' Adam was frustrated. Andrew knew he didn't mean to be nasty about Olivia, who was the person most able to get through to him, with her unobtrusive kindness. He was just angry, dealing with issues a twelve-year-old should never have to. 'It's not about Kirsty. I want this sorted. I'd do it myself if they let me!' He was almost crying now. Andrew tried to think how it was, to be that age and know that any children you had in future might be disabled in the same way your only sibling was. Never talking, never walking, never growing up. The pain of watching the world butt up against them, again and again, while you could do nothing to help. Oh God, what was he—

'What are you doing? Oh please, Adam, no!'

As Olivia came over from the kitchen, Adam was fumbling his twelve-year-old's penis out onto his place mat. 'I don't want that shit inside me!'

Olivia gave a faint scream and dropped the plates of food she held, cous-cous and chicken smashing on the floor. Andrew leapt up to shield his son, or hide him, he didn't know. Kirsty, with her vacant smile, seemed to notice nothing at all.

Later, when he went upstairs for his laptop, he saw Adam was in Kirsty's room as she napped, kneeling by her over-sized cot and stroking her hand through the bars. He pushed the door open. Adam glanced up, and said fiercely, 'I know it's not her fault, OK? I just – I don't want kids like this.'

'I understand.'

'It doesn't mean I don't want her. Does it?' That was the issue. How did you say it wasn't ideal, Kirsty being this way, or that it was very hard, crushingly so at times, without suggesting you didn't love her as she was?

'Of course not.' He hovered his hand over the boy's head, shiny and dark, and for a brief second touched it, before Adam shied away. Andrew's heart was heavy. Other families had disabled children, and divorced parents – not that he and Kate were actually divorced – but they still held together. It wasn't this constant chaos, lurching from disaster to disaster. He had to say something. This was his son, he had to keep trying even if nothing worked. 'Ads . . . '

'Don't call me that.' The boy hunched, jaw clenched.

Andrew cleared his throat. 'This can't go on. Your sister, she's enough of a worry, trying to keep her alive, and there's work, and you – well, you're the hardest thing of all.' He couldn't believe he'd said it. 'I'm sorry. I know it was rough, your mother and Kirsty and . . . everything you saw when you were little. But it doesn't excuse it. How you are. The way you hurt people. You can't – you're allowed to be angry, but no one is allowed to hurt people.' Was that true, he wondered? Had he not hurt people himself? Kate, always searching his face for something she needed, but he didn't know what it was. Olivia, looking for a different thing which he also could not give. He'd gone too far. 'I'm sorry, Ads. I just – I don't know how to help you. Tell me how, please.' Years of therapy, thousands of pounds, five different counsellors, and still this was where they were.

Adam's face had changed. The rage was gone, replaced by some snarl of pure pain. 'I can't help it,' he shouted, spit flying from his mouth. 'I don't want to be like this. I try but I can't, I just can't! It just . . . comes out! I'm sorry! I'm sorry!' He was crying.

'I know. I know. We'll get you some help, I promise. We'll – we'll keep trying.' He looked at his son as if with fresh eyes – so

154

tense with anger, the skin on his wrists laddered with thin white scars, which Andrew now suddenly recognised with a lurch – how had he not seen this before? How?

He reached out a hand to the boy, almost made contact with his bony shoulder – but Adam jerked, stood up and ran. 'Adam. Adam!' But he was gone, out to roam the streets as he did for hours now he was at secondary school. Useless to go after him, though it would be dark soon. He would come back.

Olivia was hovering in the corridor. She would not get involved in rows with Adam – not her place, she always said. 'Sandra's here. You'll be late for the train. Isn't today . . . ?'

She was right, he had to go. 'Yes. Alright, I'm off.'

The writing class, now in its final week after a year of sessions, had quickly settled in around tribal lines. There were those who went to the pub – a cool group organised by Pete, with assorted members, not always who you'd think. For a while, it was Pete and Madison, who sat together for three weeks in a row, before she moved abruptly to the other side of the classroom, under the draughty barred windows. Gossip breathed around the class, rumours that he'd finally seen fit to mention his girlfriend, a twenty-four-year-old music-production intern. There were those who worked very hard indeed – printing out everyone's pieces in neat, stapled piles, highlighting spelling and grammar errors in red circles, which seemed to baffle the younger people. What did it matter if a word was spelled differently, so long as the meaning was conveyed? Then there was Andrew, who had managed his usual trick of hovering round the edges of a group, uneasy and unsure of where he fitted. At forty, he was at an odd age to be there. All the other thirty-somethings he knew were busy with babies and jobs. The first week, he'd turned down the general pub invitation because Olivia was waiting at home with the kids, but the following week she'd urged him to go, of course he must meet his fellow creatives. She actually said that – fellow creatives. But the invitation was not repeated and so he'd watched the group move off down the corridor, trailing scarves and tote bags, already laughing and knowing each other's names and drink of choice. And he'd gone home on the cold train, blowing his nose and feeling he'd missed his chance to be young again.

He'd looked up Letitia Crowley after the first week and found himself somewhat disappointed by her pedigree. Two novels fifteen years apart, some very slender volumes of poetry, and the vague promise that she was 'working on another'. He was enough of a writer to know what that meant. But she too was a surprise. Once, as Pete squirmed reading out a piece on graphic druggy sex, she had said, 'Oh say what you really mean, dear. He put his hand in her cunt, is that it?' and during Madison's tortured reading of a college girl's gang rape, while her voice grew strangled with pain and everyone shifted uncomfortably, Letitia called out, 'Yes, but would he *really* still have an erection after all that speed he took?'

No one in the class was quite as they seemed and there was a kind of magic at work, that you got to see ordinary people and then witness the most private contents of their heads spill onto the page. He worried of course about his own. Did it reveal his pathetic clinging to his twenties, when he had first and lastly thought himself happy? And the suggestion of gay sex in the book, would people draw suppositions about him, as he had from Madison's rape scene and Derek's overuse of bondage in his thriller? (The hero got tied up with his tie *a lot*.) The odd thing about Letitia – one of the odd things – was you could never be sure whether yours would be one of the pieces she savaged, like a sated shark you get uncomfortably into a tank with. She was kind to no-hopers, Tam with his weeping eyes and

156

navvy's penmanship, and 'Veronkya' with her dodgy sex scenes involving yoghurt and chains. Yet she could viciously slam down the confident, Madison or Candace, even the radically talented Rupa on occasion. Andrew dreaded the inevitable time it would be his turn to be savaged as well, but the weeks went by, and still it hadn't come. There was a certain condescension from the young literary girls, who knew they'd be published in glossy hardback two years hence, a moody black and white photo on the jacket of them pouting beside a tree somewhere. They competed, so if one said the prose was weak the other would say it was good, but that she didn't believe in the characters. An ecstasy rush wasn't like that, proffered Candace, in her confident way. He'd be too confused to have sex with anyone. The men criticised more factual errors – that bus did not go down that road. That make of car had no boot space. The teacher orchestrated it all with flicks of her white hands.

At the end of the class, everything felt different. Andrew had peeked his head over a wall and realised it was possible – people were writing books every day, and after all, the ones in shops had to come from somewhere. Secretly, and with the same furtive excitement with which he masturbated, he'd begun adding scenes to his book. He especially didn't want Olivia to know, since she'd forced him into it, and on being proved right her face would develop a tearful red glow at having 'made a difference'. It was her overriding obsession in life. But the impression she made on people was like the ones in Kirsty's soft rubber toys when you dug your nails in – you could see them, almost visibly, forget the shape of her.

After class, at the very end, Andrew finally had the chance to meet Letitia alone. He gathered up his typed pages with her green ink scribbles, like a child in primary school. It was absurd really. She was a ditzy older woman who couldn't get the day right, and wore pink shoes, but by the magical act of having her book published, she'd become their spiritual leader.

'Andrew,' she said, with her toppled-tombstone smile. 'Hello.'

'Hello.' His hands were leaving sweat marks on the paper. Absurd.

She leafed through the pages, mouthing words as if reminding herself who he was. 'You write well,' she said, after a long time.

Andrew almost fell off the chair in relief.

'The construction, the punctuation – all excellent. Am I right in thinking this book is about you?'

He bluffed. 'I – er – I started it when I was that age, and living in a flat share.'

'And nothing bad had happened to you.'

'Well – no.'

'And now it has.'

He couldn't speak, but realised she understood anyway. Maybe not exactly, but that didn't matter. He just nodded.

'But you still write about boys who haven't lived. And if I say such and such is unrealistic, you'll say, but no, it really happened that way.' He'd done this in class a while back. 'You are a good writer, Andrew, in the most basic sense. But will you ever move on from your mundane life and write good prose – I don't know. It requires something more. An imaginative leap, a risk – I am not sure you're ready to leap, you see.'

He stared at her. The disappointment was overwhelming. 'Oh. So – it's not good.'

'I'm not saying that. You just need to find something real to write about. Perhaps not even fiction. Something to think on.'

Andrew thanked her – surely he had thanked her? – and went out into the cold and to the tube, which he took to London Bridge, and he got on the train in his usual spot outside Upper Crust. On the train he replayed her words. *You will never move on. I'm not sure you're ready. Leap.* Wasn't that what Kate had said several times – he was stuck, too afraid to ever make changes in his life? He'd have this job, this world, forever.

On the train, the blank screen stared at him like an accusing eye. He had failed as a writer, that was the truth of it. Kate had been gone five years and he had utterly failed. Their son was a delinquent and Andrew could do nothing with him. He had lived with Olivia for five years and failed to clarify their relationship either way, to touch her or ask her to leave. He'd failed to divorce his absent wife, even though the five-year mark for desertion was now past and he wouldn't even have to talk to her. They'd spent years training his daughter in a sign language she likely could not begin to comprehend. She would never grow up, and Andrew would be changing nappies until he died. He hated his job, the drab coffee-splashed interior of the local office, the dreary monotonous work. It was eighteen years since he'd started working on his novel, and it was still a miserable, half-formed thing. He was never going to finish it.

It was 2012. The Olympics would start in a few weeks, and the country was optimistic, sure of itself, confident, not afraid to hang flags and sing the national anthem. Andrew was none of those things. In fact he couldn't see a way forward at all.

In the house, Olivia was waiting. She knew he had his meeting with Letitia today, of course, she knew everything, and it made him sweat sometimes, to have no secrets at all. Kate had never cared enough to know the details of his life. 'You're back.' Her voice was full of barely supressed excitement, and that just made him angry. There was nothing to be excited about, and never would be. 'We've something to show you.'

We? Oh yes, Sandra was still there for some reason, and her presence began to affect him as he moved to the living room, the

159

crackle of hairspray in his throat, the rasp of her voice setting off some uniquely annoying vibration in his ear bones.

'Here's Daddy,' said Olivia fondly, to Kirsty, who was in her walker.

Sandra ignored him. She had Kirsty's toy horse on the sofa and was making a sign with her two hands, two fingers going through two on the other hand. 'Horsey, Kirsty. Horsey. Can you do it too?' Sandra put the toy behind her back. 'Where is it? Where's horsey? Can you ask for it?'

The child's eyes were wandering in their usual unfocused way. Andrew tensed; he felt Olivia's light hand flutter to his arm. 'Look.'

Kirsty's hands were forming the same sign as Sandra, though her eyes didn't lock onto the horse. She was doing it. She really was.

'Good girl!' Sandra gave her the toy, and her fingers closed on its tail, groping like small blind things.

'But that's nothing. She doesn't understand what a horse is, she's just copying it.' Which in itself was not something he thought Kirsty could do, he'd admit.

Sandra ignored him again. She picked up a picture book from the table. 'What's this, Kirsty? What's this?'

Kirsty did the same sign with her fingers. It was quiet, and small, but very different from her usual unformed hand gestures, like a snatch of your native language coming across a radio full of static. Sandra held up the book to Andrew and Olivia – on the page was a white horse, mane flowing and an anthropomorphised smile on its face.

'She's doing it.' Olivia's voice trembled. 'She understands, Andrew!'

Andrew was moving, something in him burning down. Olivia's habitual quiet gave him the freedom to be the one who made grand gestures, who stormed out – that must have been how Kate used to feel about him. He took down his waterproof jacket and put his hand on the door. But he could not open it. He stood in the hallway for some time then went back in, hanging the coat over the banisters. 'I'm sorry.'

Sandra was standing by the kitchen island, drinking coffee from his favourite mug. He already knew there'd be pink lip-gloss on the rim, even after it went through the dishwasher. Olivia had taken Kirsty over to her playmat. 'S'OK. Bit of a shock sometimes.'

'How did you – how?' His heart was thudding in his chest, and he wasn't sure if he might cry or laugh or be sick. How could this be happening?

She shrugged. 'Sometimes you gotta trust them. Tell your-self there must be something going on in that head. We think cos people can't talk they can't understand, but I reckon they sometimes can.'

'Oh. Will she – can she learn more signs?'

'No reason why not.'

It was the strangest sensation. As if Kirsty had been pretend-ing all this time, hiding under the table, and now she emerged, a ten-year-old who could understand. He tried to think what they'd said in front of her over the years and had to steady him-self on the counter. 'I can't take this in.'

'S'early days still. I reckon she needs her eyes sorted. See how she can't focus on things? That's her optic nerve or whatever.'

Again, something clicked in Andrew's head. When someone didn't ever look at you, you assumed they were off somewhere, not paying attention. But what if it was as simple as not being able to steer the eyes round, like a car with a snapped fan belt? Oh God. Jesus, the poor, poor child. 'I'll do anything,' he heard himself say. 'What can I do?'

'Learn this stuff. S'not hard. Go to a class.'

He was chastened. There he was, looking down on Sandra with her cloud of smoke and fraying high heels, and she had done what he and Kate had totally failed to – see the tiny waves of contact Kirsty was trying to make from inside her head. It was so awful a thought he could feel it start to crush him, knock him off his feet like a tsunami. But no. This time he wouldn't take refuge in guilt. He was going to fix it. He would make it up to her.

The front door slammed – it was Adam, back from wherever he'd been, shivering from the cold in his thin T-shirt. How thin and sad he was. 'What's going on?'

'Your sister talked,' said Sandra, easily. 'Well, signed, like.'

Adam looked to his father, sceptical. 'I thought she couldn't.'

'So did I. But—' Something was coming up in his throat, which could have been a laugh or a sob. 'She did it. She can. Things can change, Ads. They really can.' Hope, that was it, the fiery burn of it, a comet he could barely look at with the naked eye. 'Come here.' He held out a hand for his son. Adam looked at it, poised and wary as a deer. 'Come and have some tea. And there's biscuits.' Hesitation. A moment where Adam could have run again, out the door or to his room, crashing the door shut. Instead he came forward.

'She really learned?'

'She did.' Andrew risked it – he put his arm around the boy's shoulders and pulled him close. Whispered, 'We'll sort this. We'll get you help too.' Adam didn't say anything, but he didn't immediately pull away either. Hope. How it scorched.

Later, going to tidy his laptop away, Andrew looked again at his novel. It was a scene where one of the boys undresses a girl who has passed out, drugged. He'd thought it edgy and dark, but he realised now it was cruel and cold. And not even interesting, compared to what he'd just seen with his own eyes. A child being freed from the prison of no speech. A boy brought home when he'd tried to burn everything down around him. A family, reformed from the rubble of a broken one. Words, signs, like the key to a rusted-shut gate. He ran his fingers over the laptop, like a pianist about to play, and thought of what Letitia had said to him – write the truth. Write what really happened. And just as Kirsty had found the way out from the labyrinth she was stuck in, Andrew suddenly saw a way out of his own, like a miracle opening up before him.

Andrew, present day

Andrew didn't realise right away what he'd done, because his brain was so assailed with different worries, slapped with them like a pier in a storm, that it took a while to sort through. Exactly what did he feel bad about? He'd not managed to speak to Letitia yet, and there was someone from his publisher whose name he couldn't remember, and he knew he had sweat stains at the back of his shirt, but no, that wasn't it. He made his way through the party, smiling vaguely at people as they waved and hugged him, to arrive at his family. Olivia was looking miserable as she always did in crowds, and that was when he realised.

Oh, God.

She must have seen his aghast face, all the blood falling from it down to his feet. She faked a smile. 'Wonderful speech! So proud of you.'

'Livvie, I . . .'

She winced at the pet name. Delia was there, he hadn't seen her for over a year and would have liked to hug her, but the look she gave him was hostile. She put an arm around her mother. 'Let's get you a drink, Mum.' She guided her away. Andrew was left with Adam, whose face showed several different emotions braided into something unreadable. How happy he'd been, to spot them from the balcony, both of them there supporting him, these cool and beautiful young people. It almost made up for the horrible guilt that Kirsty wasn't here. But now he had ruined it all.

'I didn't . . . did I?'

'Way to go, Dad.' Adam thumped him on the shoulder in a way that was borderline painful, the only time his son ever touched him these days. 'Way to say thank you to your unpaid housekeeper and nanny for the past fifteen years.' He moved off, following Delia, pouring sparkling wine down his open throat. Andrew stood alone, bewildered, a beacon of shame at his own book launch. How could he have forgotten her? How was that even possible, the woman who'd been at his elbow all these years? A shadow in his home. Never in his bed, except for almost that one time. Oh God. Andrew was so mired in horror he could barely move, as Rupa from the writing class came over.

She wore a congratulatory smile but her eyes shone with competitiveness, and Andrew might have been pleased by that otherwise, to be seen as someone Rupa was jealous of. 'Congrats, Andrew. So pleased for you.'

'Thanks! And, eh, yours is out soon too, yes?' He'd forgotten the title of her book. His eyes were searching the room, desperate.

She tossed her shiny hair. 'Next year, spring. It's the best launch slot for a debut, apparently. They're giving it a really big push.'

'Nice, nice, well done you.' She was very young, Andrew realised. 'Do enjoy it, won't you? This is the best part. When it's all still ahead of you.' He wasn't sure if he meant the book or her life in general, and Rupa looked puzzled as he slid away from her.

Letitia was deep in conversation with an older man in yellow cords. 'Of course, Alan always loathed Sebastian, so it's hardly surprising ... oh! Here he is, the man of the hour.'

'All thanks to you,' he said automatically.

Her shrewd eyes raked him over. She was wearing some complicated layered ensemble over a pair of sack-like trousers. It occurred to him that Letitia was living in the wrong era. 'Did you leave someone out of your speech? I noticed your lady friend's heart break, it was practically audible.'

Why did she have to say that? 'She's not my ... I mean, we are friends, that's all, just friends.' Who lived together and who had raised his children at the expense of her own. Although, that was another worry, a Post-it slipped from the corkboard of his mind. Adam and Delia had arrived together, hadn't they? He hadn't known they were seeing each other at all.

Letitia drank her red wine. Her horse-like teeth were stained. 'When did avoiding the truth ever help anyone, Andrew?'

'Never,' he admitted, crestfallen.

'Exactly.' She patted him on the shoulder. 'Put it right. You won't regret it.'

Why hadn't he thanked Olivia? God, he had no idea. Was it because his head had been full of thoughts of Kate, since seeing her just for a moment earlier that day, miles away and across the Atlantic? He had only the vaguest idea of how her image actually reached him. Cables under the sea, fish swimming round in the gloom? She had been thin, in a white cotton dress, limbs gaunt and tanned, hair streaked. Face freckled by years of sun. Her body had shed itself. She hadn't spoken to him, but her eyes had widened with shock and she'd run from the room. Maybe he should turn down the option, although he really didn't want to pay the money back, and he really did want to have a film made about him. Who wouldn't?

'Drew, old boy!' He'd never been called Drew.

'Martin, hi, good of you to come.' Why had he invited his old boss, who he hated? Pride, that was it. Martin's breath was worse than ever. Did that just happen as you aged – maybe his was awful too and no one would tell him?

Martin was banging on about some CEO he'd played golf with, who had dropped dead right there in the clubhouse, 'massive heart attack, boom', and Andrew had no idea who he meant – a name from the past, when he'd had to care about such things – and suddenly he couldn't take it. He had to sort this biggest, most pressing worry first. 'Excuse me, sorry Martin, it's like a wedding at these things, can't talk to anyone properly.'

He barrelled across the room, cutting through conversations.

' . . . rather warm, isn't it . . . '

' . . . paid high six figures for it, only to find out it was plagiarised . . . '

' . . . you know how it is, takes time to finish a book . . . '

'Well you fucked up, didn't ya.' It was Sandra, swirling a glass of red wine to which she had added Diet Coke and ice, as was her wont.

'Yes, yes, I know. But I didn't – she isn't . . . '

She sighed. 'Andy, she's head over heels for you. Never could see it, could ya?'

'I . . . ' His brain refused to take it in.

'Read the book, didn't I? Not bad. You could have put in a bit more about how the signs work and all that. See—'

He didn't have time for this. 'Sorry, sorry, Sandra, talk in a minute, sorry.'

Olivia was on her own, standing, appropriately, by a shelf of self-help. She was holding her elbows in the opposite hand

166

and not even trying to hide her devastation. Andrew felt a surge of irritation. First Kate, angry and miserable at him for years, then Olivia with a quieter, more nuclear kind of sorrow. Was he incapable of making women happy? 'Will you come outside with me?'

She roused herself. 'Oh – alright.'

Always so acquiescent, even though it was freezing and he'd just broken her. 'Nice to get some air,' she said, feebly, as the door banged behind him.

'I can't believe I just did that. You must know I think of you all the time.' But was that true? Her eyes shifted away, following a bus down Marylebone High Street. 'Livvie – it was just a terrible brain slip, a lapse – God, I was so nervous I could hardly remember the name of the book. Livvie.'

'Of course it doesn't matter, Andrew. It's your night. You wrote it, not me.'

'But I wouldn't have without you. You booked the class, and found all that time for me to work, got Sandra in the first place! It was all you!'

She was trembling. 'I think perhaps I'll go now. I'm rather tired. The car is already booked for later – perhaps you can take it to the hotel and I'll—'

'No! We need to talk about this.' This was how it worked. You went on for fifteen years not mentioning things, and suddenly it was your book launch and it was time to kick your life to pieces.

'No, we don't. Tonight is for you. I'll – well, maybe I'll go back with Delia tonight.'

'To that fleapit she lives in? No way.'

'It's fine. I – I'll find a place. Another hotel.' Because Olivia, at almost forty-five, had no home of her own, no claim on his house. She'd followed him through life like some faithful handmaiden.

'Why, Livvie? Why can't we just talk it out? I know it was a terrible mistake, but that's all it was.'

She said nothing for a moment, tense as a bow-line. 'Andrew – you know the poem, the Yeats one?'

'No,' he said, impatient. 'Which?'

'*Too long a sacrifice can make a stone of the heart.* Well. It turns out mine is a stone. There's no more I could think of to do for you, be to you, and I was right there by your side all this time, and you still forget me.'

'Livvie, you can't – you never said – you've never told me you felt anything for me. Never even hinted.' That wasn't entirely true, but the hints had been faint enough for him to ignore, too faint for him to act on. 'I mean, why would you, even? I'm a broken man.' His wife had been unable to love him, his son hated him. Surely she did not love him.

She was trembling. 'Why? *Why*? I've been here all this time. Because of you. For you. And you can't even see . . . No. I can't. Excuse me.' Slowly, moving like a much older woman, Olivia began to walk down the street. Typical, Andrew thought. The moment he'd been waiting for all his life and he'd utterly fucked it up.

He was mulling over what to do – run away? Start a new life? Chase her, kiss her, like in a stupid film? – when the door of the shop jangled open, and he saw it was Delia and Adam, their faces beautiful and pale. The worries raced each other like horses to the finish line. How much time were they spending together, and in what capacity? Olivia stopped in the street, having reversed her trajectory. Her face was also now laid over with a different concern.

'Dad,' said Adam, with no trace of his usual rage or mockery. 'Delia's got something she wants to tell us all. Together, apparently.'

168

Kate, 2008

Kate put down the flute of champagne – or rather, sparkling wine, grown just a few miles away. It had quickly warmed in the blazing Californian sun and was overly sweet. She swished her legs in the turquoise water of the pool. It was a perfect scene. The sun loungers and hammocks straight from a decoration magazine, like the ones she'd bought in stacks when they first had the house in Bishopsdean. The gas fire pit waiting to be switched on when the temperature dipped. The high walls of the house overhung with fragrant pink flowers she'd never learned the name of. And casting a shadow on the pool's bright oblong, her own body baked taut and gold. Even the scars of Kirsty's birth were paled away to nothing. Catching her reflection in the house's shuttered windows, Kate knew she looked much younger than her years.

It was probably three o'clock. She tried not to open her first bottle of wine until lunchtime, but lunch was pretty early some days. Before twelve, if she was especially hungry. Or thirsty. Like most of her new LA acquaintances, Kate had learned to see food not as an absolute necessity, more of an occasional hobby. It explained why she weighed less than she had when she married Andrew. She'd caught on fast. What had seemed slim and young-ish in grey England was quickly revealed to be a flabby size twelve out here, under that merciless sun. 'I'm fat,' she'd said, horrified, to him, and being Conor, he did not contradict her. *It is what it is.* That was his motto.

What would she do that evening? He was away for another two days. Guatemala, maybe, scouting locations. She'd watch a film perhaps – she'd never learned to say *movie* – and open one of the individual packets of fish and salad in the fridge, dropped off every few days by a food service. There was no need to do any homemaking in this house. The tiled floors were kept clean by daily maids, the food delivered, the garden tended. So really there was nothing for Kate to do except exist, swim, groom herself. Shrink herself into a smaller and tighter frame with every passing day.

A bug arced lazy circles about her in the water, as inside the phone began to ring. Sighing and flicking water, she rose, dripping, to answer it. Conor? Or Trixie, whining? Or worse, Trixie's mother? Kate's heart sank at the very thought of her.

On her arrival in America the year before, Kate had so long forgotten the taste of aloneness that she was both terrified and desperate to drink it down. Conor had never offered anything more, but he had given her the means to escape. After that second time at the airport, she hadn't even considered ignoring his business card. She had emailed, and they had met again, and again, and that was it, the cadences of infidelity returning to her with breath-taking ease. They had never discussed their lives in any concrete terms, so it was a shock when he said, as she lifted her bourbon to her mouth in the hotel bar on perhaps the fifth or sixth time they had met: 'I saw you on TV.'

'Oh?'

'A documentary about disability rights.' He looked at her. He had the ability to be very still, not fiddling with anything like a beer mat or a glass. He needed no props. 'Your friend died, then.'

'Yes. Aimee. She killed herself, and her disabled son.'

'Your daughter – she's the same?' She hadn't told him this yet.

'She's a lot younger. But I think that's what did it for Aimee – the never growing up thing.'

He didn't say, I'm sorry, or I understand, or try to convince her

170

it would get better, and she appreciated that. With Conor you were always responsible for your own feelings. You brought them with you and took them away after, like a pair of worn knickers.

'Did you ever think of doing the same?' He asked it so matter-of-factly.

'Yes.' The pills in the cupboard, hoarded like secrets. 'I wouldn't though.' Not after the devastation of what happened to Aimee. The guilt that hounded her still, the anger even, that her friend had done this instead of asking for help. That Kate had failed to see before it was too late.

'You're not happy. In your life.'

'Of course not.' If she was happy would she be here with him, a man she barely knew?

'Your children, do you love them?'

She frowned. 'What choice do I have? I'm their mother.'

'There's always a choice. You chose to become a mother. Choose not to be.'

For a moment of growing dread, she didn't understand what he meant.

He swallowed his bourbon. 'Do what men do. Leave.'

It was so ridiculous it made her cross. 'You don't just leave children. Who'd look after them?'

'Your husband. Your family. Look, the thing is, if you stay in this life, you'll die too, or at least a part of you will. If it's a choice, then go and live.'

She had no idea what to say to this. 'People would hate me.'

'Let them. Do you think you've even been a good mother to them, Kate? You don't love them.'

And there it was. For five years Kate had been searching for the key that would unlock the cage she was in. Conor had just handed it to her, and it lay on the table between them, and it was this – you're a terrible mother anyway.

171

She sat for a moment, too steeped in regret to even cry. 'I don't love them.' She had never known how to, either of them, how to feel that pulsing living pull, that desperate need to be close to them, that pride or joy or whatever it was people meant by love.

Conor shrugged, as if reading her mind. 'You wouldn't have to love me. Not ever.'

'You mean—'

'How can you love someone because you have to?'

'I can't,' she whispered.

They looked at each other over the glass table, the shimmer of the candle reflecting a hundred different versions of them, a man and a woman going back into eternity. Kate formed the words very carefully. 'But it's not easy. I don't work. There's money to think about, and—'

Conor gave a little tut, as if disappointed she was so obvious. 'You want to know my terms? A good question. I approve of you asking it. I have money. I want you, right now, and most likely for a long while yet. If you decide to, you can come to LA with me next week. You can stay in my house for as long as we both want it. But you're free. You don't have to love me, or sleep with me even, although I think that you want to. You don't have to commit to me. There can be other people.'

'But I can't—' Yes, she had thought of leaving at times, but to a nearby flat, to see the kids every day. An alternative had never seemed thinkable, and here he was saying no, just go. Walk out and don't come back.

He held up a hand. 'I don't deal in *can't*. You can, so long as you're not dead. You can change your life. If I didn't believe that I'd be on the streets of Dublin, or most likely dead or a junkie.' He had hinted about his childhood, one of eight children dragged up with too little money and too much booze. Enough for her to feel the edges of horrors.

172

'I—'

'I never said it's easy. But God, Kate – the freedom. You have no idea.' He stood, threw a £20 note on the table. 'I'll leave a ticket at the desk for you next week. It's up to you.'

The last day. It was a Thursday again. Thursday seemed like the day you could still salvage the week, do something purposeful, but on the downwards slope to the weekend. Always something of joy about a Thursday, of recklessness. Kate was in the living room. Olivia had come at eight, and Kate had planned this very carefully. There was a man coming to treat the hardwood floors, she lied. Would Olivia take the children out to the park for a few hours? The day had dawned wet and grey, and Kate woke up with a terrible lurching fear – they would not be able to go out. But it brightened, and Olivia took the children with some murmurs about wet feet. Wellies. Thank God for wellies.

She'd not been able to say goodbye to the children in front of Olivia, of course. It would have looked too odd. So instead she had said it when she woke them that morning, smoothing Kirsty's hair and kissing her brow. 'I'm sorry. I'm so sorry, my darling, I really am.' What for – leaving? Bringing her into a world full of pain? Not loving her? Kirsty didn't realise of course – that made it easier. She would never even remember Kate, probably.

When she went in to Adam, he was already awake. He was sitting up in bed staring at her, as he had that day five years ago when Kirsty arrived. Seven years old. The tantrums and scratching had at least stopped, but she sensed all that rage had somehow just turned inside, that it was still there in him.

'Hello,' she said, unnerved again by this child she had birthed, the uncanny adult look in his eyes, the way he saw through her. 'Did you sleep well?'

'No,' he said. Not accusing. He couldn't possibly know.

'Have you got a kiss for Mummy?' She touched him clumsily, trying to lift him, and realised he'd got too big. She must not have picked him up for some time.

Adam ignored her advances, climbing out of bed himself. 'Leave me alone, Mum, I'm not a baby.' True. Traces of the adult he would become were already emerging. She would maybe not be here to see it. But no, she couldn't think that far ahead. She just had to go today, because something had to change, or she would die.

'OK.' She watched him pad out, thinking it happened so young, your children learning to walk away from you. Not Kirsty, she never would. Instead Kate would walk away from her.

'Adam?' He turned, confused. 'I'm sorry.' A little boy, that's all he was. He left the room.

Andrew went out not long after, in his usual panic for the train. She stood in the kitchen. Marvelling that she would maybe never see his face again, once so beloved, the red dints left by his glasses on his nose, the warm pad of his shoulder where she used to lay her cheek in bed. 'Bye, sweetheart, I . . .' What could she say? Nothing.

He turned in confusion. She hadn't used pet names in years. 'What? Shit, where's my train pass? Oh bollocks.'

Those were his last words to her. *Oh bollocks*. She consoled herself that she could hardly have kissed or hugged him, although she would have liked to, in a way, take one last draught of the comfort his body had once offered her.

The person she said goodbye to was Olivia. As her friend ushered the children out, Kate was by the door, arms crossed over her chest. 'Have fun.' Fear closed up her throat.

'You're OK, Kate?' Olivia asked it looking at Kirsty, winding a long scarf round her neck.

174

Kate didn't answer this. Instead she said, 'Thank you.'

'It's no trouble. The rain's stopped.'

'No, I mean – for all of this. You saved my life, these last years.' The words tumbled out, messy.

Olivia frowned, widened her eyes. She knew, maybe. There was a silence between them that crowded with unsaid words. She hesitated a moment, and said, 'It's really alright, Kate.' That was the last thing they said to each other.

When the door closed Kate almost collapsed. They'd gone. Now she had to do it. She went through the rooms of the house. What to take? When it came down to it, everything could be replaced. She had her passport and driving licence and birth certificate. All the money she could find – not much, she wanted no one saying she'd fleeced him. Some pictures – was she taking those for love or because she felt she should? Clothes, summer ones, all her best underwear – what would Conor expect in return for his largesse? She took off her wedding and engagement rings, and laid them on the kitchen island – paying back her debts. Then she cleaned the kitchen and took out the bin and watered the plants, because Andrew would definitely not remember to. She folded up the note she'd written the night before, while pretending to be in the bath. On the back of it she wrote *Andrew and Olivia*. It seemed natural to address them like this, as a couple almost. She called a cab. On the outskirts of town she asked the driver to stop, engine running, as she cracked open her phone and threw the pieces into a bin. That was it.

She had expected some reciprocal gesture from Conor to match hers, when she'd run through the airport breathless, dodging luggage carts, only to find him queuing for check-in, a coat over his arm and a magazine open in his hand. She'd skidded up, red, panting, tears crusted round her eyes. 'You made it,' he said easily. As if the salient fact was that she'd caught the plane in time, rather than that she'd come at all. He did not kiss her. He ushered her onto the plane, politely. Business class – Kate would never fly economy with him.

Conor was utterly at home with this luxury, his childhood home with the seven siblings on the back streets of Dublin long forgotten. He said no to champagne – too dehydrating – and put on his sleep mask. It was an expensive silk one that he'd brought himself. Kate gaped at him as they took off. Was he really – could he honestly – did he realise she had left, not just on a holiday but for life, her children, her husband? A sick weight settled on her chest that perhaps she had misunderstood the situation. That was why you had to state it outright in marriage. *I take you.* Not I take you for a night, or a month, or as a mistress, but I take you, full stop. For the first time, and not the last, she had a pang of missing it, the concrete walls of its certainties.

When the seatbelt sign went off, she undid hers and dashed to the loo. She'd always found airline lighting, along with that in clothes shops for teenage girls, to be the least flattering in the world, and it showed Kate in her all her thirty-five-year-old reality. Tired, swollen. Lank, over-bleached hair. Unfashionable mumsy clothes and under the waistline, a small roll of flab. At 30,000 feet, Kate clutched the small sink, caught in her own bout of turbulence. Of course Conor would not want her. He could have women ten years younger, fifteen years younger, groomed and gorgeous like the perma-tanned lovelies she'd glimpsed in the other seats. What had she done?

She crept back miserably to her seat and watched him sleep, while she flicked channels and drank and dozed off, waking dry-eyed, with a blocked nose and a hefty dose of heartburn, as chill light whooshed into the cabin. Conor had clearly been up

176

and shaved, cleaned his teeth, changed into a fresh jumper. She smacked her gummy mouth. 'What time is it?'

He didn't remove his headphones. 'Four pm local time. We land in twenty.'

At passport control, Conor passed through a US citizens portal, while Kate cringed in the long, slow, suspicious queue for foreigners. Would he even be there when she got through? He had not touched her at all. The border guard seemed to pick up on her nerves. Where was she staying? How long for? She wasn't sure. Did she plan to do any paid work? She knew enough to say no, since she didn't have a green card, but that sent her into another spiral of fear. She had no money to her name, and now no means to earn it. What was she going to do?

The guard handed back her passport. 'Next time you come, lady, you get some better answers. Have a nice day.'

Conor was in Arrivals, looking at his watch. She scuttered up to him, miserable and sweating, then out into the rank tropical heat for three paces, then an air-conditioned car, with a smell of dry-cleaning fluids and a driver up front. Conor settled in and began stabbing at his Blackberry. Kate shrank into the leather. 'Is this yours?'

'Limo service,' he said, not looking up.

'Conor – I—' Her voice broke, the weight of what she'd done crushed further by travel and strangeness and no sleep. 'What's happening? Please will you tell me?'

'We're going to my house.' Outside, unbelievable lines of traffic and hills and a sky blue as denim. Her skin goose-pimpled in the aircon.

'Are you glad I came?' She almost whispered it.

'Are *you*?'

Kate had no answer for that.

*

There was a brightness to LA, Kate would discover, that made it hard to see anything. Everything was too much to look at directly, the landscape, the house they drove up to – a mirage in white – and the fact she was with Conor, but no idea if she was with him or not. She told herself she would adopt his 'in the moment' approach. In Bishopsdean she had planned for the coming forty years, only to wake up one day and find she couldn't get through the next ten minutes.

He was on the phone again, not looking at her. 'I need to catch up on work. You can shower. Everything should be in there.' He really wanted her to wash, it seemed, so Kate did, in what was clearly a guest room, clean and impersonal, letting expensive toiletries in frosted glass scour all the dirt and sleep from her skin and hair. Mindful of her on-plane revelation, she found scissors and cut her toenails and raggedy pubic hair, creating an unattractive drift in the previously spotless shower. In her head she began a list – manicure. Waxing. Dentist. Hair. That was easier and more manageable than things like job – life – divorce. Moulding and scraping the body was always possible. Moulding the self, less so. There wasn't much in her suitcase, but a sundress seemed right. Pink and splashed with flowers, it was a struggle to get the zip up, and the length was too Bishopsdean Mum for LA, but she had to start somewhere. *It's done*, she told her red-eyed reflection. *It's done and the hard part is over. It will get easier.* She would become slimmer, more tanned, more fashionable. These things were all in her grasp, whereas being a good wife and mother seemed beyond her.

Conor was in his study with the door open, a hot airless room full of high-tech computer equipment. Her feet made no sound on the rug. He looked up but said nothing.

'Can we talk?' she said, unwittingly adopting the motto of nineties America.

'Are you tired? I make it a rule never to talk when tired.'

'I'm fine. Slept on the plane.' Another lie – was this new thing, whatever it was, also to be based on untruth? 'I just need to know – on what basis I'm here, if that makes sense.'

'I invited you.'

It was an early lesson in the fact that with Conor, you only got an answer to the precise question you asked. 'Do you know anything about me? I'm thirty-five. I have two children. One is disabled and I had to care for her round the clock or she'd die. About three years ago I realised I didn't love my husband and maybe never had. I had an affair. This is who I am.' Her fingers fumbled. She took off the dress over her head. 'I literally have nothing, Conor. I had a career and a brain and a good body, but they went, and instead I have two children and a husband, except now I have nothing because I've left them. I'm like – a package you bought on the internet. So why did you ask me here?'

He watched her with interest, but no warmth. 'I wanted to see what you'd do. I felt you were on the edge of a cliff and you might jump off.'

'I did.' The air was beginning to chill her naked flesh, her stomach with the scars and pouches, and she hugged her arms over her breasts. She realised she could never totally leave her children behind, because there they were, the marks of their mouths and bodies tearing through her. 'Was that the only reason?'

He opened his mouth, shut it again. 'My mother. She – well. She never got her escape.'

'Oh.' The sense of a vast country inside him, a lifetime of stories to tell her, or perhaps he never would.

'Also you're – Kate, you're very beautiful. And intelligent. And sad. I wanted you. I want you.' He said this in a detached way. He unbuttoned his shirt and slid it over the planes of his body, the flat lines of muscle, the veins in his arm. He unbuttoned his trousers and folded them. She thought, like an infidelity, of Andrew, who always seemed genuinely surprised that they had a laundry basket, so would leave his socks wherever they fell. As she came to him, Conor put out a finger and draped a wet lock of hair over her naked shoulder. 'Are you sure about this? I don't play nice.'

Remembering the disaster with David, Kate was suddenly terrified. The first time with someone was always like simultaneously taking part in a gymnastics competition and judging one too. Her body insisted that time had gone mad, it must be night outside, she was so far beyond tired. She put her hands on his shoulders, smelling him, the bitter lemon and musk. 'I've had enough nice to last me twenty lifetimes,' she said. 'Do it.'

That was a year ago. Her immigration difficulties had been smoothed out for her by some string-pulling at Conor's production company, and a lot of money, but she had simply surrendered to the process, filled in forms, signed things. She didn't actually do any work, not knowing where to start in this whole new country, who to email or call even. She lived in his house, and she knew that to stay there required a daily effort to maintain her body, her brain. She felt something like terror, a slippage, knowing there was nothing to lean on, no good will built up. She would not be excused the smallest mistake. It was at these times she almost missed the strong cradle of marriage, the ropes lashed together after years of toiling side by side. A marriage was a long book she'd not had the patience to finish, and now here she was, stuck in the short-term.

*

The landline had stopped before she got to it, but Kate was suddenly dizzy with the relentless sun, seeing spots. She went inside to the clean, cold, sterile interior of the house. She didn't have to talk to Trixie, who was not her daughter or even her stepdaughter. She didn't have to do anything. The night and next day stretched ahead of her, no work to do, barely even any household chores, no children to care for. She wasn't really a mother and was only a wife in the technical sense that she hadn't divorced Andrew.

Once she would have given anything for five minutes alone – now she had nothing but time. She wondered how on earth she would get through the rest of her life like this. She supposed just like all the years up to now – one minute at a time.

Kate, present day

'Screw them all.' It was Suzi's standard response to everything. 'It's men, isn't it. The problem. With everything.'

Kate gave her a wan smile over the top of her iced tea, in an enormous plastic cup with a printed label bearing her name. Everything was so sealed-off here. 'I still have to work with them. And live with one.'

'You don't, you know.' They'd had this conversation many times over the years since she'd met Suzi. Her friend pulled her wheelchair closer to the pavement table at the Silver Lake café. Kate had stopped off on her drive home, finding herself shaking in the seat. She'd hunted out a parking spot at a meter, rung Suzi in a flap. It was one of the many things Kate liked about her, that she was willing to stop work and be called out for an emergency coffee, in a city where people were so over-scheduled they'd cancel a meeting while you were already driving there. 'I mean. Life's been a lot easier since I stopped dating them, switched to a female doctor, a female agent.' Suzi was a writer for late-night talk shows, and refused to work with anyone who wasn't liberal, left, and female-identifying, which limited her options somewhat. Kate admired her political certainty, but could never quite manage it herself. A life without men made no sense to her at all.

She also couldn't finish her drink – everything in America was at least twice as big as you needed. She'd learned over the years to ask for a 'box' to take food home, a habit Conor hated, thought cheap. 'I better go and face the music. Thanks for listening. I never even asked about you. Did you take the late-night gig in the end?' Since abandoning her family to Olivia she was more conscious of the reciprocity of female friendships, the debts, the deposits.

Suzi drained her frappé with a loud slurp. 'Crisis card. We can do me next time.'

Kate stooped to hug her, thinking: *this is real, I have a real life here. People care about me. The last fifteen years haven't been a dream.*

She drove home, mind and stomach churning. You had to drive everywhere in LA, no matter how drunk or upset you were, or else leave your car and then pick it up the next day. It seemed a city of uniquely poor design, on an inhuman scale, the freeway an encircling beast ready to squeeze the town to death.

She hadn't been fired, of course. Just given a gentle hint to take some time off, she'd been working so hard, and Isabelle could cover for her (Isabelle was twenty-seven and would be only too delighted to sit in Kate's chair, preferably forever). She hadn't had an unspecified amount of time off in years, not since she first arrived in the city, those strange empty days when she wondered sometimes if she'd died and just hadn't realised it. Unseen, therefore non-existent. What to do now, with her unexpected time? She could drive up the coast, rent a cottage by the sea on Airbnb. Instagram it and say she was having a wonderful time unplugging, except from Instagram clearly, and relishing the solitude. Take time away from Conor and his latest act of cruelty, disengage.

She could go to London, of course. Conor was flying out in just a few hours; for him getting on a plane was as routine as taking the bus. She could go with him – she was his wife, after all. She could see her family. Even stop this from happening. But how? The book was already published. She could still stop the film, though, limit the damage – how many people would read a memoir about a disabled child, really? A film, though. Every idiot from here to Nebraska would see that in their local multiplex, crying into their too-big popcorn. They'd come out and say to each other – but what about the mother? How could she leave them?

Conor would not be happy. He wanted to make this film, thought it would earn him money and maybe some Oscars, and so he was going to. Why couldn't it just be easy? Why couldn't she have a husband who was on her side?

You had Andrew, said her inner voice, the one that so often sounded like her sister. Her sister, who had kids now that Kate had never met. She googled her family from time to time, looked on Facebook to check her parents were still alive and well. She had deleted her account when she fled, but much of Elizabeth's profile was public and she'd taken to Instagram as if born for it. Kate was glad of her sister's over-sharing impulses as they allowed her to keep a small connection to her family, a capillary that only flowed one way. So much she had left behind when she went, pulling herself out by the roots, losing fifteen years of birthdays and Christmases and family days out, the

183

chance to hold her newborn niece and nephew, slide a sure hand around their wobbly heads. If she went with Conor, perhaps she would see them too.

Kate swung her car into the driveway, again barely thinking about it, barely noticing the opulence, the ease of her life. None of it really made a difference. She had been an angry, unhappy person and she still was, just one with a swimming pool and regular, heated sex. If only she'd been able to combine the two men, Conor and Andrew, the passion and drive of one and the peace and reliability of the other. A jigsaw man, a Frankenstein's monster but in a nice way. Unfortunately this kind of man did not exist.

As if to nudge her decision, there was a copy of Andrew's book on the counter when she went into the kitchen, everything wiped clean of any drop of water or crumb of food, the plants on the window watered and standing to attention. She picked it up. The cover was nice enough, a generic child's hand in an adult's. On the back, a flattering picture of Andrew that must be quite old, leaning his chin on his hand, in a tweed jacket. The copy read, *The uplifting true story. When Andrew Waters found himself alone with two small children, one severely disabled, he thought his life was over. But through a chance encounter with a ground-breaking speech therapist, that all changed. Gradually, his daughter Kirsty, mute since birth, learned to communicate through sign language. This is the remarkable story of family, of never giving up, of finding a way to connect when all the odds are stacked against you.*

She sniffed, sat the book down. No mention of her. She jumped as the back door opened and Conor came in from the terrace, phone in hand. He was wearing a jumper and jeans, as if it wasn't eighty outside. She had learned, finally, to think in Fahrenheit. 'You're here,' she said, meaninglessly.

'You're back early.'

'Um, yes, they – I decided to take some time off.' Conor's eyebrows went up. He knew her too well to believe this, but he didn't ask and she didn't tell. 'So. I'm free for the next few days.'

'I'm going to England, I told you that.' Impatient. Reaching for the coffee machine.

'I know you're going to England. What I'm saying is I might go too.'

He stared at her. She had surprised him, something that was increasingly hard to do. 'You want to see them? Your husband, your kids?' She let the *husband* go. He was just needling her.

'If you're discussing a film about me, I should be there.'

'Oh, so that's it, is it? Anyway, the book's not about you. It starts after you left.'

'But I'll be in it. I'll be ... backstory.'

He poured out coffee, tearing off kitchen roll to wipe a minuscule drip from the pot, throwing it away. So wasteful, so thoroughly American and so far from the council flat in Dublin where he'd been raised on scrimped and saved scraps. 'If you want to come, I can't stop you.'

Did she want to? Was that mad? 'Gracious invitation, thank you.'

'What did you expect?'

'No. You're right. Would you at least sit beside me on the plane?'

'Have Charlotte book you a seat, if you really insist.' That meant first class, which she wouldn't necessarily want to pay for herself, although she'd become embarrassingly used to it.

'And the hotel?'

'I have a hotel booked in London, yes.'

'You want me to stay with you?' It was a loaded question. Two meanings, really. He knew what she was saying. He was not obtuse, Conor, though he might pretend to be at times.

185

'I'll be taking meetings the whole time. Including with your husband. What I don't want is any awkwardness.' *He* was her husband.

'You mean you don't want to *see* any awkwardness. You don't care if it happens.' She reached for an apple just to have something to do. No one ever ate these, and yet the housekeeper set them out each week. Did they get thrown away? That was a terrible waste too. This country.

'I don't want my film derailed. If you try to do that, I'll have to push back, Kate.' So reasonable. As if she were a producer or screenwriter he worked with, not his wife.

'That's not what this is.' It was, of course, but if she told him that he wouldn't let her come. Or he'd let her and just be so unspeakably cold that she would wish she hadn't. Conor was good at getting his own way like that.

He said, 'What's your plan then? Are you going to see them?'

'I just want to know what happens, with the film. I just want to be there.' She hadn't got much further than that. If by some chance she could talk Andrew round and kill the film, Conor would never forgive her, so their marriage, such as it was, would likely die too. That was the choice she was really making by going to England, after so many years circling round it like a maypole. In a way, she was almost glad her hand had been forced. Nowhere to go but forward. Hadn't she once owned a cushion that said something similar? Left behind like everything else. 'I can come then?'

'Kate, it's not up to me.' He often said things like this, that were factually but not emotionally true. 'I'm leaving in one hour, if you're coming.'

'Alright. I'll – let you know.'

He turned away, then turned back, ready to say something. 'I'm not doing this to hurt you. It's a story that needs to be told, that's all. And yes, my personal connection will probably help get it made. But it's not about you.'

How could he say that, when this was her life, her past, her family? She studied his face, the lines and curves of it, as she had for years now, trying to work him out and still not managing. Was that what kept her here? He was a man she could never get to the end of. 'What about Trixie?' His face went blank. 'Someone needs to visit her, if we're both away.'

'She's very well looked after. Believe me, it's paid for.'

'I wouldn't want her to think she's totally abandoned. Perhaps you could—'

Conor left the room, coffee in hand. That was how he handled conflict, just refused to engage and there was nothing you could do about it. She told herself it didn't matter. It was all just ballast for the decision she was finally ready to make. If she was going back, it was time to face a few things, starting with the least painful, which still packed a hefty punch. Kate took out her phone and prepared to speak to someone whose voice she hadn't heard in fifteen years.

Kate, 2010

There was too much space in Los Angeles. She'd study a map, or peer down a long straight road, and think somewhere looked close enough to walk, ten minutes maybe. Then half an hour later she'd still be struggling along, weighed down somehow, as if everything was being pulled apart instead of pushed together. The fabled glamour of the place always seemed over the next hill, down the next street. It wasn't the people living in tents under every bridge or passed out on the streets of Downtown.

It wasn't the crumbling freeways or the honking traffic slow-downs, crumpled cars at the side of the road. It wasn't the drifts of rubbish by the side of the interstate. Where then?

She had lived here now for almost three years. They'd been exciting years, riding a wave of optimism about the country, surprised and delighted at its own progressiveness in electing a black president. She never knew where she was with Conor – she had no title, no place in his life. She was afraid to raise it with him, the fact they still slept in different rooms, the way he often went out of town and left her for weeks on her own. He had said early on there could be other people, and Kate had never taken him up on the offer, or asked if he was, but it gnawed at her mind. He was away a lot. There were many things she didn't ask him. Their relationship was mostly sex and going to restaurants, all the things she'd missed with Andrew. Sometimes he took her to parties, where she touched up her makeup next to emerging starlets snorting coke from hundred-dollar bills. She had a whole set of clothes, in fabrics she'd never touched before, and thanks to swimming every day and eating salads in the sun, a layer had been stripped from her, the fat melted off, the body hair removed, the skin scraped down to the lovely bones. This was LA Kate. At parties she was sometimes introduced as Conor's 'partner', but he always said, 'And this is Kate McKenna.' Simple. She was who she was, no one's mother or wife.

At one party, drunk on slimline vodkas and no food, she found herself up close to a producer. Someone in TV. It was flattering when his eyes assessed her, because there were women in the room who were almost twenty years younger than Kate, and who appeared to have sprayed on their clothes. He was older but attractive if you didn't look too close, his eyes strangely smooth compared to the skin on his hands.

'Is that a British accent? It's a-dor-a-ble.' He had a strong New York accent himself.

'Oh thanks. Half the time people just think I'm toffee-nosed.' She didn't know why but when speaking to non-Brits, she trotted out all the idioms her mind had ever picked up.

'I think it's goddamn *awe*-some. What do you do, Kate?'

Sometimes she thought of making up lies – astronaut. Courtesan. Tonight she said, 'I used to be on TV. In England. I did the news.' Not entirely true, since she'd only been on camera three times, but he didn't know.

Conor usually abandoned her at parties, sweeping off to network, and she couldn't even protest because he'd once said he trusted her to take care of herself, and wasn't that what she'd wanted? Kate would stand with her vodka, a terrible and exquisite pain blooming under her heart as she watched him laugh, lean in to whisper in a woman's ear, hand on her waist. At home she'd been everyone's root – their meal, their home in her body, and now she was adrift. But when the producer leaned in to shout to her above the din, so close his breath was on her neck, Conor was suddenly there. 'Michael. How lovely to see you.' They sized each other up, gorillas stamping feet in the forest. 'I see you've met my Kate.'

My Kate? Possession without purchasing? She bristled.

'I've just been listening to that great British accent. Katherine here tells me she's in TV.'

'She's not in anything.' Ouch, Conor.

'I was on TV in England,' Kate said, with a plastic smile. 'Since moving here I've not been working.' Technically she was allowed to, but had no idea where to even start.

The producer's bushy eyebrows went up. 'Maybe you won't know, being from out of town, but I produce a little show called *West Coast Wake Up*.'

'Oh! I've seen it.' She really had, and she slopped out some of her drink in un-LA-like enthusiasm. 'I mean I watch it every day, since I came here. It sort of reminds me of home.'

It was like an American *This Morning*, she meant, with cooking bits and interviews and all of it feather-light. The producer had never been so touched in his life, his face said. 'Say, why don't you drop by the studio one day and I'll give you a tour? Seeing as you're in the biz.'

'She just did local news,' said Conor coldly. 'Research.'

Kate did her professional smile again. 'I was on camera too. There was talk of anchoring, though of course I'd have missed the journalism. I have a Masters,' she said, faux-modest. Conor had never gone to university.

'What a lady!' The producer actually held her hand as he pressed his card into it. 'You gotta call me, Katherine. And you never know. We might have a little something for a talent like yours.'

Kate was giddy – she'd been hit on *and* offered a job, like a real actual person, and it all felt like good fun, until she looked at Conor. She raised her chin in defiance. He said nothing, just turned and stalked off. She followed in her heels, the skirt forcing her knees together. She'd have liked to stay, glittery and admired, go home alone and have Conor call her the next day sheepish and chastened, but damnit, she lived on his good will and she'd punctured that. A kind of fear sent her tripping to the door after him, where the efficient valets had already brought his car. She opened the door for herself and tried to get in in her tight dress. The valet helped while Conor ignored her, starting the engine. He pulled off before she had her belt on, frigid air belching into the car. The leather seats stuck to the bit of her leg exposed by the skirt.

She pondered a long time on her opening gambit, settling for, 'I'm *your* Kate, am I? No job description?'

He drove faster.

'So he might offer me a job! Wouldn't that be exciting? I'd have money again. It's been so hard, never knowing whether you'll throw me out if I mess up—'

'When have I ever said I would throw you out?'

She shrugged. 'Never. I just feel like you might. I'm not your girlfriend or your partner. Just your "Kate". And you – well, you always say there can be other people. I don't know if that's something you've been ... doing.' And it wasn't fair, was it, to rush to her side as soon as another man showed an interest? He said nothing for a while, and she felt it enter her, the desolate emptiness of the canyons, the black of an LA night, but couldn't stop all the same. 'I'd like my own job. I'd like to give something back.'

'Look, he just wanted in your knickers.'

Knickers, he'd said, not panties, as if the American slipped when he got angry.

'Do you want me, Conor? Otherwise, why care?'

'I don't care. I just don't want you to make a fool of yourself.'

'I think you're jealous.' Kate watched her own ghost in the window as they slid through the dead town, the makeup and glitz of her surface, but somewhere in there her own steely self.

'I don't get jealous.' Like it was a strength, to be emotionless. Like anger was not an emotion.

'Then you don't mind what I do, I suppose.' Laying down a gauntlet. She had triumphed in this bout, but once again the knowledge of winning the battle and losing the war. If he really wasn't jealous, perhaps he did not love her at all, and could ditch her at any moment. At least the sex was good. As soon as they got in, he set the car keys down on the hall table. Stared at her in the semi-dark, lit only by the pool lights outside, and below them the glittering city.

'Well?' she challenged.

'Come here.'

She did, her feet sweating on the floorboards, leaving prints of body heat which evaporated like breath. He took off her dress and 'knickers'. Kate let him assess her, shattered stomach and collapsing breasts and the stripe of hair she'd missed under her armpit. He walked her to the stairs, undoing his trousers with one hand, and he pressed her back and suddenly he was inside her. The feeling of it shocked her like a punch to the jaw and she realised it was the only true way to know someone. 'Oh God. Fuck, Kate.'

Was that an example of the performative? She reached up and dug her nails into his hips as he thrust them against her, the slap of flesh on flesh hard and brutal. 'Harder,' she commanded. 'Fuck me. Fuck me harder.'

He did. His hand scrabbled in her pubic hair, the other bracing himself against her as he stood. She let him do it, where before she'd have pushed him away. It might actually work this way. For the first time ever.

'Wait!' He stopped, sweating inside her, panting in her ear. 'Come for me. Come.'

Wait, wait – she guided his finger against her, where it was slippery-hard, and it was almost, almost – ALMOST.

A few seconds. He began to move against her and as she suddenly came, he caught up, and he screamed into her hair. 'Jesus! Kate!' As if to remind himself who she was. She liked to be told her name during sex, in the middle of losing herself, like an island to make for out of an immense wave.

Whatever she said was lost in his mouth. Everything between them slick with sweat, sticking and breaking each time as they moved. He sounded like he was crying. 'Oh God. Oh God. You're – oh God, ahhh.' Her body was soaked in

192

his sweat. 'This is real,' he said, his voice returning to normal. 'Isn't it?'

'Yu-yes.' She braced her arm on his shoulder but didn't move her hips. They stayed like that for some time, plugged in, eyes searching eyes. 'Well?' she panted.

'Well what?'

'Well, was it good?'

He laughed. 'Do you want a score? Insecurity, Kate. It was fucking great. Surely you know that.'

A smile spread through her. 'For me, too. That was the best, I think. The best ever.' She didn't watch his face as she said it. Conor was not driven to adumbrate their experiences, climbing the precarious of ladder of I like you, you're great, there's no one like you, I think I'm falling for you, no I have fallen for you, will you marry me? Maybe he was right. Where was there to go after that? Forty years of slow death.

'Why?' she said, picking up her limbs, moving into the downstairs bathroom to pee. 'What was all that about?' He was outside, buckling his trousers. Her face in the mirror was flushed with wild blood – she thought she had never looked better.

'You slept with your last boss,' he said. He'd listened. He'd remembered. Somehow this touched her, that he cared enough to be jealous. She followed him into the kitchen, where he switched on the coffee maker. He could drink it at any hour, ran on it like fuel.

'That's got nothing to do with this.'

'Doesn't it? He wanted you.'

Kate folded her arms. How much easier it would be to fight now she had a box to stand on. 'I want to work. I'm tired of being your kept woman.'

For a moment they stared at each other, across the white expanse of a kitchen where nothing was ever cooked. Who would back down first? Then Conor rubbed his eyes. 'I'm sorry. I don't want you to feel like that. I just – I don't want to lose you.'

He thought he might lose *her*? That didn't fit the narrative she'd written herself. 'What?'

'I know you don't love me – you just came here to escape.'

Kate digested this. 'You're saying – you think I'm only here because I've nowhere else to go?' This man, so attractive, so rich, so clever, his drive to succeed straining in the sinews of his neck, he thought *she* might leave *him*?

He shrugged. 'It's true, isn't it?'

'But—' She didn't know what to say next. She should say that she loved him. But did she? Or was she afraid to, assuming at any moment he would tire of her and kick her out? She moved across the kitchen, her bare feet cold on the clean tiles. She stood opposite him, resting her hand near his on the counter, but not touching him. 'That doesn't make any sense, Conor. You know that. I left for you.'

He grasped at it hungrily, and she was stunned by what she was seeing, the mass of insecurity underneath the expensive clothes and muscled body of this man. 'Did you? Really?'

It wasn't entirely true, but there are kind lies sometimes, between people. 'Of course. This way, if I work too, we can be more equal. We can be a real couple.' She wouldn't have dared to say this to him before today, or even to ask if they were a couple. After three years, it was ridiculous.

He hesitated, and she could feel the struggle in him, the pull to be cold and distant and shut down, the hints of a rawness underneath, to be protected at all costs. It felt like some pivotal moment, where her life would go one way or the other. She'd need the work visa his company had arranged, should she get this job. Without it, without his patronage, she would have to leave the country. Go back to the life she had burned down. For a moment she thought about saying it all – *I don't want there to be other people, if indeed there are others* – but no. This was enough for now. It was so fragile.

She reached out and touched his hand, cold in the chill of the air conditioning. After a moment, Conor moved his thumb and stroked hers back. Only a small thing, but it was enough for now.

Adam, present day

Finally, the launch was over. Adam was angry. Angry at his father, for fucking up the most simple of tasks, so now Olivia was in core-reactor meltdown mode. Angry at himself, for going to this stupid party in the first place, at his mother for choosing now to resurface and overturn his life. But mostly at Delia, for dropping the bombshell that she had big news, and still refusing to tell him what was up. Not that he could really be angry with her, which made him even crosser.

He and Delia and Olivia and his dad were huddled on the pavement outside the shop as people left, waiting for a clear moment so Delia could finally share her news. The launch had clearly been a success, stacks of copies sold, lots of people there, a buzz about the film deal. People were so happy to be out again after the years before, they would turn up to anything. But the four of them, a sorrowful little knot, knew it had really been a huge catastrophe. Even Olivia could not overlook a snub as big as that one, so what did that mean for them all?

Olivia was twittering with anxiety about some car service she'd already reserved, to take her and his dad to the hotel they'd booked for themselves, a pathetic treat for the night.

Surely she wouldn't go with Andrew now though? Where would she sleep – at Delia's? He felt stupidly disappointed that he might not get her for the night. 'I hope the car will be here soon, they promised they would ...'

Delia said, 'Mum, it's fine. There's no hurry.'

'I do hope they have the right branch, I told them there are several and ...'

'Mum!' Olivia's head swung round at the crack of Delia's voice. 'Will you just ...' She was losing it. She never lost it. Part of Adam was very interested in seeing what happened next. Another part was terrified.

The last of Andrew's acolytes had gone ambling towards Baker Street, heads swivelling, keen to know what was going on. Andrew said, voice full of fear: 'What is it you have to tell us? What's the matter, Delia?'

She laughed. 'What's the matter? You're asking *me* what the matter is?'

He paled. 'Obviously I know I ... made a mistake, but ...'

'A mistake.'

'I'm terribly grateful to your mother, of course ...'

'Grateful?' Was she going to echo everything he said? 'Andrew. My mother has raised your children for you – instead of raising her own, I might add. She has washed your socks and made your meals and run your life for you, without which you wouldn't have been able to even write this book, and look, as soon as your ex-wife pops up again you've forgotten all about her. You didn't even *thank* her.'

Was that it? Was the old fool distracted by what was going on with Adam's mother? He couldn't still be in love with her. No one was that stupid. 'I ...'

'Isn't that the reason? Or does Mum mean so little to you you'd have forgotten her anyway?'

Olivia was still staring up the road, as if this conversation wasn't about her. Adam was entranced. All this time knowing Delia, her grace, her silences, her calm, and it turned out she had a tiger inside her. Good God, he could never walk away from this girl, stepsister or semi-stepsister, or whatever she was. There was no one like her. She went on. 'You've never even slept with her, Andrew, in all these years. Have you?'

Olivia flinched. Andrew went red. 'Delia! You've no right to speak to me like this. You're upsetting your mother, and ruining my big night!'

He'd never known his father talk to Delia like that – she was his special girl, the talented lovely daughter he'd never got to have. Adam let out a burst of laughter. 'What are you, five? Come on Dad, she's right. What are you to Olivia? What is she to you?'

'I – eh . . .'

Delia had shot him a grateful look, and it was so beautiful he almost reached for her hand, but then she put hers on either side of her face, like that painting with the screaming man. 'Oh my God. You need to decide, Andrew. For all of us. We're all affected here, by Kate coming back and you forgetting to thank Mum and, oh, all your actions. You forget that. We're all affected, especially now.'

Andrew looked baffled. 'What do you mean?'

Delia took a deep breath, and looked at Adam, and he saw she was going to say it, the thing she wouldn't say before. His stomach dropped, roller-coaster style. 'Because,' she said, and her voice shook. 'I'm pregnant. I'm pregnant and it's Adam's, and yes, that does mean it might be like Kirsty is, so we need to decide. What are we all, to each other? Are we a family or something else? Are we just . . . people?'

197

Kate, 2012

The night Trixie almost died, Kate had a good day at the chat show. It hadn't all gone smoothly to begin with – she'd started scripting her pieces, and sometimes fluffed the autocue, and her jokes were screened beforehand for the sensibilities of the American housewife. Nothing really funny was left in, and her skin felt clogged with all the makeup, but God it was nice to have somewhere to go each day, anecdotes to bring to Conor about the silly runner girls and diva lead presenter, Ann Jacobs, who allegedly had her hair insured for half a million dollars. Being in the business, he knew everything and everyone, and she felt they were equals, a power couple, like she'd always wanted. More often than not, he'd sleep in her room now, and Kate noticed he even left things behind – books, half-empty glasses, tissues which she had to pick up. His own room remained a shrine, and on nights when he didn't come to her, she itched and burned for him, turning over and over and wondering why she couldn't let herself go to him. She was never sure he'd allow her in, for one. It was a game. Perhaps that was why she still wanted him so much, after almost five years.

Sex remained the one place they could say anything. She'd called him a cold bastard, a control freak, in between kisses that felt like she was sucking the breath right from him. He pulled her hair, slapped her while taking her from behind, and she wanted it, she begged for it. What she'd never realised all those years with Andrew was that sex was a foreign country, with its own rules. But afterwards she would lie awake wondering about his coldness, if they'd ever go out with friends, go on holiday, decorate a Christmas tree together. She began to hallucinate words never said between them – *I love you*. Words she'd swept

198

away in a disgusted pile when Andrew said them. From Conor, they were precious coin. Then she'd think no, it was OK, he was just a man, and it suited them both to be free. It didn't matter that she was forty. If you wanted no more babies, life had no timetable. You could roller-skate through it with abandon. Waste a decade or two on a man you weren't sure loved you.

Then came the day it all changed. She was winding down after the show, shivering with adrenaline and sweat. They had covered the Olympics, and she was much in demand as a bona fide Brit to talk about the country, London landmarks, British customs, the home team's success, and the strange pang of pride it gave her, when she had so long left. Her eyes behind the layers of makeup glittering hollow. Then Michael Gold, the big-shot producer who'd hired her, was in the dressing room. She was annoyed for a moment he hadn't knocked, then realised how quickly her old instincts had come back. She was important. She deserved a lot, and maybe better tea. She opened her mouth to ask him to leave, then saw his face.

'Kate. We gotta problem here.'

Her stomach collapsed and reassembled itself. 'With the show?'

He shut the door. 'Show's good. Feedback is positive, 'specially now you've toned it down a bit.'

A flare of anger. 'Then what?'

'Why'dya not tell me you didn't have a green card?'

Kate had never thought of it in those terms. She'd had an O-1 visa for three years initially, but it had been renewed when it ran out, handled by someone at Conor's company, and she'd assumed the same would apply when it came up again next year. 'Firstly, Michael, you asked me to work here, not the other way round. And you know I'm British. You must have known I'd need a visa, but you never asked.'

He squeezed his forehead with fleshy fingers. 'I gotta phone call from goddamn immigration today. They'll be in tomorrow to see you. I'm telling you these guys don't mess about. They might not renew you – O-1, that's a shitty goddamn visa. You never even told them you worked here!' It was true she didn't work for Conor's company, as her visa said, but she'd never thought it mattered.

'So what will happen?' It seemed unreal, like when they were told about Kirsty.

'I can't get you a green card now. I coulda before the show, maybe.'

'So what else can I do?'

He looked at her in exasperation. 'I donno Kate. You could get married. Get that goddamn Irish guy to marry you. He's a citizen, yeah?'

She stood very still. She was a professional. No weeping in the workplace. 'Alright, Michael. I will sort this out. I apologise for the inconvenience.'

English over-apologising seemed to work on him, and she walked out calmly through the studio, although she was shaking. They'd send her back to England, maybe in cuffs and an orange jumpsuit, like in American films. She drove to the house, concentrating intensely, thinking how she would phrase it to Conor. *Will you marry me?* God, and he'd said a hundred times he would never get married again, after his disastrous first attempt. She'd have to go back to England and face what she'd done, maybe live with her sister and Elizabeth's new baby she had only seen online, if her sister would even talk to her after all these years of silence. Crawl back to her family. Andrew. The children – but no, she couldn't face even thinking about that. There had to be options.

The automatic gates let her in but there seemed to be no one home. No lights. She tried to think where Conor would be – a party, perhaps, or working late in his office in Santa Monica, overlooking the beach, a place she had only been once. She took her keys from the expensive bag he'd bought her, and then she heard the noise. A sort of mewling, like a dog or a person with their mouth gagged, in pain. Oh God. A serial killer? It was what you always heard about in the LA hills. A bobcat, a coyote? She moved through the house, its air brushing her skin like cold water. She set the keys on the table with a chink, holding her breath. If she shouted *hello* the killer might find her. The back security lights came on, and the pool's underwater ones, so it shone like a milky eye. Beside it, slumped up against the patio doors, was a body. Kate fumbled the door open and in fell Trixie.

Kate had first met Trixie in the empty months after she'd moved to LA, padding about Conor's house like a ghost, never wearing more than a bikini or one of his shirts. She ate strange, overseasoned American foodstuffs, ice cream and twizzlers and cereals like sweets. Because it wasn't real, this life, none of the calories counted. She didn't think about England at all. When the maids came she shut herself in the bathroom while listening to pillows being plumped and a hoover going, then crept downstairs, making wet footprints on the wooden stairs. Later, they would somehow have cleaned the bath too, like a mist settling over the house and leaving all pristine.

One day she was watching a romcom from Conor's towering DVD library, and spooning Ben & Jerry's into her mouth. She'd had to adjust the thermostat so the house's ambient chill didn't keep it rock-hard. Conor hated that. He worked hard to control such things as the temperature, and his life. Kate leapt up like a startled animal – she'd heard a door opening, a noise

201

somewhere. Conor was out, so who was it? A blob of ice cream fell from her spoon onto the hessian sofa. Shit. She was about to bolt when a figure appeared beside the pool. No one should be able to get in that way, not without a key fob. It was a skinny teenage girl in extremely tight denim shorts and a vest top, red hair plaited around her head in an arrangement that looked very heavy. She wore large expensive sunglasses and had a phone stuck to her ear, pausing to trail a small foot in the crystal water of the pool.

Despite her panic, Kate still went into the kitchen and put away the tub in the freezer, a measure of how much she feared making Conor angry. The girl had yanked open the patio doors and now came in, her flip-flops slapping on the tiles. Kate wore only a T-shirt that didn't cover her pants. It was like those dreams where you accidentally go to school in your underwear.

'Oh this is just fucking great! Another skank.' The girl said this almost to herself, before snatching up her phone again. 'Mom? He's doing it again. There's some ho here in her panties. No, she's old. Like as old as you nearly. Ew.'

Kate stood right there for all of this exchange. Who was this girl? Her mind was pedalling hard, pushing against nothing.

'I dunno where he is. Probably naked.' She began to cry. 'It's every time, Mom! What is wrong with him?'

Then Conor was there, home from wherever he'd been, not naked but in a white shirt and jeans. 'What are you doing here?' he said to the girl.

'You gave me a key! I'll give it back if you don't want me.'

'No, no. Is that your mother?' Conor took the girl's phone. He hadn't looked at Kate yet. 'Hello. No, I have a friend staying is all. She's over-reacting again. Jesus Christ. Fine, fine. Right, fine. I'll drop her back later.' He gave the phone back. 'Have you eaten? You're skin and bone.'

'Thanks.' The girl continued to stare at Kate, chewing on the end of one of the plaits which had come down from her head. Who was she? An actress Conor was working with? Would he speak to her like that if so?

Conor opened the fridge. 'I'll make you something. I bet you skipped lunch.'

In a sudden switch-around, the girl went to him, wrapping her arms about her waist, resting her head on his back. 'Thank you, Daddy.'

Daddy. *Daddy*. Kate put down the ice-cream spoon, trying to creep from the room, and it made a small noise. Conor looked up. 'Kate. Why don't you put some trousers on?' *Trousers* he had said, not pants, which was how she knew he wasn't as calm as he seemed.

Was this girl his *daughter*? Why hadn't he introduced her then, or indeed mentioned her existence? 'I'll go if you want,' she said. Stupid. To where?

'Of course not. It's time you met Trixie anyway.'

Trixie. And on the phone, that must have been her mother, presumably Conor's ex-wife. *Trixie*. Red snaky locks, a pinched white face spread with makeup. She was, it turned out, only fourteen on the day she stumped into the house and broke the fragile peace of Kate's refuge. Just allowed to run riot by her mother, Alanna, the woman who'd put Conor off marriage for life, just soured already by drugs, and bulimia, and pain.

After the awkward lunch, during which no one spoke to Kate at all, Trixie left, in a car summoned for her by Conor. Kate waited for him to say something as he washed up the dishes. Watching his precise, mathematical strokes of the cloth, she wondered if perhaps the house's eerie cleanliness was because he got up at night and tidied.

'Are you sorry she saw me?'

'She gets upset sometimes.'

'What's her mother like?' Wipe wipe wipe. He swiped under her elbows. She lifted them. 'Conor. I met your daughter today. I'm – well, I'm basically hiding out in your house. All I do is eat and sleep and watch Meg Ryan films.' She paused. 'I spilled ice cream on the sofa.'

His head whipped up. 'I should have said I don't like eating in the other rooms.'

'No, you should have said you have a daughter.' It was hard to take it in. She had left her life, run away with a man who hadn't even told her he had a child.

'I believe I mentioned her.' Had he? No, she would have remembered. That would have changed everything. Wouldn't it? She didn't know.

The chrome chair was hard, cold. It had nowhere to burrow the feet. She tucked them up, realising that the angry daughter had had lovely manicured toenails. In LA even unstable people looked better than she did. 'You said in a very vague way you'd been married. Was that to her mother?'

'Beatrice's mother and I were married, yes.' He held the word away from him syntactically, like a piece of sink debris.

'And her name?'

'The mother?'

'Your wife. Your ex-wife, if she is.'

'Alanna.' His mouth had grown tight.

'I told you about my husband. I told you everything about him, and why I had to leave. You said nothing. You didn't say you had a daughter called Beatrice – who chose that?'

'It's from Dante. So, me. Of course her mother called her "Trixie".'

'It's a nice name.' He went back to wiping, though it looked spotless to Kate. 'Conor. Are we ever going to talk, or – I mean,

204

I don't know what I'm doing here. When Trixie asked who I was, I didn't know what to tell her. I'm nothing.' She realised her voice had taken on the same shrill hectoring tone she'd used with Andrew, trying to penetrate those spongy layers of male denial. She softened it. 'I'm sorry. It's just been an odd time. I feel like I don't exist.'

Conor was cleaning the sink filter. 'She's my daughter, and she has a key to my house. She's entitled to make a claim on me if she wants. I allowed her to be born, so it's my responsibility to ensure she copes as well as she can in the world. But her mother and I should never have had a child, let alone got married.'

'Why did you?'

'Why does anyone? It's what you do. We got on OK. She's an actress and did well for a while. You can see her in old high-school movies. I wanted into the business, she helped me. I needed a visa, so we got married. Vegas. Seemed appropriate. But then I realised I'd shackled my life to someone who has multiple mental health issues, a cocaine problem, a painkiller addiction. Who took drugs throughout her pregnancy. Who left Trixie on her own to go to auditions. It's why I promised myself I'd always be free, from then on.'

'Oh.' For some reason the news hit her right in the stomach; she began to shake. What was it about marriage, that even when it had gone rotten, teeming with maggots, and you'd found yourself in a three-legged race with a corpse, you still wanted that from the next person you met? 'You give her money, Alanna?'

He looked at her. 'I don't think that's your business.'

'No.' She got down from the stool, her feet cold on the tile. This house was so cold. 'I don't know if anything's my business.'

Conor was folding the cloth into little squares. 'Children can't be unthought, Kate. Even if you don't want them, and

205

can't love them, there they are. I do my best for Trixie. I hope she doesn't feel unloved, at least.' It was how he was – he'd just casually say the unthinkable, the worst thing ever, that he did not love this girl and had not wanted her in the first place.

'OK. So what do I do?' What happens next, she meant. How can I live here with you when you didn't even tell me you had a child? 'Do you even want me here – do I – Conor, should I leave? If you don't let me into the most basic parts of your life?'

'I want you to stay.'

'I can't go on like this.' But the fight had gone out of her. Where else would she go? Really she was saying, please, love me a little. Let me in.

He shrugged. His tone softened. 'You're right – I've been neglecting you, leaving you here alone too much. That will change, I promise.'

'You want me here.'

'Of course I do. Now, tell me where you spilled the ice cream.'

When Trixie fell in the door on her five years later, Kate's first thought was irritation – *this bloody kid*. Then she saw Trixie was not breathing. Her face below the makeup was green, and a halo of white foam caked her mouth, as if she'd choked on vomit. In her miniskirt and ripped band T-shirt, she was tiny as a child, goose-bumped skin. Kate was able to pick her up and lie her on the sofa. The first aid course came back to her, the one she'd taken when it was clear Kirsty might die at any moment. She opened Trixie's mouth and a sour, rotten smell came out. Wincing, she reached in, jabbed at the airway. The intimacy was shocking. When else do you put your finger in the mouth of another adult, all muscle and spit, the uvula fluttering like a caught butterfly? 'Come on, Trixie,' she said. 'You need to be sick. Be sick and you'll feel much better.'

She pressed down on the girl's stomach at the same time. Nothing. Her body flopped like a boned fish. 'Trixie. You need to throw up. Come on, I know you throw up every day. Just puke.' She pressed hard and felt a resistance, insides locking together, and then Trixie was spasming and white foam welled up, stinking. Kate marched her to the downstairs loo, where she threw up and up, on her knees. She moaned, trying to lie down, but Kate grasped her fast between her own legs, holding back the girl's ratty red hair. 'Come on, Trixie. Get it all out. What did you take? Did you take drugs?' Panicked, she looked through to the phone in the hall. She needed an ambulance. 'Stay here. Keep puking. Good girl.'

She went to the phone and tried to explain. They didn't understand her accent. She spelled out the address several times. 'A girl is having an overdose.' She thought that's what it was.

'And is this your daughter, ma'am?'

She glanced in. Trixie had slid over so she knelt with her face to the wall, vomit running down the tiles. 'She's my stepdaughter. Please hurry.'

She went to the girl. 'Come on, love.' Where did it come from, the tenderness? Trixie was crying now, which Kate took as a good sign. 'You're OK. Have you got it all up?' Trixie shook her head weakly, pushing Kate away, but no more came up. 'Let's clean you. You'll feel better.' She put her under the shower, and planned to go out, give her privacy, but saw the girl was under it, shivering and insensate, her underwear dark with water. So Kate took down the shower attachment and washed her, wiping soap over her face, arms and front where she'd puked, then wrapping her in a towel, soon smeared with mascara. Then she took her out and just rocked her, as she had when Kirsty was smaller and ran those awful fevers, and you had to hold her every moment in case she died.

Trixie weighed no more than a child, her bones hollow, her eyes taking up half her face. Clearly, she had not been eating. She mewled like an unhappy cat. This was not her daughter or even her stepdaughter. She was nothing to Trixie. But all the same she walked the floor with her all night. 'You have to stay awake. Don't sleep, darling.' She had to slap her sometimes, on her white painted face. 'Trixie! Don't go to sleep.' The ambulance didn't come. Maybe they'd misunderstood her. Conor didn't come. She'd annoyed him the night before, arguing with him over work. He was most likely out with some other woman, and she couldn't even protest because he'd promised her nothing, he owed her nothing, and she had the right to do it too except she, serial adulterer that she was, had never wanted to. Except it was deep in the night and here she was keeping his child alive.

When Trixie ceased her flailing or vomiting for long enough, Kate thought of driving to hospital, but she didn't know where it was and was still afraid of the freeways at night. She called Conor again and again on his mobile, even calling from Trixie's phone, in case it was only her he was avoiding. She called the ambulance five, ten times, giving her address again and again, each time being told it had gone out. '543 Laurel Canyon Drive! But no one's come. They have to ring the buzzer, there's a gate – please, my stepdaughter, she's very ill – very sick I mean. She's overdosing. Yes, I've made her throw up. Oh – wait.' Trixie was pushing herself up on an elbow, and Kate flung down the phone and rushed her to the bathroom again, holding back her red hair as she hoofed up strings of phlegm, her thin body shaking like a dog. She moaned, rolling into a foetal ball on the floor. Kate pulled her up. 'I know, darling. You'll feel better soon, I promise.'

She wondered if this was how nurses felt. A sort of temporary mad love, fighting the night and the sickness, you against it, across the battlefield of one frail human body. She who barely knew the girl, resented her whole existence, could not even love her own children, and yet she cradled and whispered, kissing her clammy forehead. Thinking that fresh air would help, she walked Trixie around the pool. It was very late, but the lights burned like an early dawn. Sirens screeched. She stopped believing in ambulances. It was just her to keep Trixie alive, no one was coming. The pool was a costume jewel. The night was endless. Time came and went. Kate woke. Oh God – she was dead, the girl was—

Kate was on the tiled surround of the pool. It was cold beneath her face and she pushed herself up, unsticking her eyes. A grey and concrete dawn. An American light that told you you were very far from home and no going back. Conor was standing over her, in a jumper and jeans.

'Trixie – she's sick.'

'I know. They've taken her.' He held out a hand to her.

'I went to sleep. God. I wasn't supposed to sleep.'

'She's alright. They said she threw it all up. I got your messages.'

'Oh.' The was a lapping of water in the pool and the crickets in the garden and the first breath of traffic below. She was shivering and frantic.

'You made her throw up?'

'I put my fingers down her throat. She was sick – oh, a dozen times. I don't know. I walked her. She wanted to sleep. No one came.'

'You gave the wrong address. It's Laurel Canyon Road.'

'What?'

'Road, not Drive.'

'Oh.' Drive was her home back in England. No longer her home. Under stress, it had come to her mouth. 'I'm sorry.'

He sighed. 'Will you get up? We need to follow them.' He saw her look. 'She's alright. She'll be fine, they said.'

Kate scrubbed her hands over her face. She had the exhausted but exalted feeling of lack of sleep. She'd saved a life. She couldn't stop shivering, so for the first time in five years she put on the jeans and jumper in which she'd fled England. It felt appropriate.

At the hospital, Alanna was by Trixie's bed, humming to herself with her eyes closed. Kate had met her only a handful of times, picking up or dropping off Trixie at their apartment.

'What are you doing?' said Conor, too loudly.

'I'm chanting for her.' Alanna's eyes stayed closed. She was heavily made up, her auburn hair long and artificially glossy. She wore a skin-tight lime green jumpsuit, as if she'd just come from a film set. Kate knew she still worked, sometimes, low-budget films and the odd episode of TV, eking out the sad end of brief stardom.

'You'd have been better off actually being there for her.'

'I work, Conor. I don't sit round the house in my panties like your little friend here.'

Kate opened her mouth to say she did work, but demurred.

'She saved your daughter's life, by the way.'

'My daughter? Yours too, asshole. And where were you all night? Sniffing out more pussy, I guess.'

It was so close to what Kate thought herself that she blocked it out, stared at Trixie in the bed, so tiny and white against the pillows. She had tubes in her arm, mouth, hand. Her fingers twitched feebly, as if she could barely stand the fluids going into her.

Conor was saying, 'You're a neglectful mother and you taught her to take drugs. Where'd she even get them?'

'Grow up, Conor. Every kid in her class takes coke.'

210

'Do they take crystal meth? Jesus, she's going to end up toothless on the street, whoring herself. And look how thin she is – puking up every day again, just like you.'

'Fuck you. You weren't there for her either. I have to work, seeing as you give me fuck-all alimony.'

'I give you a fortune! A fortune! No wonder the kid's so fucked up, your sleazy boyfriends, coke when you were pregnant, for Christ's sake, spending all my money on boob jobs and juice diets so you can pretend to be thirty again – well, no one's gonna have you, Alanna. You'll be playing people's grandmas before you know it, if you aren't already.'

There was a crack as Alanna smacked him across the face. Conor seized her wrist. 'Stop.'

'Fuck you, that's assault. I'm calling the cops.'

'Try it. I'll send them round for your knicker-drawer full of pills.'

Alanna burst into tears so angry and loud they were almost a weapon. 'You fucking bastard. I'm calling my lawyer. You'll never see her again.'

'Fine by me. I'll never pay a penny again.'

The girl's eyelids had moved. Kate was at her side before she knew it. Trixie opened her eyes in a look of abject terror. Her hand trembled. Kate knew what she wanted and took the hand. The girl's thin arms went around her like someone trying to climb out of a pool, her bird heart fluttering. 'Please,' she croaked from her charcoal-burned throat. 'Stop them.'

Alanna and Conor had not noticed their daughter wake up. 'Fuck you, you raddled druggie tart—'

'—You piece of shit, coming in here with your whore—'

'Will you two pack it in? She nearly died, for God's sake.'

Trixie whimpered, and Kate hugged her, and they both

watched, and Kate felt a strange tug of joy, something she couldn't remember feeling before, but which was as familiar as a baby latching onto a breast. She was needed. She could help. 'Tell the doctor she's awake,' she instructed Alanna. 'Stop thinking of yourself for once.' Trixie's mother pouted but went, her stupid six-inch heels stomping on the floor. Kate addressed Conor over the bony back of his half-dead child. 'You've been awful tonight. Worse than useless as a father, a partner – anything. You should be ashamed.'

'I am,' he said, shortly. 'I wasn't there. She almost died. Of course I'm ashamed.' She blinked. There was more to say, much more about how he'd taken Kate but not committed to her, how Alanna's slur of *whore* was not very far off how she actually felt. Where he had been all night, another conversation they would have to have. But it didn't matter, because she had quite literally held someone's life in her hands. She thought, fleetingly, of Adam, in a way she rarely allowed herself to. He'd be twelve now. Was he like Trixie, a wreck who had to be propped up on all sides? But she couldn't think about that.

'This isn't working,' she went on. 'The way you are – it wouldn't work for anyone. You're not human.'

He rubbed his nose, his shoulders sagging. 'I know. Believe me, I know. I want to be different. I want . . .' He reached out and touched a lock of Trixie's hair, matted and lank. Kate wasn't sure the girl could feel it – her eyes had drooped again, she was barely conscious. 'I know all of this, Kate, and you're right, again. But this isn't the place to talk about it.'

'No. But I'm afraid I can't just move out as nice and quiet as I moved in.' She pressed her cheek to Trixie's sweat-beaded forehead. 'You see, I need you to marry me, Conor.'

Andrew, present day

8am. Andrew woke up and didn't know where he was for a horrible moment. His head ached, his eyes were scratchy and his mouth sour. The bed was too large, and outside he heard the noise of traffic instead of twittering birds. Of course, he was in the shockingly expensive hotel he'd booked for himself and Olivia after the launch. To have a treat. Two rooms, naturally. And then he'd forgotten to thank her in his speech and Delia had dropped her bombshell, and Olivia had fled alone in the booked car, which had finally turned up just as Delia said what she said. Olivia had jumped in, slammed the door behind her, and driven off into the night. It had taken Andrew several moments to understand what had happened – she had left him. Not left-him, left-him – could that even happen when you weren't together? But she was gone. He'd slept, eventually, in this expensive room, calculating that every minute was costing him a pound. He checked his phone – no answer to his increasingly frantic text messages to Olivia. They veered between recrimination – how could she do this on his big day? – and worry. *Please, this isn't like you.* Where could she have gone? She wasn't with Delia, he knew that much. He texted Adam again just in case.

Heard anything?

Nothing.

How's Delia?

Dunno. I'm not with her.

So, Adam had gone back to his own house. Was Delia his girlfriend, or was it just another of his son's flings, using young women like tissues? Not Delia, surely. She was his sister, almost, although not of course in the ways that mattered. Not related. Not legally either. If Olivia was nothing to Andrew, then Adam was nothing to Delia, that was how it worked. It had shocked him, all the same, as if he was Delia's real father and Adam some loutish youth who'd knocked her up. What would Adam do now? Impossible to imagine the boy with a child of his own. Would he take off, as his mother had? Would Delia even have the baby? Of course there were options. And the biggest question of all – would the baby be alright? The odds were fifty-fifty that any child of Adam's would have what Kirsty had, not that it had a name – far too rare for that. He still recalled the conversation with the geneticist all those years ago, one of the worst of his life. Kate radiating hatred at the doctor and him and the world, refusing to cry. Crying, now that he could have comforted. But that bottomless, unfathomable anger of hers, he had never known what to do with that.

He pecked out another text to his son. *We need to talk about all this*. He waited, but Adam did not respond, and fair enough, Andrew had no idea what he'd even say. Have the baby? Don't have it? Get the baby tested, for God's sake? Could they do that now, before the birth? He was sure they could, though he didn't know how. Poor Delia. But perhaps she'd done it on purpose – young people didn't just get pregnant nowadays, did they? They were all so woke and clued-up, not like his generation, still embarrassed to buy condoms.

A knock at the door roused him. Olivia! She had come back, oh thank God, thank God, because he couldn't do without her. He sprang from bed, realising too late he was only wearing his boxer shorts.

But at the door was a kid in a white jacket and black face mask, with a huge tray on which sat silver-topped tureens, a bowl of chopped fruit, a pot of coffee, rolls wrapped in a white cloth, butter, dinky pots of jam. The smell of fried meat filled the room. 'Mr Waters?' Of course. He'd ordered a room service breakfast in advance, imagining how he'd lie there pleasantly hungover, surveying his triumph. A book published; his life's dream achieved. A new life ahead of him, someone who stayed in five-star hotels and ordered breakfast to the room and thought nothing of it. Someone with a loving family, children who looked up to him – including Delia, who'd been so helpful at the launch. And of course, he had ordered breakfast for two, picturing Olivia sitting opposite him, as she did every morning. Stupid.

As the waiter left, Andrew fretting over whether he should have tipped, he realised there was no point to any of it. Nothing had changed. Here he was, a published author, waking up in a five-hundred-quid-a-night room, about to eat pancakes and bacon, meeting a Hollywood producer in just a few hours to talk about a film adaptation of his work, and he had never felt more unhappy in his life.

Kate, 2014

It was her wedding day. She was getting married, after making such a terrible hash of it the first time. Kate was semi-hysterical and kept bursting out laughing as she caught sight of herself in the mirrors of the ranch's dressing room. She was in a ballet-length white lace dress. White! A bride! She was forty-two years old. Up until the previous month, she had still been married to a man in England, who she hadn't seen in seven years. Even arranging the divorce had made her uncomfortable, handled by lawyers so she wouldn't have to talk to Andrew at all. It was still a signal from her new life to her old. A connection. A communication, of sorts, when she would rather have vanished without a trace. She had two children, the older practically grown now, fourteen years old, and she had not seen him in half his life. She had a stepdaughter, official as of today, a girl of twenty-one who had almost died three times already from overdoses, from bulimia, from slashing at her thin arms, but who was here by her side. The whole wedding had been Trixie's idea – Kate and Conor would have rather slunk off to City Hall, vaguely embarrassed at being forced to yoke themselves together like this. Conor was furious about it, she knew, but when it came down to it, he'd also not been willing to have her deported. With the looming election, the mood on immigration, even of blonde English ladies, had darkened. He had kept her in the country by marrying her. That was romantic in its own way, she supposed. She'd take what she could get.

When Trixie heard about the engagement, if you could even call it that, she had been unaccountably delighted. 'Can I be a bridesmaid! Oh, please say yes.' And then it had snowballed into a gathering at a tasteful Malibu ranch, once Conor realised he could use the event to schmooze actors and industry people. Now, she had a Marvel superhero at her wedding, as well as a hundred other movers and shakers, including the people from the studio, Michael Gold having conveniently forgotten the row that had precipitated this wedding in the first place. The only thing missing was family. Kate's sister, her parents, her niece and nephew, never even seen. Her son and daughter. Olivia. Trixie was the only representative of Conor's family, thin and scarred in a pink slip dress. But she was smiling as she came into the dressing room. Kate had done her own hair and makeup, although her studio artist had offered. She wanted to look like herself today. To make sure Conor knew what he was getting.

Trixie slammed the door, making the mirrors rattle. 'I got

your bouquet! OMG, there's like three Oscar winners out there.' Kate was touched at her excitement – the girl had grown up with stars, she wasn't easily impressed. Since the almost-dying incident two years before, she and Trixie had become . . . something. There was no real word for it. Kate didn't feel like her stepmother, not even close. Something like a friend, maybe. She cared for the girl, she wanted the best for her, she would have knocked down anyone who hurt her. Was that love? Or something in the same terrain?

'You look lovely,' she said, which was at least partly true. Trixie had gained a little weight, helping out with menu tastings. Maybe this would continue, and she would heal. Maybe this could be Kate's chance to win at motherhood, or a sort of motherhood. To do better.

'You look *awesome.*' Trixie was so sweet to her these days. It was hard to take in, that she'd somehow got this right, that this hostile, troubled girl actually liked her. 'Kate . . . you'll be kind of my mom after this, right?'

'Well . . . kind of. I mean, there's your actual mum.'

'That bitch. She didn't want me to come today, you know? Made a whole scene. She – I'm sorry but she hates you, Kate.'

'Oh.' She had known it, but it still stung. She had not seen Alanna since that day at the hospital, and they communicated with her via Trixie, or occasionally lawyers when she became dissatisfied with the ever-increasing amount of money Conor paid her. Kate did her best to say nothing, never even comment on the situation. Trixie stayed with them more and more, and somewhere dark inside Kate felt a stab of pride. See, she couldn't be such a terrible mother, if Trixie would choose to be with her instead of the woman who'd given birth to her. Alanna's dry spell of acting had turned into a desert now she was forty-five, and Kate felt grateful she'd chosen a career that wasn't entirely dependent on how well her face kept its collagen. 'Well, sometimes we can't help people, Trix. We just have to help ourselves. And I'll always be here for you, if you need me.' Did she mean it? She'd try her best to mean it. That would have to be enough.

A knock on the door – Conor. Trixie squealed. She was thoroughly unlike herself today. Kate wondered briefly if she had taken something. 'Dad! You can't see the dress.'

'What? Oh, don't be silly, Trixie.' He didn't like her calling him Dad. He did his best by the girl, ensuring she had money and clothes and whatever support she needed. If he couldn't give it, he would pay someone to fill the breach. Was *that* love? Or the closest semblance of it possible? 'I need to speak to Kate. Go and sit down.'

'Duh, I'm walking down the aisle in front of her, I'm the bridesmaid! Have you never been to a wedding?' Trixie clattered off, feet awkward in silly flimsy shoes. Out the door, Kate could see a slice of shining Pacific, the dipping sun golden on the hills, and marvelled again that this was her life, her country. Weddings were held so late in America – hers to Andrew had started at noon. Her stomach roiled. Was she mad, to do it again, when the last time went so badly wrong? Was hope always an insanity?

When Trixie was out of earshot, Conor said, 'I thought we should talk.'

Oh no. He's going to call it off. He had never looked better to her, red hair cropped short and faded to a faint ginger, like spice in a jar. A grey suit, every line of it whispering good taste and money, a new silk tie. Stupid. Of course he wouldn't want her, when he could have anyone. 'Oh?'

'I know that this – we're kind of forced into it, and I know I've not – I haven't been exactly – I'm not romantic.' She'd never

218

heard him so inarticulate. 'I just want to say that, what I say up there, that's for other people. It's expected. Or, you know, the law. But I want to say to you, just for us – I swore I would never do this again. And I'd still rather not. But if I have to – I – well. I'm happy it's with you.'

She didn't know what to say. A lump had come to her throat. Conor looked almost wild-eyed. 'Alright. Thank you.' He nodded. That was all. She said, 'I – I'll see you in a minute.' He left. She drew in a breath in the suddenly silent room, alone for a second before her life changed again. Part of her was wondering if, in its ham-fisted, brutally honest way, this was maybe the most romantic moment of her entire life.

She was picking her way to the aisle between the erected chairs – stupid heels, why had she bothered – when she heard the commotion, saw the pink sheen of Trixie's dress over to the side, not ahead of her on the white carpet where she should have been. 'Mom. You can't be here. Oh God, Mom.'

She looked over – Conor was already in place at the head of the aisle she would walk down. At the edge of the car park, a few metres away, Trixie was remonstrating with a woman. Alanna, she could see now it was Alanna, but she looked different. She was wearing a tracksuit – sweats, as they called them here. Her hair had an inch of grey at the roots and she must have put on, oh wow, twenty pounds, maybe? Why was she here? 'Mom, please. It's not right. It's Dad and Kate's day.'

Alanna's shrill twang rose to Kate on the warm air. She was drunk, clearly, or on something, back to her old ways. Please God they'd save Trixie from that. '*Dad!* Yeah right. He's not your dad, you stupid bitch. Never was. That's why I'm here. He's not your father at all.'

Kate, present day

The airplane noise surrounded her, the white noise almost womb-like. In the seat opposite, Conor had layered a silk eye mask with a similar face mask, covering his entire face. Various people around them wore masks too, but most had abandoned the practice already. Kate sat back, her own mask suckered to her face with each breath, and felt the relief of taking some kind of action, while still putting off a serious decision. She was going to the UK, yes, but perhaps would still not see her children, or Andrew. She was ostensibly going to see her father, who'd apparently had a heart attack the month before. When she'd told Conor this, he had narrowed his eyes, sensing a ruse, but hadn't been able to protest, so here she was alongside him. Kate, of course, had not known about the heart attack, since no one had told her, until she had rung her sister out of the blue a few hours before. Perhaps this was the place to start anyway, with her family of origin, who were supposed to love her no matter what terrible thing she had done. Ha! Only kidding, of course it wouldn't be like that. But perhaps the trauma of seeing her parents and sister would distract from the even worse one of seeing her children again.

Earlier, Kate had steeled herself to make the call. Her sister had the same phone number as fifteen years before, and in any case was extremely findable, with accounts on Facebook, Twitter, and Instagram. Kate had always rationed her stalking of these, knowing it would only cause her pain, but since searing pain was on its way to her in any case, she often found herself scrolling, careful not to click on anything. There was so much! Her sister posted several times a day, professional-looking shots that must have taken time to arrange. Bunches of flowers, books, her own feet in socks, her hands clasping a mug (who took it?). Her children, Alice and Benjamin, photographed endlessly. Any stranger could easily have worked out their dates of birth, their ages, what school they went to, their address, their likes and dislikes. Kate allowed her irritation at this, her judgement of her sister, to muffle the hurt. She had a nephew and niece, who were eight and ten, and she had never even seen them. And they were lovely children, fresh-skinned and happy, cuddling dogs or splashing in the sea or taking part in improving craft sessions, all photographed by their mother, who didn't appear to work any more. Was this what she did all day, took photos?

Elizabeth had over ten thousand followers, which seemed an astonishing number to Kate. There was a lot of pressure on her to be on Twitter for work, but from what she'd heard of it, there was no way. She wasn't ready to let strangers say whatever they wanted to her. And what if it surfaced, what she'd done, how she'd abandoned her family? That was enough to get someone 'cancelled', as the younger people at the studio were always talking about. How did people run away any more? She remembered throwing her phone in the bin that day back in Bishopsdean, driving off, the dizzying freedom of it. Would anyone do that now, or would it feel like hacking off a limb?

The judgemental scrolling was quite soothing, however, and she had been relieved to see her parents in some of the pictures, with Elizabeth's children – more aches, but at least they were alive and well. She'd never been entirely sure if she'd be told or not, were her parents to die. Perhaps they would not be able to get hold of her – after all, no one from her past had her email or phone number. But everything was alright. There was no sign of Adam or Kirsty or Andrew in any of the pictures, which she was grateful for. Maybe they'd fallen out of touch with her family.

But maybe, with all the ease and joy and hashtags of her life, her sister would be receptive to a phone call. Maybe. Unlikely. She could only bring herself to do it because all the alternatives were so much worse. She swallowed hard, gritted herself to it. It was just a call, but it felt like rolling back the stone of a tomb. The number rang, the unfamiliar UK dial tone. It was getting late there, perhaps Elizabeth would be asleep. Then her sister's voice, a little breathless, high and girlish still. 'Hello?'

'It's Kate.' Her heart was whirring.

A silence. '*Kate* Kate?'

'Kate, your sister, Kate.'

'Jesus Christ.'

More silence. What to say after fifteen years? 'I know.'

'Are you . . . is everything OK?'

'Well . . . that's a very relative question, in the circumstances. Nothing's immediately wrong, no, not on my side. You – you seem well? I saw Instagram.'

'Oh, yes, I have a lot of followers.' Attempting to say it casually, pride breaking through. 'Why are you calling me?'

'I'm thinking of coming to the UK.' Did they even know she was in LA? Andrew could have guessed, from the divorce papers her lawyers had handled. 'Um . . . it's a long story why, but I'm coming. Today. Well, it'll be tomorrow when I get there.'

'Jesus Christ. Just hop on a plane today, like you do.'

Kate said nothing. In her world, this was normal. 'I'd like to see you. And Mum and Dad.'

'Oh! Now you remember they exist? After leaving me to look after them for fifteen years?'

She sensed this was the nursery slope of a very long ramping up of recrimination. 'Are they alright?'

'Well, apart from Dad's *heart attack*.'

'What?' A sudden lurch of pain that surprised her.

222

'Dad had a heart attack last month. Not that you'd know, of course, since we don't even have a number for you. We can see you on TV, but we can't even ring you when your own dad has a heart attack.'

'Jesus, is he OK?'

'As well as can be expected,' Elizabeth said, huffily.

'What does that mean? Is he in hospital?'

'No. I mean they hardly keep you in nowadays. He's at home, he has pills. Can't get stressed.'

'You mean I'd stress him out, if I visited?'

'Would you? Depends on you, I suppose.'

Kate felt battered by waves of guilt and hidden meaning, unable to keep her head up. 'Look, I'd really like to see them, and I know there's a lot that – there's a lot more to say, really years' worth, and I . . . ' She was reluctant to say sorry, because once she started, she'd never stop. 'If it's alright with you, and them, I'd like to visit.'

'What, like, *tomorrow*? They wouldn't like me dropping in next week with no notice, and I live ten minutes away.'

'I won't expect anything. I just want to come.'

'Well, that's all very well, but you know how they are, they'll make a massive fuss, and guess who'll have to do the shopping since Dad's ill, and Mum can't read the labels without her glasses and keeps buying non-fat stuff, that's right, muggins here.' Kate sensed that her sister was enjoying the role reversal, that she could be the organised downtrodden one for once.

'Don't go to any trouble. But will you ask them? If I can?'

'But how will you get here?' Elizabeth sounded bewildered. Her helplessness had always been a source of annoyance. She had two children, presumably she had some awareness of how to exist in the world.

'Get a train. Hire a car at the airport, I don't know.'

223

'Just like that.'

'Well, yes, that's how it works, that's what people do.'

'Not people I know.' No, they would have reserved a car months back off a discount website, printed out maps, hired a sat nav. It was exhausting, the amount of fretting her family did. Kate refused to get drawn back in.

'Thank you. I'd really appreciate it, and – I would love to see you too. And maybe the kids?'

'Your niece and nephew, you mean. Who you've never met!'

'I know. I'd like to do that now. I'm sorry but I have to go and book my flight.'

'You haven't even *booked*?' Elizabeth screeched. 'Jesus, I have no idea what world you live in.'

'Well, let me worry about that. This is my number – text me the details maybe? Thanks.' And she hung up, before the true volleys could be fired. There was a lot of artillery on the other side, she knew.

She looked now at the facing airplane seat, which contained her husband. He had put up his screen after take-off, as if she was a stranger, and not spoken a word to her, likely annoyed that she'd weaselled her way into coming with him. Just like that trip over to LA, when she had left her life. Restless and masochistic, she took out the ARC of Andrew's book, which she'd packed into her hand luggage. Her fingers traced his name on the cover before she dipped in, like someone diving into deep water.

The doctors couldn't tell us much. They were kind, supportive, but working in the dark. When a condition has no name, what can you do to treat it?

Huh. Kate didn't remember it that way at all. The doctors had all been high-handed and patronising when Kirsty was born,

224

if not downright cruel. Was this book just a tissue of lies? She flipped on.

I'll admit I didn't believe Kirsty could ever learn to communicate. Hope had been in short supply during her early years. It was Olivia who urged me to try it.

Olivia. The same Olivia – her Olivia? Could she really still be hanging about, exactly where Kate had left her? God, in her note she'd meant look after the kids for a day, a week at most, not for fifteen years! What did it mean – they couldn't be together, could they? The idea was unthinkable. But what did Kate know? This was why she hadn't wanted to go back, even to look over her shoulder. The people she'd left frozen in amber clearly had not stayed frozen.

Andrew and Olivia. It couldn't be. No.

Kate turned back to the book, hunting for references to herself. *I had become a single parent to Adam and Kirsty when they were seven and five, and those were not easy years.* That was it. She wasn't even a pronoun.

She skimmed on, dipping in and out, too tensed for pain to read it properly. Was this real, the Kirsty he described here? With likes and dislikes, a bubbling laugh, a little personality all of her own? Who'd blow him kisses and smile to see him? Who could say if she was hungry or cold, or wanted a particular toy?

It's not fair. An old thought that hit Kate sidewise. She had left, she'd forfeited any right to fairness. But this child bore no resemblance to her memories of Kirsty, the screaming and howling and seizures. The feeling no one was in there, the failure to connect, the constant terror of death. She'd got none of it, the love and laughing and the communication. Just to feel Kirsty knew who she was. She'd have given anything for that, back then. Had she just not been patient enough? Kirsty was only five when she left. They'd been told she would never talk, but was that not true? Should she have tried harder to hope?

Kate sighed and stuffed the book away, out of sight. Speculation was useless until she got there and saw the truth for herself. Not that she was sure she'd see them. Or they'd see her. She toyed with the idea of logging onto the wi-fi, so she could check on Trixie, and maybe email Suzi. Suzi would be supportive, she was sure, with a stream of memes based on misquotes of Persian mystics. She was attending yet another protest today, which Kate had ducked out of, against the recent rumours the Supreme Court were going to strike down Roe v Wade. Although it was intensely depressing that all their fears of six years earlier were so rapidly coming to pass, part of Kate was relieved she wasn't there. As much as she supported the cause, and had more reason to than most, she always felt she was acting a role when at a protest. She didn't know if she was the kind of person who could care about the fates of strangers enough to march and wave banners. Suzi seemed to have an inexhaustible supply of concern and rage, maybe because she stayed single and childless herself. Suzi, Kate realised, was her new Olivia, although the two women were about as different as it was possible to be. She comforted herself that her life in LA was a real one, not a pale shadow of what she'd had in England. There were friends, family even. There were always people, however many you had left behind.

Kate, 2016

The pressure of the crowd around her was like water, surging, flowing. Dangerous. 'Alright?' Suzi mouthed at her. Kate nodded. She reached up to adjust the 'pussy hat' she was wearing, a knitted pink thing shaped vaguely like vagina, if a vagina could be said to have a shape. The hats were silly, she felt. They undermined the serious point.

Kate tried not to mind the growing agitation of the crowd, the unwashed smell of some of the protestors, the misspelled banners they waved. They were excited as well as angry, trying on this role of activist, fighting for something their generation had always taken for granted. But none of them knew how to ask for things, to write letters or run phone trees. They hadn't had to fight. Privilege had dulled them into submission. Kate was not sure exactly what they were asking for today. That man was going to the White House no matter what. There were murmurs of the Russians hacking the voting machines, but Kate didn't really believe that. As in her own country, things were simply lurching off the rails. The good years were over. So they were marching to show they did not like it. Underneath the rage was a real current of terror. Could this, like, actually, really, you know, happen to us? Kate had heard a lot recently about *The Handmaid's Tale*, a book she had read at college years ago, but life in America felt like it was actually going that way. People liked to say this, as a joke or internet meme, but the fear was real and growing. There was talk of abortion being banned, contraception even, gay marriage going almost as soon as it had arrived. Was that how things went wrong – you joked and joked, and then one terrible moment you looked up and it was true?

After the wedding neither she nor Conor had really wanted, ruined by Alanna turning up like someone in Greek tragedy and claiming Trixie was not Conor's daughter after all, nothing had changed right away. Alanna had been dispatched by security and thence to rehab; Trixie had walked down the aisle in front

227

of Kate, unsteady, tears running through her mascara. Kate and Conor said words, signed papers, were yoked together. The next day Conor stood over Trixie while she swabbed her cheek for a DNA test. 'Is this necessary?' Kate had murmured in the kitchen, as Trixie wept into her hands. 'She's still your daughter either way.'

Conor had glared at her – 'You must be stupid.' Her husband, this was how he spoke to her. The test came back, and Alanna was right – Conor was not Trixie's father. Alanna said it was some actor, whose name she couldn't remember, so drug-addled had she been back then. Conor never said one more word about it, but everything was different. When Kate invited Trixie over to the house, Conor would simply walk out of the room. He still paid her allowance and he hadn't taken back her key, but he would not spend a second in the girl's company, or answer a message from her, or speak to her on the phone. He had shut down entirely.

She tried to soothe Trixie. 'He'll come round. It's just a shock.' This was why she hadn't wanted to get married again, or one reason anyway. To have to excuse someone else's behaviour. To be responsible for them. She saw the way the girl's sad eyes followed Conor round the house, beaten, knowing she had no claim on him, and Kate tried to make up for it. But could a well-meaning stepmother replace a biological parent? She didn't know, and didn't want to wonder too closely, who might be caring for her own children.

Then, something else happened. Eight years after she left her husband, and her son and her daughter, ended that part of her life, Kate got pregnant again. So unlikely did it seem that it took her a long time to admit it, too long. Conor was better at tracking her cycle than she was, and he asked why her period hadn't started two months in a row. She'd given some vague response about always being irregular. His watchful eyes. One morning, as she filled her metal coffee cup ready to whizz off to the studio, he looked her full in the face. It was remarkable how seldom that happened, when you lived with someone. 'Kate.'

'What?'

'You're late.'

She glanced at the clock. 'No I'm not.' Even with traffic, there was plenty of time to get to the studio in Burbank.

He sighed. The same 'you are so stupid' sigh she used to give to Andrew. 'Your period.'

'What?'

'It's been eight weeks. Since you bled.'

'And how do you know that?' They still had sex, but less often since the wedding, not so often that he'd know for sure.

'I'm not stupid. Laundry, your mood. And you have the same box of tampons in your bathroom as three months ago.'

So many things went through her head – rage – violation – a strange kind of pleasure that he knew her so well, maybe? 'Well, I'm just getting older, that's all.' She'd never even considered she might get pregnant again – that part of her life seemed over forever.

'You're forty-three. Too young for menopause.'

'Not necessarily.'

'All the same. I'll feel better if you take a test.'

He wasn't serious, surely. It was so unlikely. 'I have to go to work, Conor.'

'We'll stop at the store and get one. You can pee on it there and then we'll know.' And he had done it, marched her to his car, driven her to Walgreens, found the pregnancy test aisle, bought one, and sent her off to the bleach-reeking loo. Not even allowing her to go home, to their beautiful separate bathrooms cleaned twice weekly by someone else. This action of doing it, unwrapping the test, awkwardly angling it beneath her, peeing a few drops, sent her back in time to 2000. The year of Adam's birth. She'd been so pleased that time, pregnant within two months of trying – another obstacle cleared with ease by champion life-hurdler Kate McKenna. But surely not this time. She couldn't be. It took her a long time to see the lines. Two lines. Yes, definitely two. She read the little paper leaflet again. Two.

Outside, Conor was impatient, checking his phone. 'Well?'

'Um ...' She just handed it to him, stained with her pee as it was. She thought she might pass out. The edges of her vision were blurry and the music on the tannoy seemed to fade in and out.

His face wiped out. White, featureless. He said, 'How could you let this happen?'

Maybe that was the beginning of the end, for her.

Kate had not even considered that she was now living in a country with a dystopian approach to women's rights. Back home, had she ever needed to end a pregnancy, it would have been easy. A quick trip to a clinic and the job was done. How did it work here? Even her Pill came via the studio health insurance, and lucky for her that she worked for a liberal coastal-elite company, because, she was learning, some big corporations were already trying to remove contraception from employees' plans. And it wasn't just six quid like a prescription in the UK, it was hundreds of dollars.

A tense night had passed after the test result, as Conor tried to figure out, pointlessly, how and when this might have happened. Had she been sloppy with her Pill? Drunk too much, had a stomach upset? As if it was only down to her. By the next day, he had already found a clinic, somewhere in Sherman Oaks, and made an appointment and was driving her there. He had applied all his speed and problem-solving ability to this, the growth of his child in her womb. There was a small niggle in the back of her mind, like a tiny hand pulling at her. Shouldn't they at least discuss it? He had no biological child now, and she had left hers. Irritating chemicals were flooding her body, images of a baby with his red hair, who she would love this time, who would be well-behaved and sweet. An angel-child, like Delia.

'Conor,' she tried, sitting in the car beside him. 'This has all been so fast.'

He glanced over. 'Isn't that for the best? You're already probably three months along. You're lucky we're in Cali – some states have a six-week limit.'

'Six weeks? But – you might not even know by then!'

'Exactly. It's the right-wing agenda, they want it all but banned, even if they can't outright overturn Roe v Wade. Though I'm sure they're going to try, if they win this next election.' A flash of admiration for him, how smart and informed he was. Was that the same as love? This man was taking her to abort their child. She couldn't help but think of Andrew, who would never have proposed such a thing, who would have dissolved with tearful joy at the sight of the pee-stained stick. Imagine Conor, driven and successful and handsome as he was, but softened by a child. Holding the baby over her hospital bed, smiling at her with love in his eyes.

She tried again. 'I just – I think we should at least talk.'

Conor pulled suddenly off the road, with a spin of the wheel that shocked her, and she braced herself against the side of the car. For a moment she thought – the baby. How stupid. It was the parking lot of a drive-in Starbucks. 'What?' he said. 'Talk, then.'

'It's just – after Trixie, you know … don't you want to at least think about it?'

He sneered. 'You must be joking, Kate. You, a terrible mother, want another child?'

Was that true? It hit her like a slap in the face. 'I – I'm not saying that, I just – want to talk about it. It's our baby, Conor. And now you – you don't ... ' Now he had no children, she meant, not biologically. Did he even care about such things?

It was a sentimental thing to say and she was rewarded with a scornful look. 'It's cells. Blood. I never even wanted a first child, and now I don't have one.'

'But ... ' She knew it was pointless. Yes, she had struggled with motherhood. But maybe here was a chance to get it right. Show that she was not a failure, a bad mother. It had been the other people involved who were the problem.

'You left your children, do I have to remind you?'

'No.' Did leaving your kids always mean you were a bad mother? Was there a world where it could be the best thing for them, where no mother at all was better than a bad one? She pressed her hands against the cold leather seat of the car. It was 100 degrees outside, but inside they were insulated, cut off. LA was like that.

'And Kirsty.' Conor had never said her daughter's name before, she didn't think. 'The thing she has, isn't that from your side of the family?' Kate had not even thought of that. Of course it was. 'The risk is huge, especially at your age. Surely you don't want that, another child with special needs.'

'But – there are tests now ... ' She only had a vague sense of this. She'd never planned to have another child, of course she hadn't. But now it had fallen into her lap, wasn't that a different matter?

'Kate.' He turned to look at her. 'I'm telling you, I won't do this. I can't force you not to have it, but if you do that's me out. For good. I'll pay for it but I won't be involved.' He paused, and

232

she could see him swallowing hard. 'Trixie – to have her, that was one thing. I didn't want her but then I – well. I'm not made of stone, whatever you may think. I loved her where I could. And to find out she isn't mine . . .'

There it was, her chance to get to him, comfort him for his loss, burrow inside to all the hidden parts of him she'd always sensed were there, never reached. She'd known he must feel something. He must love Trixie, to have cared for her all her life. He couldn't be so dead inside. It seemed like a trade-off. All she had to do was give up this child, and perhaps he would let her in, and they could love each other like she'd always wanted.

What a choice he was giving her, right here in this cracked parking lot in a city she had never expected to find herself living in. Stay with him, a man she kept thinking she'd worked out only to find out there were yet more levels, or have this baby, go through it all again, losing her body and her mind and her job, her friends, her life, and doing it alone in a foreign country this time, where her health insurance didn't cover maternity care. An overwhelming sense of pointlessness washed over her. She could not persuade him, she wouldn't even try. She could not overturn her life again for that. And he was right. She carried a genetic disease, and she was a terrible mother. It was not meant to be. 'OK. Fine.'

'Alright then.' He nudged the car out into traffic, and half an hour later they were at the clinic.

The first thing she saw were the protestors. Although she knew there was a huge and vocal anti-abortion movement in America, somehow she hadn't expected it. This was Los Angeles, one of the world's most liberal cities. She froze in the car. Conor was already out and glanced back, irritated. 'Ignore them. They're loons.'

233

She recalled one day years ago walking through London, passing the Marie Stopes clinic, shouldering aside a handful of protestors with nasty banners. But this was ... so many people. Fifty, sixty. They saw her and were on her. 'Your baby can feel pain!'

'Stop now, before you commit murder!' A vague impression of contorted faces, bodies in drab clothing, NHS-style glasses. A lot of middle-aged men, cream slacks, phone-holsters. Women too. Pictures of embryos, impressions of blood and mangled limbs. She started to pant with fear. Conor marched her through, like someone going on trial for murder. Which was how these people saw her. They had closed off her route to the door of the clinic, a nondescript glass-walled building, and she just wanted to turn and run, which was surely their intention and ...

Another group of people, behind the first. As Kate watched, the group – mostly women, some men – fanned out and made a kind of corridor for her. They were wearing bright red reflective tabards that said STEWARD on the back. Undercuts, tattoos, horn-rim glasses, kind and determined faces. She was surrounded by them. One woman, in a wheelchair, rolled herself with determination through the crowd, scattering protestors, and hooked Kate's arm in her strong and muscled one. 'It's OK,' she said. 'We have you. Ignore the lifers. It's just a bunch of nutjobs.'

That was how Kate first met Suzi, on the day she aborted her third child.

'The fetishisation of motherhood is one of the most subtle forms of patriarchy, Kate.' Suzi dipped a biscuit – a *cookie* – into a cup of coffee the size of a small bucket.

Kate's head was spinning. 'How do you mean?'

'Think about it – if having children is some kind of sacred fulfilment for women, no one can say it's plain hard work.'

'Oh.' When she came out of the clinic that day, parts of her body numb, like when you had a filling, she had seen a flyer on the ground. *Be a volunteer steward.* Someone had trodden on it, leaving a large dirty footrprint, but all the same Kate stooped – hard to do – and picked it up. They had been volunteers, the people who'd protected her, there as a buffer to the protestors, as a shield. How strange, when Kate's own thoughts about her abortion erred more to those of the other side. Of course she believed in a woman's right to choose, always had done. But had she chosen it, herself? Or had Conor done it for her? She'd never said anything to him, over the following week while she bled quietly into her clothes, but she had gone online and found the latest information session for stewards, and here she was. She'd almost turned away at the door – Kate was not a joiner, as the Bishopsdean support group had confirmed for her – but she had to do something with the rage that was still growing inside her, where the baby wasn't.

It was a shabby room, plastic chairs stacked around the walls, high dirty windows, a coffee urn on a folding table – Kate experienced the same feeling she'd had all those years ago in Bishopsdean, of wanting to turn on her heels and run. These weren't her people – there was not a highlight or a designer label in sight. But they were, weren't they? They had led her through the throng, their hands safe and sure on her body.

The first person she recognised, parked by the coffee, was her rescuer from that day. Kate smiled shyly. 'Hi – I'm – you helped me. At the clinic.'

Suzi was stocky, with a partially shaved head and tattoo sleeves. She'd had a leg amputated from untreated diabetes, after losing her health insurance and not being able to pay for her insulin. Kate had to ask her to repeat that, because how could it be true in a country like this, where you could buy ten-dollar coffees? Suzi, like poor Aimee but even more so, was miles away from Kate's former friends, those polite English women, or even the polished LA execs she sometimes got lunch with. She assumed at first Suzi was gay, although in fact she identified as pansexual. She exuded an air of calm confidence Kate found dizzying. Like she just didn't care what people, or more specifically men, thought of her. That, in itself, seemed a revolutionary act. On that first day she had just begun to speak, to tell Kate about herself and the pro-choice movement, and she had not stopped talking for close to ten minutes, another painful echo of Aimee, who'd poured out so many words, only to silence them forever. 'Motherhood is a job with impossible requirements. It's possible to love your children and still feel unable to look after them.'

It was the first time anyone had ever seemed to understand. It was complicated. There had been love, sometimes – hadn't there? – and there had been pain, and in the end the pain won. If she'd stayed, she might have hurt them, or herself, or both. Like Aimee. She had done it for them – or was that just a get-out clause? Because maybe she didn't love them at all? 'I left mine,' she heard herself say. 'In England. I have two children. I left them.' Suzi had taken this with the same equanimity with which she'd told Kate about her own tubal ligation, which she'd had to pay for herself because no one could believe a woman in her twenties didn't want children. The effect was extraordinary. Kate felt she could have told this woman, whom she'd only just met over coffee and doughnuts in a run-down community centre, any thought in her head. How was it some people could be that way, their lack of judgement leaching all the truth out of you? Old Kate, pre-Kirsty Kate, had been the most judgemental

236

of them all, sizing up people's clothes and haircuts and makeup, their jobs, the contents of their fridge. Now she had found herself miles from that, her old identity lost at sea. Maybe, just maybe, her people were not who she'd thought, because she was not who she'd thought.

Suzi crunched her cookie. 'I was like twenny. Abusive relationship, I got knocked up, I was in that damn abortion clinic soon as I could. The diabetes was already bad, and I thought another time might kill me, so I got my tubes done right after. Shit, I'm not cut out for kids.'

Something was welling up in Kate. 'I didn't want them. I thought I did, but I didn't.' Suzi was still nodding. Welcoming the confidence, almost driving Kate to compete, say the worst thing. 'I couldn't love them,' Kate said, admitting it in a rush. 'Not enough, anyway. The boy, he was always so angry, so difficult. And the girl – she's disabled. I'm not sure she even knows who I am.' Why was she using the present tense for her? Kirsty was in the past, with her old life. Kate was remembering small hands clutching at her. 'It was just so hard, coping with her needs. Knowing that she'd always be so, so ...' Suddenly she realised Suzi was disabled too. She'd always thought of disability as something all-encompassing, life-altering, but clearly it could be this too, just a woman who sometimes used a wheelchair and sometimes a crutch. She faltered, guilt-ridden, but Suzi only looked interested.

She said, 'But is it like as simple as, disabled and not disabled? Everyone has something, I think. Mental health, bad childhood, allergies ... you know. You don't have to, like, think of us as a different type of person.'

She'd never seen it that way before. 'I suppose. Yeah. But when I got pregnant this time – I mean, I was a bad mother. I was angry all the time, I thought about – I thought about

237

hurting myself, I . . . So – I guess it was right to have the abortion.' She was looking for validation, she realised. Of the choice that had not been hers, not really.

'It's the biggest myth there is,' said Suzi stridently. 'That they always love us, and we love them. You think of all those women who don't feel it, and they feel like shit, like they're freaks of nature. Just cos the chemicals in their brains aren't firing. Or they have like, like post-natal or something.'

Maybe she'd had post-natal depression after Kirsty, with such a difficult birth and what happened after? Certainly she had felt as if all hope had drained from the world, for the rest of her life. No one had ever even suggested it back then. Kate found she was shaking. She'd finally spoken the words she thought she'd never say, and Suzi had taken it in her stride. She felt like one of those French women after the war, tarred and feathered, laid out for all to see. But she couldn't feel bad either. Maybe those women didn't care. Maybe they were proud. Maybe they thought, *This is what I am. I won't lie so the rest of you can feel secure.*

She was fortunate, she now realised, a year on, to have got that abortion, to be living in a liberal city. There were women without her means who'd have to drive all day to get to the one clinic in their state, assuming they had a car and could get off work. It was too easy to say it was dystopian. Never one to call herself a feminist, while benefitting from it of course, she noticed things more and more now. She even enjoyed being politicised, aligning herself with what she saw as the side of good, in a country sliding hard towards opposite corners. The activist identity was an anchor, when she'd slipped all the others she'd once had, job, husband, children, nationality, name even. And perhaps it really was for the best, the abortion. Today, her T-shirt fit snugly over her

238

stomach and breasts – her body would surely not have recovered from a pregnancy in her forties. Besides, she had been no good at it, so why bring another child into the world to mess up even more, and one whose father would also be cold this time? No, it was for the best. It was just that she could not entirely put it out of her mind. The disappointment, that even conceiving their child – a miracle, in the circumstances – had not broken Conor down. Had not made him turn to her with love in his eyes, and open to her at last. If the loss of his daughter and their own baby had not managed it, maybe nothing would. Doing this, protesting for the right of other women to do what she hadn't really wanted to, helped in some obscure way. Choice. If she could convince herself she had chosen all of this, to be a mother in the first place, and then to leave England and be with Conor, marry him and not have his baby, perhaps she would feel better.

She surged forward with the crowd at the LA Women's March. She had lost sight of Suzi's chair long ago, her head lower than most people's. Her hands were sore carrying her banner, a piece of plywood with a bit of card taped around it, and she wondered what she'd do when she needed to pee. She had been handed it as they walked down Wilshire, past the fancy shops, and it made her hands smell of sawdust –a sense memory that took her back to visiting the butcher's shop with her mother as a child. What would her mother say about this? She'd never wanted a fuss. She'd taken her husband's name and given up work and waited on people all her life.

'Our bodies, our lives!' someone screamed, and the women whooped and cheered. How strange it was, to walk down the middle of the road where traffic normally roared. To pass shops and landmarks so slowly, moving at the speed of the crowd. The staff from chi-chi stores and restaurants out on their doorsteps, staring at the women, some bemused, some applauding.

Overhead, the cloudless LA sky, like a flat lid. Conor had not wanted her to come today – he wasn't political, refused to pass judgement on this country that had let him reinvent himself. There was something unseemly about anger, he thought. It was yet another wedge between them. That brief time before their wedding, when she felt she'd known him, that he had loved her, it seemed a dream now. He wouldn't talk about Trixie, about the abortion, about anything.

So this was all she had left. Walking with strangers, angry about something she couldn't really formulate. The protest was orderly. A few whistles and loudspeakers, but camaraderie, love. Sadness. Squeezed hands and worried smiles. A few people openly weeping. The older women, grey-haired, who'd fought this in the seventies, and here it was back again. The little girls on shoulders, who didn't know yet what lay ahead. Kate thought of Trixie at college, where the girls starved themselves and gave blowjobs like they were shaking hands. As someone whipped out a loudspeaker and began to honk about the election and women's rights and Roe v Wade, Kate experienced a moment of dissonance. How had she ended up here, in an another country, trying on all these different lives for size? It was dizzying, sometimes, the choices open to her, the freedom even in her marriage to Conor. Once you had left your family, your children, you knew nothing could ever really hold you down again, and sometimes that was the most terrifying thing Kate could think of.

Adam, present day

Adam was lying in his bed, looking at the damp stains on the ceiling, listening to Barry shower next door. Why did he make so much noise? What was he doing in there? Or was that a question Adam didn't want answered?

He had, of course, considered the possibility that one day he would get a girl pregnant. When you had as much sex as he did, it was almost inevitable. He was baffled by his friends who did their best to wheedle girls out of using condoms. Why be so stupid? Why risk ending up caring for some wailing kid, paying for it, yoked together with its mother, both of you hating each other, and your kid hating you too? No thanks. At the age of twelve, he'd asked if he could have a vasectomy, but it wasn't allowed. His stupid father, saying *You'll change your mind, Ads*. And now look. Delia was pregnant, and the baby would probably have what Kirsty had. He imagined the two of them, stuck in some boxy house in the suburbs, full of Ikea furniture, the baby crying and crying and pooping and pooping, staring at each other in the frazzle of 4am, realising their love had been squashed, trampled all over by this child they'd made exist. Delia's face rough from tiredness and disappointment, like his mother's had been. Himself hiding away in some garage, telling himself he was still a musician, only to have to stop and heat up baked beans or take the bins out, like his father all those years.

She must have known this could happen. The thought crossed his mind, lying alone in his small, spartan room. The only colour in it came from her, some art prints she'd bought him that sat propped against the wall, unframed, a green cardigan she'd left behind the last time she was here, months before. That must have been when it happened. Delia, Delia. Had she done this on purpose? He thought back to how it was between them, the madness of each other's bodies, the rush of being fully alive in a moment, so strong it almost knocked you out. Had they been careful? Not especially. Even he could get carried away, and they were young, only just in their twenties.

241

This was supposed to happen. The human body was designed to get you carried away, drugged by each other, aiming to make a baby, and they had. God, they were stupid. He knew. They both knew what could happen, what was twisted up in his DNA.

At least something could still be done. It couldn't be that far along, her body was still flat and slender. And she'd agree, she'd have to agree. She couldn't want to risk it, what were the chances, one in two? That was insane. There were tests they could do now. There'd been no warning for Kirsty, nothing showing up on the scan. That wouldn't happen now, twenty years later. And even if – he let himself imagine the worst here – even if Delia had inherited her mother's near-suicidal selflessness, he didn't have to be involved, did he? He could just leave, like Kate had. Just refuse. No one could make him pay out his love, his time – the most precious thing, worth more than money. If the worst happened, he would only lose his family. And Delia. He'd lose Delia, any future they might have had, a funky loft flat in the centre of town, which perhaps he had let himself think about once or twice. But never kids. Not with the thing in his genes.

But what now? She was pregnant already, something was growing to life in her. It had to be stopped, and Olivia had vanished, and Andrew was too weak to put his foot down, and both of them would support Delia in whatever she wanted. There was only one person who'd be on Adam's side – he was sure of this. His mother.

Adam had spent several hours like this, moping and ruminating and googling tests and abortion and fathers' rights, before he heard an unfamiliar noise, and realised his phone, usually always on silent, was ringing. He leapt for it. Delia? No, it was his aunt Elizabeth. Weird. She hadn't heard about the pregnancy somehow, had she? Adam didn't have much time for his aunt.

After Kate left, she'd tried to keep the connection up, with such an obvious sense of duty he bet she marked it off in a calendar, and now he rarely saw her or her annoying children, his cousins, or even his mother's parents. They were scared of London and Adam had long since refused to go to their tiny house in Birmingham that always smelled of soup. But it was a distraction from the endless prowling of his thoughts, and so he answered.

'Adam?' Her voice was high and childish, though she was in her forties. He hated frilly Insta-mums like her.

'Yeah?' She couldn't possibly know. Likely she'd no idea Delia existed; she had never even met Olivia, as far as he knew, since Livvie hadn't come on the occasional excruciating trips to Birmingham his dad had dragged them on. It was all too embarrassing for anyone to look directly at. So what could she want to tell him, and why would she call him out of the blue, on the very day his life was turning upside down?

Adam, 2017

'Well that's it then. It's all over. That's it.'

Olivia had actual tears in her eyes as she reached to mute the television, showing footage of the ill-attended windswept inauguration. She had chilled out a lot over the past ten years, was less uptight about drinking and snacks and had even allowed her no-TV rule to slide, thank fuck, except all she ever wanted to watch was rolling news, a live scene-by-scene play of how completely on fire the world they'd left him was. It was all very well for them to wring their hands over Brexit, and now America, but he was seventeen. He hadn't even gone to uni yet and this was the world he had to grow up in.

243

Olivia's tears were irritating him. She'd be alright, she was rich and posh. 'It's America,' he grunted, from the saggy armchair he threw himself into when forced to spend 'family time'. 'I don't know what you're so upset about.'

She blinked at him. 'But the world, darling. It's taken such a dark turn.'

He wanted to say the world had always been dark, just look at Kirsty and his mum's friend who'd killed herself from lack of support, and Olivia just didn't know that because she was privileged, but in truth he felt laden down by it too. Everything was shit, ruined by climate change and pollution, and now the adults of the world had to go and do all this.

Before this, he had to admit, things had been a bit better for years. Sandra had found Adam a therapist, some friend of hers from her degree, a twenty-something man with a hipster beard and glasses who called him 'pal'. He didn't mind Laurence, actually. Mostly they talked about music and films, and sometimes Adam would come out of the session and realise he'd actually talked about Kirsty or his mum or why he scratched up his own arms, and feel tricked but also think, fair play, mate, you did your job. He'd settled down at school too, stopped causing havoc. He was angry but he wasn't stupid – if he didn't pass his exams he'd never get away from this boring town with its dead-eyed commuters. He'd stopped cutting himself, except when things got a bit too much, and then he just hid it better. People asked too many questions when they saw the scars, it wasn't worth it. Anyway, everyone did it now, it was becoming basic. And he was seventeen and soon he'd be out of this dump and starting his new life.

The rest of the family, if you could call them that, had settled down too. Kirsty could speak to them a bit now, ask for things, respond to them – or so his dad and Olivia thought, Adam

244

wasn't convinced yet. His dad was working hard and actually seemed to be writing a book this time, after years of talking about it, and Olivia, thrilled by the success of Kirsty's speech therapy, after many hard years, hadn't had an episode since a wobble in 2014 when his mother had sent divorce papers from America. Adam wasn't supposed to know about this, but he'd long ago learned to find out what he needed by snooping. His dad didn't even think to put a password on his computer, so really Adam could not be blamed. And Olivia even saw Delia sometimes, though hardly ever at the house, something Adam knew was his fault. Lately, he'd been thinking about Delia in a kind of different way, not just as a perfect little angel who everyone preferred to Adam, but as something else. It was confusing.

On the TV screen, there were repeated images of people open-mouthed, shouting in silent rage. Everyone was so angry, and Adam understood that; he'd been angry since birth. 'I'm going to bed.' He pushed himself out of the chair with what felt like more effort than usual and trudged up the stairs. Was nothing ever going to get better? Kirsty with no clue what was happening to the world, his father and Olivia sitting apart on the sofa every night as if a ghost had pushed between them, and it was true in a way, the ghost of his mother.

His father was in his 'office', tapping away at his book behind a closed door. Adam didn't know what it was about, since Andrew wouldn't talk about it and had hidden it somewhere on his hard drive where it couldn't be found by, say, a nosy teenager. Probably crap. He wandered the upstairs rooms. In Olivia's, plain and spartan, was a picture of Delia, framed. She was on a horse, her fair hair in a plait, tight jodhpurs. He picked it up, leaving a smeary fingerprint. Set it down askew. It was depressing. Olivia had lived here ten years and it still looked like a guest room.

He heard a door open, then the bathroom light go on and its lock slide back. His dad'd be in there at least ten minutes, taking advantage of a quiet moment to scroll through Twitter, no doubt. Adam slipped into the so-called office, where, as far as he could see, his father spent most of his time playing Candy Crush and googling things like 'problem teen' and 'signs of ADHD'. Sometimes he put the signs on, just for a laugh. A jiggle of the mouse brought up what Andrew was working on, not yet shut down. Something called *Your Hand in Mine*. Not a bad title, Adam had to admit, if soppy. He scanned the words on screen.

The day we realised we were wrong about Kirsty is etched on my memory. My son was behind me on the stairs – Dad, is she really doing it? he asked. And I was stunned into silence. Because it seemed like she was.

Shit! It was a non-fiction book, about Kirsty learning to sign (which was all thanks to Olivia and Sandra, not his dad, but of course the old fool would take credit for it). He read a few more lines. It wasn't bad. Shocker. Reluctantly, Adam had to admit that 'stunned into silence' was about right for how he'd felt that day. You grow up your whole life being told your only sister can't understand you, will never talk to you, has no idea what's going on, then there she is making the word *horse*. Other signs came next – hungry, daddy, toilet, dog. Love. It had been a strange time of everything suddenly getting better, a time of miracles.

He bet Andrew had no backup for his files. He could delete it right now and it would be lost, and likely his father wouldn't even know it was Adam. He'd assume it had been eaten by some vague computer failure.

His finger hovered. Shit. No, he couldn't do it. It would crush the idiot. What if this book was actually good and he managed to get it published? The world tilted slightly at the thought, his father doing something, creating something. Not failing.

He went out, leaving everything as he'd found it. The door to Kirsty's room was open, her nightlight turning with its slow, slightly sinister music. She was awake, holding her hands up to make patterns in the shadows. 'Hey Kirsty.' Stupid. She couldn't understand speech, could she? But she did look over. He went to her bed, which had high sides and bars to stop her falling out. She was dressed in a fleecy sleepsuit, like a baby, though she was fifteen now. She was tiny still. People usually thought she was seven or eight at most.

How strange it was that he could get through to her. Such a simple thing, to form a word and be understood, but they'd never thought she could manage it. He remembered his mother crying in the kitchen, clutching her face in her hands, because Kirsty would never say mummy. She could say it now – she signed *daddy* to Andrew – but Kate had not stuck around to know that. He had picked up some of the hand signs from watching Sandra, who he quite liked. She had three sons who were into everything, drugs and minor theft and vandalism, and she smoked like a chimney, but all the same he thought she was one of the smartest people he'd ever met. Much smarter than his artistic-pretensions father, who was enjoyably rattled by her. Cautiously, feeling stupid, he shaped his hands into an easy sign, arms crossed over his chest. *I love you*. Kirsty wouldn't know, and no one else could see. He only did that one because it was easy to remember. How could you love someone who barely knew who you were? Her unfocused eyes probably hadn't even taken it in. Sometimes he doubted it all. Just because she could copy or repeat a few simple signs, that didn't mean she knew him, or understood more than the basics.

But look. She was raising her hands, doing it too. That was the same sign. Oh God. She was saying she loved him. Did she really? Adam almost stumbled back against the door. He went out, slamming it angrily, then opening it again a fraction. Kirsty's gaze had drifted back to her lights. Was it just copying? Or was she really saying it to him? Had she understood, all this time, and really known him? Seen all his outbursts, his cruelties, his tricks and meanness, and still loved him, her brother? Somehow, he wasn't sure if he could bear that.

In his own room, Adam threw himself on his bed and opened his laptop. MacBook, top of the range, a guilt present for his birthday. His notifications buzzed with messages from the various girls he was running at the moment. He approached it a bit like farming – some would be almost ready to bear fruit, some would be on their way to the bin, worn out, and some he'd just be starting to flirt with. But tonight he wasn't interested in that, the girls he had learned to use as an outlet instead of losing his temper and acting up at school and slashing his own skin. He went to the site he opened so often he just kept it in his tabs – *West Coast Wake Up*. He wanted to hear his mother's thoughts on what had happened in her adopted country.

Adam was thirteen when he found his mother. Olivia being ineffectual and Andrew oblivious, it was very easy for a sly and clever child to get up to anything, and Adam was both. He'd finally got his own phone after years of lobbying, and even though his father was supposed to check it regularly, Adam knew they wouldn't be able to rein him in. At first he hadn't known what to search for – naked women, his weird friend Barry suggested. Boobies. But something stopped Adam. Maybe some vague idea it was sad, that he wanted to see boobs for the first time in the flesh. Instead, he found himself typing in a name from the past, a ghost he had never named but thought of only as a concept – *Kate McKenna*. He'd learned from the divorce papers he'd found that this had been her maiden name, like a secret identity he'd never known.

He'd waited as the computer did its work. Some stuff came up about her old life, before him. She'd been pretty, smiling in her fake-looking way, getting some naff award, as if being on local TV was something to be proud of. Anyway, Adam had no interest in the world before he was born. He clicked on the images tab, the usual random internet scurf, along with other pictures of her looking happy. Before him. Before Kirsty. Somehow, he knew it was really him who'd changed her. Then his eye was caught by something – his mother with short hair. Waved to her ears, and streaked blonde. He hadn't seen her like this. He clicked on the photo and was taken to an American celebrity page. It was a gallery from some stupid awards event, all teeth and tan, and he had to hunt to find it, but there it was – *Kate McKenna of West Coast Wake Up at the Tropical Tans TV awards*. His mother was in America. She was in America, and she was back on TV.

That had been four years ago, and he'd searched for her on average once a day, every day, for all that time.

Now, he refreshed the page until a new video clip appeared. She looked different than in the pictures he had of her, which Olivia was careful to remind him were OK to look at. Thinner, shinier all over, her face and hair and yes, her teeth too. His heart was racing as he pressed play, as if he was going to talk to her on the phone or something. As if she could see him. She looked troubled on the screen, not her usual fake smile. 'Well viewers. What can I say? I'm not American, and I can't vote in this country. And my own country has made, let's say, some pretty big errors of judgement this year. And it's not for me to say who you elect. But I know some of you will be scared, and hurt, and sad tonight, and I want to acknowledge that, and say it's alright. I've had moments like that in my life. Where you

249

feel like all hope is gone and you can't see a way to take a single step in the dark. What's important is that you do something. Anything. Even if it's the wrong thing. Anything's better than just . . . stagnating.'

He switched to Twitter, which normally he disdained because it was full of arguing millennials, searched for her name, saw the clip was being shared over and over. *Finally someone has the balls to say it. The moment Californian TV anchor says what we've all been thinking.* His mother was out there in the world, not just a figment of his imagination. He wondered if when she made this statement, she'd been thinking about the decision to leave him, if that had been for her a choice to do something rather than lie down and die. He wondered if she meant she'd made the wrong decision, doing that. Leaving Kirsty, and Andrew, and him.

A soft knock at the door and he quickly minimised his screen. Olivia, with cocoa and a fan of homemade biscuits on a tray. 'I thought you might be feeling worried.'

'I'm not. It's not even going to affect me.'

'No. But these kinds of moods can be . . . catching. The anxiety.'

'I'm OK.' He looked at the little display, the tray with a steaming mug and biscuits crunchy with sugar, the way she'd even folded a napkin under the tray, and for some reason, he wanted to cry. She was too good to them all, so good it was painful. She took care, Olivia. Wasn't that what a mother was supposed to do? And yet his own never had. That wasn't fair, exactly. She had fed him and clothed him and made him do his homework. She just hadn't loved him. She wouldn't have left if she had.

He decided to give Olivia a sop in return. 'I suppose, yeah, it is a bit worrying. What kind of world there'll be when I finish uni. What kind of job I'll get.'

She sat down on his bed and tentatively patted his arm. 'Of course, darling. It's perfectly natural to think that. But you know, we felt the same at your age. There's always something to worry about. I shouldn't have been so down about it all – there's always good things. Look at your sister, how much she's learned! It's more than I ever hoped for.'

'Yeah.'

'And, you know. We'll always take care of you. Your father and I.'

Money, she meant. He didn't want her to think that was all she had to offer. 'The music, you know. I really want to do it. Give it a try.' Olivia had bought him a guitar for Christmas one year, and it was one of the few things Adam had stuck at, strumming alone in his bedroom for hours.

'And you should. You're very talented.' She would say that. Praise from Olivia, who always saw the good in him, meant very little. Praise from his mother, who he remembered as cross and exacting – now that would count. But she would likely never know about his music. Unless he got really famous, and that annoyed him, to think so transparently. *I'll have a hit single then Mummy will love me!*

He bent to pick up the cocoa from the tray, blew on it. 'Thanks, Livvie. For this. Thank you.' And watched the pleasure flush over her, from this absolute bare minimum of decent behaviour, and was ashamed.

Andrew, present day

Being Andrew, he massively overthought the meeting with the producer. Conor Ryan. His ex-wife's husband! Would they

251

talk about it, or pretend it wasn't true? Part of Andrew felt that indeed it couldn't be true, because Kate was still *his* wife, wasn't she? The divorce, done at a distance via lawyers, didn't seem real. She had initiated it without ever contacting him herself, and even that had been strange – an indication she was still out there in the world. America. California. He hadn't told Adam – better to let the boy forget. Presumably she'd divorced him then because she'd wanted to get remarried, to this Conor.

He'd stayed in bed a long time, eating his breakfast, smearing ketchup on the covers and feeling sorry for himself. Getting ready in the hotel room felt lonely somehow, no Olivia to tweak his lapels and smooth his hair, tell him he looked smart. He'd decided to wear jeans and a shirt, a jacket with no tie. They weren't formal, were they, these LA people? He slicked his hair down, nervously, that one cowlick that always refused to sit flat, and looked mournfully at his phone. Nothing. Had he gone this long without speaking to Olivia ever, at least since Kate went? He didn't think so. They lived together. They slept in separate rooms and didn't have sex. Of course, a lot of married couples didn't either. So what did it even mean, to be married? Did it mean you became family? He considered Delia his daughter, in a way, and his heart wrenched when he thought of her, alone and scared, having a baby with Adam of all people. He'd messaged her, but there was no reply from anyone, not Olivia, not Delia, not his son.

Andrew held onto the wall as a wave of self-pity swept him. He should be happy. He should have a smiling photogenic family gathered around him, toasting him with champagne. Good old dad, the published author. Meeting with Hollywood producers! Getting overseas deals! He'd sweep them all out to dinner at Hawksmoor, finally feel happy for once in his life. He wouldn't though, would he? His guilt permeated everything.

That Kirsty wasn't here, and without her there would be no book. That Kate had left. That he'd somehow let Olivia down all these years, and he didn't even quite know how.

'I'm off then,' he said, to the empty air, and felt quite silly. He'd been obsessively watching the time on the clock, not wanting to be too early or too late, but now it was time to leave the hotel and go to another hotel to meet his ex-wife's husband. Would Kate be there as well? He had no idea. Into the lift, catching sight of his ageing face again. God. He had to get a grip – this was supposed to be the crowning glory of his life. But all he could think of was Olivia, Delia. Olivia. Adam. That he might be losing what remained of his family too. Where the hell was Olivia?

He walked the few streets to the other hotel, noticing as he went through the revolving walnut doors that it was nicer than his, a different layer of nice altogether, hushed carpets and uniformed porters and a gentle hum of well-being. The tinkle of a grand piano. 'Sir?' A young woman in a suit was at his elbow, eastern European accent.

'Um, yes, hi, I'm here to meet Conor Ryan? He's a producer. From Hollywood.' *Oh shut up Andrew, you berk.*

'Of course, sir, Mr Ryan's in the lounge.' She indicated the way, and Andrew bumbled over. He was too hot in his jacket and already felt clammy, should he take it off? Or would that only reveal sweat stains? He paused half-in and half-out of it and felt her eyes on him. He grinned, a rictus.

There, that must be him. The kind of man Andrew always envied, comfortable in his space, even if it was public. He wore jeans and a light cotton jumper, one leg resting on the other at right angles, revealing snazzy socks. An expensive watch. How could he look so fresh and rested, when he was literally just off a transatlantic flight? First class, probably. Andrew had never even been in business. Overseas travel wasn't possible with Kirsty, of course. The man looked up and saw Andrew, who hurriedly extracted his other arm from the jacket and moved forward. 'Hi! Hi! Conor, is it . . . I'm – Andrew?'

'Of course, I recognise you.' Soft Irish accent, more pronounced in person than on Zoom. They shook hands, and Andrew worried his was sweaty. 'Can I get you coffee?'

'Oh – yes, thank you.' Andrew sat on the opposite sofa, which was very squishy, and worried he'd fall into its depths. A different suited girl came over.

'I'll have another cortado, and . . . Andrew? Anything?'

His mind was blank. A menu would have helped, but that was gauche. What was a cortado? 'A latte?' Was that too feminine? He had an obscure sense of scrabbling for power like he was scrabbling to stay upright on the sofa. The woman smiled and went to get it. Silence fell. 'Um – I'm so pleased about the option.' Andrew stretched his face into a smile.

'Me too, me too. I just loved it when I read it. Then I realised – the name. I knew it.'

Oh. They were just going to talk about it then? 'Right. Right.'

'But I saw it would make a wonderful movie, and you know, I really feel the personal link, it will make all the difference. So it can be done sensitively. I hope you agree?'

Andrew couldn't think how to even start processing this. It was all very crazy, the web of connections between total strangers. His mind jumped back to Olivia. Where could she be? With her parents, perhaps? But she hated it there, though she'd never have said so. A hotel? She would baulk at spending money on herself, surely. Would she manage alone? It was years since she'd been anywhere by herself. He wanted to check his phone, but Conor was already watching him, as if he'd missed something. 'Sorry. Yes, well, it depends on . . . things.'

'On Kate?' Conor said calmly. The name of his wife, of Andrew's wife too. It was so strange. Was Kate here in the hotel? He resented it suddenly, the way she could upturn his life, gain the upper hand, after all these years gone. 'She was . . . surprised, yes. But I believe she'll come round when she sees how well it can be done.'

'Can she stop it? If she doesn't?'

Conor shifted in his seat, his expensive watch rattling. 'Well. Let's hope it doesn't come to that.' Andrew was totally floored by this dilemma, and just sat in silence for a moment. Was he being unfair to Kate, by writing this book? Imagine if they got embroiled in legal issues, that was the worst thing he could think of, the fuss, the guilt. Luckily, the efficient girl came back then with his coffee, and one for Conor too, plus a little plate of round shortbread, glistening with sugar. Definitely nicer than his hotel.

Conor smiled at the girl as she withdrew. Then he snapped back into business mode. 'Let's talk film roles. Tell me about your son. About Adam.'

Adam, 2018

'Oh my God, you need to leave me alone or I'm gonna break something. I mean it.'

His father pushed his glasses up his nose. 'It's just . . . we should talk about it, no?'

'What's the point?' He hunched down in the seat of the car. 'We always knew I had it.'

'Well, it was fifty-fifty, so . . .'

'And I have it. So. I wasn't going to reproduce anyway.'

255

'But all the same, Ads, it must be ... hard.' They were nearing the house now, after the short car trip from the hospital, where he'd heard what he had been telling himself he was going to hear. He carried the gene that made Kirsty how she was. Meaning if he had a kid, they could be that way too.

He slammed the door and got out almost before his father had parked, stomping into the house. He didn't want anyone to talk to him or look at him, but there was his sister in her wheelchair, now sixteen, though she still couldn't talk, or feed herself, or go to the toilet. Yes, she could sign a few words, but she was never going to grow up, not properly. She was dressed up, in a pink flouncy skirt, because today was Olivia's fortieth birthday, and despite no one wanting it, least of all Olivia, his father had insisted on throwing a party for her. Olivia was not to lift a finger – not even to know who was invited – and even Adam could see this would cause her anxiety. She was standing in the hall as they went in, hands wringing together, face stricken. Dopey Dad must have texted her the news. She too was wearing some kind of flowery dress, and behind her Adam could see bunting, and flowers, and dishes from the caterer – he remembered his mother once sneering at people who didn't cook for their own parties. He felt a stone of guilt in his stomach – he had ruined Olivia's day with his bad news. He should have waited to get it, moved the appointment, but his dad had insisted, they both had.

'Oh Ads.'

'For fuck's sake! Will you two just fuck off and stop feeling sorry for me! I don't want kids anyway! Look at the shitty parents I have for role models!' He meant her too, of course, and she knew it.

She took a step back, her face clouding over. 'Right. OK. It's terrible timing – we can cancel the party, of course ...'

'No. Don't be stupid.'

'But darling, you don't . . .'

'Get it into your head, I don't care! Have your stupid party, this makes no difference to me.' He just wanted to be away from them and their pity. It was the worst thing he could imagine, letting them see he felt anything but rage or contempt. He pounded up the stairs away from them, kicking his shoes off so they bounced down the steps behind him. One of Olivia's stupid rules, no shoes on carpets. He slammed his door and lay on his single bed. Babyish. He'd already slept with three girls – it was easy when you knew what buttons to press, which ones were the most insecure, who just wanted to hear they were desired. He'd been careful about condoms, more careful than any boy he knew. He'd always known there was a chance this shit was in his DNA. And yes, he was a carrier, they'd told him today, some annoying pretty doctor with a soft sympathetic voice and a huge engagement ring, but what was the big deal, he'd always thought he must be? He looked up at his ceiling, the old star stickers he'd scraped off two years ago, then secretly missed their soft glow. He carried the gene. Any kids of his might be like Kirsty. Big deal. He wasn't going to have any anyway.

Adam was eighteen. He had a place at a medium-good university to study Politics – it was stupid too, but he liked the pointless rage it generated. And no way was he going to apply to Oxford or something, though his teachers had pleaded with him to. What message would that send to the adults in his life, Olivia and Andrew and his teachers and irritating grandparents? He didn't want them thinking they'd done a good job. They refused to give up on him, no matter how cruel he was. Their own fault, really.

'What's up with you?' said a voice from his doorway. There she was, the one girl who had never forgiven him and usually refused to speak to him, even on the various awkward occasions they'd had 'family lunch' over the years. Delia. She had never come to stay again after the wasp had stung her, and when Adam thought about that a strange shaky feeling came over him. He'd done that. Kept Olivia and her kid apart, although Olivia never seemed to blame him. He'd wanted to be blamed. Delia obviously did, since she'd never again so much as looked him in the face, and so she was the only woman, apart from his mother, who really intrigued him. He googled her sometimes when he was bored. Delia Addison. She wasn't on Facebook, typical, but there were a few articles about her in the local press, piano competitions she'd won or dance recitals as a teenager, the prize she got for an essay on The World I Want to Live In. She was such a good girl. Adam wanted very much to change that.

He sat up. 'Nothing.'

'Well that's not true. I heard Olivia talking about it. I'm sorry.' She didn't sound very sorry.

'Doesn't matter. Can you shut the door?'

Ignoring his signals, Delia actually came in and sat on his bed. Adam froze – normally he'd be very happy to be on a bed with a pretty blonde girl in a short denim dress showing her long pale legs, but this was weird. She was Olivia's daughter. 'Look, you can say when things suck. Sometimes it helps.'

'What would you know about it?' he snarled.

She smoothed down the duvet cover, her hair hanging over her face. 'Well, my mum won't live with me, and I don't even know who my father was. So you've got the mum who fucked off, and your sister's – well, I know it's hard – but I've got that. I reckon we're about even.'

He blinked; he'd never heard her swear before. 'But my dad's so fucking square. So wet.'

She tutted. 'You don't see how good he is. Being the same

258

every day, that's something, you know. Mum was totally nuts before he calmed her down. She'd hardly even see me, she was so afraid I'd get hurt.'

'I guess that's – hard.'

'You've no idea. Why do you think I do all this stuff – riding, and studying, and winning prizes? At least you know your dad won't leave you, however bad you are. Me, I have to work for it.'

There was maybe two feet of space between them, and he was edging away without quite knowing why. As if he was afraid of her. 'You really don't know who your dad was?' He was intrigued by the idea of saintly Olivia having a past. He'd never actually wondered before who Delia's father was.

'Nah. Someone married is all I know.'

'Huh.'

She smiled, a sly and ironic smile he'd never seen on her before. 'I know. Mum was a slut.'

He couldn't help it. Delia, the good little girl, saying these things, was so unexpected. He burst out laughing, which brought his father to the door, half in and half out of a tie. He looked confused to see them in the same room, though Delia was sitting decorously at the end of the bed, feet on the floor and legs crossed. 'Oh. Are you ready, Ads?'

'What are you expecting, black tie? I'll change my shirt.' Delia wouldn't stay for that, would she? A strange shiver went through him. But no, she stood up, gathered her hair up over one shoulder. Switched back to her good-girl persona, which up until about three seconds ago he'd thought was all there was.

'I'll come down and help, Andrew.' After she left, Adam and his father looked at each for a moment in confusion, defensiveness, fear. Then Adam stood up and shut the door in his dad's face.

When he went down, Olivia was hovering. Her eyes were kind but red. 'Sorry,' he muttered. 'Didn't mean it.'

259

'That's alright. Whatever you feel right now is alright, Adam.'

'I don't feel anything.'

'That's OK too.'

People had already arrived, standing in awkward groups on the patio, holding flute glasses of what they were calling champagne, but which wasn't actually. Adam had a vague idea that when he went to university he'd become a massive snob, maybe get into whiskey or something. Use it as a yardstick to judge people by. He could already hear Sandra outside, talking loudly about bunions.

Delia was standing at the door, greeting people politely, taking their jackets. Adam sidled over. 'This is so shit,' he hissed to her. She smiled tightly.

'It's for Mum. Just make an effort, she does enough for you.'

A couple were coming in now, old, like in their fifties, the woman bony and angular, the man tall, with a loud Scottish voice. 'Young Adam, is that you? You've shot up!'

Why did old people think this was an original statement? 'Yeah. Who are you?'

Delia shot him a look but the man laughed. 'David McGregor. I work with Olivia at the TV station. And this is my wife, Elaine.' Elaine pressed out a paper-thin smile. He vaguely remembered this man, Adam thought, though with something like dislike – why? Of course, he would have worked with his mother as well. Her boss and Olivia's boss. It was strange to meet a new person who'd known her, when she was so long gone – part of him wanted to ask what she'd been like at work, was it true she was really good on screen like she'd said, or was she deluding herself? But no, it must have been true, she had a show in LA now.

'Drinks are over there,' said Delia. 'Mum's just gone outside, such a lovely day! Have a good time.' Adam shot a look back at her – *faker*. She gave a slight shake of her head, making her fair hair flick, so he could smell her shampoo. It was the same one Olivia used, confusingly.

The wife had marched off, but the man was lingering. 'You'll have to forgive me, but I can't place you, love.' To Delia. Charming smile.

'Oh! I'm her daughter. I don't think we've met. Delia.' Delia put out her hand, being well brought up.

Adam had spent most of his life trying to predict his mother's moods, and then Olivia's. So he noticed the man's reaction to this – slight tightening of his hand on hers, jerk of the bushy eyebrows. 'Oh! You're – ah, of course. I didn't realise you would be ... well, it's nice to meet you at last!'

'You too. Drinks over there, do have fun.' The man went, but Adam saw him look back at Delia, pale and rattled. And the germ of an idea began to sprout in his head. Could it be? When did Livvie start at *Look South*? He had the vague idea it was before his mum, who'd got the job just after having him. And Delia was a year younger than him so ...

'Oh! David.' He heard Olivia's voice from round by the kitchen island. 'I didn't know that you – I'd no idea you were coming! How lovely!' Her tone went up and down several octaves.

Delia hadn't noticed anything, it seemed. She was walking away, heading for the glasses of what she called 'fizz'. But Adam saw Olivia's face, turned the colour of the semifreddo melting on the counter – stupid name, it was just ice cream – and he knew his hunch had been right.

Olivia looked over at him, visibly collecting herself, fumbling her hands in her dress. 'Darling, do come outside, there's no need to answer the door. You'll never guess what Kirsty just did – Sandra's wearing a T-shirt with a pig on it, and she made

261

the sign for it! She only learned that one for the first time last week. It's amazing. She's amazing, she really is.'

'We just met your boss,' said Adam, stirring. 'That David guy? Said he'd never seen Delia before.'

'Oh.' Her eyes went wide with fear. Adam knew he could push it, make a scene, tell Delia in front of everyone this was quite possibly her father – clearly, he knew she'd existed, though he hadn't expected her to be here, since Olivia had kept her discreetly out of sight all these years. He could ruin this man's marriage, ruin his life, and Olivia's. Damage whatever fragile trust Delia had in her mother. He could do all that.

But no. Not today. He took Olivia's arm, unheard of for him. 'Come on, let's get you something to eat. It's your birthday, take it bloody easy for a change.'

Kate, present day

Family was like a time machine. As soon as she stepped into that house – tired from the flight on which she hadn't slept a second, despite the flat-lay bed – it was like being thirteen again. When they arrived in London Conor strode away with his luggage, towards the car that would be waiting for him in Arrivals. Humiliated, Kate had called him back. 'What am I supposed do to?'

'You're your own person, Kate.' What he always said. But did that have to mean he couldn't care for her at all? Did that have to mean the yawning loneliness of total independence?

'Can I at least ride into town with you? I'm taking a train north.' She'd looked it up in the airport before they left, with trepidation, as if planning a journey across some developing country. It was very expensive, the train, at such short notice – how could normal people afford it?

'I'm not stopping you.' What did that mean? How could he be so closed off? Why was he like this? She thought again of that brief interlude, the years when they'd almost had each other, practically nothing between them, and then Alanna had dropped her bombshell and he'd closed off the tiny portal in his heart that had only been open to her and to Trixie. Then he'd made her have the abortion and she wasn't sure she would ever forgive him for that. She was ashamed of this feeling, given her pro-choice beliefs, but all the same, extremely aware every March that the baby would be a year older. Six, now. It hurt inside, somewhere old and boring and aching, that he had not allowed her this second chance, had not loved her enough to try. And now he had done something even worse, optioned the story of her worst pain as if it was fiction. She would visit her parents, accept whatever recriminations she had to face, and then she would travel to London and try to stop this film however she could.

The car journey into central London had been interminable, grinding in traffic past endless houses, shops, lives she would never touch. She'd always hated that feeling, like being in a bubble where you couldn't reach anyone. She was stale and tired, despite freshening up in the first-class lounge at Heathrow. Conor had buried himself in emails, ignoring her until the driver pulled up outside Euston station, which now looked totally different, half-demolished. 'So – I'll see you later?'

'You know where I'm staying.' He didn't look up from his phone.

She didn't know what that meant either. It was crazy, but she wasn't about to ask and lose the game of chicken they'd been playing since they flew the opposite way across the Atlantic, fifteen years before. She got out, smiled awkwardly as the driver opened the door for her, dragged her little case through the shabby terminal. She'd not been on a train, or any form of public transport, since she left the UK, and was almost relieved to find it still shonky, with an unexplained twenty-minute delay. Kate, having dieted for years, had been stuffing her face since she set foot on the plane, and didn't stop now, visiting a Pret to buy sandwiches, crisps, a proper cup of tea. In the first-class carriage, she was handed Mini Cheddars and a tiny bottle of water by the attendant, and the train shot north, through the fields and canals and rivers of her home country. Two hours ticked away as she failed to read her magazines or even scroll through the news, eating steadily through her snacks then ordering more. Trying to fill some aching hole inside. What was going to happen? What was she doing?

The station sign – Birmingham – made her heart lurch in her chest. Time melted away as the taxi nudged towards her parents' house. She was so utterly different, how could all this be the same? But it was. Kate began to feel sick, either from stress-eating Mini Cheddars or nerves, or both. She was going home. What kind of reception would she get? Even the broken gate was the same. Why had they never fixed it? Why were some people happy to never change a thing and others, like herself, had to rip it all up and start again?

Elizabeth answered the door of the small terraced house, in yoga pants. She was thin, her hair nicely done, diamonds on her fingers, but otherwise exactly the same. 'It's you.'

'Yes.' They stared at each other. Did they hug? There seemed to be too much between them for that.

Elizabeth laughed. 'I can't really believe it. You're so thin.'

'*You're* so thin.'

'Oh, do you think so? It's paleo, honestly, it's changed my life. If you want, I sell these supplements ... ' Of course her sister was in a multi-level marketing scheme. Kate changed the subject before they could immediately fall out.

'Is Dad here?'

'Don't excite him, he needs to stay calm.' How Elizabeth was enjoying this role of hers, the dutiful daughter. Kate followed her sister into the hallway – same old flocked wallpaper – and through to the lounge, with the same hideous white leather sofa. Her father was in an armchair in front of the TV, which was playing *This Morning*. Was that Philip Schofield? She'd had such a crush on him. Like her father, Philip looked older. Her dad wore a cardigan which she thought he'd also had fifteen years ago, which had something crusted on it. Egg, perhaps. 'Dad, it's me.'

'Oh.' A very low-key reaction to the return of a long-lost daughter. 'Did you have lunch?'

'I ate something on the train.' Her stomach had no idea what time it was. The TV was apparently not going to be turned off or even muted.

'I'll make tea,' said Elizabeth, and disappeared. Kate sat down on the squeaky edge of the sofa.

'How are you, Dad?' On the mantelpiece was a picture she'd never seen before, of Adam in a graduation robe. Her son tall and handsome, scowling of course. He'd been such an angry child. No sign of Kirsty in any of the pictures. God, there was her and Andrew's wedding shot! They might have hidden that for her visit. How young and pretty she looked, her face bright with hope. It was almost crowded out by many, many pictures of Elizabeth and her kids. They were so cute. She'd missed so much of their lives.

'I'll be right,' he said, eyes on the TV. 'Journey OK?'

'Good thanks.' Her father had barely been on a plane, let alone first class. 'Where's Mum?'

'It's her day at the food bank. Volunteering like.'

'Oh. That's nice of her.' Could she not have changed it, given that her daughter was home for the first time in fifteen years? Kate didn't know what she'd expected. In some ways it was a comfort, that they were right here where she'd left them. That no one was going to cry or shout or say they'd missed her. Had she missed them? It felt like a more complicated sensation than that. Like putting on old shoes and discovering they remembered your feet.

Elizabeth ducked her head in. 'There's only skimmed milk, it's all Mum drinks. OK?'

Kate hadn't drunk milk in years. 'Sure.' When the tea came, she was surprised by her enjoyment of it, the deep warmth. American tea was always made with lukewarm water and little better than herbal. 'Mm. That's good.'

'It's just tea, Kate. You don't have that over there?' Elizabeth perched on the edge of her father's chair, as if she might get up any minute and start plumping cushions.

'Not really. It's all massive, very strong coffees. Actually that might explain something about the national character.' She stopped herself – she was doing a bit already. This was not the time for bits. 'I'm sorry you were poorly, Dad.' There was a word she hadn't used in years. 'Is there anything I can do?'

Elizabeth sniffed. 'We're fine, aren't we, Dad? We don't have fancy coffee but we manage.'

Kate shot daggers at her sister. 'Thought you quite liked an Instagram latte. With drawings on top.'

Elizabeth twisted her mouth up. 'Mum should be back soon.'

Kate smiled into her tea at the point she'd scored, and then remembered it was 2022 and her dad was recovering from a heart attack and her second marriage was maybe over, and she might soon have to see the children she'd abandoned years before, and stopped.

Adam, 2019

'Great,' said Adam, stepping from the van. 'Today Norwich, tomorrow the world.'

Barry snickered. Barry snickered at everything Adam said, and sometimes uploaded it to Facebook as quotes, with the word 'classic' or 'legend' after it. It was getting annoying. Adam liked adoration from girls, but he wasn't about to stick his cock in Barry any time soon, so it seemed a waste. He'd set the band up in his first term at uni, spurred on perhaps by the revelation that even his ridiculous father was making headway with his creative endeavours. Adam wasn't one to get excited, but it was going better than he could have thought – they were already booked for this ten-uni tour, and he'd had a few emails from record companies.

'Give us a hand, guys,' said Matt ineffectually, struggling with kit. As drummer he had the most stuff and the least valued role in the band. Adam liked to think that had he been a drummer, he'd have enough stage presence to also lead-sing, like that bloke out of Genesis. Barry jumped down to help – as bassist he didn't have much to do – but Adam stayed where he was, shouldering his guitar. He didn't lift things. He was the draw and he knew it. Pete, the supposed lead guitarist – they duked it out for rhythm – knew this too and it was why he was glowering from the front seat. With his curtain hair and friendship bracelets, girls liked Pete until Adam walked in with his shiny dark hair, leather jacket, black jeans tucked into army boots, and their eyes slid away. 'You never help.'

Adam plucked a chord, which was swallowed in the chill air of the university car park. 'Don't see you helping either, Pete mate.'

'I've hurt my back.'

'Shame. Guess you can't do that solo then.'

'Of course I fucking can.'

Adam played on, morphing into the big guitar solo from 'Malevolent', one of their best songs, which he'd written, of course. He played it perfectly, just to piss Pete off. Adam could put a lot of time and effort into pissing people off, more than anything else.

'Not bad here,' Barry was enthusing. The campus was new built, with a large sports centre and fake lake.

'It's effing freezing,' scowled Pete. It was true: icy winds rolled in across the fens, making Norwich a city without shelter, huddled in on itself.

'It's bourgeois,' said Adam, in rare agreement with his band-mate. 'How can you learn anything stuck out here with all these public school rahs?'

Matt was the sensible one. 'They pay OK though. Let's get set up.' He shouldered the drum kit with their name etched on, a sign of commitment, when they'd started actually getting paid for gigs. PANIC, etched in green. Adam liked to look at it, sometimes running his fingers over it when no one could see. He was distracted though by his antenna swivelling, the one which was always attuned and lived between his legs. A gaggle of girls had passed, in shapeless hoodies with their names on the back, damaged blonde hair, good teeth. Poshos. Most likely called Charlotte or Victoria. They looked the band over, pretending not to. Barry straightened up, dropping a cymbal, and the girls streamed off, their laughter rising on the cold bright air. Adam smiled. The one good thing about campus gigs – stuck out of town, the girls would take anyone who was fresh blood. And Adam, up on stage, eyes closed as he sang, was the very freshest, the very bloodiest there was.

On stage, Adam felt like a god. It was a cliché, he knew, and if Barry had said it, he'd have mocked him and said *we're not fucking Coldplay*, but it was true all the same. He could barely see their faces in the dark, the girls, the fanboys, his adoring crowds. The sweat and beer in the small bar of the students' union, the sticky stage, the feedback of the guitars. It was all as potent as any sacred ground. He even smiled over at Pete. In this they were united. Pete and Matt had a good hit-rate with uni girls – Adam couldn't take them all himself – the grubby kind. Too much eyeliner and chipped black nail polish, usually a guitar back in their room on which they would pick out a few chords when they took you there after too many Snakebites, and shyly removed their Mumford & Sons T-shirts under posters of the Beatles.

Adam made it a rule never to shag a girl with a poster of the Beatles – it meant they had no imagination and no real taste in music. Besides, he went for more exotic species. The Valerias, the Annabelles – foreign students, polished posh girls who'd be running the civil service in three years' time, lecturers if possible. It always annoyed him he couldn't see into the crowd to spot tonight's girl, and the first bit of the set was accordingly belted out in angry impatience. 'They started with such energy', reviewers often said, and it was mainly Adam's libido providing this. They did their top songs – 'Now Please', 'Everybody Sucks', and 'Girl with the Night in her Eyes' (most of his conquests liked this best, as if they thought it was about them). Then he announced with relief they were going to take a break. Applause. Some geek from the entz committee rushing over with beer in plastic cups, slopping it onto his Ramones T-shirt. Adam looked at his beer in disgust. 'Is there whiskey?'

'Er – I'll ask. Great set guys! Woo!'

Then he saw her. Tonight's girl.

He just knew, always did, and she hadn't even turned around yet. She was at the bar. She wore a dress, unlike the pasty indie girls in jeans, who'd turn out to be virgins and start crying over long-dead pets after too many beers. Her legs were long and pale, bony almost, and her leather jacket too big. Unkempt blonde hair ran down her back and over her shoulders, so much of it, untamed, you wanted to gather it all up like a scarf. Adam had gone very still.

'Fucking hell, mate, good crowd tonight, I—' Barry followed his gaze. 'Aw, I saw her first.'

Adam ignored him. 'Any of these indie chicks will drop their knickers for you. So long as you don't open your mouth.'

'OK.' He recovered quickly.

'Who is she?'

'Think she's going out with the entz guy, that snooty twat who signed us up. Rupert.'

'What's her name?' It didn't matter. It never mattered. If she'd only turn around so he could see if her face matched the rest of her, the sea green dress floating round her narrow hips, the white hands studded in silver rings.

'Eh – forget. He did say. Something weird.'

Turn. Turn. She turned. Adam felt something he barely recognised, it was so rare to him – fear.

'Delia,' said Barry, pleased to be helping. 'That's her name. Short for Cordelia.'

*

270

It was much later, somehow. Lust, Adam thought, was like some kind of drug that changed time. Six hours had passed since he'd first looked at Delia's hair, and it was as if he'd blinked and here he was, in her student bedroom. The entz guy, if he'd ever been a thing, had melted away. Low music played – Mazzy Star. He couldn't even disapprove of it. It was something he did, scrolling through their Spotify likes and sneering at the Spice Girls and Madonna, as a prelude to discarding their clothes. Delia's room was actually OK. It smelled of the incense she burned on a little plate, and she'd tied scarves over the lights in a fire-hazard way of making the place dim. There were fairy lights round the noticeboard, which was pinned over with postcards. Books piled everywhere – she was studying Fine Art, she said, and he couldn't remember if he'd known that already. Olivia rarely talked about her, and Adam hadn't seen her since the year before, but surely he knew she was at Norwich. Was that why he'd pushed for this gig, on some level? He didn't remember. A bicycle propped up in the corner. A collection of spirits they were working their way through – gin now, in teacups, mixed with orange juice. He was finding all this slightly put-on, too boho chic, but actually, he was only trying to. Really, he was thinking – *God, she does it well.* Most students spent their time studying, clubbing, and moaning about cash. Not Delia. They were sitting on her bed, as they had once sat on his, her long legs drawn up under her. She was rubbing at the nub of her ankle. 'Mum never said you were coming here.'

'Why would she know?'

'She's your stepmother.'

He tutted. 'No she's not.'

Delia shrugged. 'May as well be.'

He swallowed gin, wished for a bottle of whiskey. He liked to drink from the mouth like some parody of a rock star. 'Don't you mind? She's your mother, and she didn't see you for years.'

He said mother like some people say *homeopath* – a dangerous delusion he didn't believe in.

Delia didn't react. Most girls with bad pasts exploited them to their full dramatic potential, carving up their arms and crying black eyeliner tears. 'I saw her. Just not with you. Anyway, it was you who hurt me. When we were little. That's why she wouldn't let me come.'

'Cos I'm so bad.' He had a vague memory of this, his mother dragging him off, her nails digging into his arm.

'You scarred me. See?' She tilted her face to him and it seemed natural to take it in his hands. Her skin was like the underside of velvet. There was a faint white mark on her perfect cheek.

'I was a little bastard. Still am.'

'I actually am,' she contested. 'At least your parents were married.'

'You never found out who your dad was?' He hadn't told her of his hunch. Even he had limits. Over the past year, he had often found himself wondering how she was, if he'd been right about her parentage.

She squinted at him. 'You know, don't you? That it was that guy? David. I worked it out from how Mum acted around him. And the dates, I suppose, when she worked there.'

'I . . . kind of guessed at the party that time, yeah.'

'Well. It was him, yeah.'

Something stirred in Adam's brain – something about his mother and the same man, David, a memory maybe of meeting him on the street one time, his mother upset after – but he let it go. 'And?'

'I wrote him a letter.' She laughed, painfully. 'He said he wished me well but he had three kids already and he'd . . . well, he hadn't thought Olivia was stable enough to have a child at the time. In other words, he'd never wanted me.'

'Thought she was stable enough to fuck though.'

'Well. Yeah. So.' She shrugged again. 'No point in pushing, is there? At least I know who he was now.'

'Those other kids, you ever . . . '

Delia shifted, her hair falling so he couldn't see her face. 'One time I went to their house. They're in the phone book – so retro. And they were all there in the garden, back from uni I guess – they're older than us. They were having this big family lunch, all laughing and there were these dogs running about, and one of them had a baby, one of the girls. And it was like – this could have been my family. But it isn't, is it? I don't really have one. So I just left.'

Adam watched her. In many ways she'd had it rougher than him, and he didn't really like that idea. He'd hoarded his pain, mined it for capital, whereas she had just . . . got on with life. Excelled. Been the good girl. Maybe she'd felt she had no choice. 'At least Andrew never did anything like that. Shit, he's never even slept with your ma, has he.'

'I think she'd like him to.'

'He's a twat.'

'He's always sweet to me. When I came that time – then you hurt me again. The wasp, remember.'

'Jesus. Have you got a list or something, all the bad things I've ever done?'

'No. Just a working memory.'

'Hold a grudge much?'

'Not a grudge. It's just some things that happened, is all.' She smiled through her fall of hair. 'No need to take it so personally, *Ads*. People say that but it's bullshit, isn't it. It's your life. you can hardly not take it personally.'

He did feel bad about it. 'Look, I didn't mean to hurt you. Either time.'

273

'I know. You were just in pain, weren't you.'

He was going to do something he never did. 'I – I'm sorry, alright.'

'I know you are.'

Was that worse, being understood? Would he rather be reviled? He heard himself say, 'You turned out pretty damn hot.'

'Hot,' she mocked. 'Poetic.'

'Beautiful.'

'You too.' She peeped up at him. His hand was on her face again, and she leant into it, and he felt something so strange he almost didn't want to fuck her. But he would.

He could feel the time between them, slowed down so every breath took hours, and at the same time gulping away like water down a plughole. 'If my stupid father had married Olivia, you'd be my sister,' he said, mumbling into her hair, which smelled of coconut. Something rose up in him – his libido, rearing its head, sniffing about.

'They didn't,' said Delia. It was impossible to tell from her face what she was thinking. What interest could such a good girl have in him, dangerous, messed-up? Was it as basic and boring as liking a bad boy? Maybe he'd read it all wrong. But she was here, wasn't she, with her legs bared and her dress ridden up on her pale thighs. 'I wouldn't be your sister, anyway. You've got a sister.'

He didn't want to think of Kirsty now. Not here with the incense and soft lights glowing on the skin of Delia's legs. 'This would really piss them off,' he risked. 'You and me like this.'

'So what? Maybe they deserve a bit of a jolt. Mum, anyway.'

'But you're always so good to her.' He didn't understand it.

She sighed. 'It's complicated. I'm angry, yeah, but I know she couldn't help it. Or maybe I just know if I make it too hard for her she'll leave me again. I don't know. Who cares, anyway?'

274

He was afraid to stop talking, of what might happen. 'I didn't know you were like this. I thought you were so perfect.'

She smiled. 'We're the opposite. You seem all cold and fucked-up, but inside you're kind of . . . vulnerable.'

'I am not, fuck off.'

'And me, I seem – good on the outside, but inside I'm raging, sometimes. So we're different, you see, but the same.' She leaned forward to put down her cup and suddenly she was very close, and he knew he was going to kiss her, and just as he did, he saw again how he'd made a white line on her face. Like he'd marked her as his, all those years ago.

Adam, present day

'Wow, Aunt Liz, slow down.' Why had she called him? He didn't know if he'd even spoken to his aunt on the phone before – maybe to thank her for Christmas presents, something Olivia had enforced with all the pressure of her social class. 'She's there with you?' His mother. Actually back in the country.

'She was. She's gone back to London now, got a taxi to the station.'

'Alright. And Granddad had a heart attack?' Had he known this? Would he have cared, being honest?

'Yes, but that was last month, he's fine now. She said she'd come all the same. I think she wanted an excuse, maybe?' His mother was in the same country as him. On her way back to London, where he was still lying in his small room, staring at the ceiling, his bed unmade beneath him. Delia was not answering any of his messages, and Adam hated it, hated breaking his usual rules about contacting women twice in a row, but she'd left him no choice. She was *pregnant*, for God's sake. The worst thing. 'Is she coming to see us?'

'Adam, I've no idea. I asked her and she got huffy and left. Poor Dad's very upset, he can't even concentrate on *Cash in the Attic*.'

Adam's brain was whirring. His mother would understand why this pregnancy couldn't go ahead. She was clear-minded – ruthless, really. Not woolly like his father or weak like Olivia, soppy like Delia, who'd probably already done an Instagram post with the due date written on a chalk board, cradling a flower over her stomach. Who'd been abandoned by her mother and rejected by her father, and so maybe, in her brain, saw some logic in having her own child now, someone who was truly hers and would not leave.

His aunt was still talking so he interrupted her. 'What train did she get, do you know?' He couldn't bring himself to say *Mum*.

'How should I know? The 2.15, I imagine. Such a short visit, I don't know why she bothered. She'd have had plenty of time for that, unless the taxi went past the roadworks . . .'

He interrupted her ramblings. 'Alright. Thanks for the heads-up.'

'Are you coming to see your grandfather any time soon?' she demanded, shrill. 'I did tell your father he was ill, but I suppose he's too taken up with his *book*.'

'Um – sure. Why not.' Deal with that later. One emotional disaster at a time. Adam checked the time – his mother's train should be getting into Euston in forty minutes or so. He could make it. He jammed his feet into his Converse, found his wallet and keys. God. His hair was a state. Not how he wanted to see his mother after all this time. The last time, he'd been heading out to the park with Olivia, and she had bent down to kiss him,

276

which was how he'd known something was wrong. He'd been seven. She'd had the guts to turn around and walk away from a seven-year-old, a disabled five-year-old. What would she be like now? His stomach was in knots as he dashed out the door, almost falling over his flatmate's stupid scooter as he did.

Short tube ride, glancing anxiously at the time, willing it on. Did it always stop for so long between stations? God, hurry up, slowcoach tourists. Did their IQs get siphoned off at the airport or something? Finally he was at Euston, plunging out the doors and up the escalators before the rest of the sheep could move. What platform? He scanned the arrivals board. Four. Would he even recognise her, after so long? Or her him? God, he felt sick. Maybe this was dumb. He just didn't know if he'd see her otherwise, and wasn't that ridiculous, knowing your mother was in the country, the city even, and you weren't sure if she'd try to see you or not? Part of him maybe admired her for that, how little of a shit she gave about social norms. He was on the platform now, squinting at everyone. Would she be the first off, rushing to the tube, or was she American now, slow like a tourist, taking ages to put on her coat and pick up her bag? He didn't know. He had no idea who his mother was these days. Really, he'd never known.

Woman after woman. She'd be, what, fifty now? He knew from sneaking looks at her show that she was thin, glamorous, Californian with her tan and streaked hair. Was that her? God, he didn't know. People looked different in real life. What if he missed her? He was reminded unpleasantly of waiting for Tinder dates, those few minutes where you weren't sure if that was them with the latte or not, and didn't want to look a twat by asking some total random, all the time worried their pictures wouldn't be realistic.

In the end, he realised he could not have missed her. He knew her right away. She was walking down the platform, at a decent but not brisk pace, her face scowling as if deep in thought. Expensive jeans, ankle boots, some kind of soft jumper. She didn't see him – of course, she'd no idea he was there. He moved forward. She saw him from the corner of her eye, and for a split-second she frowned, held her bag tighter, as if he was going to rob her.

'Um . . . ' He wasn't going to say *Mum*. 'Kate.'

She stopped. She stared at him, right there in the concourse at Euston, a river of people parting around them, some tutting impatiently. 'Adam?' Her voice faltered. She wasn't sure. She'd last seen him at seven, now he was taller than her.

'Yeah.'

She blinked. Her eyes were like his. 'What are you doing here?'

'Aunt Liz rang me.'

She rolled her eyes. 'God. She's even worse than she was.'

'Where are you going? To see Dad?'

'Oh. I don't know, to be honest. I'm going to my hotel. Where my – to meet my, eh, my husband.' That was the film producer.

'I think Dad's with him.' It was all so weird. It seemed there should be laws against it.

'OK. Where are you going?' Meaning, what the hell are you doing here, my long-lost son, meeting me off the train like we're in *Brief Encounter* or some such soppy shit?

'Um – I don't know either. I need your help with something.'

He saw from her face that this was the absolute last thing she had expected today, and to be honest, he was in the same fucking boat.

Adam, 2020

Adam looked at the marks he had started scratching into the paint of his skirting board, like a prisoner, feeling the need to mark his incarceration by destroying his father's house. Forty-seven days he'd been stuck in here, and no sign of it ending. Lockdown. Quarantine. The Great Disaster, The Thing. Lots of names for it. There he was, his band taking off, playing campuses all over the UK, his degree totally neglected because who needed that in the current market of zero-contract jobs, and boom – live music was totally destroyed by a Biblical pandemic, of all things. It was almost funny, except it wasn't. His university had shut down within a week, sent them all home, lecturers talking to empty rooms, confusing drifts of emails, students collected by panicked parents, painful attempts by Boomer-era teachers to give video lectures. *You're on mute, Professor.* Olivia had come to collect him. She'd insisted. And now he was here, locked down with his father, not-stepmother, and sister. Delia, his not-sister and not-girlfriend, had gone home to take care of her grandparents who, being ancient, weren't even allowed out to the shops. She was such a fucking martyr, posting endless Instagrams about making the most of the time, baking bread and boiling up jam with fruit from her grandparents' massive garden, teaching them gentle yoga and praising how sweet they were. Easy to have a good lockdown in a mansion with an orchard. He hated how much he missed her.

It made no sense to him, what had happened between them that night on campus a year before, and was still happening from time to time. It had started as a bit of a two-fingers up to his dad, even to Olivia, a transgression, a sexy crossing of boundaries, but now it was something more. God, of course he liked

279

her – she was beautiful, clever, sophisticated, immune to his bullshit, and all but taboo given their family relationship. But what did she want with him? He knew she saw him as broken in a hot way, funny and sharp and handsome, and she felt he understood her like no one else did. The fact that despite her high achieving and perfect blonde looks and growing Instagram following, she was broken too. But was that enough? Could he hold onto her, especially if he didn't see her for months? It was maddening, to feel with each day ticking past, he was losing his music and his future and – well, his girl. How embarrassing to think of her that way, when she wasn't. But he wished she was.

Adam had mentioned once or twice to Olivia, casually, that maybe she would like to see her daughter at *this difficult time*, as everyone had started calling it in their emails, but couldn't push it further as Delia didn't want her mother to know that she and Adam were in touch (a euphemism for screwing every time they could get away from their not-easily-connected universities). Olivia just insisted they must follow the rules, no matter how much they might personally wish to see people. Adam got the feeling she was relieved about having a cast-iron excuse to stay at home, avoid her parents and yes, even Delia.

He wanted to see her. He'd never felt this way about a girl before – all too often they were puzzles he could unlock in one or, at the most, three dates, smart girls, dumb girls, posh girls and chavvy girls, rich city girls, poor country girls, he knew them all, and none of them surprised him, but Delia somehow did. Maybe the secrecy, the slight wrongness. Maybe her long pale hair, her smell of hand cream and herbs, the locked-up inner core of her, that he couldn't touch, as if she was always holding herself back from him. He had hurt her twice before as a child. She wouldn't let him do it again, and that, to be honest, was a relief. He was tired of having things break in his hands.

But God, it was boring being stuck here, twenty years old and no sex, no drinking, no music, no fun. Some nights his dad would open a bottle of wine and Olivia would visibly wince, so they'd end up only having a glass or two then recorking it. It would sit in the kitchen all week, then only be good for cooking, as they all tried hard to prove they didn't have a drinking problem, even when there was literally nothing else to do. Olivia had them on a strict lockdown routine, out for a walk at 9am when it might be less busy, for no more or less than a government-sanctioned hour, shying away if anyone veered too close to them on the street, Kirsty grizzling in her adapted buggy under a plastic hood, strictly masked up, hand sanitiser squirted, daggers shot at anyone walking two or three abreast. God, people were selfish morons. All they had to do was sit home for a month or two, not stand too close, not block up the paths with their kids and dogs and scooters, and they still couldn't. Kirsty was high-risk. She had to be protected, they kept saying, Olivia and Andrew. Their worry for her was tangible, like something pushing the walls closer together.

On these walks, Adam trailed behind, embarrassed and bored and wishing someone else was with them, or better, that he was somewhere else. Life felt stopped. When they got home it was a continuing programme of events. Bread-making, craft projects, working in the garden, all so wholesome it made Adam want to suffocate himself with Olivia's flowered kneeling mat. Lunch. Study time for all of them – Kirsty learning more signs all the time, to the point where they'd almost taken it for granted she could communicate with them, and wasn't that something, to take a miracle for granted. His father's stupid book still progressing, and apparently there was 'agent interest', Olivia studying Mandarin off Duolingo, Adam supposedly revising for his exams, though nothing seemed more pointless

281

when the world had been metaphorically and literally on fire for the past four years. Even before all this, there were floods and fires and destruction, and that was only up to March when the whole world ended. All he wanted was to see Delia. He'd suggested it a few times, a sneaky meet-up halfway between them, perhaps even a shag in his dad's car, but she was too good to break the rules. They had to think of the vulnerable, her grandparents and Kirsty. The fact she was probably right just made him even more angry, that she didn't seem to need it as much as he did. Maybe she just didn't feel the same – had she done it only to piss off Olivia? Not that Olivia knew of course. He had to admit, this was the worst thing. That he who had trained himself not to need anyone, after his own mother walked out on him and never came back, had ended up with feelings all the same.

Bored, he went downstairs so he could look out of a slightly different set of windows. He was surprised to find his father and Olivia there, standing around the kitchen island, talking in low voices. Olivia was holding her elbows in that way she did when she was stressed, her face frozen. 'What's up?' It was study time now, they shouldn't be downstairs at all. God forbid they'd break into the homemade biscuit stash before 4pm.

His father looked up. He wasn't touching Olivia – they never touched – but he was standing close to her, almost but not quite patting her back. 'Olivia's had some upsetting news, Ads.'

Not Delia *not Delia* but maybe a grandparent then he could see Delia maybe? God, that was a terrible thought. 'What?'

'Her boss has passed away rather unexpectedly.'

'Oh. From the . . .'

'Yes. From covid.' It was strange to think of someone actually dying it from it, not on the news but in real life.

Olivia spoke, her voice strangled. 'He'd been having

treatment for cancer apparently . . . I didn't know. Prostate. I – well, it's a shock. He wasn't even sixty.'

'Your boss, you said?' Who was that? 'Oh – that guy David? Delia's dad, you mean?' The bluff Scottish one with the crushing handshake, who'd told poor Dee to get lost. Idiot.

Then he realised what he'd said, and could have kicked himself. Olivia didn't realise Delia knew, of course.

Andrew looked up, shocked. 'What? But Ads, we don't know who . . . ' He trailed off, looking at his son, who shrugged, and then Olivia, who was shaking like a leaf in the wind. He blinked. 'Oh. Well that . . . I didn't realise . . . Wait, does Delia know?'

'She worked it out, yeah. After your fortieth.' Adam was looking at Olivia, wanting to take back what he'd said so casually, but not able to. 'Look, it's no big deal. She's over it.' That was a lie, but it might make Olivia feel better, stop a full-blown collapse. The last time she'd had one was in 2014, and even then Andrew had managed to soothe her through it. This was different though. Everything felt more fragile now, the entire world.

Olivia rushed from the room, making a small noise in her throat. Andrew leant on the kitchen island, exhaling hard. 'God, I should have known. Bloody David! I never liked that man – I mean I shouldn't speak ill of . . . but he sniffed around your mother too, I know he did, and . . . ' He stopped, as if realising he was speaking to his twenty-year-old son. 'I should go up to her.'

'No. Leave her for now.' He knew instinctively it was better not to crowd Livvie when she got like this.

'And Delia? She'll need to know.' His father shook his head. 'I can't believe you all knew and I . . . well, never mind.'

'I'll – look, I'll tell her he's gone.' It would give him an excuse to speak to her, and while she might be angry he'd so

283

thoughtlessly blurted it out to Olivia, at least he'd hear her voice. Suddenly he was cross. 'Anyway, is it so bad if the truth comes out? Christ, why do we have to keep so many secrets in this family? Who cares if he was her dad? She's got a right to know. Isn't it better to be honest, even if it sucks?'

His father took off his glasses and very slowly began to clean them on his jumper. After a moment he said, 'Honestly, Ads, I've asked myself that many times. And I have to say, I still have no idea.'

Andrew, present day

His first thought when she walked into the hotel lobby was, oh, it's Kate. As if no time had gone by since he'd seen her, as if she was simply coming to meet him here after a shopping trip, or maybe to say hello to his film producer, as a wife might. But Adam was with her. Why were they together? It didn't make sense. His head hurt at seeing all these people in the same room. Conor also looked surprised. He spoke to Kate. Of course, because he was her husband. Not Andrew. 'I didn't realise you were coming here.'

Kate seemed annoyed. 'Well, I didn't know what else to do. This is Adam, he's ... well, you know who he is. I gather there's been some kind of emergency?' She looked at Andrew then, addressing him directly. He quailed. Couldn't speak. Looked at Adam to explain what was going on.

'You're the producer,' said his son, to Conor.

'Yes. Conor.' He stood, held out his hand to Adam.

'You're my stepfather.'

Conor flinched. He actually flinched. 'I suppose I am.' Kate

284

made a noise, a bit like a 'huh'. Conor flinched again.

Adam said, 'Basically we need to find my ... Christ, I don't even know what to call her. Olivia. Like my stepmother but not that, not at all. And Delia, her daughter. They've both gone off-grid or something.'

'I can't believe Delia's all grown up,' said Kate, wondering. 'In my head she's still two.'

Conor was looking between them with guarded confusion. 'She's not in the book, this Delia.'

'No,' said Andrew wearily. 'Olivia didn't want her mentioned.'

Conor looked at Andrew. 'And you and Olivia, you're not a couple? I got the impression ...'

'A lot of people get that,' said Adam, impatiently. Andrew avoided Kate's gaze, that same blue stare that had always broken him. How to even begin to talk to her? So much he had to say. How could you. Why did you. Sorry, maybe, even. Adam went on, 'That's kind of the problem. Delia's pregnant, it's my baby, it might have what my sister has, and Olivia's lost it and run off somewhere and I need her to persuade Dee she's not having the baby, but I don't know where either of them are.'

'She's not having it?' Andrew was surprised at feeling a pang. Perhaps he had allowed himself to think of grandkids. A chance to do it better, for all of them. A joint grandchild, for him and Olivia, as if they were actually a couple.

Adam shot him a poisonous look. 'You really think another kid like Kirsty is a good idea?'

Conor was like a tennis-match spectator. He spoke to Andrew. 'Wait, I'm not following this. Can someone explain?' Andrew opened his mouth, found he couldn't speak.

Talking over him, as she always used to, Kate said, 'Basically, Adam's girlfriend ...'

'She's not my girlfriend.'

'Well, alright. A girl Adam's been seeing . . .'

'She's not just a *girl*,' said Andrew hotly, and he saw Kate's face change. Genetics, family, the worst type of tangle. 'I mean, she's family.'

'No she isn't,' objected Adam. 'How is she? That's stupid.'

Conor's head was on a swivel. 'Well, what about her, whoever she is?'

'She's pregnant,' said Kate, matching Adam's impatient tone. 'And the baby – well, it might be like – how Kirsty is.'

Conor said, addressing Andrew again: 'So wait. Your partner's daughter is pregnant, with your son's baby?'

All these connections. 'She's not my part . . . yes, basically.' So aware of Kate's eyes burning into him. *How could you. My best friend*. Even though he never had, even though she'd left, and she'd specifically asked Olivia to look after them all. Maybe she wasn't thinking that at all. Maybe he had never understood what Kate was thinking.

'And the kid might have the same condition your daughter has?'

'Well, yes. There's a chance. Fifty-fifty.'

Conor looked shell-shocked. 'Christ, talk about a third act.'

Finally, Kate seemed to realise something. Her brow was knit with hard thinking. She looked right at him, and he thought his lungs might collapse. 'Andrew – where's Kirsty? Who's with her, if Olivia's gone?'

Adam, 2021

It was Adam who noticed that Kirsty was sick. Not her usual problems, but something else. Sometimes, when he was young, his teachers had explained to classmates that Adam's sister was 'sick', although sick meant you could get better and that was not the case. But she was of course sick at times too, like everyone. It was just harder to tell because her normal skewed so far to the left of the scatter graph.

The year had started hopefully, an end to the Bad Times in sight. Kirsty had a vaccination in March, being in a high-risk group, and Olivia and Andrew relaxed about taking her out of the house, stopped washing their hands twenty times a day. His father had, against all the odds and to Adam's ongoing astonishment, sold his book to a publisher, for a large sum of money, so large he was able to give up the law job he'd always hated. Adam went back to university after Easter, such as it was, with spaced-out lecture theatres, bars enforcing capacity levels, no gigs still, lots of online teaching. When would live music start up again? At least he could finish his degree, get it over with then move to London, like Delia was planning to. Her grandparents were buying her a house so she could finish her last uni year remotely. He could be in the same city as her, after barely seeing her at all for the past year.

Kirsty would be turning nineteen that year, and the news that she was losing her regular day-care, as most kids did at that age, felt muted – her day-care had not operated anyway in over a year. Services for disabled adults were much worse even than for children, and scuppered entirely by covid. Adam knew his father was thinking about what to do next – put her in long-term care? Olivia would not stand for it. But it wasn't up to Olivia, was it. He hated that martyrdom. The way people didn't know how to be happy, or even to try. What would Kirsty herself like? Assuming she could have opinions either way. It was a new field, the question of what Kirsty could and could not do. For years it had seemed clear (almost nothing), but now it was less so. She learned more signs all the time, and when she flashed them at Adam, a kind of fear clenched in his stomach. If she understood, if she was capable of that, anything was possible. Maybe she knew he had failed her all those years. Maybe he needed to help with her more, stay behind at home instead of running off to London. But what could he do?

He came home from his final year of university for a reading week, because no one else would be around on campus, but he dreaded it. He had considered staying in his cramped little room above the rooftops of Brighton, going to the library every day and eating in the dining hall with the overseas students paying exorbitant fees to be there. He liked the city, the feeling of being on the edge of things, easy to escape. The music venues, the various bands he'd put together in his time there and discarded as not serious enough. The slight undercurrent of sleaze and panic. But it was too sad in the end to be there alone, with shops and cafés shuttered, and so home he went, masked up, with a single rucksack. As the train drew into Bishopsdean, he imagined staying on it, heading north. Hopping on a boat to the Scottish islands, as far away as possible. Running from this life, this family, just as his mother had done.

His return was predictably embarrassing – Olivia hugging him after a rigorous hand-washing, bony under his reluctant arms, a special spread of lunch dishes and even a banner, for Christ's sake. On the table were all the foods she had once seen him eat and so assumed were his favourites, and Kirsty spruced up in jeans and a jumper with a cat on it, her fair hair plaited by Olivia, wheeled to the table, presentable for few seconds before she dribbled down herself again. Olivia pressing her hands together in anxiety, his father hanging back awkwardly. He hated it. He wished he'd stayed at uni and eaten Pot Noodles instead. There were bound to be some townie girls he could have had a crack at. So he told himself, knowing all the while there was only one girl he actually wanted.

'Kirsty's so excited to see you,' said Olivia, and anger doubled his chest over like a hinge. Even with her new signs, there was no way she could have communicated such a complicated sentiment. But then she waved her hands towards him, sticky with spit, signing *hello, hello, hello*, and he felt a surge of guilt, because maybe she really was excited to see him. 'Hey Kirsty. You OK?' He took her hand in his and frowned, a sudden current of fear down his spine.

'She's really warm,' he said. Her skin felt like she'd been out in the sun all day, though it was a cold and rainy day, one of the chilliest springs on record, as everyone kept saying glumly, crouched in miserable outdoor dining areas pretending to have fun. His father's brow creased, but he did nothing.

'Is she?' Olivia reached for Kirsty's forehead, which had strands of hair stuck to it. 'Should we get the thermometer, Andrew?' They just looked at each other, and Adam gave a sigh, wondering how the hell this house kept running when neither of them could make a decision.

'I'll get it.' Opening the door to the high cupboard where the medicine box lived triggered some memory in him – his mother, her cold hand resting on his head like Olivia had just done to Kirsty. Getting down this exact same thermometer that had been in all of their mouths, hopefully washed. The bulby feel of the glass in his cheek. Kirsty fought him, not wanting it, and putting it under her tongue was not pleasant, but it made him feel like more of a proper person, this contact with someone else's spit and skin. It made him feel he was doing something real. He stroked her head to calm her. 'It's OK. Just a second, there we go. What's normal?' he said, waving the thermometer as he'd seen his mother do, realising he had no idea what it was meant to read.

'Um, thirty-seven or below I think,' said his father, vaguely. He said everything vaguely. Since selling the book he seemed even more anxious than before. Happy, yes, but also terrified, which Adam could sort of understand.

'Thirty-nine. Is that bad?'

Adam looked at them. They were the adults, it was on them to decide if this was serious or not. 'We'll see how she is in the morning,' said Andrew, uncertainly, glancing at Olivia to bolster this lack of decision. No one seemed to want to say the word, *covid*. 'She's been jabbed, after all. Probably more of a risk to go to hospital.'

'And she isn't coughing,' said Olivia, biting her lip. 'Is she?'

No one answered.

Olivia washed up, although Adam would have rather done that than sit with his father in front of the TV. 'Anything you'd like to watch?' Andrew fingered the remote nervously.

'Oh. No, I'm kind of out of the loop on TV.' He'd been going through a series on Netflix, but of course they didn't have it. Too expensive, even at less than a tenner a month, even though Olivia was loaded. He hated this pointless penny-pinching.

'Olivia and I are watching a boxset. Swedish thing on Channel Four.'

'Oh. Well, go ahead with that. I don't mind.'

'Or we could watch a film or . . . ?'

Adam felt it weigh him down, the lack of decision, the killing politeness of this house. At least his mother and father had fought, from what he could remember. At least his mother had lost her temper, with Andrew, and with him and Kirsty, who really didn't deserve it. But it was better than this.

Olivia came in, rubbing cream into her thin hands. 'So! Did we want to watch a film or . . . ?' He could tell no one would decide and his taste would be too violent for them or there'd be a sex scene and it would be too embarrassing, and he'd have already seen all the things they wanted to watch, so in the end he just said he was tired and went up to bed. Lying awake for hours texting girls from his course to see were they up and similarly bored with their families. Feeling guilty, because of Delia, but why should he when she refused to meet up with him or classify their relationship in any way? Lots of pictures on Facebook from his friends, barbecues in the garden, holiday homes and canal boats and smiling healthy siblings. Life getting back to normal, people grabbing it with both hands.

When he woke up in the night to pee, he heard Kirsty moaning and went into her room to find she was twisted up in her high-sided bed. Her breathing sounded funny. Like something being torn. It wasn't supposed to sound like that, was it? As if something heavy sat on her chest and she couldn't get the air in. He put his hand on her head as Olivia had done – pulled it away, another worm of panic down his back. She was so warm. Worse than before. She had to be sick, right? She smelled sick. She was red and hot and whimpering. But why hadn't his dad or Olivia noticed?

'Dad?' He went out on the landing. 'Olivia?' They emerged, from separate bedrooms, in sensible pyjamas, staid and chaste. 'It's Kirsty. She's – I think something's wrong.'

He would remember afterwards that he could almost see the fear slice through his father's fogginess, like a glass cutter, a perfect circle breaking in.

Kate, present day

Kate's head was sore with all that had happened in the past twenty-four hours, like a long dream of the past she could not wake up from. She had cried on the train, in a brief furious spurt, aching with it all. Her father, her sister, briefly her mother when she came back from the food bank, washing her hands vigorously and looking quietly shocked to see her daughter. They had talked of nothing important. Her niece and nephew, who she wouldn't get to meet on this occasion. Maybe never, then. Everyone's experience of the pandemic, which felt largely over now, unbelievably. Home-schooling, Elizabeth's husband's furlough, the long queues for vaccine boosters earlier in the year. Her job – they had seen her on TV. Her mother's volunteering and her father's health. No mention of Kate's life in LA, or the family she had abandoned. The names Kirsty, Andrew, and Adam did not pass their lips at all. Wouldn't they have said, if something was wrong with one of them? Clearly not. Because she was here now, in the lobby of a smart London hotel, and Andrew did not want to tell her something.

'Where's Kirsty?' she had said. She should have asked this first, but even saying her daughter's name was painful, like a small stabbing. It was so odd. Her son was here. And both her husbands, in the same room. Sharing a plate of fancy biscuits, by the looks of it. What was going on? Andrew couldn't look at her, and Conor had an unreadable expression. Mild annoyance, probably, at being embroiled in the messiness of this family. Well, he was the one who'd bought his way in, let him deal with it. 'If this book's about Kirsty, where is she?'

Andrew gaped. 'She ...' God, what was wrong? 'There's something you need to know about Kirsty. She ... um ...'

Kate was frowning at him. The old expression she would always use – *God, spit it out, Andrew* – rose in her mouth.

'What is it?' Oh God. A sudden fear, piercing a mineshaft into her, places she had thought long dead and calcified. 'I – please tell me, Andrew.'

So he did. Words broke over Kate. 'You see – she got sick, last year. Covid. We thought the danger was past, she had her jab early of course, but then – well. Adam spotted it. She had it. Quite bad.'

Kate stared at her son, who was looking at his shoes, furious, and her ex-husband, spilling words from his mouth. Kirsty was dead. Was that what they were saying? Oh God, the guilt would drag her under. 'I . . . just say it! Where is she?' *Dead.* She waited for the sound of it. *She's dead.* It seemed inevitable. So many disabled people had died of covid, why not her child too?

A short pause. Adam and Andrew exchanged a look. 'In a home,' said Andrew. 'We – I had to put her into residential care.'

'Oh.' First relief, a pure burst of it, quickly coloured by other feelings. Kate did not know what to think about this. In her head, Kirsty was still a small child, and the idea of putting her in a home was abhorrent, but she was twenty now. Had she expected Andrew to care for Kirsty all her life? 'So, she's not – she got through it?'

'Barely,' snarled Adam. 'She could hardly breathe and no one even noticed. She couldn't tell us and her oxygen dropped way down. She was on a ventilator for weeks. She's not the same as she was.'

'We don't know that . . .'

'We do, Dad. Just stop being in denial for once, OK? She's . . . lost what she learned. A lot of it. You know she can't – do what she did. She's gone backwards.'

Kate was trying to arrange her face but didn't know what

expression to use. She had scarcely got used to the idea that Kirsty could communicate – were they saying she'd lost it already? *And I missed it. I'm too late.*

'Look, Ads, I know . . . ' Andrew blinked suddenly. 'God. I've just realised where Liv must be.'

Adam's expression changed. 'Ah. Yeah. Makes sense.'

Kate felt very left out, a reminder which could not be more tangible that she was no longer part of this family, because she had no idea what they were talking about. Andrew was fumbling about for his jacket. 'It's not far to drive – maybe I can get an Uber or . . . '

'Take the car,' said Conor, who Kate had almost forgotten was there. Her husband. 'It's just outside, and the driver. Please. Take it where you need to go.' Showing off, even in a moment like this. Or perhaps that was unkind, perhaps he really did want to help. He could easily have asked what this meant for the film, if the story of the book didn't end with hope after all, if events carried on once it was finished and signed off, if Kirsty's progress had not survived. But Kate looked inside herself and found her leeway for Conor was almost completely exhausted.

'I'm coming with you,' she heard herself saying.

Andrew, present day

In films, people always knew where an absconded loved one might have run off to, what particular place held the most significance for them. All day Andrew hadn't been able to shake the feeling that if only he'd paid more attention, if only he had given Olivia what he knew she'd wanted all these years, perhaps the answer would drop into his head like the solution to a crossword clue. What mattered to Olivia? Who did she love? Adam, but the boy was here with him. Delia, but Delia was also unfindable. Him, Andrew. She loved him, he knew she did, so why had he held her off all this time? Afraid, perhaps, to accept that a woman could actually see all his faults and not run away. Of the mess of it all, the heartbreak that was inevitable once you let yourself love people, because one day they'd either die or leave you. Where else could she have gone? Her parents were in France at their holiday home, and he didn't think she would go to them in any case.

But the answer had come to him. The only other person he could think of who Olivia loved was Kirsty. Of course, Olivia would not have wanted her left alone for too long. And now here he was, in the car on the way to her care home, in the next town over from Bishopsdean. Barely an hour's drive from London. Travelling along with his son, his ex-wife, and his ex-wife's new husband. No one was saying anything. The driver was separated from them by a smoked-glass panel, the seats cool leather, bottles of water in the seat pockets. What a life Kate must have been living since she left. Comfortable, cosseted. He found his eyes kept crawling to her and her husband. The glow of wealth about them. Her skin was tanned, though more lined than it had been, her hair highlighted. He knew nothing about women's clothes but there was a sheen of wealth on her ankle boots and jeans and light jumper. Conor was the same – just jeans and a jumper, but somehow nicer than anything Andrew owned. His skin was pale despite living in LA, his hair well-cut. Silver watch on his wrist. Rings on Kate's fingers. No wedding ring on either of them though. Why was that? Andrew had taken his own off the year she'd gone, and it was still in the drawer of the bedside table, where he sometimes came across it while searching for antacids. It probably didn't fit any more.

Kate caught him looking at her. 'So ... it's a nice place, where she is?'

'Well. Nice as possible.'

The care home was pleasant enough, geraniums round the door and a badly painted mural of balloons in the lobby. Yet the guilt was appalling, at putting her in there. The doctors said there might be brain damage from her time on a ventilator, though they had no real way to tell. He could hardly bear to think of that time last year, rushing her to hospital after Adam spotted she was ill, the terrible shame of missing it. The shortage of ventilators, the over-worked, wide-eyed staff with dents from masks etched onto their faces. The decisions that would have to be made, explained to them in careful words, but the gist of it being, Kirsty was not a priority. If the ICU was swamped, and someone needed a ventilator more, a healthy person say, young and strong or with a family, they might be treated instead of his daughter. That even if she got a ventilator, she might not be strong enough to survive it. It took a great toll, and she wouldn't understand, she would fight it. The starkness of it, the horror of weighing up her life like that, of knowing despite his pain and rage the hospital had no choice. There was only such much help to go around. Even Olivia had been shocked out of her lifelong quietness by it and had gone on screen at her own news programme for the first time ever, railing against government policies and shortages that left disabled people to die. She was still in a campaign group even now.

Somehow, Kirsty had pulled through, after two terrible weeks. It was true she seemed to have lost some of the signs she'd learned, it was true they were struggling to care for her by themselves, it was true few families kept disabled adults at home still, with this level of need. The home seemed the best solution, even though he worried about the covid outbreaks that had swept such places in 2020. So he'd explained to Kate, wondering why on earth he felt so bad about it. Kate had left, after all, she had no right to comment on his choices. Kirsty would live there now, in a place where people would look after her, stimulate her, never resent her or weep over her since they were being paid to do what parents did for love. How much easier it was to stay cheerful, to hope for someone, when you weren't their family. And just like that, his life had suddenly been handed back to him. Adam was grown and gone. Kirsty was being cared for. It was just him, and Olivia, and he no longer needed her to look after him and his children. But that didn't mean he didn't need her. It didn't mean that at all. What a mess.

They were almost at the town now. He saw Kate stiffen slightly at the familiar turn-off from the M25. He could almost hear her thoughts, clear as a radio – the surrealness of coming back to a life she had left so completely. He glanced at Adam, scowling out the window, and wondered what would happen to him and Delia. The children, Olivia called them. As if they belonged to both of them. It hurt that Adam had not asked for his help in the matter of Delia's pregnancy, turning instead to his absent mother, but in a way he understood. He was the not the man to go to when you needed things done. And yet he was here, trying to do a thing.

Adam, present day

Adam cleared his throat, needing to break the silence in the car. No one had said anything since London, and no wonder, because it was like being trapped in a nightmare, his dad and mother and her new husband, who Adam grudgingly had to admit was cool for an old guy, expensive watch, fancy clothes. But he couldn't stop thinking about Delia.

'Livvie will know where she is. Right?' He wasn't sure who he was addressing, but his father answered. He looked like he hadn't slept at all, and there was a tie hanging out of his jacket pocket like a thirsty tongue.

'Um. I hope so. Delia wouldn't want to worry her.'

'She had enough to deal with last night, didn't she.' Adam watched his father wince at the dig, but it didn't make him feel any better. 'I just – I don't know what's going on in Delia's head. About this – the baby.'

His mother had been looking out the window, as if embarrassed to be overhearing this conversation, as if knowing she'd given up any right to know his business. Now she turned, her groomed eyebrows going up. 'Delia's, what, twenty-one? She'll hardly want a baby, will she?'

Adam chewed on a hangnail. 'She's not like other girls though, is she? Her mum left her.'

'Oh, she didn't . . . ' Kate stopped. 'Well, I suppose she did, yes. I never thought of it that way.'

'Livvie tried at least.' Adam didn't want his mother letting herself off the hook, just because Olivia had also not been able to live with her child. 'Thing is, Delia's dad dying, not wanting her and then it was too late, it really threw her. She might – well, she might want a kid to make up for that. For not having parents really.'

Kate looked confused. 'Delia's father? I thought she didn't . . . '

Here it was. Adam stared her straight in the eyes. 'Yeah, your old boss, you know.'

Her face changed. 'David? David was Delia's . . . oh.' He could see her working it out, running the dates in her head. 'Oh my God, I had no idea.'

'He carked it, you know. Two years back.' He felt like being

298

cruel. Somehow he knew this news would hurt his mother, without wanting to get into why.

'What?'

His dad cleared his throat. 'Covid, sadly. He'd been ill with cancer, and . . . well. It was before the vaccines and he just . . . didn't make it.'

Kate had gone white. 'But he was . . . he was young!'

'Sixty, or almost. It's no age.'

'Oh. That's . . . God. How sad.' She bit her lip, and looked out the window again, but he could see her hands were shaking. Conor took one of them, held it fast on the leather seat, and she looked at him briefly, her blue eyes wet with tears. Another relationship Adam could not begin to understand – an hour ago he'd have said they were clearly on the brink of divorce, and no wonder when the man had optioned a book about her life without even telling her. And yet he was here with them all, trying to help.

His mind turned back to Delia. She had to be OK, she just had to. He couldn't have lost her too. Adam was so worried he would have prayed, even, if he'd ever for a second thought someone was listening.

Kate, present day

This was intolerable. The life she'd escaped from, she was being driven back to it, inexorably. Signs for Bishopsdean made her feel physically ill, as if the past fifteen years were an illusion and she'd be led to the same house, presented with the same life, the same children to raise. Even though one was here right now, tall and grown and still angry, giving her the news that David was dead. David.

They couldn't know, could they? Andrew, or Adam? He'd been a child, how could he know? But Andrew was looking at her from the corner of his eye in a way that made her think he at least suspected. Would things be different if he'd confronted her back then, during her first affair, before she'd even met Conor? Could they have fixed things between them? Might she never have done the terrible thing she'd done?

It didn't matter. Things were not different, that was the important thing. It was impossible to think of it, David, who she'd loved, gone forever. His body, the angles and corners of it, cold and in the ground. His voice, the Scottish purr of it that had curdled her, silent for always. And he had slept with Olivia too? Of course he had. How stupid she was, to think herself special, the only recipient of his slow-voiced charm. Likely he'd gone through every young woman in the office, and he must have known Olivia was pregnant, since she'd come back to work after her maternity leave, but he'd never even ... had he seen Delia ever? Did he care? She remembered what Olivia had said, the story of leaving the baby on the father's doorstep, but he didn't want to know. So Kate had risked her family, betrayed her husband, for a man who wasn't even marginally good. *No. Don't think about that.* She had other worries in this exact moment, because they were almost there and she was going to have to see her daughter, as well as the woman she had abandoned her family to, all those years ago.

Andrew, present day

The staff at the care home knew him, those kind, underpaid girls in pink smocks, who always felt the need to say they'd had a lovely time with Kirsty, describing her as *gorgeous* and *such a character*. He was allowed in no questions asked, mask on and a quick squirt of sanitiser, although they still enforced a two-visitor limit. For a long time after Kirsty went in they had barely been able to see her at all, and that had been hard, so much guilt. One of the girls – Julia, or maybe it was spelled Yulia? – led him into reception, with its faded blue carpet and bunches of dried flowers, streaks of purple in her red ponytail. 'Your wife, she is in lounge with Kirsty. If she comes out you can go in, both.'

'My wife?' Andrew didn't understand. His first thought was of Kate, hovering behind him, fiddling with her phone, shaking uncontrollably, having hooked a silk mask over her pale face. Conor – her husband! – had opted to stay in the car, without any discussion, just a look between him and Kate. Somehow that look had made Andrew feel the worst he had all day. It was a married look. The kind where a small act resonates deep in the mines between you, because of a million other actions and words. Not accompanying your spouse into a care home meant something to these two. Something not good. Adam too had not come in. It upset him to see Kirsty here, the way she had gone downhill, the fact he could have noticed sooner she was ill. They had never spoken of it, but Andrew knew all of this anyway.

'Yes?' Julia looked confused. 'She come earlier.'

Then he realised – they thought Olivia was his wife. Like everyone did. Because she was, essentially. At least that meant he was right, and she was here.

Kate said, 'Um. I won't yet. I'll let you go in.'

And there Olivia was in the lounge, holding Kirsty's hand as she sat in her chair, eyes flickering between the various sources of noise in the room. Olivia saw him standing in the doorway but didn't let go of Kirsty's hand. Walking towards them, Andrew felt awkward. Such a public place, under the eyes of the staff who thought they were married, and the residents and some

301

of the other relatives he recognised, who likely thought so too. Why else would Olivia have spent years caring for a disabled girl, if she wasn't her stepmother? Good question. 'I thought you might be here,' he said, awkwardly. Standing there awkwardly. His voice awkward. Never just comfortable in his skin.

'Yes.' Olivia's eyes moved behind him to reception and she convulsed slightly. 'Kate's here?'

'Um. Yes. She wanted to come. We can't all be in here.'

Olivia nodded, and stood, like someone going to the gallows. She squeezed Kirsty's hand. 'I'll be back in a minute, darling.' And she followed Andrew towards Kate, her former best friend, his former wife.

As the distance between them shortened, Andrew's anxiety was pitched so tight he could hardly breathe. The two women didn't hug – they hadn't really done that even when they were friends, as far as he remembered. Olivia's voice was several notes higher than usual. 'Kate. You look wonderful.'

Kate looked wrong-footed. 'Oh – thank you. Um, you too.' It didn't sound sincere, and it was true the difference between them was stark. Kate glowing and tanned, Olivia grey and mousy, faded like the British light outside. 'We've come – well, Adam's very worried about Delia. And about you. So – we came to find you.'

Olivia spread her hands. 'Here I am. But you don't need to worry about Delia, Kate. She's *my* daughter and you haven't seen her in almost twenty years.'

Kate looked stung. 'I know. I just – Adam asked me to come.'

Olivia gave a small bitter laugh, one he had never heard from her before. He started to be afraid. 'Did he? I see how it is. Even a bad mother's better than no mother. Better than a pretend one, no matter how hard she tried all these years.'

'Livvie . . .' He began, but she shot him a look.

'No, Andrew. I don't like to make a fuss, as you know, but sometimes a fuss just has to be made. She can't swan in here and take the family back. Because a family isn't just something you're born into. It's something you have to earn, every day, and I earned. I *earned* it.' Her voice cracked. 'Delia will be fine, thank you. I'm taking care of it.'

Kate nodded cautiously. 'I'm very aware that you – how much you've done for the family. I honestly never meant for you to. I just meant – could you see they're OK for the first day. The first week maybe.'

'You left them in my care, Kate. What did you expect me to do? Someone had to be there. Andrew was broken when you went. Those children would hardly have survived.'

Was that fair? He felt he'd done alright, but perhaps now was not the time to say it.

Kate was saying, 'Look, I haven't come to . . . interfere in any of that. I just came . . .'

'To stop the truth getting out? There's not a word in Andrew's book that isn't what really happened, the fallout from what you did. You can try to stop it, stop the film, but if I were you I'd be too ashamed.'

'I am ashamed,' said Kate quietly. 'But. Here we are. I can't change the past.'

Olivia subsided, her startling anger like a flash flood, wreaking devastation and then retreating. 'No. Well. That's all I . . . that's all I wanted to say. Kirsty's in there, if you want to see her.'

'Oh.' Kate paused. Andrew wondered if she had thought this through, if she actually wanted to see her daughter. What it would be like, after so many years. What to expect, when Kirsty hadn't grown up like other children did. 'How is she?'

'Oh, she's fine. We had a scare last year, but she pulled through.'

'Thank you. For – well.' It was so inadequate, Andrew suddenly understood why he might have forgotten to thank Olivia himself the night before. There was simply too much to thank her for. 'Now that I'm here – I don't think I can see her, no. It's just – too much. To know she might have . . . understood things all along, and I had no idea. I just – we were told it wasn't possible. So I had no hope. And now I hear she did, but maybe it's gone already, and I missed it, and I just – can't.'

'What? Don't you want to see her at all?' said Andrew, a little shocked at this despite his long knowledge of Kate. But Olivia was nodding her comprehension. Kate had gone too far; she could not come back now.

'I – I'm sorry, I can't. Not today, anyway. I'm glad she's well. I'm glad you've – taken care of her all this time.' Kate gulped. 'Look, Oliva's right. Do what you want with the film, the book. I won't get involved.' She looked at him, her face unreadable. 'You can do what you like,' she repeated. 'I . . .' She faltered. 'I just want you to know, I had to do it. What I did. But all the same I'm sorry. I'm so sorry.'

Andrew might have said something back – another apology, an absolution, a denunciation – save for Adam suddenly entering reception, looking furious. It was the first time he'd ever been inside this care home. He was holding a surgical mask over his face, voice muffled as all of theirs were.

'Liv, there you are. Where did you go?'

Olivia composed her face into the fond smile she always wore for Adam. 'I'm sorry darling. I just – had to be with Kirsty.'

'Where's Delia? You must know. She wouldn't worry you by vanishing entirely, I know her.'

Olivia hesitated, then inclined her head. 'She did tell me where she is, yes. But she wouldn't let me go to her.'

'I fucking knew it. Tell me!'

'She – well, the thing is, she had an appointment today. For a test. To see if everything's alright. With the – the baby. It's why she wanted to tell us all last night.'

Adam breathed out hard. 'She's getting the test now? Without me?'

'In an hour or so, yes.'

'You know where?'

'I believe ... there's a facility near her house. The East London clinic.'

Adam looked between his parents – three of them, really. Andrew waited for him to ask for help, lean on him, the father who'd done his best all these years, even if it wasn't enough. Or Olivia, who'd cared for him so well and so long. 'Mum,' said Adam. To Kate. 'What should I do?'

Kate, present day

Bits of her were breaking off. It was too much, all of this. To walk into her old life, find Olivia in her place, caring for her children. Her son looking up to another woman, who called him *darling*. She had chosen this. This was all her fault. But then Adam had asked for her help – he'd even called her Mum! And now, before she could answer, Conor had wandered in too, casually at ease, as if he went into suburban care homes all the time. She saw Olivia look at him, and knew she should make introductions, but simply could not face it. They belonged in different worlds, and she was stuck between the two. She should not have come back here.

'She's ... I have to go to her.' Adam looked about him,

frantic after this news about Delia. 'I need an Uber . . . God, I don't know.'

'You can have the car,' said Conor, apparently casting himself in the role of benefactor for the day.

'How will you get back?' said Kate, glaring at him.

He shrugged. 'There's trains, I'm sure.' As if Conor would ever get on a train.

'I'll go with you,' said Kate to her son. She wasn't sure why – some strange old mother instinct, which she'd thought long dead in herself. He had asked her for help, after all. She still had some use, even if she'd no idea what he should do. 'I mean, if you want.'

Adam nodded. 'I'll wait in the car. Don't be long.'

How to leave this situation, with both her husbands and Olivia, her former best friend? How to say anything at all? Behind that door was Kate's daughter. A person she had carried, and given birth to, and cried over for five years until she couldn't do it any more. She could not see Kirsty today, not now. Maybe another time, if there was another time. 'I . . . better go.'

Now she was with Adam, her son, driving in Conor's car towards East London, not far from where she had met Andrew all those years ago. She was a little shocked by how trendified it was, the fancy coffee shops and boys and girls with large-rimmed glasses and baggy clothes. It looked like Silver Lake in LA.

She was trying to process what had just happened. She had not been able to face her daughter, or the guilt that Olivia had mothered her children for her. Well, that was her penance. She felt the significance of it from far away, coming towards her like a comet of guilt. *Don't think about that now.* There was nothing she could do. Focus on the task in hand – find Delia. 'So, you know where she is?' Kate had not imagined seeing Olivia or

Delia again, her former best friend and patsy, and the perfect little girl Adam had injured that day when she realised she did not love either of her children.

Adam just shrugged. 'Think so.'

She tried again. 'I don't understand the set-up. Your father and Olivia, they're not a couple?'

He shrugged again. 'Don't think anything's ever happened between them.'

That seemed insane, in fifteen years. She had slept with Conor within an hour of arriving at his house. 'And you and Delia . . . ?'

'Not a couple either. But.' He shrugged yet again. Meaning, she supposed, they weren't a couple as such, but they were sleeping together. Kate tried to sort out her feelings. He and Delia were not related, of course, not even by marriage. They hadn't been brought up together. But something felt fateful about it all the same. As if Adam was still somehow ruining that bright perfect girl. A baby on its way, maybe with Kate's tainted DNA. What had she expected – Adam to never have children? Honestly, yes, that seemed likely, given the anti-social, angry little boy she'd left behind.

Kate was a whirlwind of guilt, picking at her cuticles in fear. Conor would tell her off for it. But maybe it wasn't Conor's business what she did any more, if she picked her nails or did anything at all? Because maybe they were over, after he'd made it clear once and for all his work mattered above everything, above his daughter, above her? Could she live like that? Could she, who had cut off all her ties once before, survive with none? And yet he had taken her hand in the car, had known she would be blindsided by the news of David's death, even after all these years. That counted for something, yes it did. But was it enough?

The car was slowing, and she felt a terrible nervousness,

almost unbearable. A red-brick building with a blue NHS sign outside. 'Will I go in with you?'

He shot her an irritated look, one she knew she gave people herself. 'Why else did you come? I need you to talk her round.'

'It's what you want – not to have it, if it has the thing?' She couldn't say *baby*.

'Well, of course! What else can we do? But I guess – I guess it's up to her. It's her body.'

Kate felt herself pale at the thought there might be another outcome. 'But Adam, why would anyone do that, if they had the choice? I didn't have the choice.'

'I don't know. Maybe that's why. The choice.' He looked at her, his eyes like her own. 'Look. Just because I don't want this, it doesn't mean I don't love Kirsty, you know. That I don't want her as she is. OK?'

'I know that.' It was something she'd often struggled with herself, how to say she didn't want this life, wouldn't have chosen it, without erasing her daughter entirely. The fact that Kirsty existed as herself, no matter what choice Kate would have made to have her or not. In a way she envied Delia the ability to decide. But it was a weighty decision, all the same, and a small twinge inside reminded her of the baby who'd never been.

She didn't even know the driver's name – poor man, witnessing all this – but she spoke to him briefly, apologising for the difficulty of parking in this area, as he pulled over to let them out.

'Don't worry, ma'am.' A face she would instantly forget. Too late to worry about that. She followed Adam in from the sunlit street. Inside, a dingy NHS waiting room, various women sitting about with hands resting on their stomachs. It could have been her, if she'd known that there was a gene to look for before Kirsty's birth, if she'd not been living in stupid

308

and happy ignorance. They could perhaps have prevented all this, the years of hurt, the leaving, the family she had blown apart. Could she live with herself for thinking that way, wishing a person unborn? Not that it made any difference. You could not unpick the past. You just had to live with what you'd done.

Adam was arguing with the receptionist. '... I don't care about data protection, it's my baby. It's my baby!' How strange to hear her child say that, when he was only a boy himself.

Then Kate's phone went, and she was so detached from reality, so far in the past, that she had no idea what the sound was for a moment. A message from the Mountainview Treatment Clinic. She clicked on it.

When Adam came back over, Kate had processed it already and decided what to do. Why did people dither so much over choices, when really you knew in an instant which one to make, if you forgot about guilt and obligation and politeness? 'I've had a message,' she said.

She saw his face. He had allowed himself to trust her a tiny bit, after all she'd done, and she was letting him down again already. Her son, the tall young man he had become. 'What about?'

'Asking me to go back. To LA. There's this girl and she's sick and – well, she needs me.'

'You can't even stay one more night?'

'Of course, it's just ... there's – an emergency. Trixie. Well, she's near your age, older actually. But she's in a sort of hospital, and she's taken a turn for the worse. She's not eating. She wants me with her, and I can help her, maybe.'

He looked confused. 'Who is she?'

'She's my ...' Kate hesitated. Stepdaughter no longer seemed

309

to cover it. Ex-stepdaughter? Ex-step girl-who's-no-relation-to-either-me-or-Conor? 'She's family. She's my family.'

Had that hurt Adam's feelings? It didn't mean he wasn't her family. It just meant family was bigger and wider and more elastic than she ever could have thought. It was Kirsty, who she couldn't even bear to see right now, but who was still her daughter. It was hostile Elizabeth with her Instagram shots, the niece and nephew Kate might meet some day in the future. It was Conor, whatever he would now be to her. And it was a young woman starving away in a hospital in the Malibu hills, eating even less now because Kate hadn't visited her in two days. 'I – Adam, I'm so sorry.' Adam was looking at her now. Taller than her, his blue eyes exactly like her own. She stammered, 'I won't go if you want me here. If you think I can help.' But she felt the tug across the Atlantic all the same. That pull of love that had always eluded her, she felt it now for Trixie, she realised, fear that it would be too late if she didn't get to her in time. And she felt it for Adam, in a darker, more complicated way, tinged with unbearable guilt.

'This girl, she really needs you?'

'I think so. She's – sort of your stepsister.' But that was Delia also, who was somewhere in this clinic, carrying his child. 'I won't go if you don't want me to. I can stay, of course I can.' It was true, she didn't need to rush off right now, did she? She could say hello to Delia at least. But it was too much, encountering these people from the past, these grown-up children. Who was she to tell the girl what to do with her life, her baby? People had to make their own mistakes. And what did Adam need her for, when he'd learned to do without her at seven? She was thinking of what Olivia had said, that a bad mother was better than none. Kate had left because she'd thought the opposite. But had she been wrong? Was there any way to tell? 'I

310

think – Adam, it's not up to me. This choice. It's easy for me to say what I'd do, but I didn't have the chance to make it. I don't know what I would have done back then, and that's the truth. So I can't help you. I'm sorry.'

He straightened his spine, nodded. 'You should go.'

'Really?'

'Yeah. You're right, there's nothing you can do here.'

Kate took this as a blow, as what she deserved. 'I'll leave you the car anyway. Maybe you could – maybe you might visit me out there. You can meet Trixie.'

Another Adam shrug. He was re-aligning his world already, erasing her from it, as he had learned to do for so long. 'Yeah, maybe,' he said. 'Bye, Mum.' He'd called her Mum again. That was something, at least.

Adam, present day

What a day it had been. For someone who didn't like drama, it was following him around. His dad and Olivia, whatever was going on there. His mum and her new husband, the slick producer guy, and the weird currents of tension he'd picked up between them. Seeing his mother again when he'd thought he never would. Her decision to not see Kirsty, after coming all this way, not to walk the remaining ten steps into the room to look at her. And now Delia. Chasing after her like some wanker in a romcom, to ask her – what? Don't have the baby? He couldn't do that. He loved her. He just needed to be here, while she got this news, whatever it was.

Of course his mother was leaving already. He'd never been able to imagine a future where she moved back here and behaved like an actual parent, because it didn't exist. She was just a fireball through his life, streaking the skies for a moment. He wasn't even angry. Go, he'd said, when she told him. There's nothing for you here. Not true, but he had a little pride left still.

Come and visit, she'd said. You could meet Trixie.

Who was this Trixie? Someone else his mother was choosing over him. My family, she'd said. Did that mean Adam wasn't? He was so tired of feeling angry at his mother, for buggering off back then and again now, going to some girl he'd never heard of instead of him. What did he know? Maybe he'd do the same in her place. He'd thought about running when he heard Delia's news, of course he had. Adam saw the nurse hovering. Shit. Delia was about to get the test. Time to decide, to answer the question or not, throw the dice, spin the wheel. Risk it all. Was that what life was really about, in the end? After all, the worst had already happened to his family, and here they were, fractured and messed up, but alive. Still a family, of sorts. And he'd shown up, he hadn't run like Kate had. That had to count for something.

He stepped towards the ultrasound room. Maybe he would visit LA after all – the visions of the turquoise pool and girls in bikinis – or maybe he would just stay here and never see his mother again. A dad at twenty-two. Get a job to support Delia, some kind of office horror that would drain him away. Or maybe he'd like it. Being with her, their child. His mother coming over, or them going to see her, the baby playing in the water, or just cutting her out entirely. It could go either way. But if the baby wasn't OK, would Delia have it anyway? He just didn't know.

Delia was lying back on a bed, her legs splayed frog-like, her top rolled up to show her stomach, shiny with gel. Her lower

312

half covered by some rough blue paper. She didn't say anything for a moment. 'Hi.'

'Your mum said you were here.'

The ultrasound woman was irate. 'You can't just barge in! Who are you?'

'He's the father,' said Delia. 'The baby's father.' A role he'd never imagined for himself. He was Andrew's difficult son, Kate's abandoned son, Olivia's not-even son. Not someone's father. He'd never even been a boyfriend. He wasn't ready for this. But whatever was happening inside Delia's still-flat stomach, he had no control over it. He had set it in motion and it would play itself out, whatever he did.

'Can you give us a minute?' he said to the tech. 'Sorry.' He knew he was being rude, that people saw him as a rough and angry young man. He had to work on that. To be in the world you had to at least play by some rules. And he wasn't a kid now. He couldn't use his missing mother as an excuse. She was back, for a start, at least in some capacity. Everything he'd taken for granted was upside down. His revenge shagging, trying to hurt his father, mother, Olivia, it had all led to consequences. He hadn't got an STD, and the baby wasn't even the biggest problem. It was that he had somehow developed love. He had love for her there, under blue paper, her pale legs with the hairs standing up from the cold, the chipped polish on her bony feet. He had love for Kirsty, stuck in that home, and he knew he had to get over himself and visit her more. Love for his dappy father, who'd never left, and for Olivia, who'd raised him. Even maybe his mother, running hard to save herself and leave him behind, maybe he had some love left for her, or least some compassion, and maybe that was the same. He loved all of them. It was annoying, but it was the truth.

Kate, present day

After leaving the clinic Delia was in, without even seeing the young woman she'd become, Kate stepped out on the busy London street – hit in the face by the life of it all – and called an Uber, leaving the car for the kids. She was running again. She'd failed to see Kirsty or Delia, she'd failed to stop the film, she'd failed with Adam again, one of a million ways she'd let him down. This was who she was, apparently. She'd go straight to Heathrow and book a stand-by flight, business class at least. After all, she was rich now in her own right, she was successful and independent and had no need of a man in her life. The Uber arrived in two minutes – the almost unbearable convenience of modern life. It was too easy just to do things once you had set your mind on them, without the time to even think it through. She climbed in, remembering that her luggage was at the hotel with Conor. It hardly mattered. Everything could be replaced, and her passport was in her handbag. Travelling light, she had always been good at that. Once you'd left children and husbands and parents, it was easy to leave face cream and socks.

In the air-conditioned back of the car, travelling through London yet sealed off from it, she rang Conor. She listened to the dial tone, not at all sure he would answer. But he did, his voice hesitant. 'Yes.' She wondered what he was doing, if he had simply summoned a cab back to London and set to work in the back, unbothered by the emotional crises engulfing the rest of the family. Not part of it.

'Hi.'

'Are you OK? I offered them a lift home. Andrew and Olivia. They wanted to stay, they said.' How strange to hear their names in his mouth.

'Alright. Thank you.' He had done what a husband would, today. He had helped. Again she asked herself – was it enough? 'I'm going to LA. The clinic messaged. Trixie, she's in a bad way, she needs someone, to be there for her.'

No answer. His breath down the line. 'I told you I don't think we can help her any more.'

'You did. But I won't leave another child.'

He breathed a bitter laugh. 'Not even yours. Not even mine.'

'It . . . doesn't matter. She is, anyway.' And it was him paying for the clinic, so he didn't really mean it. It was hard work, to truly give up on someone.

She heard him suck in air. 'Kate. I don't – I never wanted it to be this way. I know I haven't – these past few years have been bad.' He faltered, and she heard how hard he was trying, the strain in his voice just to say something, anything. 'I . . . I'm sorry. For all this. The film. I won't make it if you don't want. I don't think I realised until I saw that care home, what you were up against. How much pain you were in. You should know I'll never judge you for leaving. Even if you judge yourself. And the rest of it – the baby, and Trixie, and . . . all of it. I'm sorry. '

It wasn't a thing he said often. The thing was, she realised, in a car speeding away from him, or as much as you could speed in London, that they both did love each other. It just wasn't enough, maybe. Maybe neither of them knew how to make it enough. She said, 'When you come back to LA – where will we be?' Somehow the fear of asking had left her. She had blown a hole in her family, and still they were standing, the people she had met today. Adam was an angry young man, that was clear, but perhaps he had always been that way, screaming and bloody against her chest after he'd fought his way out of her. He loved Delia, she could see that, so he couldn't be all bad. Maybe they would work it out. Andrew and Olivia – she had been right to leave them together. Maybe now they could actually find out what they were to each other, instead of living with her ghost. Maybe some other time she would see Delia, the angelic child from way back then, and perhaps the baby she might have. Maybe it would be born healthy, or maybe Delia would not have it, but there might be other children in the future, Adam's or Delia's or both. And then there was Kirsty, but Kate's mind failed her then, a weight of guilt so great it might break. There was always next time, another chance for Kate to be her better self, face the daughter she had abandoned. She would not give up on herself just yet.

Conor said, 'I want us to be us. Together. Married.'

'And Trixie?'

'If you want I can – I can make an effort with her. And your kids. We can be – some kind of family. Or we can try at least.' He would try, she would try, but should you have to try in these matters, to love people, to be a family?

'It's not so easy.'

'No. All we can do is our best. So what do you say? I'll fly back tomorrow. Will you start again with me?'

She hadn't answered his question. She could hear him down the line, waiting. Perhaps it was all over for them – a second divorce, alone at fifty. She could move in with Suzi for a bit, seek out the comfort of women, friends. Throw herself into activism, pretend she was a good person whose actions had value. She had work, she had friends. Family, romantic love, it wasn't everything. Her life had been divided in two by husbands, one she'd given up, one she'd never really had, not entirely. In a way, she had been alone for years. She had left her children for that luxury, to know where her own self stopped and began. And here she was. The car inched on through London traffic, as several miles away her husband sat on the phone, and still she made no reply.

Andrew, present day

'I was so worried when you went,' he said, then realised that might be guilt-tripping. 'I mean – I'm glad you're alright.'

'There was no need to worry,' Olivia said, still looking at Kirsty. They had gone back inside and now sat by her chair in uncomfortable armchairs, the fabric torn and stained. She was utterly oblivious that her mother had been so close and not come to see her. Or was she? Andrew stroked her hand, the soft skin, the close-trimmed nails to stop her scratching herself. Olivia took her other one. 'Kirsty's the only one I can talk to, you see. Delia, of course I love her like my life, but it's all so complicated. I can't tell her what do to about the baby. It's not my right. Adam is always so angry. And you ...'

'I'm useless,' he said. 'Aren't I?'

She sighed. 'I'm tired of the self-pity, Andrew.'

'I know. I am too.'

'You got what you wanted. A book, a film deal. Kate to come back.'

He almost laughed. 'You think that's what I want?'

'Haven't you been waiting for her all this time? Isn't that why you and I, we never – well. Why we're like this?' Tenderly, she wiped saliva off Kirsty's face. Kirsty seemed to have registered his presence, and waved her arms, gurgled towards him. Did she know he was her father? He'd come to trust in it during the good years, the simple fact that she knew him, and now he doubted again. Maybe it didn't matter if she recognised him or not. Why could neither of her parents care for her with the self-sacrifice that Olivia did? Perhaps it was easier for someone not related. Less of the pain, the imagined child you could have had, though of course you never could. That child did not exist.

He said, 'No. Olivia, of course not. I ... I never thought she'd come back.'

'Well, she has.'

'She hasn't. Not like that. She isn't staying. I doubt I'll see her again.' Though she had said, maybe next time. So who knew?

Kirsty made a noise, perhaps of annoyance or pain. Now at least there was something he could do, to speak to her. Still feeling awkward, he made the sign for *what's wrong*. For years, he would never have asked his daughter this question, because she couldn't answer or even understand, he thought. But now, tentatively, she shaped her fingers into something. *Hungry*. She was hungry. It made his heart hammer, that one little sign, its meaning. Even after her illness, her losses, she was trying to communicate, something still remained. Perhaps she would get them all back again, learn even more. He would give her something to eat, a rice cake or a banana, or something like that, and she would stop being upset. They spoke a language now, however basic. Kirsty could, in her limited way, talk to them, and even that was such a miracle, to peer into the fathomless depths of her and realise she did have thoughts, she did want things.

But how could he explain to Kirsty, in primitive finger signs, that her mother was back? Did she even remember she had a mother, or did she think Olivia was it? One woman had cared for her since she was a baby. The other had left before her sixth birthday. What did a mother mean, really? Was it the one who gave birth to you, or the one who stayed?

He found a biscuit in his pocket, one of the little packets from the hotel which he had unthinkingly swiped from years of habit, always carrying snacks to stop Adam's meltdowns, and he broke it into bits for her, fed them to her. As Kirsty devoured it with squeaks of pleasure, he tried again. 'Olivia. I can't apologise

318

enough for last night. And for everything. For years and years. I shouldn't have let you do all you did for us. Move in, become a stepmum and a wife except ... '

'Except not.'

'Right.' A long silence between them, in this too-hot room full of voices and smells. 'Is that what you wanted? To get married?'

She hunched her shoulders, and he could see how she'd be as an old woman. Spare, and starveling, and nervy, increasingly stuck in routine and order. Always there. Always kind. When he thought of the future she was always in it, and he saw now how wrong he'd been to take that for granted. The love she gave so freely, to grab it in handfuls and not acknowledge it. 'I only ever wanted what you wanted.'

'I want you. Back with me. Not as a pseudo-mother, not to look after Kirsty – just to be with me. Until we get old.' He imagined them. Passing the paper to and fro, assuming papers existed in the future. Filling in bits of the crossword. Taking turns to make the dinner. Quiet evenings. Looking up from his laptop to find her there with a herbal tea. A good life. Adam and Delia perhaps a couple, and that might be a little strange, but they weren't related after all. This baby, or some other baby in the future. If it was like Kirsty. But it might not be. And if it was, if that's what Delia chose, well, people managed. People managed with so much more than you could think.

Olivia was quivering. 'I thought I was safe. Hiding in your family, like a cuckoo or something, caring for children I knew couldn't love me anyway, trying to make up for Delia, for leaving my own daughter ... This is my fault. If she has this baby.'

'Of course it isn't! It's Adam's fault.'

'Adam doesn't want it. It's Delia, her need for something to love. Because I left her, didn't even tell her who her father was. You know, I'm as bad as Kate. All these years it was safe to judge her, to tell myself at least I'm better than her, but no. She was just braver.'

'But none of that matters. Delia knows you love her. Adam loves you too, and Kirsty . . . ' There he went, with the kind lies himself. Could she love, Kirsty? Where did love come from, what capacity did you need to feel it? He had no idea.

'And you?'

He had wondered this for years, trying to identify love, searching for the feeling. But what else could it be except this, the feeling that another person was your home? 'I always have, I think. Please, Olivia. Come back to me. Marry me. Be with me properly, and I know I should have done this fifteen years ago, but I didn't, and here we are now. Will you?'

No answer. Her face seemed flat, and he couldn't read it. Sitting in the bright noisy room, his child between them, after fifteen years not asking the question, Andrew waited for her answer.

Adam, present day

Delia was watching him, steadily. There was that strange confidence in her, she never looked away or doubted herself. 'So. You found me.'

He sat down beside her on an uncomfortable plastic seat. 'Are you OK?'

'I've been a bit sick and bloated, amazing how quickly it happens. Otherwise, alright.' She'd always been this way, pretending everything was fine, serene as a swan on the outside at least. Maybe that was why she loved him, when he didn't deserve it, because he was the only one who understood how

320

things were. If she even did love him. He had no idea what she felt in this moment.

'Not physically. I mean, are you *OK*? How long have you known about this?'

She wrinkled up her nose. 'Few weeks, maybe. I put off doing the pregnancy test.'

'Why?'

'Because I knew everyone would want to talk me out of it. That's why you're here, right? To talk me out of it.' She rested her hand on her stomach as she spoke. Like someone pregnant, who wanted to be. 'I wanted to make my own decision, at least.'

'Dee, you're twenty-one. I'm twenty-two. This, it's for life. Aren't there things you want to do? You haven't even finished your degree!'

She shrugged. 'What's the point? There aren't any jobs, unless you want a corporate grind, no soul, burning out by thirty. Or would I work in a coffee shop for pennies? Post more yoga videos on Insta? It's all so pointless. At least this, it's real. I'm young, I'm healthy. Why shouldn't I have a baby now?'

Anger snapped in him. 'Because it's not that easy! It might not be ... OK.'

'Right, so that's why I'm here getting the test. They have to take my blood – things might not show up on a scan yet. I thought I at least owed you that.'

'At least!'

'You don't have to do anything. There's no obligation.'

'Fuck's sake, Dee. I'm not my mother! I can't have a kid and have nothing to do with it!' Though that had been his first thought, hadn't it? 'And what if the test says yes? Will you?'

She paused. 'Honestly, I don't know. I'll need to check in with my feelings, if that's the case.'

What utter bollocks. 'I wanted my mum to talk to you. Tell

321

you what it's like. Giving birth, and then finding out there's something wrong, and it's forever.'

'She's here?' Delia raised her head from the couch.

'Outside. Or, she was.' He felt too tired to explain it all. Older than his years.

'Oh. I'd like to see her again. But not like this. Adam, it has to be our decision.'

'Your decision,' he said bitterly.

'Well, yes. That's just how it works. And Kirsty ... I know it's hard, but ...'

'You don't know! You weren't even there all those years! Maybe it's OK seeing her now when she's all cleaned up and signing away, talking to us, but you weren't around for the shit years, the screaming and being sick, her legs in casts to try and straighten them, but she doesn't understand so she's howling in pain, and she's having seizures every day and not breathing and almost dying, and ... Christ, Delia. And don't give me that about do I wish she was never born. It's not the same, imagining a person not existing, your whole life different.' His mother would never have left, probably. He might be less angry, a happy young man, with a good career ahead of him. No Olivia. No Delia, probably.

'I know it wasn't easy.'

'So why, then? Why not just end it?'

'Because, I don't know what's right, Adam!' Her voice had sharpened. 'Is it up to me to say who can live and who can't? Who deserves a chance?'

'Oh for God's sake. You're not turning into some pro-lifer on me. What's this about really? You want some cute little thing to love, is that it?'

'And why shouldn't I?' They were both shouting now, probably upsetting the other women outside. 'I barely had a mother,

322

I didn't have a father. I have no family, just my grandparents, and they won't be here much longer.'

'You've got me!'

'I don't have you, Adam. What even are we to each other? You never wanted a relationship, or a family. You said often enough how stupid it was. For God's sake, you asked for a vasectomy at twelve! As if you'd want to raise a child with me.'

He was getting angrier and angrier. 'I didn't want any of that, no. But I want you. I want whatever you want. Can you not see that? It's you who's been holding me off the last three years.'

She bit her lip. He thought she had never looked more beautiful, pale and scared and cross. 'I couldn't risk it. To love you and lose you, when I knew you didn't want any of that. A real relationship. Love.'

'People can change,' he heard himself say. 'Look at our parents. Are you saying you do love me after all?'

She rolled her eyes. 'For God's sake, Adam. Of course I do. That's not the point.'

There was a moment of joy, a harsh spike amid the rage of pain and fear. She loved him. 'So at least talk to me about what to do.'

'I know what you'll say. You won't want me to have it, if it's got the gene.'

'Dee, most people wouldn't want that, if they had the choice. You must know that.'

'But Kirsty. She has a life, she's loved.' Her lip was trembling.

'Don't bring Kirsty into this. Don't you dare.'

'But we have to think about . . .'

'This isn't the same as wishing her gone, and you know it. I just, I just . . .'

Something was happening to Adam's face. His nose ached, like really burned, and his throat was closing up. Oh shit. He was crying. God almighty. Delia reached out her arms, and he laid his head on her stomach, just above the cold gel. He could smell it, and underneath, the warmth of her skin. A miracle was happening in there. Someone that hadn't existed now did, at least in a tiny way. 'What do we do?' he cried, choked. 'What do we do?'

She stroked his hair, as his tears ran over her stomach, warm and salt, washing away the gel. 'I really don't know. That's why I didn't tell you.'

'I don't know either.'

'What if we don't find out?'

'What?'

'Just … don't find out. It might be alright.' Thoughts went through his head. He didn't want a baby anyway, even a healthy one. That was crazy, Russian roulette with a bullet in every other chamber. But he wanted her. And he wanted, after an entire life staying cold and distant, something human. He wanted to feel. He wasn't his mother, already heading to the airport and out of his life. And perhaps it had been right for her to go – perhaps she would have died if she'd stayed with them, like her friend Aimee, lost her mind. Who knew. 'God. Sorry.' He hadn't cried since he was twelve years old.

'Don't be.' Delia's face was serene again. 'It's up to you, Adam. If you want, we'll get the test. If not, we just … won't.'

Jesus Christ. Who even knew what was right? How she could drop this choice in his lap – risking it all, having a baby he didn't want, maybe one with serious disabilities? Or making her end it, and risk losing her? Crushing her heart, the good pure heart that he loved? Adam lay there, feeling her fingers in his hair, the tick of her pulse through the stretched skin of her stomach. 'Alright,' he mumbled. He was exhausted by today, his mother, Olivia, this. He gave up.

'What?'

'Alright, let's not find out. Let's just go home.' Not that they even had a home together. Not that they were even a couple, or maybe they were now she'd said she loved him. Maybe that was enough, or maybe they'd get the test another day, although they would run out of time soon, and then it would just be waiting, and hoping. He really had no idea.

Adam had always thought hope was stupid. Just another way to get hurt. But Kirsty had learned to speak, and he had learned to love, and his mother had come back, and none of those things had seemed possible before. So who knew what would happen. Nobody did.

He took her hand to help her off the table and into her jeans, and led her out of the small featureless room where a question might have been answered, into a future he could not make out at all. Her thin hand was in his, clasped tight, and he did not let it go.

Kate, 1997

It so nearly did not happen.

She had gone to the pub with a friend whose name she would later struggle to remember, but which was Maria. Not even a friend but a work colleague, from the newsroom where Kate was on the absolute bottom rung, getting water in paper cups for people and escorting guests through the labyrinth of corridors. She didn't care – she was where she was supposed to be, and she was already applying for reporter jobs in newsrooms outside London. She had almost cancelled on Maria, who she didn't much like – too posh, called dinner supper, breath smelled like sardines – but there'd been a rumour the reporting team were out in this pub celebrating someone's birthday, and Kate wanted to network. Then, they had almost not gone in – Maria had objected at the last minute to how crowded the pub was and insisted the team had meant the one on the other side of the square, but Kate had overruled her. She wasn't sure why. Maybe because she liked to win, or because something about the lights of the pub, the happy murmur of post-work voices, called her in.

Then, so many other things might not have happened. They might have left when they realised the reporters weren't there after all. They might have stood on the other side of the bar, since there were no free seats, protecting their handbags and gym stuff with their bodies, Maria complaining about the crush. Kate might have bought the first round of small white wines, so then Maria would have been at the bar for the second, not her. She might have got served a little faster. Or he might not have bought a drink at that exact time, he might have been talking to someone else, or neither of them might have felt like chatting to a stranger. As it was, all these things did align, and at around 8.23pm, on Friday, 14th March, 1997, Kate had found herself waiting at the counter of a pub near St Paul's, waving a tenner and failing to catch the eye of the barmaid, who was busy serving a group of city lawyers who'd actually tip. She had just let out a long sigh when a voice spoke in her ear. 'I could add it to our tab, if you like. I don't think anyone would notice. They've just ordered ten bottles of Moët.'

The person speaking was a young man about her age, which was twenty-five. One of the lawyers, but his suit was not expensive and his shaving indiscriminate, so she quickly surmised he was a trainee and about to be spat back out from the upper echelons of corporate law. He wore glasses, which she liked, and had an open, artless manner. 'Well, thank you. It was just two white wines.' She looked over at Maria, who was now chatting to another lawyer, and had thawed out somewhat. She was one of those women who only came alive when men were nearby.

'Sure thing.' The man caught the barmaid's eye with ease, something he would never be able to do again, though of course Kate did not know that then. She would sometimes think of this moment in later years, how she had the wrong idea of him, and wonder how much difference that had made. 'Two white wines, please, thank you very much. On the same tab, yeah. And a pint of Boddingtons, why not.' He didn't specify type of wine, which confirmed her guess that he was not from this world, not really. Like her. He'd been polite to the barmaid, not patronising or sleazy like so many of the men she worked with.

He passed over the glasses of wine. 'Well, here you are.'

Kate took them. 'You're sure I can't give you cash?'

'Honestly, it would make me feel a bit better about the fact I spent the day basically helping an arms dealer not to pay tax.'

'Oh, well, in that case ...'

She hesitated. Did she want to talk to him, or did she want to go home and watch the news, take notes on the breaking stories, go in tomorrow full of ideas? Wake up refreshed? What good could a not-top lawyer do her, how did he fit her life plan? He wasn't her type, anyway, she tended to go more for rugby boys, loud and confident. But that had never worked out, and he was still smiling at her, in an expectant but not pressured way, and so she found herself saying, 'I'm Kate.'

'Andrew. Hi.'

'Hi.' She put the cold glass to her mouth, the sharp tang of cheap alcohol, and he raised his own pint to her in a cheers.

'It's nice to meet you. You're the first woman I've talked to all week who hasn't looked right through me.'

Kate could see why that was – he wasn't tall, or loud-voiced, or even especially handsome, but he was nice-looking, and seemed kind, and he was meeting her gaze fully and frankly, without flirtation or hustle. Suddenly weary from months of trying to get somewhere other than where she was, she thought it might be nice to stand here for a moment and talk to him. Restful. Just for a moment.

Later on, when she had time to think over this encounter and all the ways it might not have happened, she would remember looking out the large windows of the pub and seeing their reflections imposed over the view of the wet black street, bright with the shifting colours of a nearby traffic light, and she would think: would I stop it, if I could? Would I take that girl, so sure she knew it all, but who really knew nothing, and march her back out onto the street? Set her feet on another path? If only she had seen all that lay ahead of them, the children and lovers and betrayals and hurts, would she do it differently? The truth was, Kate would never know the answer.

Acknowledgements

This was a hard and a long book to write, so I'm grateful to everyone who kept me going along the way.

Firstly thanks to my wonderful agent Diana Beaumont, who never seems to mind me veering wildly from one type of writing to another!

Thank you for Corsair for providing such a good home, especially James Gurbutt, and Olivia Hutchings and Alison Griffiths for such a sensitive edit. We really were on the same page which is such a gift with material like this.

Thank you to my writer friends Sarah Day, Angela Clarke, Laura Barnett for reading early drafts, and thank you to Dana Massey for reading (even though you don't really read!) and telling me it was good.

And finally thank you to my family who said it was OK for me to publish this book. It isn't based on us but the feelings contained within are certainly inspired by real events. To everyone in a similar situation, you are the strongest people in the world, and I send you all my admiration and love.